SEASONAL STORMS

Spring Showers—the Bloom

STEVE WEATHERSPOON

Copyright © 2022 Steve Weatherspoon
All rights reserved
First Edition

PAGE PUBLISHING
Conneaut Lake, PA

First originally published by Page Publishing 2022

ISBN 978-1-6624-7058-5 (pbk)
ISBN 978-1-6624-7060-8 (hc)
ISBN 978-1-6624-7059-2 (digital)

Printed in the United States of America

To those I've loved so far, those I still love, and those I have yet to love. Without you, this isn't possible.

Chapter 1

The sun slightly peeked from behind the clouds as it shone brightly, quite contrary to MaKayla's mood. A small breeze flowed through the slightly cracked window. She closed her eyes as its rays brushed along her face. The sweet scent of a morning after it rained, followed quickly behind the breeze. The birds were chirping rather vigorously back and forth. She sat, staring out the window, her eyes heavy, she was tired. *I wish I had your energy,* MaKayla thought as she stared at the birds chasing after one another through the air. She was in her own world. There were other students around, but her attention was outside.

"Hey MaKayla!" yelled Liyah from the entrance of the classroom after spotting her best friend.

Liyah's loud voice caused everyone to stop for a moment, and it brought MaKayla back to reality. After realizing that she had drifted off into her thoughts, she responded, "Hey, how have you been? I've missed you." She got up, smiled, and gave Liyah a hug.

"Mmm, you smell good. What are you wearing?" Liyah didn't wait for her friend to answer. "And speaking of missing, you know I miss you more, right?" she said as she smiled at MaKayla.

"Yeah, I know. I'm sorry that I've been so out of touch. I've just been so tied up with school and my internship. Plus, you know I've been working all this overtime to keep everything together," replied MaKayla in a somber tone.

"Yeah, I've noticed you take forever to get back to me when I text you. Sometimes, you don't even return my calls," said Liyah as she pressed her lips together to make a pouty face.

"I'm so sorry. You know you're my girl. If that's how bad it's gotten, you know it has to be really hectic for me, because that's not like me at all." MaKayla knew her friend had every right to tell her about herself and how she had been neglecting their friendship. "Shoot, I'm even tired right now. The day just started, and I'm ready for it to be over already!" She chuckled lightly, then smiled.

"You know I forgive you. There's really no need to apologize. I really do understand." Liyah paused for a few seconds. "It's just that we have to get back to how we used to be. I just want my best friend and sister back. I've really missed you!" She made a pouty face while she folded her arms playfully across her chest.

"Don't act like that. I feel the same way. I hate that it's gotten so out of hand. I'm just trying to get everything in order and hoping it all comes together the way I want it to," said MaKayla as she pouted to mimic her friend's actions.

"I know you are. With all that you have going on and the hard work you've been putting in, things will come together sooner than you think," Liyah responded as she flashed another big smile.

"Thanks sis. I'm patiently waiting, as I've always been," answered MaKayla. She tried to bring herself to smile, but it was hard. She had become so engulfed in getting things together the way she wanted that she had lost track of a lot of what she used to do. She could barely recognize the person she had turned into. It bothered her that she had allowed herself to slip so far away from who she had always been.

"I'm serious. You deserve every bit of goodness that comes your way," Liyah replied, noticing the disappointment setting in on her friend's face.

"Aww, don't go getting me all emotional, because you know it's hard for me to stop once it starts." MaKayla started tearing up as the depth of Liyah's words sank in.

"I'm just being real with you. Just don't push yourself too hard," said Liyah, giving MaKayla another hug. "You know, you can always ask them for help. There's no need to overwork yourself. I mean, that's what our parents are here for—to help. You've got school, work, and your internship. I just hope that you're not overdoing it. I don't want you getting sick or anything like that." She began to rub MaKayla's back.

"I know, but I'm okay. It is hard, but I got it under control. It feels good being able to stand on my own and accomplish this. I think, when it's all said and done, they'll be even more proud of me for being able to do it on my own."

Liyah paused and began grinning. "They'll be proud of you no matter what, but that's why I love you girl, that mentality right there. I wish I could do that because you know me. I'm calling my daddy as soon as I feel the stress trying to come." The girls laughed.

"Yeah, I know," said MaKayla.

The professor entered the class, had the students take notes, and assigned some work. That was all he had for them, so class ended early. The students were free to stay and talk or ask questions if they needed to, but they didn't have to. MaKayla and Liyah talked to the professor for a few minutes before leaving the classroom. They were both doing great in the class, so they only wanted to check in with him.

"Well, we have some time now, so we can catch up a bit on life. Let's go to the café for lunch since we have to work today anyway," said MaKayla excitedly. Both of them laughed and left the class. They worked at the café that was several blocks away from the school. With Liyah's car being in the shop and it being such a nice day outside, they figured they would walk as opposed to taking a cab, as MaKayla often did.

MaKayla and Liyah grew up together. Born only two days apart to parents who had been good friends, they were basically raised together. It was a running joke that their parents had planned both of their children's births so that they would be the same age. When the girls were younger, they made a promise to each other that they would do as much as they could together no matter what the circumstances were. Thus far, this was a promise that still held true.

Growing up, MaKayla and Liyah attended the same elementary, middle, and high schools. They both played on the track and volleyball teams and performed on the dance team together in high school. Now as young adults, they were attending the same college. Although MaKayla and Liyah had a similar upbringing, they went about things differently. Even while working toward similar ideas and goals, they each had their own way of tackling problems and finding solutions.

MaKayla's and Liyah's families were well-off, so they were able to pay for their schooling. Liyah, who followed in her parents' footsteps by studying accounting, accepted the help. MaKayla declined the assistance. She wanted to experience what it was like to truly be independent, so she refused to allow her parents to assist her financially. She did, however, follow in her father's footsteps by going to school for business management.

Her father even called her at times to discuss potential business decisions. It was his way of still helping her, even though she wouldn't let him financially contribute to Her education. He wanted to prepare her for the vicious world that she was about to be thrust into. MaKayla had done pretty well thus far. Making it to her second-to-last semester without needing any help, she was on the path to graduating early. It wasn't that difficult, though. With all the scholarship and grant money she had earned, a large portion of the financial burden was off MaKayla's shoulders.

Liyah was also in her second-to-last semester of college, and she looked forward to graduating the following semester as well. In true form, she and MaKayla had taken a majority of the same general education classes before they began courses in their majors. Then to help them get ahead, they took summer classes.

Initially, MaKayla and Liyah lived together, but they decided to get their own places before the semester started. MaKayla initiated the conversation about them living apart because she wanted to know what true independence felt like. She didn't have any issues living with Liyah, but she wanted to fully experience having to live life on her own.

They worked at the same café, but their schedules were different now that they were in their major classes. It was rare for them to see each other for more than a few hours on any given day. Before, they used to catch up when they were at home together, but that was no longer an option. Although they had keys to each other's places, they rarely had the opportunity to spend quality time with each other.

On this particular Tuesday, it seemed as if everything was working in their favor. The one class that they did have together was optional to attend in person. However, the professor required all students to show up in class to receive their assignments. By chance, their other courses were canceled or rescheduled on this Tuesday, so they were able to grab lunch and catch up.

On the walk to the café, MaKayla began talking. "So? Tell me what's new with you. I know we have a lot to catch up on. Tell me everything!"

"Okay. So where do I start? Hmm, let me think. Oh, okay. So you know how I have always talked about the perfect living room set that would make my place look fabulous? So I finally ordered it, and I almost feel like my place is complete," Liyah said quickly as if she only had a limited amount of time to talk.

MaKayla paused and began smiling. "You're lucky I can understand you with the speed in which you talk, because if I couldn't, I'd ask you to repeat all that again. Slow down, though. We have a couple hours before we have to actually go in for work, so stop rushing." She gave her best friend the side-eye, then let out a laugh. Over the years, she had tried to get Liyah to speak slower, but it never worked.

"My bad. You know how excited I get talking about furniture and fashion. Plus, I feel like we haven't talked like this in forever!" Liyah said before immediately continuing the conversation. "I said *almost* complete because I need a few pictures to throw along the walls—you know, a few extra things to really make it pop."

"Aw, okay. That's cool. I just recently ordered a living room set too. Look at us, still thinking alike." MaKayla looked at Liyah, and they both started to laugh. "If you have some free time tomorrow, you should drop by and see it. I'm expecting it to arrive in the morning. I have class from noon to five o'clock, but I'll be free after that. I'll just be at home, packing."

"What'd you say? A day off?" Liyah asked before cackling.

"Yeah, just so I can get my furniture." MaKayla wanted to know more about Liyah's place, curious of the vision she saw for it. "What are the colors of the pieces that you ordered?"

"I ordered a living room set that's dark brown and tan. I have ideas about how I want to paint and everything. I'm going to get the paint this week and take care of that." Liyah paused for a few seconds. "Well, I'm going to have my brother paint. I can't be doing all of that—working, internship, school, and painting on top of that. Nothing would get finished."

"I can understand that. I would paint my living room too, but the wall color already complements my furniture. I have a gray sectional that comes with gray, black, and white pillows. When it gets here tomorrow, I'll see what else I need to get to go with it. I ordered my bedroom set too. I can't wait for the pieces to get here. Anyhoo, I want to go to the museum. I know that's off-topic, but I just wanted to let you know." There was a short pause before laughter broke out between them.

"Now where did that come from? We aren't even talking about that right now. You're always so random," said Liyah jokingly. "Let's get back on the subject."

"Okay, okay," said MaKayla, smiling and shaking her head.

"Anyways, something else that's new with me is who I'm seeing!" blurted out Liyah excitedly. She looked at MaKayla for a reaction but didn't get one.

MaKayla had drifted off into another one of her zones and started thinking about the last time they had gone to the museum together. A slight smile crossed her face as she remembered how much fun they'd had that day. Once she realized what Liyah had just told her, she perked up. "Oh, really? So who's the lucky guy?"

"His name is Darrell. He's so handsome and sweet. I'm thinking he's one of those too-good-to-be-true guys."

Like a true best friend, MaKayla interjected. "Stop thinking like that! There's no need to jump to that assumption unless you have a reason to feel that way. Do you?"

"No, not really. He just seems like he's too good to be true, but who knows?" Liyah shrugged her shoulders.

"How long have you been talking to him?" asked MaKayla with curiosity in her voice.

"We met a little more than a month ago at that bar and grill over on Ninth—you know, the one by the bowling alley. He approached me respectfully, so I felt like I should give him a shot, not to mention he had a smile to die for." Liyah raised her right hand to her forehead and pretended to faint.

Makayla's smile increased as she shook her head at Liyah's antics. "Well, yeah, he better approach you with respect. You're not just anybody. You're special. Now you know me. I need all the details." MaKayla leaned in as she pressed her friend for more information about her new boyfriend. "What did he say? What was he wearing? How did he approach you? I wanna know everything."

Liyah began to smile because she had missed having these chats with MaKayla. "Well, I was there with Donna and Patrice. They were sitting at the table, and I was at the bar, getting me a drink. I noticed him when he walked in with some other guys. He definitely stood out in the crowd, though. He's tall. You know I'm not good at estimating stuff, but about this tall," said Liyah, gesturing with her hands.

"I'm assuming he had just gotten off of work because he was casually dressed with a gray peacoat. Come to think of it, I never asked. But anyway, we made eye contact, and he flashed me a smile. And man, that smile of his was to die for. I got my drink and went back to sit down. We were having a good old conversation, and about fifteen minutes goes by, and he comes to our table." They were both completely engaged in the conversation, MaKayla hanging on to every word and Liyah gesturing with excitement when she spoke.

"Now this made me nervous because I could see his table from where we were sitting, and the guys he came in with were all staring at us. So I was thinking, 'Here we go with the whole "We want to buy you ladies some drinks" line,' but that's not what happened. He got up from their table and started walking over to our table. I tried not to pay attention to him, but like I said, that smile was just so captivating.

"He said, 'Excuse me. I don't mean to interrupt, but may I sit for a second?' Of course, you know Donna. She was too excited. She said, 'Yeah, yeah, sure. Have a seat.' He sits down and turns directly toward me and says, 'I don't want to interrupt your ladies' night, but I just couldn't let an opportunity like this pass me by. I sat over there and fought with myself about coming over here since I saw you at the bar. I thought to myself, "Surely someone as stunningly beautiful as that has someone who cherishes and adores her, but who knows, maybe she's just waiting on the right man to treat her like the queen she is.'"" MaKayla was quiet, her mouth wide open with a huge grin.

"So we all were sitting there quietly. I had this big, dumb, goofy smile on my face, and he's just looking as if he's waiting for my response. I could barely bring myself to talk, but when I did, all I could say was, 'Are you talking to me?' He responded, 'No offense, ladies, but is there anyone else in this place that could meet such a standard?'

"Then you know Donna and Patrice. They got all loud. 'Ooh, he's laying it on thick. You better take advantage of that.' He smiled. 'I'm not trying to embarrass you. I was just hoping that if you didn't have that man who cherished and adored you, maybe you'd allow me the pleasure of having your number.' I was silent and stuck. I couldn't speak. So he says, 'Forgive me. Maybe I was too forthcoming. Would it be all right if I leave you mine and you call me? Is that something you'd be okay with doing?'

"I still couldn't bring myself to utter a word, so I just nodded my head yes, still sitting there with this goofy smile on my face, and I only know that because that's what Donna and Patrice told me later that night. He wrote down his number, got up, and walked around to where I was sitting. He handed me his number and held my hand ever so gently, but firm at the same time. 'I never got your name,' he said through that big smile of his. 'It's Aaliyah, but everyone calls me Liyah.' That was all I could say because I couldn't stop smiling," Liyah said, shaking her head while smiling in embarrassment.

"'My name is Darrell. It's a pleasure to meet you, and I look forward to hearing from you.' I sat there holding his hand for a while before I realized it was past the point where I should let it go. I didn't want to let his hand go, but I had to. I just wanted to freeze time, stay in that moment. It was perfect, unreal, and I felt—I don't know—lifted somehow if you know what I mean. He left me floating.

"It's crazy because after he went back to his table, I'd catch him staring, and our eyes would meet. Then he'd smile, and we'd break the eye contact. I called him that very next day, and we've been talking ever since. Would you believe that I actually had to build up my confidence to talk to him, to even call him?" said Liyah through a stern smile.

"What? Are you serious? Not you!" said MaKayla, smiling. "You're always talking tough. Now look at you. He had you stuck," she said, shaking her head. "I'm not surprised, though. I've been telling you for years that you would meet someone that would stun you. Plus, you know that I'm rarely wrong about those things."

"I know, but you just don't know. I mean, how could you know? How do you always know?" asked Liyah, smiling.

"I know that's not a serious question. Being around each other since Pampers and sticky fingers, I know everything there is to know about you. We are one and the same, cut from the same cloth, two peas in a pod. Just like you told me in so many words, you deserve the best and nothing short of it," MaKayla stated, smiling.

Liyah's eyes slowly began to fill from hearing those words come out of MaKayla's mouth. It had been so long since they had a real conversation, and she missed hearing those types of encouraging words from her. "Awww bestie, that's the reason you hold that title. You're trying to make me cry," she said, wiping her face.

"Not at all love. I'm just stating facts. But man, a month? Plus, he had you stumped, and I wasn't there to see it. I didn't even get a call or a text about this guy. Where have I been?" said MaKayla, shaking her head.

"Wait. Hold up. I called you twice that night. You said you were tired and had a test in the morning so you would call me after you finished it, but you never did," said Liyah matter-of-factly.

"Oh, I do remember that. I'm slacking for real. I can't believe I'm this far behind on what's going on with my best friend," said MaKayla, her somber mood beginning to return.

"I understand. Don't beat yourself up over it. What matters is that we're talking right now and catching up, so now you know." Liyah smiled. "So what's this guy's name that's been keeping you from me?" she asked slyly.

MaKayla laughed. "Which one are you talking about—the author of those textbooks, the men on the money I've been trying to make for these bills, the professors, or what?" They both started laughing. "I don't have time for a guy right now. I have to stay focused," replied MaKayla, although it wasn't how she really felt.

"You're so silly, but I do hear what you're saying. It's just, sometimes, you need something that will take your mind off of all of that, something to give you a break from the monotony and stress—you know, someone who might be able to help you relieve some of that built-up pressure, if you know what I mean."

MaKayla looked at Liyah, and they both erupted into laughter. "Something is seriously wrong with you," said MaKayla after catching her breath.

"I just realized what you said, though!" said Liyah curiously.

"What I said when?" asked MaKayla.

"Earlier, you said that you're going to be packing tomorrow. You're going somewhere?" asked Liyah.

"Oh yeah, but I thought I told you. I'm going to visit my parents for spring break. I just have to make it through these last few days, and I'll be able to really relax. Plus, I'm really starting to miss them again. I haven't really been able to keep in touch with them as much as I'd like because of how busy I've been," replied MaKayla, dropping her head a little.

"A vacation sounds nice. I need to see my parents too. I wish I had known earlier. I would've tried to go with you. How long do you think you'll be gone? Are you sure Mr. Stacy is going to let you leave?" asked Liyah, smiling.

"I'm going to be gone for both weeks of spring break, and yeah, he understood. I mean, after all, I have been working almost every day now and putting in my internship hours there too. He's been trying to get me to take some time off for a while. You should ask him if you can get the time too," said MaKayla, perking up.

"I'll see about the second week, but the first week, I already have plans. I want to try to get in a lot of hours at my internship so I don't have to worry about that so much after the break," said Liyah.

"Oh, I understand. That makes a lot of sense. My load will be a little lighter after break because I've put in so many internship hours already. I don't have many left," replied MaKayla.

"See? I'm trying to get like you," said Liyah, laughing.

"How is William by the way? I haven't seen him in a while. I forgot to ask you about him earlier when you brought him up, saying he was going to paint for you." MaKayla perked up again. This got her excited. She really enjoyed hearing everything about Liyah and her family, especially since they hadn't been keeping in touch as often. She still wanted to hold on to the things and people that were important to her. She felt like she was losing sight of those things while trying to handle the new aspects of her life.

"Oh, William, he's fine. He's into sports and things of that sort. You know, he does things that guys do." Liyah laughed. "That's why I said I'll get him to paint for me because he enjoys doing things like that. He doesn't know he's going to do it, but he will soon enough." They both laughed.

"I'm sure he won't mind," said MaKayla.

"He won't have a choice." Liyah smiled. "You know, with him owning the construction company and all, he does the jobs he wants and lets his employees do the others. I guess he enjoys the fact that he's the boss, but I don't know about all that." She shrugged.

"Well, I can't wait until I'm the boss and owner of my own establishment. You make your own schedule and can work when or if you please. I mean, instead of having to work every day and meeting certain quotas yourself, you have a team of people striving to meet those quotas with you. Are you honestly telling me you wouldn't want to be your own boss? I mean, I really like Mr. Stacy, and he treats us good, but can you tell me that you wouldn't want his position?" MaKayla smiled.

"I don't know, honestly. I guess it would depend on where I'm working. You know I enjoy dealing with numbers, but I'm not too sure about the managing aspect. I mean, I could imagine having my own accounting firm. But at the same time, I wouldn't mind working for someone. Having your own company or business is a lot of work and pressure. You know that's like some superhero type of stuff—'With great power comes great responsibility!'" said Liyah in a deep, manly voice. They both laughed loudly. "But anyways, enough about me and William. How are you really?" she asked, looking sincerely at MaKayla.

"I'm good. Really, I am. I've started running in the mornings to help clear my mind when I start my day, and it's been helping," replied MaKayla.

"What's been on your mind that heavy that you need to clear it when you start your day? I would expect that when you end your day, but not when you start it," said Liyah with a confused face.

"Well, that's my way of relieving that built-up pressure you were talking about." They both laughed again. "Seriously, though, other than school, work, and internship stuff, I've really been missing my brother lately. I try not to get myself worked up about it, because I know for sure it'll affect my day at work or school. I know he wouldn't want that," said MaKayla, sighing. "I can honestly say he and William would've definitely been partners in the work field or something close to it. Remember how they always did everything together back then?" she asked through a smile.

"I miss him too, and that's weird because I was just thinking about him the other day just out of the blue. And I'm sure you're right, they would've. They were glued together as if they were brothers. Our parents didn't help either. If one was in a basketball camp, so was the other. If one was going to the movies, get the other one ready, because he was going too!" said Liyah, shaking her head, smiling.

"Well, we don't have much room to talk," said MaKayla. "We were the same way and still are. Look at us now." She laughed.

"Shh!" said Liyah, putting her finger to her mouth. "No one has to know." MaKayla smiled and shook her head. "Sometimes, I think about how things would have been if he were still here. You know, William took it so hard. He still talks about that day. Somehow, he still thinks that if he had gone to the park with Marcus that day instead of being sick, he would still be here. He always tells me he could've saved him, or maybe they would've gotten to that baby faster if they both were going to save him. He still has all those pictures of him and Marcus posted everywhere. I swear he was the brother he never had," she said, sadly staring at the ground.

Marcus was MaKayla's older brother by two years and was the same age as William, who was Liyah's older brother. Marcus went to the park one day, one of the few times he ever did without William.

He saw a baby chasing a ball into the street and ran after the baby. He made it in time to push the baby out of the way of an oncoming truck but consequently couldn't get out of the way himself. He died several hours later in the hospital from internal bleeding.

"That's why he was so big on us coming to school out here so that he could be close to us in case we need anything," said Liyah, shaking her head.

"Okay. Let's change the subject. I'm beginning to become sad, and I don't want to shift the mood like that," said MaKayla as she wiped her eyes.

"You're right," replied Liyah, placing her arm around MaKayla and smiling as she stared into her eyes. "What time are you supposed to be getting off tonight?" she asked, smiling.

MaKayla paused and smiled while looking at Liyah. "Now you know I'm going to be there until closing again!" she said, and they both laughed softly.

They went into the café and ate their food in the back, still conversing about things that had been going on in their respective lives. It wasn't very busy inside the café, so they were able to talk to a few employees as well. "Let's get ready to start our shift," said Liyah. "I'm ready to get today over with too." They laughed and gathered their things, and the workday started.

The only thing MaKayla could think about was how she would be able to get a few more hours of sleep knowing that her schoolwork was done. She had really enjoyed her conversation with Liyah. It was so good to talk and laugh with her again. She knew she would always be there no matter what. She didn't have any other friends like that in her life. She was also looking forward to taking that run in the morning. The weather had finally begun breaking, and it was starting to warm up. It should be a good run. *But no sense in thinking about tomorrow when I still have to get through today,* she thought.

This workday in particular seemed to drag. MaKayla found herself drained halfway through her shift. *A few more hours,* she thought. *Then I'll be able to rest up.* The café wasn't busy at all, so MaKayla did a lot of thinking as she took care of the small things around the café, such as refilling the salt and pepper shakers, ensuring there were enough sugar and napkins at every table, and things like that.

She thought about her conversation with Liyah, about how she had talked about Darrell. *I hope he's really the one for her. She really deserves it. She always manages to find herself caught up with someone who doesn't appreciate or cherish her. Hopefully, this one is different. I can tell from the way she talks about him that she really likes him.* MaKayla thought about how she said that she didn't have time for a guy right now. But actually, she wished she had that one person, who could make sense of all the confusion, and calm the calamity.

She figured it would be nice to have someone to come home to after all the stress she went through day in and day out. Someone who would just hold her and allow her to forget about everything else, to just melt away in his arms. *I can't wait to find love, like, real love,* she thought. *I feel like I've been through enough over my twenty-two years of living, and I hope my time is near. I just want to have that one person there for me through everything, us uplifting each other and pushing each other to our furthest potential.*

MaKayla sighed and smiled while shaking her head. *Wishful thinking, I suppose. Where will I find something like that?* She laughed at herself. *Maybe in a million years or another lifetime,* her conscience retorted. *Yeah, you're right. What was I thinking anyway?*

Before MaKayla knew it, her shift was close to ending. *I guess all that thinking helped me make it through this day.* She spoke to Liyah as she was getting ready to leave.

"Do you want me to wait for you?" asked Liyah.

"Girl, don't you have to be here to open tomorrow? You need to go home and get some sleep. I'll close everything down and lock up," said MaKayla confidently.

"You sure? You know it's no biggie for me. You don't need a ride? It's too late for you to be trying to take a bus," said Liyah as she leaned on the counter, keys in hand.

"Yeah, I'm sure. I haven't taken the bus in quite some time now. I already called a cab, and yes, it's the same cab driver that always takes me home." MaKayla smiled before Liyah got a chance to ask.

Liyah smiled back. "You know I was going to ask."

"Sure did. Now are you going to try to come by tomorrow?" asked MaKayla as she continued to look over the daily receipts.

"Yeah. After my last class at seven, I'll try to stop by if that's okay," said Liyah as she stood up, stretching.

"That works for me," MaKayla said, coming around the counter to the side Liyah was on.

"Okay. See you then." They hugged, then she left.

*****

After locking up, MaKayla headed home for the night. The cab ride was very quiet, and although this was her routine cab driver, they did not talk aside from them greeting each other. Instead, MaKayla stared out the window, at the night sky, how the moon peered from behind the rolling clouds. The clouds drifted across the sky aimlessly.

She noticed that there weren't many cars on the road and even less people walking. They were all probably at home, getting ready for tomorrow. A smile crept on her face. *I'm almost done with this chapter of my life. Just a few more months and the real journey begins.* She was excited to see what the future held for her, to see where all her hard work and effort would take her.

MaKayla thought about how proud her parents would be of her, envisioning the smiles on their faces as they embraced her. *Soon, this part of my life will be nothing but a memory, a story to tell my kids one day,* she thought. She let out a laugh unintentionally.

The driver looked at her curiously. "You okay?" he asked through a smile.

"Yeah, yeah. It's nothing," she said, waving her hand as if she was saying hello. *Me with kids,* she thought. *I think I'm getting ahead of myself. One thing at a time. One thing at a time.*

MaKayla made it home around ten thirty. She ate some leftover chicken wings and hopped in the shower. *Now let's see how much sleep I'll really get,* she thought. Then she was fast asleep before she knew it.

*****

SPRING SHOWERS—THE BLOOM

The next morning, she woke up a little after seven and went for her run. It was about fifty degrees and sunny, which made it feel warmer. There were a lot of people running this day. She assumed it would be like this a lot more with the weather getting warmer. She took a different route this morning, one that took her through the park. It was really becoming so beautiful. The flowers were beginning to bloom, and all the ends of the tree branches were covered with green buds.

The animals seemed to be so happy too. It was like a scene from a Disney movie. They were all running and jumping around playfully while the birds sang beautiful songs from the trees. MaKayla figured she would make this a permanent part of her route. *I could get used to starting my days with such happiness and beauty.* She smiled as she watched two rabbits run after each other. She returned home feeling refreshed and invigorated after her run. *Might as well keep this day going,* she thought.

After taking a shower and eating breakfast, her furniture arrived. She had the movers put the furniture in a manageable position, seeing how she didn't have time to organize it the way she wanted. She knew it would take her a while and a few different positions before she settled on one that she liked. She got her things ready, and she left for class.

MaKayla couldn't focus for some reason. Her mind drifted in and out of the lectures her professors were giving. *Man, I even had a great run. Why can't I focus? Maybe I need this vacation even more than I thought. I might just need a complete reset and change of scenery for a while,* she thought. She got a text from Liyah at four thirty: "I'll definitely be there after my class. I got a surprise. Well, some good news to tell you."

"I can't wait to hear it!" replied MaKayla. She figured it would be something about Darrell or about William painting for her. The simplest things always made Liyah happy. But the fact that Liyah was so happy and excited made MaKayla happy as well, and she couldn't help but put a smile on her face.

After class, MaKayla went home, put on some music, and began situating her furniture. To her surprise, she got it in a position of her liking a lot quicker than she anticipated, so she began packing for her trip. Before she knew it, time had flown by. She received a message from Liyah. "Have you eaten? I'm stopping to get tacos. Want some?"

MaKayla realized that she hadn't eaten since breakfast. Plus, she loved tacos. Liyah, of course, knew that. Even if she had already eaten, she would eat again if it meant that she got to eat tacos. "Of course. You know I want some. 2 steak, 2 chicken. You know how I like them," she responded.

Within thirty minutes, her doorbell was going crazy. As she opened the door, in rushed Liyah. "Now why didn't you use that key I gave you?" asked MaKayla.

"Oh yeah, I forgot. Plus, my hands were pretty full, as you can see, and I have to use the bathroom pretty bad. Where is it again?" asked Liyah hurriedly as she set down the bags of food and took off her coat.

"Second door on the left down that hall," MaKayla said, pointing.

"Okay. Your food is the one on the left," said Liyah as she rushed off. She returned a few minutes later. "Whew!" she said.

MaKayla was already stuffing her face with tacos. "I tried to wait for you, but you took too long," she said through a mouthful of tacos.

"I was only gone for, like, two or three minutes, girl," said Liyah, shaking her head, smiling.

"I was hungry. I hadn't eaten since this morning, and you shouldn't have told me which bag was mine if you didn't want me to start eating without you," said MaKayla, smiling with a mouthful of tacos. "Now what's this surprise you have to tell me? You and Darrell getting married?" she asked, smiling, as she took another bite of her taco.

"Nooooo!" Liyah said smiling. She put her head down, almost blushing. "But I did talk to Mr. Stacy and he said I can get the second week off. I already bought my ticket so I'll be down there with you for the second week of spring break!" she said excitedly.

"Oh my God, are you serious?" asked MaKayla excitedly. "I'm so happy right now."

SPRING SHOWERS—THE BLOOM

They hugged, and Liyah pulled out her food. "We have to do everything. That week will be our comeback. Girl, we're going to…" Liyah stopped midsentence.

"What's wrong? Why are you looking like that?" asked MaKayla, worried.

"This furniture is gorgeous, and you are so right, it goes perfect with the walls," said Liyah, peering around the room.

MaKayla threw a napkin at her. "Man, don't scare me like that. I was worried for a minute."

"Oh, sorry. You know how I am about this stuff. All you need is some wall decorations, and it'll be perfect. We should do that while we're on our vacation," said Liyah as if she just had the best idea.

"Sounds like a plan to me," said MaKayla as she took another bite.

They sat and talked for hours as MaKayla packed. Before they knew it, it was 2:00 a.m., so Liyah just spent the night. Neither had anything to do before ten, and they would both be heading to the school at that time anyway. They figured they would just go together since Liyah's place was on the way to the school, even though they would be going to different classes.

*****

Thursday went by fast for MaKayla. It was very hectic between school and work. She even forgot that she had an assignment due on Friday morning, and since she had work, she promised her professor she would turn it in by Thursday night. Her professors knew her situation pretty well and the load she had on her plate. So whenever they could, they would cut a few corners to help her out, trying to lighten her load and ease her stress.

This was one of those times, but she knew being late with the assignment would not look good. She didn't want to make it appear as if she was taking advantage of the situation, so she stayed up until three to complete the assignment although she had to be at the café to open by eight. She figured she would get up at six thirty and try to get in a quick run to start her day. It usually gave her an extra boost of energy. She hoped it would do the same tomorrow because she would definitely need it.

After a quick shower, MaKayla set her alarm and allowed her bed to take her away to the place of sleep, hoping it would also equal rest.

Chapter 2

Alarm clock buzzing, in walked Jaron, his towel wrapped around his waist, wet from head to toe. *Today's going to be a good day,* he thought as he turned off the alarm. *Why do I still use this alarm seeing as I haven't slept through an entire night for almost two years now, not even when the guys and I have one of those crazy nights? Force of habit, I suppose.* He shrugged his shoulders as he turned off his phone.

The playlist was still going from when he was in the shower. He turned on the TV—SportsCenter, as usual. Then he walked into his closet and was surrounded by a plethora of different-colored suits, shirts, and shoes. He grabbed a dark-gray suit and a lightly tinted purple shirt with shoes to match, then laid it on the bed and grabbed his underclothes as he finished drying off.

Before getting completely dressed, he walked downstairs into the kitchen. *I think I'll have a light breakfast,* he thought. Grabbing the eggs and sausages from the refrigerator, he turned on the stove and began cooking. It didn't take long. After grabbing some OJ, he headed back to his bedroom. He got dressed as he ate, watching highlights from last night's games. "Dang," he said. "I knew we should've gone to that game. I knew it was going to be a good one. That's what we get for listening to Xavier."

Jaron looked at his watch. "Seven o'clock," he said. "I guess I'll be a little early today." His phone rang. He looked down and saw his mom's smiling picture and couldn't help but smile back. "Good morning, Mom," he said with a smile as he answered the phone.

"Good morning, baby. How'd you sleep?" she replied.

"Eh, up and down, but I don't feel tired. How are you?" asked Jaron.

"I'm okay. Getting ready to go to breakfast with my friend Tracy. You remember Tracy, don't you?" asked his mom.

"Yeah, I remember Tracy. Tell her I said hi. You got today off, or are you going in late?" asked Jaron as he began buttoning up his shirt.

"I'm off today. Remember, I told you I have to go in for my checkup," she replied.

"Oh yeah, I forgot. What time is your appointment again?" he asked.

"One o'clock," replied his mom.

"Oh, okay. Maybe I'll try to stop by when I get off," he said, fastening his sleeves.

"Okay. Well, have a good day at work. I love you," she said through a smile.

"I love you too," he said before they hung up.

Jaron took his plate to the garbage and put a few things back in place that he had moved the night before. Grabbing his briefcase and laptop bag, he headed out the door. Outside, the weather was beginning to warm up. Spring was approaching, but he could still see his breath. He surveyed the neighborhood, taking in the beauty, as he often did before going to work.

He noticed that everything was still. No one was up or moving along the streets, which was pretty awkward for a Tuesday morning. He would often see the Johnsons and their kids, who were usually running late for some reason. *Must have been on time today,* he thought as he walked to his car. The pavement was dark gray and still damp from the overnight showers that had passed through. He stood by the car, closed his eyes, and inhaled. The smell of nature after the rain was one of his favorite scents. He allowed the smell to fill him, and a smile rose onto his face.

He sat down in his car, placing his bags on the passenger seat, and skimmed his playlists, looking for something that would go with his mood. "This will definitely do it. Mellow but hits hard—that's how I'm feeling today," he said as he drove down the street.

*****

SPRING SHOWERS—THE BLOOM

Traffic was about average, and he arrived at work in a timely manner. He got out of the car and stretched before walking around to get his briefcase and computer bag from the other side.

"Good morning, Mr. Coleman. You're here early today," greeted the receptionist as he entered the building.

"Good morning, Krystal. Yeah, I figured I'd get a jump-start on the day. Is everything good with you?" he asked through a smile.

"Yeah, it's going good. No complaints from me," she replied, smiling back.

"That's what I like to hear. Enjoy your day," he replied as he headed to the elevator.

"Sure thing," she replied as the elevator doors closed.

Jaron arrived at his floor. It was mostly empty, except for a few people at their desks and Tina, his assistant. "Good morning, Mr. Coleman," she greeted him from her desk. "Getting an early start on the day, huh?"

"Yeah. You know, no reason to sit around wasting time when I could be trying to—"

"Save the world," they both said at the same time. They laughed together. "I know, I know," said Tina.

"I know it's early, but do I have any messages?" he asked.

"Yes, you have three, two from our suppliers—you know, order confirmations—and one from Mr. Wynstead," she said, handing him a couple of papers.

"Okay. Thanks. I'll get right on it," he said, looking at the papers.

"You sure about this?" asked Tina.

"About what?" he asked curiously.

"This whole Wynstead deal," she replied with a nasty undertone as she turned up her lip. "There's just something about him that doesn't sit right with me."

Jaron laughed. "You sound like Dad," he said, shaking his head, smiling. "It's about time that we moved forward, and I think he's the one to help us do that. Change is never easy—"

"But it's always necessary," they said together. They laughed together again. "I know, I know," Tina said.

Jaron walked into his office and placed his bags down. He was the owner and CEO of Coleman Industries, one of the leaders in innovative medical advancements. His company only dealt with natural ingredients. All their medicines and vaccines contained no artificial or man-made ingredients, which cost more, but Jaron always felt it was worth it to help people in that way. They had a lot of regional success, but he was looking to expand the business to go nationwide and at some point, hopefully, global. He really hoped Mr. Wynstead would be the key to making that happen.

He stood there in his office, looking out of the huge floor-to-ceiling picture windows, appreciating the beautiful view he had. He would often sit there and stare. *All those people,* he thought. *So much to be done, so much change needed.* He picked up a picture he had sitting on his desk. "I hope I'm doing the right thing," he said out loud, looking at the picture of his dad.

His father was the one who began the business when Jaron was in college. It had always been a dream of Jaron's, something his dad had promised to help him achieve. Initially, he was part owner with him, his father being the CEO and him being the co-CEO. They were like Batman and Robin, the dynamic duo, as they often called themselves. Jaron smiled. He and his father had discussed the potential of doing business with Mr. Wynstead before the accident.

His father died in a car crash caused by a drunk driver as he was returning from work late one night almost two years ago. His father left his portion of the business to Jaron, and he became the CEO and sole owner. It was the hardest thing that Jaron ever had to endure. He and his father were close. He was like his best friend.

He struggled to sleep at night. It was as if his mind never rested, like his mind was doing everything it could to ensure that Jaron would never forget him. Or maybe it was so busy trying to find some way for him to be closer to his father, he often thought. So he would be up and down throughout the night, tossing and turning from thinking about his dad and anything else his mind chose to add to his load.

He remembered going around as a kid, always trying to help people feel better. His dad got him a little medical bag on his tenth birthday that he carried all his supplies in back then. He had told his dad that he was going to change the world. His dad never doubted or questioned him. He just simply asked, "What can I do to help? How can I be a part of it?"

So even back then, he and his father would sit for hours, just planning the business and what they wanted to accomplish. His father would always say how amazed he was by his knack for business at such a young age. "Just never forget why you're doing it, what started you on this path in the beginning. It will come in handy when you least expect it. Sometimes, it's okay to make decisions with your heart and not your head. Your heart cares more. Your head is always worried, cautious, and sometimes, even afraid," his father would say.

His dad was just a regular businessman. He had no medical ties outside of his mother, who was a pediatrician at the time. His mom was the one who connected his father with the medical people to start the business. His dad wasn't sure about Mr. Wynstead either. "Something just doesn't sit right with me," he would say.

Wynstead was one of those businessmen who really only cared about the bottom line, not so much about the product or consumer, or at least that was what they gathered from the few meetings and phone conversations. That wasn't necessarily their way of going about things, but seeing as they spent more on supplies and sold their products for less than their competitors, turning a profit and growth became somewhat of a struggle.

They held off on brokering a deal to look for other options and do more research. Jaron wasn't 100 percent sure, but if it meant helping more people, he felt he had to do it. Plus, he wanted his father to be proud of him. He felt that he was watching. His father's loss had drawn him and his mom a lot closer—all his immediate family, actually.

Jaron felt that he had to step up now, really keep the family together. His mom would tell him time and time again, "It's okay. We're okay. You can relax." Yet it was still hard for him to do so. His father was a great man in every way that he could remember, and in his mind, he had to be just as great.

His phone buzzed and brought him back to reality. He looked at it. There was a text message from Xavier. "Dinner and drinks tonight with the guys. You in?" it read. "Yeah. I'll call you when I'm leaving my mom's house," Jaron replied. "Cool," replied Xavier. He picked up his work phone and called Mr. Wynstead. Wynstead's assistant answered the phone. "Please hold, Mr. Coleman, while I transfer you." The phone rang twice before a very deep male voice answered. It was Wynstead.

"Mr. Coleman, ah, I see you got my message. Sorry to call so early, but my workday begins at five. You know money never sleeps, so why should we?"

"Yes, I understand, Mr. Wynstead. How are you doing?" asked Jaron in an upbeat tone.

"I'm very good, very good. Thanks for asking. I trust we are still on for this Friday, right?" asked Wynstead.

"Yes, we are. Is twelve thirty still good for you?" asked Jaron.

"Give me one moment." Jaron heard Wynstead's voice. "Jennifer, am I still free Friday at twelve thirty?" he asked rather loudly. "Yes, that will work just fine!" he replied to Jaron several seconds later.

"Okay. Then—" Jaron was cut off by Wynstead.

"Sorry I didn't make it to your father's funeral. I had an early tee time that day, which had a pretty big business deal riding on it. You know how business is. I trust you got the flowers. I suppose I should've said something before now, but seeing as though we'll be partners soon, I figured I'd clear that up."

"Yes, I did. Thank you," replied Jaron. The conversation didn't feel right. He wasn't sure what to think about the abrupt nature in which Wynstead brought up his father's funeral. His tone felt somewhat dismissive. He figured it was something he had read too deeply into.

"Well, I'm sorry for your loss, but I'm glad we're able to finally get the ball back rolling on this deal. It'll be huge for both of us," replied Wynstead quickly.

"Thank you. And so am I. So I'll see you Friday," said Jaron.

"Yes, see you Friday!" said Wynstead before hanging up.

After hanging up, Jaron took out his laptop and began checking and responding to emails. Shortly after, Tina knocked and walked in.

"I'm going to run to the cafeteria for tea. Do you want something?" she asked.

"Yeah. Can you bring me a bottle of water and an apple if you please?" he replied.

"All right. I'll be back in a sec," she replied, closing his door as she left.

"Oh, Tina."

"Yes, Mr. Coleman?" she said, smiling, as the door slowly opened again.

"Can you make sure that my schedule is cleared Friday from twelve to three? I have a meeting with Wynstead at twelve thirty."

"Can do," she replied. "Is that all, or is there something else?"

Jaron looked up from his laptop, smiling. "That's all for now."

"Okay then. I'll be back in a sec," she said, smiling, as she closed the door.

Jaron called the suppliers to confirm his orders and ensure the quantities were correct. After the calls, he went about his daily business until about eleven forty-five. He got up and grabbed his coat. "I'm going to lunch Tina. Do you need anything before I go?"

"No, I'm okay, but can you bring me back one of those pastrami sandwiches?"

"Wait. How do you know that where I'm going for lunch has pastrami sandwiches?" he asked through a grin.

"You go to the same place every day. They probably know you by name and you're like a member or something." They both laughed.

"Okay, okay. You got me. How do you want it?"

"Just plain with mustard."

"All right. I'll be back in about an hour."

"Sounds good," she replied, smiling.

As Jaron walked out the front door, he could tell that it had warmed up significantly. It was still cool enough for a coat, but not cold enough to have it closed. He liked to walk to the little café that he went to just about every day for lunch unless the weather was inclement. Then he would drive. It wasn't far anyway, about four to five blocks away.

He went into the cozy little café and sat by the window. He loved this place. It reminded him of how the simplest things could be wonderful, how something so small could make your day. He enjoyed sitting by the window because he got to watch life. All those people and their lives, he imagined that they were all happy and enjoying their day. It made him feel better, especially on those really trying days.

He ordered his regular—ham and turkey on white bread, lightly toasted, extra mayo, extra mustard, one slice of American cheese, one slice of Swiss cheese, two tomato slices, two leaves of lettuce, a glass of water, and a lemonade with a lot of ice. He smiled as the waitress walked away. He figured that everyone knew his order by now because of how much he came and ordered it. *Maybe they could make a special just for me,* he thought.

Jaron was in an unusually good mood, and he couldn't quite put his finger on it. *Does this little café make me this happy? Or maybe it's the impending deal with Mr. Wynstead. Nah, that usually worries me or makes me nervous. What is it? I mean, sure, it's nice outside, but I'm never this happy over the weather. Oh well, I'll just go with it,* he thought.

Just then, she walked out of the back room; and at that moment, it was as if time froze, just for the briefest of moments. Like the gods, smiling down, knew his predicament, how much the very sight of her complemented his day. He smiled at the thought of it. Surely no one would care so much about him to do something like this. Well, maybe his mom or dad did. The thought of his dad up there, pulling strings for him, gave him an added level of happiness. He let out a slight chuckle at the thought, and the sound of it caught the attention of a few people sitting close by. He quickly composed himself and smiled off the attention.

Regardless of why or how it was happening, he was grateful to be able to appreciate such magnificent beauty, to simply be allowed to bask in her presence. Now he always saw her, but he never knew her name. Even after coming in for so long, she had never served him. He tried a few times to get a glimpse of her name tag, but the fear of being caught staring always deterred him. He had never even heard anyone call her, but it was probably because he spent so much time deep in thoughts and daydreams when she was around. He was sure he had missed it several times over by now.

Sure, they spoke in passing, a regular "Hi" or "Have a nice day," but nothing more than that. He was infatuated with her, even if it was only the sight of her. The sight of her, he thought, just taking a moment to save another image of her to his memory bank. This was the reason he came to this little café every day. He just hoped to see her, hoped she would serve him and he could maybe start up a conversation. It would seem that fate, however, would not have this in the cards for him.

Sure, Jaron could have approached her himself, but that wasn't in his nature. He didn't want to be too forthcoming, so he waited, hoping for the perfect opportunity, hoping they would be placed in one big, serendipitous situation. *It could all be so simple,* he thought. He caught himself staring and quickly looked away, but his eyes slowly moved back in her direction.

He couldn't help it. She was so beautiful. It was like he was a magnet drawn to some precious metal. He never thought he had a type, but if he did, he figured she was definitely it. No, scratch that. She broke the mold, was immensely better than the prototype. *Simply one of a kind,* he thought.

She had black dreads that faded into a reddish-brown color the farther they went down, falling just past her shoulder blades and coming to rest on her back. She had a smile that lit up the room whenever she walked in, and those cheeks, perfectly round, became plump whenever she smiled. She was short, probably coming to his chest or shoulders, maybe a little smaller. He figured she was somewhere between five and five-four, petite but not skinny, just right in all the right places. She moved as models moved, but it was effortless, just graceful.

He imagined them sitting for hours, just talking. They would talk about everything and nothing, but it wouldn't matter. They would be happy, engulfed in each other's presence. They would be home. Her laugh eased his nerves. That was what her laugh did for him. It made him feel that everything was okay even if he only heard it from a distance or in passing. There was a comforting nature to it. He could feel his entire body relax when he heard it. He would stare into those deep-brown eyes and get lost for eternity.

Jaron slowly drifted back to reality as the waitress appeared with his food. He sat there, shaking his head, smiling. "Is something funny?" the waitress asked.

He smiled. "It's nothing. Just thinking, that's all."

"Oh, okay," she said through a smile. "Will that be all for now?"

"Yeah. Oh, wait. Can I get a pastrami sandwich to go?"

"What would you like on it?" she asked.

"Just mustard, and that's all."

"Okay. You can pick it up on your way out the door if that's okay."

"Sounds like a plan."

"Okay. Just let me know if you need anything else."

"All right," he replied before taking a bite from his sandwich.

As Jaron ate, he fell back into his thoughts about her. He figured she was intelligent and cultured. Probably into the arts and loved music. She was probably athletic and loved to dance. He smiled as these thoughts danced in his head. He began wondering if she was okay, if she was happy, if she lived close by, and why she worked here.

These were thoughts that ran through his head almost every time he saw her. He often felt bad, as if he was stalking her or something. He shook his head. *Nah*, he thought. *They do have great sandwiches.* He smiled again, taking another bite of the sandwich. *I've got to get her off my mind. She probably has a guy anyway. I mean, someone as beautiful as that... And I'm sure she's intelligent. It's obvious from how she runs things here. Her mere presence commands the room. No way any guy would let her go.*

He finished eating and left the café, hoping he would see her on his way out, but he wasn't so lucky. The sky had gotten a little cloudy, but you could still see the sun peeking from behind them. He changed his thoughts to business and the impending meeting with Mr. Wynstead. He suddenly felt a little weird and uneasy, not as confident as before.

He shook it off the best he could and made his way to the office. Once he exited the elevator on his floor, he noticed that things were a lot busier than that morning. There were a lot of conversations and several phones ringing. He smiled. He loved his employees and how hard they worked to keep the company going. He hoped that this deal with Wynstead would allow him to show them how much he truly valued them.

Jaron walked toward his office and was stopped by a tall, slender man wearing glasses and suspenders. "I put that report you asked for on your desk, Mr. Coleman."

"How were the numbers, Gerry?"

"A little higher than we anticipated actually."

"Can we still make it work?"

"It'll be tight, but I believe so."

"That's all I needed to hear. Thanks again."

"You're welcome," said Gerry as the two men parted ways.

"Tina," said Jaron, "pastrami plain, just mustard, as you requested." He handed her a brown paper bag.

Tina smiled. "Why, thank you. What do I owe you?" she asked.

"Eh, don't worry about it. Just pay it forward," he said, lightly hitting his hand at her.

"Sure thing, boss."

"Hey, what did we say about you calling me boss?" he asked with a serious look on his face.

"I know, I know. Don't do it. We're all working together, and everyone matters just as much as the next person. Yada yada yada," she said, removing her sandwich from her bag and smiling.

"That's right," he said with a smile as he opened his office door.

Jaron had known Tina for as long as the company had been around. She began as the receptionist, but after his father's untimely passing, she became his assistant. His father's old assistant couldn't continue after what happened. She said the building reminded her too much of his father. Tina was more like a sister than an assistant, though, and he would prefer it if she viewed it that way as well.

"Oh yeah, you got a call from a Mr. Thomas while you were out. He asked if you can give him a call at your earliest convenience. I put the number on your desk, next to your report," she said, taking a bite out of her sandwich.

"Okay. Thanks, Tina," he replied, looking at the number on his desk.

"Sure thing," she mumbled through a mouthful of food.

Jaron smiled, closing his door. He picked up the report Gerry set on his desk. He skimmed a few pages and set it down. He sat back in his chair, a look of deep thought on his face, then sat up and dialed Mr. Thomas's number. The phone rang several times, and he got ready to hang up before a man answered the phone.

"Hello," said the man on the other end.

"Yes, hello. This is Jaron Coleman calling for Mr. Thomas."

"Oh, Jaron, hi. This is me. Well, you know, it's…" They both laughed before he finished his sentence. "My secretary just ran to the bathroom, so I had to run to answer the phone. How are you?" asked Mr. Thomas excitedly.

"That's quite all right," said Jaron, sitting back in his chair. "I'm doing pretty good. Just returning from lunch. How are you?"

"I'm doing well on this end too."

"That is good to hear. So what can I do for you?"

"Well, I know we haven't spoken in a while. I didn't want to appear insensitive to the loss of your father. I know what he meant to you, and he was a great man. I wasn't too sure where you were or where you were trying to go business-wise. It's just that a few things came open for me, and I was wondering if you were still interested in discussing a possible business deal. Forgive me if it is too soon to discuss these things. I completely understand."

"I truly appreciate that. It means a lot to me hearing those words from you. My father always spoke very highly and had great admiration for you and the manner in which you conduct business. I also appreciate you thinking of me and my company with the desire to do business with us. But actually, Mr. Thomas, I have an appointment this Friday to finalize a deal that I already have in place."

"That's completely understandable, and I wish you the best with that. I know you're destined for great things, Jaron. There's no doubt in my mind. I just figured I'd see if you'd allow me to go along for the ride," replied Mr. Thomas, laughing. "If anything should change or you need anything, give me a call, will you?"

"I definitely will."

"All right. Enjoy the rest of your day," said Mr. Thomas.

"Thank you. And you do the same," replied Jaron. They hung up.

Jaron sat back in his chair again, that same look of deep thought on his face. His mind was working through a number of different things, and he needed to take a moment to sort it all out. Mr. Thomas was a front-runner on his dad's list of potential business partners. He didn't have the financial backing of Mr. Wynstead, but he had that it factor, as his dad always called it.

Mr. Thomas cared about people. He cared about the bottom line as well, but not as much as the people he serviced. "It's pretty difficult to find that in the business world," his dad used to say. "Most people are just ruthless and care about themselves, so when you meet a good person, you have to keep them by your side."

Jaron sat up, smiling. He loved thinking about his dad and all the advice he had given him. They helped him hold things together and make better decisions. He sat there for a while, thinking of the decisions he had before him. He thought about his dad and wondered what he would have done. *No use stressing,* he thought. *We have a deal in place, so why not see where it takes us?*

He opened back up his laptop and began checking his emails again. He continued working throughout the rest of the day, making calls and updating reports. It was a pretty productive day, and he felt good as he began ending things. He went out of his office to Tina's desk.

"Anything else on the docket for today?"

"Nope, not on my agenda for you, unless you want to do my job."

"Nope. That's quite all right." They both laughed. "Do you need anything? If not, I'm going to get ready to leave."

"No, I'm good. I have a few things I need to finish up, and then I'll be heading home too," she said. "I should be out of here in about an hour or so."

"Okay. Sounds like a plan," he said.

Jaron walked back into his office and packed up his laptop and suitcase. He looked around the room, making sure everything was where it should be. Then he walked out, speaking and saying his goodbyes as he got on the elevator. Once he made it back to his car, he called his mom to make sure she was home and to let her know he was on the way.

Traffic was pretty bad, so it took him longer than he anticipated to make it to his mom's house. He figured it was probably because the weather was starting to get nice. He pulled into the driveway and got out of the car. His mom stayed in a two-story redbrick home with a big picture window in the front and a white door. There was an outdoor porch that had eight concrete steps leading up to it. There were short bushes at the bottom of the porch, followed by a bed of flowers, then the grass. On the left side was a driveway that led all the way to the back of the house.

Jaron stopped halfway up and went in through the side door. Inside, there were five bedrooms—three upstairs and two downstairs—plus a full basement. He had many memories in this house. He and his sisters grew up here. Even though none of them lived there now, his mom refused to sell the house after his dad's passing. She just couldn't bear letting it go. It was the first thing they purchased together, and it held much sentimental value. She wanted somewhere they could all come back to. Plus, it was paid for.

Jaron walked in and began calling his mom's name to let her know he was there. "In the kitchen," he heard his mom call out to him. He walked in and gave his mom a big hug and a kiss but didn't say anything because she was on the phone. He walked into the living room and began looking at the pictures on the mantle. There were pictures everywhere in the living room—on the walls, on the tables, and in a huge glass-and-wood cabinet that his parents had had for as long as he could remember.

He grabbed a picture and let out a chuckle. It was an old picture with him and his sisters taken maybe fifteen years ago. Even though it was so long ago, he remembered the day vividly. His dad had taken them all to the beach. They all built sandcastles and then took pictures of them all together, their individual sandcastles with the person who made it next to it.

There was his older sister, Kelly, who was two years older than him. Her sandcastle was small but very neat and detailed. On the other side, there was his younger sister, Shannon, who was two years younger than him. Her sandcastle was the biggest of all. She always had to have the biggest of everything. She didn't like the fact that she was the youngest, so that was her way of compensating, they always said. Then there was his castle. It was just normal. There was nothing special about it. It was just a regular castle in the middle.

"What are you doing?" asked his mom through a smile as she entered the room.

"Do you remember this day, Mom, when you guys took us to the beach and we all made sandcastles and then took pictures with them? Look at how neat and detailed Kelly's was, even back then, and of course, Shannon's had to be the biggest." They both smiled.

"I sure do remember this day," his mom said, smiling, as she took the picture and stared at it. "Even then, you can see all three of your personalities on display. Your dad and I used to talk about this day all the time. His babies, his talented babies, he always said."

The mood grew somewhat somber, and Jaron felt it. He decided to quickly change the subject. "So how was your checkup?"

"Oh, you know how those things are," replied his mom as she put the picture back on the mantle. "Everything was well. They want me to come back in a few weeks for some blood work."

"So the doctor didn't tell you that you need to relax more or anything about your blood pressure?"

"Well, of course, he suggested it," she said through a smile. "But I'm okay. Stop worrying."

Jaron's mom had begun having really high blood pressure over the past year, and he was determined to help her get a hold on it. "It's not so much of a worry, Mom, but you know that if Dad were here, you wouldn't be up and about as much as you are. You relaxed more when he was here." He said it before he could stop himself.

She looked at him with a smile on her face, but sadness filled her eyes. "I know," she said. "But I can't just sit around and do nothing. I'll go crazy. I have to keep busy. It's how I keep things together. I'm okay. I'm taking the necessary precautions. Plus, the supplements you gave me have been helping. Nothing is going to happen, okay?"

"All right, Mom. If you say so," he said with a smile. "How's Tracy? How was your breakfast?"

"It was good, and she's just as crazy as always. Kept me laughing the whole time. She said I should go on this cruise to Jamaica with her and some of the other ladies, but I don't know."

"What don't you know? It'll be good for you to just relax and be around people that keep you laughing. Just make sure you don't go trying to get your groove back," he said through a laugh.

"Get it back? Shoot, I never lost it," she said, chuckling. "But yeah, maybe it'll be good. How was your day? Did you talk to that girl yet?"

Jaron had told his mom about the waitress at the café, and she hadn't let him hear the last of it since. "My day was good and productive," he said, hoping to avoid the other question.

"So I take it that you didn't talk to her, then?"

"Well, Mom, there really wasn't an opportunity, you know?"

"You went to the café today, right?"

"Yes, but—"

"Then there was an opportunity," she said, smiling. "I'm surprised. You're usually confident and determined, not to be turned away."

"I am Mom, when it comes to business, with her, it's—I don't know—it's different."

"It's okay baby," she said, smiling. "All in due time. Come go into the kitchen so I can finish these dishes."

"Oh yeah, I have a meeting with Mr. Wynstead on Friday," he said as they walked into the kitchen.

"Oh, that's good, right?"

"I really hope so. You know it's my first major meeting since he's been gone. It'll be weird with it being just me by myself. I don't want to mess up Dad's name or anything like that."

She turned around with a look of concern on her face. "Now you listen here! This was your dream, not your father's. This is your company, not your father's."

"I know, but—"

"Don't interrupt when I'm talking, Jaron Coleman," she said sternly.

She hadn't used his middle name, so Jaron knew he wasn't in too much trouble. "Sorry," he said, taking a seat.

"You have to live your life for you. He lived his, so you can't live yours off of your father. You can't live just for him. There has to be you in there as well, living it for you. He's already proud of you. He used to tell me every day after work how smart you were and how much he knew you were going to accomplish. He used to tell me like I didn't know. I mean, you are my son, and you did get your brains from me," she said through a smile, turning back around to start back on the dishes.

"This is your choice to make. Whether success or failure, you learn from it and move forward. You take it in stride. You can't change the world if you're too busy beating yourself up over something you view as a mistake. There's a lesson in everything Jaron. You just have to open your eyes and allow yourself to learn it."

"I know, Mom. I just wish he were here, you know? We worked so great in everything together. He always knew exactly what to say when I was uncertain."

"Then he gave you the tools baby. Now it's up to you to use them."

"I just want this to be right. I don't want to make a mistake. I really feel that Wynstead can help me take us to the next level, but Dad wasn't sure about him, so it makes me wonder if I'm jumping the gun."

She chuckled. "I know his flaws. I discussed them with your father. But it's been almost two years. If you feel this is the move, then you stand on it with confidence. And if not, I promise, something just as good, if not better, will come through for you."

He smiled. "Thanks Mom. I don't know what I'd do without you." His phone began buzzing.

"Who is that?" his mom asked.

"Xavier. I'm supposed to be meeting him and the guys when I leave here."

"Oh, okay. Well, answer it," she said, smiling.

"Yooo," he said. "Nah, I'm still at Mom's. What about you? Mom, X said hi."

"Hey baby," she said.

"She said, 'Hey baby,'" said Jaron, laughing. "Nah, I'm not sure. What time are you guys going to head up there? All right cool. Well, I'll meet you guys up there around then. Yeah, I'll shoot you a text when I'm leaving. Cool. One," he said as he hung up.

"How is he?" she asked.

"You know X Mom. Still crazy as ever. He's got this new girl he's been talking about settling down with, but you know X, so we'll see how that goes."

"Well, maybe that's just what he needs."

"Here Mom, let me help you with these dishes," said Jaron, getting up and grabbing a dish from the sink. "You wash, and I'll rinse and dry. Deal?"

"You just think you're slick," she said, smiling.

"What?" he said through a smile.

"It's just dishes Jaron. It's not going to kill me. But come on then."

They talked as they finished the dishes, laughing and reminiscing. An hour later, he got ready to leave. "Okay Mom, I'll talk to you later. Love you," he said, giving her a hug. Then he opened the door to walk out.

"I love you too," she said. "And you better talk to that girl next time you see her."

"I'll think about it," he said, smiling, as he closed the door.

The temperature had dropped, and it had gotten windy. He could see that it was really cloudy, and he wondered if it would try to rain or snow. "Oh well," he said as he got in the car and backed out the driveway.

The bar and grill was about thirty minutes from his mom's house. There really wasn't any traffic, so he got there in about twenty-five minutes. As he pulled in, he noticed an opening between William's and Xavier's cars, so he parked there. He got out and walked into the bar and grill. It was pretty crowded for a Tuesday, but since they came there often, he already knew where the guys would be.

He walked toward the back and noticed Tony and Daniel walking back from the bar with drinks. As they got to the table, Jaron said, "I hope you guys got enough for me too."

"Oh, what's up man?" said Tony as he turned around to face him. Jaron did his normal greetings with the guys.

"What took you so long?" asked Troy.

"I was at Mom's house. You know how that goes—talking and helping with the dishes."

"Yeah man, I feel you."

"Okay, check this out man. So I say this is the last time we're going to listen to Xavier when it comes to going to a game," said William.

"I was just thinking that same thing this morning after watching those highlights," said Jaron. "I tried to tell you guys that it was going to be a good game."

"Hey, hey, hey now. Players mess up too. Who would've thought that game would be that good?" asked Xavier.

Jaron raised his hand. "Um, I did," he said. They all laughed.

"All right, all right," said Xavier.

"We should really try to make one of these games in the next couple weeks, though, before this season's out, because it's only going to get better," said Daniel. Without a second thought, they all agreed.

"So I see everyone's got drinks. I'm about to go grab me something. Y'all ordered food yet?" asked Jaron.

"Yeah, pizza, wings, and fries. Should be out in a little while," said Troy.

"All right. Cool. I'll be back in a minute."

After returning from the bar and taking his seat, Jaron noticed a sly grin on the other guys' faces. "Why are you guys looking at me like that?" he asked, smiling. They all started laughing.

"Well, we have this little wager that we figured maybe you could help us out with," said Tony.

"All right. What's up?" asked Jaron hesitantly.

"Okay, so we were wondering, out of all of us, who do you think Kelly would be the most interested in?" asked Tony.

Jaron paused and shook his head. He had known his friends all liked his sister for as long as he could remember. He hated indulging in these conversations, but he figured, what the heck? "I don't know why you guys keep going down this road, but okay," he said, shaking his head. "What's the wager?"

"Winner doesn't have to pay tonight," said Tony.

Jaron laughed. "Okay. Well, she always told me that Tony was the most handsome or nicest looking out of all of my friends."

Tony got really loud. "See? I told you it was me! Women can't resist my looks. I be killin' 'em before they even know it. Just one look and they're mine," he said. Everyone started laughing.

"The thing is, Tony, my sister doesn't like pretty boys." The guys loved poking fun at Tony at every opportunity they could. "She says they're too cocky, full of themselves, and believe they're God's gift to women." All the guys except Tony burst into laughter.

Tony, looking a little embarrassed, said, "Hey, I can't help it if God put me here for that sole purpose." He began laughing with them.

"If I had to say, it would most likely be Danny Boy," said Jaron. The name was a nickname they had given Daniel years ago as a joke, but it just stuck. "She always said he seemed the most polite and down-to-earth out of all of us. Plus, he has a nice smile, and my sister loves polite guys with nice smiles." Everyone was quiet for a while.

"Are you serious dude? Danny Boy?" said Xavier. "No offense or anything, but you weren't even really in this. You didn't even make a stance for why it would be you."

"None taken," replied Daniel, shrugging his shoulders. He was a really reserved person and didn't take much to heart.

"Yep, that's who I'd have to say, but it doesn't matter, because none of you have a chance! My sister would never date one of my friends. You guys are like family."

"Except for me though, right?" Daniel smiled. Jokingly.

"She's dating some guy now anyway, and she claims to really like him. James or Jimmy or Justin. I don't know. Something like that."

"That's all I needed to hear," said Daniel. "Pass me the drink menu William. I think I'll have another one considering I didn't drive and my tab's on you guys tonight."

SPRING SHOWERS—THE BLOOM

"Yeah, yeah, yeah," said William as he passed the menu.

"I really thought it would be me," said Xavier. "I'm always around, and your family loves me. This is all wrong." Everyone started laughing.

"Why do you care? I said none of you really have a shot. And aren't you still with Candace?" asked Jaron.

"Yeah, I am, but you know, what she doesn't know won't hurt her," said Xavier, smiling.

"That's why your relationships never last," said Troy, "because eventually, they always know."

"Oh, so I should be more like you," asked Xavier, "letting some woman control my life?"

"Nina doesn't control my life. I enjoy doing the things necessary to make and keep her happy, thank you very much."

There was a brief pause and then an eruption of laughter. Although Jaron laughed, he completely understood what Troy was saying. He wanted that as well and even envied him at times, but he was happy for him and Nina.

"Yeah, all right. You laugh now, but we'll see who's laughing when you're all fat and lonely while I'm happy at home with my family."

"Fat," said Tony. "I can never get fat. Don't you see this physique?" There was another pause, followed by more laughter.

"I feel you though," said Daniel. "We all want that eventually, but you and Nina have been together since what, like sophomore year of high school? Don't you ever wonder how it feels to be with someone else?"

"Why would I want to see how it feels when she does everything I need and more? I'm too busy keeping my grass green to be worried about if it's greener on the other side, although we have been throwing around the idea of adding someone to the equation, if you know what I mean." The guys sat there, stunned. "What? Why are you looking like that?" asked Troy curiously.

"It's a trap. Don't do it," said William, shaking his head.

"A trap?" asked Troy. "How could it possibly be a trap when it was her idea in the first place?"

"Okay, look, there are only a few ways this can go, none of which is good for you," said William. "First, you do it. Then come the questions. 'Did she do it better than me? Were you more attracted to her than to me? Whose body looked the best?' None of these questions you can answer and say anything against Nina, so that means you might have to lie, which starts even more issues. Then what if you want to do it again? You could never ask or bring it up. Why not, you may be wondering. Because then come more questions: 'Am I not enough? Are you tired of me? Are you not attracted to me?' Once again, it's going to be bad."

Troy laughed. "You don't know Nina. She's not like that at all. She wouldn't do that. We talk and have open conversations about everything without allowing our emotions to get the best of us."

"Yeah, that's until you stick your friend inside of another woman and she watches her get the best of you," said William, bringing the whole table to laughter.

Troy laughed again. "It's not like that man. I'm trying to tell you."

"Hey, I'm just trying to help, but if you say so."

"So what about you, big dog?" asked Tony to Jaron. "You got some special lady that's going to help you make some heirs to that Coleman empire you're building?"

"Nah. If he did, I would at least know about her," said Xavier.

"Yeah, there's no one right now. I'm just focused on work. Got a few things in the pipeline that could be huge for the future." Although that was what Jaron said, his mind really went to the waitress from the small café, but he hadn't told anyone other than his mom about her.

"Oh, that's what's up, but you know what they say," said Xavier.

"Nope, but I'm sure you're going to tell us," said Jaron, laughing.

"Can't be all work and no play," Xavier said through a smile.

"True, but Dad always told me that if I do what I have to do right now, I'll be able to do what I want to do later."

"Oooohhhhh, I think he just killed your argument right there, Xavier," said William.

"Yeah, yeah, yeah," said Xavier. "Well, I'll have enough fun for the both of us then. And don't bring up your dad to school me. You know I was there for many lessons."

"But did you listen?" asked Troy, and they all began laughing again.

Just then, three waiters arrived with what could have been compared to a smorgasbord of food. The guys all let out a cheer.

"Yeah, see, this is what I'm talking about. I'm starving," said Daniel.

"You're always hungry," said Tony.

"This is true, this is true," replied Daniel as he grabbed a slice of pizza with one hand and bit into a wing from the other hand.

The guys sat, ate, laughed, and joked the rest of the night. After eating and having a few more drinks, they said their goodbyes and went home. Jaron had a better sleep that night than the one before.

*****

Wednesday flew by. Thursday was also somewhat of a blur. Jaron did a lot of preparation for the big meeting, getting together the necessary documents and going over his presentation. He wanted everything to be perfect. He was more nervous than he had ever been seeing that this was the first time he had to prepare or decide on a deal of this magnitude without his father. "This can be the deal that puts us over the top, right where we want and need to be," he kept telling himself. He stayed later than normal at work and didn't even make his usual trip to the café. He really wanted this for his employees and the people he worked for. They deserved it.

On his way home, he called Xavier. He hadn't talked to him about the meeting yet and figured he would discuss it with him.

"What's going on man?" asked Xavier after answering the phone.

"Nothing much. Just leaving the office."

"Man, it's kinda late. Why are you still at work?"

"Yeah, that's why I called you. I actually got a meeting tomorrow with Wynstead."

"Wynstead, Wynstead, Wynstead," repeated Xavier out loud. "It sounds familiar, but I can't remember where I know the name from. Who's that?"

"You remember the guy I told you my dad and I were thinking about going into business with?"

"Oh yeah, now I remember. But I thought your dad wasn't too fond of him."

"Well, it wasn't that. He just wasn't sure about some of his business methods, mostly his lack of concern for the people he worked for. I just think this will be a good opportunity for me to push us to the next level."

"Well, I know your dad's opinion meant a lot to you, so if you feel like this is the one, go for it man. You've always had an eye for opportunities and ways to improve things. I'm sure you've crossed your t's and dotted your i's."

"Yeah. The numbers are solid, and we should see immediate growth once everything goes through."

"That's what's up. I'm happy for you. Hit me up once it's over, I'll get the guys, and we'll go out and celebrate."

Jaron laughed. "All right. I'll hit you once I finalize everything."

"Cool. Look at you, steady making moves. I like seeing that. I think all the guys do too. It's motivation and definitely makes me want to push myself even harder."

"Yeah. I have to do it, and I'm glad it pushes you to go harder too. That's what we have to do for each other."

"Yeah, I hear you on that."

"Yeah. But what's been up with you? Everything good?"

"Yeah. You know me. Same old, same. I'm actually on my way to go get Candace. A little dinner and maybe a late movie, but who knows, we might call it a night after dinner."

"Oh, okay. That's what's up. Tell her I said hey, and enjoy. I'll talk to you tomorrow."

"All right. Cool. One."

"One," said Jaron as he hung up.

Jaron picked up some Chinese food on the way to the house and watched his favorite movie while eating. Before calling it a night, he jumped in the shower, but he didn't take long, just a quick refresher, something to help clear his mind, calm his nerves, and help him sleep better. He put on something to sleep in and climbed into bed. His mind briefly went to the café and the waitress, and a smile crawled across his face. *Man, I'd love to meet her,* he thought. Then the thought was gone.

His mind was blank—no thoughts, just darkness, just like the room, which was also dark aside from the tiny beam of moonlight that was streaming in through the curtains. He watched it for a while and began to think about what tomorrow might hold. He envisioned his employees applauding as he told them of the deal he had finalized, all the smiling faces, all the cheers. The last thing he remembered thinking was, *Man, Dad, I hope I'm making the right move,* before his eyes shut, and he was fast asleep.

Chapter 3

Jaron sat on the edge of his bed, staring at the picture of his dad that he had hung on the wall. His thoughts raced back and forth. It was only six twenty-seven, but he couldn't get back to sleep. He had tossed and turned all night, but it was not like most nights when he just thought about his dad. No, this was a little more complex. There was his dad, but there was also the impending deal. He couldn't calm the thoughts, so he just stared, hoping that maybe, just by looking at the picture, he would gain some insight, that some calming factor would present itself. Still, nothing presented itself. There were only his thoughts.

He got up and got into the shower, figuring it would help him clear his mind. He stayed in the shower for a little over forty-five minutes. He stood under the water and attempted to let the thoughts be rinsed away. It helped somewhat, and his mood began to turn positive, as opposed to concerned, once he was ready to get out.

After getting out and drying off, he stood in his closet, thinking of what would be the best suit to wear. *The blue one,* he thought. *Yeah, that's me and Dad's favorite color. It'll bring me luck.* He pulled out his blue suit, tan shirt, and tan shoes. "Yeah, this will work," he said as he laid the clothes on his bed. No music and no TV today. He felt that he had to focus on the task at hand. He had to be at the top of his game for this deal.

"The first big business deal I have to do without you Dad," he said, looking at the picture once again. "I think this is the one to take us where we need to go, or at least I hope so," he said in an unsure tone. He went over some things in his head as he got dressed, thinking of the presentation and how he wanted things to go. He went over every detail and then went over it again, making sure he had it down the way it needed to be.

After getting dressed, he went to the kitchen, grabbed an apple, and rinsed it off. He ate it as he walked around the house to ensure that everything was in its proper place and that he wasn't forgetting anything. He grabbed a bottle of water on his way out the door.

*****

It was seven fifteen, and the alarm clock was blaring. "Shoot!" yelled MaKayla, rubbing her eyes. "I overslept." She jumped out of bed and turned off her alarm, then ran into the bathroom. *I'll take a quick shower and then be out the door. Looks like I won't be running this morning.* She tried to calm herself while she was in the shower. She hated running late, because it threw her whole day and mood off. After her shower, she quickly got dressed and ran out of the door. There was more traffic than she anticipated, which only made everything worse. The deep-gray sky completely coincided with her mood. Although she attempted to change her thought process, hoping that it would brighten things up, it continually went downhill.

When MaKayla got to work, Mr. Stacy was already there. "You're not on vacation yet. Let's get things ready to open up. You're already late," he said, seemingly annoyed. MaKayla arrived at eight fifteen and expected his reaction to be this way. She went to the back room without replying and collected herself while gathering the necessary items to begin setting up the tables.

Mr. Stacy was a short, stumpy black man with a very full beard. He always wore pants and suspenders, shirt with a tie, and black shoes. He was a very simple man in his appearance, in his business, and just overall. He was always very nice, but when it came to business, he had certain expectations and required them to be met. So when they weren't met, like when someone was late, his entire mood changed. She learned a lot from him and aspired to have similar qualities when she began her own business.

*****

Jaron stood on the porch for a while to take in everything—the people, the weather, the beauty, and just everything. There were the Johnsons, speeding down the street as usual. "They must be running late again," he said to himself. He waved, but they were moving too fast and didn't notice him. Mrs. Miller was sitting on her front porch a few houses down. She was an older woman in her midfifties, salt-and-pepper hair. She had on an old floral housecoat, which came from underneath her overcoat. Her arms were folded to keep them closed, a coffee mug in one hand and a half-smoked cigarette in the other. There was a Mr. Miller, but that was why she was on the porch, because he couldn't stand the smell of cigarettes, so to keep the peace, she smoked outside, on the porch.

Jaron waved. She flashed a smile and waved back. He began to feel calmer and more relaxed. He made his way down the stairs and looked up at the sky. It was really gray and cloudy. *Maybe it's going to rain,* he thought. The temperature had slowly risen over the last few days, even getting up to fifty-seven yesterday. Today was a little colder, in the low fifties. Jaron had on a waist-length peacoat, skullcap, driving gloves, and scarf. Everything he had on was black. It made him feel like he was going to a funeral, but he pretended he was a part of the mob. He laughed as the thought rolled through his mind. *Me in the mob.* He laughed lightly. *Nah.*

As he drove in to work, he kept it quiet in the car and just thought about what the day had in store. Once he got into the building, he was greeted by Krystal with a very big smile.

"Good morning, Mr. Coleman. Big day ahead of you, huh?"

"Every day is a big day," he said through a smile, "because every day, we have an opportunity to change things for the better."

"Hmm, I never thought about it that way. It really makes sense when you put it like that."

"How's everything with you today? All good?"

"All good," she replied. "Good luck today," she said as he entered the elevator.

"Thanks," he said, waving as the elevator doors closed.

Once the elevator door opened, Jaron was struck by the business of his employees. He paused for a second and smiled. *This is what I do it for,* he thought. He exited the elevator and made his way toward Tina, who sat staring at him curiously as he approached. "And how are you this morning?" she asked with a smirk on her face.

"I'm okay. Pretty nervous, but I'm okay."

"You sure? Because you look a little shaken."

"Really?" he asked. A look of shock and disappointment rose over his face.

"I'm just joking. Just joking," she said. "Just relax. Everything is going to be fine. Don't worry."

A smile crept on Jaron's face. "I'm trying to, I'm trying to. Any messages for me today?" he asked as he walked into his office.

Tina followed, holding a few stacks of papers in her hand. "Yep. Mr. Wynstead called and asked where you would like him to meet you. He doesn't remember if you set an exact location."

"Okay. Call him and tell him to meet me here, and we'll discuss things over lunch. I'll drive."

"Okay. Accounting called. They wanted to know if you ever finished looking over the numbers from the last report, because they haven't received a final draft."

"Can you call Gerry and have him fax them a copy of the report? Tell him that the numbers are solid, and we'll go with it."

"Okay. And the last four are from vendors and stores—shipment confirmations and such."

"Okay. Thank you. Set them on my desk."

"All right. Would you like the door closed?"

"Yes, please," he said as he finished taking off his coat and sat down.

Jaron let out a sigh and began to focus his thoughts. *Well, today's the day, Pop,* he thought. He turned and looked out the window. It was busy down there. *I wonder if there's anyone on their way to an important meeting.* He imagined they were and silently wished them luck. "You're going to do great," he said to them.

He turned back to his desk and picked up the papers that Tina had left. He began calling them one by one. This wasn't usually the role of a CEO, but he liked having a close working relationship with his vendors and the people he supplied. "It makes for better business, and it'll help out in the long run," he always said.

*****

This day, the café seemed to be overly crowded, and MaKayla was running around like crazy. She was happy when eleven o'clock rolled around and in strolled Liyah, smiling as usual.

"Hey gorgeous. You look like you're having a great time," said Liyah sarcastically.

"Girl, you don't know the half," MaKayla said, shaking her head. "I was up extremely late last night, finishing up an assignment that was due yesterday. I woke up late and got here late today, so you know Mr. Stacy didn't like that. Plus, on top of all that, it's been extremely busy since those doors opened. Like, this day has been ahhhh." MaKayla let out a sound of frustration.

"Come here," said Liyah as she hugged her. "All you have to do is think about the fact that you are about to be on a two-week vacation, and this is the home stretch, okay?"

"I hear you, but I feel like I'm close to my breaking point today."

"Don't worry girl. I got your back," said Liyah, smiling, as she patted her back.

"Okay. Now that you've got all the pleasantries out of the way, you ladies want to start taking care of these tables?" said Mr. Stacy, who had been standing close by the whole time.

"We're on it boss," said Liyah, smiling and giving a playful salute.

"MaKayla," called Mr. Stacy, "I apologize for this morning and my attitude. I just had a rough night. I know you've been putting in a lot of work lately, and you're probably exhausted, but trust me, it'll all be worth it in the end. Flowers need water to grow. It has to rain. Your season to bloom is very close."

"Thank you Mr. Stacy. I really needed that. I had a rough night too, and I'm really looking forward to this break. It's much needed."

"Well, let's get through this day so you can get to that much-needed break," he said, smiling.

"Okay," she said as they exited the back room.

*****

After finishing up his calls, Jaron pulled out his laptop and pulled up his presentation. He made several paper copies, but he also had the hard copy backed up on his laptop. *Just in case,* he thought. *You never know what might happen.* He went over everything again, making sure it was all in order. Before he knew it, time had flown by.

"Mr. Coleman," said Tina, knocking on the door.

"Yes, come in."

"You do know it's twelve fifteen, don't you?" she asked.

He quickly got up and began putting his things away. "I got so caught up in making sure everything was correct that I lost track of time. Thanks for coming in and letting me know."

"No problem. We're a team, you know. Now stop," she said, putting her hand on his chest. "Calm down and take a few breaths. Don't overthink it. The last thing I want you to do is rush. You still have time."

He stopped, closed his eyes, and took three deep breaths. "Okay. How do I look?" he asked.

She straightened his tie. "Like a man destined to change the world."

He smiled. "Thank you," he said as he began walking out of the office, briefcase and laptop bag in hand. She smiled as he made his way to the elevator.

Once downstairs, Jaron was greeted by Mr. Wynstead, a burly white man with a bald head and gray beard. He wore a black-and-white pinstripe suit, black shoes, black tie, white shirt, and white handkerchief.

"Ah, Jaron, how are you? I was just about to have this young lady give you a call for me."

"I'm good," he said, shaking Wynstead's hand. "If you'll follow me, we can go get my car."

"Oh, I almost forgot. This is Wilfred, my lawyer. He'll be handling the legalities of our deal."

Wilfred was a tall, thin man with a head full of oily black hair. He was dressed exactly the same as Wynstead, but Jaron thought nothing of it. He stretched out his hand. "A pleasure to meet you," he said, but Wilfred only nodded.

"Now if we can get to it," said Wynstead.

"Yes, right this way." As they made their way outside and toward the side of the building, Jaron noticed a puzzled look on Wynstead's face. "Is everything okay?" he asked.

"Where are we going?" Wynstead asked.

"To get my car."

"You mean you don't have a driver, or is he just sick? Why didn't they bring your car around for you?"

Jaron smiled. "No, I don't have a driver or anyone to bring my car around. I drive myself. And where we're going isn't far. Most of the time I walk."

"Well, I insist you allow my driver to take us then."

"That's alright. We'll be fine. I'm sure he isn't close by anymore anyway."

"Nonsense. I won't have it." Wynstead pulled out his cell phone and pressed a button. "Yes, Charles. Come pick us up from in front of the building. You'll be driving us." Wynstead said to Jaron as he hung up the phone, "See how simple that was? Now come on." Wilfred still didn't speak, and his expression hadn't changed either. He just blankly watched the engagement.

They made their way back to the front of the building, and there was a clean black Lincoln Continental. A rather short man in a driver's attire stood outside the car. Jaron assumed this was Charles. "Wilfred, you ride up front with Charles. Jaron and I will ride in the back." The driver opened the door, and they entered. Jaron told the driver how to get to the café, which was very simple. He only had to make one turn after going down three blocks, and then two more blocks and they were there.

Although it was a short ride, a million thoughts went through Jaron's mind. *Is he outta my league? I mean, he has his own driver, for crying out loud. But what do I need a driver for? I love driving myself. Seems like overkill now that I think about it.*

"Looks like it might rain," said Jaron, trying to break the silence.

"Yes, I suppose it does. You said you usually walk here," asked Wynstead curiously.

"Yeah. It's not far. Plus, it's good exercise, and I love being able to see the people I work for, to see the happiness."

Wynstead turned his nose up. "I'd rather see them from a distance. It's all the same anyway, and you have it all wrong."

"How so?" asked Jaron curiously.

"You don't work for them. They work for you. If it's the other way around, you'll never get ahead. I'm sure that's a lesson your father taught you, or perhaps he didn't have enough time to get around to that one."

Jaron was once again caught off guard by the comment from Wynstead. He felt his stomach drop. He wasn't sure if Wynstead was taking a shot at his father's teaching or his untimely death. "We are here, sir," said Charles from the front before Jaron had the opportunity to respond.

*****

MaKayla finished up with the table she was working on. "I got the next one," she said, letting her coworkers know that she was free to take the next customer who came in. Things had become a little slower, and she was starting to feel better after talking with Liyah and Mr. Stacy. She had finished all her tables and actually had a moment to rest since there was no one waiting to be seated. She allowed herself to think about how great it would be to be home with her mom and dad again, to not have to think about work or school or anything, and to just relax. *Man, I can't wait,* she thought through a smile.

*****

They were parked outside the small café. "This is where we are going?" asked Wynstead in a condescending tone.

"Yes. I know it's small, but they have great food, and it has a good atmosphere. You'll see." The fact that Jaron had to sell the café to Wynstead only added to the growing feeling of uneasiness that he was now feeling.

"Oh, I suppose," said Wynstead stiffly. They exited the car. "I'll call you when we are ready to leave, so stay close by," Wynstead said to Charles as he closed the door, not even waiting for a reply.

They entered the café, Wynstead first, then Jaron and Wilfred right behind him. "How may I help you?" came a voice from in front of them. *I know that voice,* thought Jaron. He moved from behind Wynstead to see who it was, and there she was.

Out of all the days, this was the day she would serve him. Now this was definitely a serendipitous surprise. He stood there staring, not saying anything. He was in disbelief. Was this some cruel joke being played on him? Surely the gods must have a sense of humor to put him in such a predicament.

Something was different this time. He had never really gotten to see her like this—only from a distance, only in passing. She didn't look like herself. She looked like she was tired or drained, disheveled. He noticed the silence and then felt the eyes upon him. Everyone was waiting for him to speak.

"Are you okay?" asked Wynstead.

"Uh, yeah, sure," said Jaron hurriedly. "Uh, yeah, a table for three please—by the window, if you have one."

"Right this way," she said. "How's this?"

"This will be fine."

"Okay. Well, my name is MaKayla, and I'll be your waitress for today. Can I start you off with something to drink—tea, coffee, Coke products—or should I just bring water and give you a minute?" She smiled, but it looked forced, like she needed a break, but she had a determined look at the same time.

"MaKayla is it?" asked Jaron as he let her name dance on his tongue. "I'll have a lemonade with a lot of ice. And can you bring me water as well?"

"Yes, and okay. What about for you two gentlemen?" asked MaKayla as she wrote down Jaron's drink order.

"I'll have a cappuccino, extra whip cream, and Wilfred will have tea with honey and lemon."

"Okay. I'll be right back with those," MaKayla said as she finished writing down their orders and walked away.

"Actually," said Wynstead before she could walk away, "if you know what you want"—he was talking to Jaron—"we can order our food too."

"Yeah, sure," said Jaron, somewhat surprised, but he just went with it. "I'll have a ham and turkey sandwich on white bread, lightly toasted, extra mayo, extra mustard, one slice of American cheese and one slice of Swiss cheese, two tomato slices, and two leaves of lettuce."

There was a slight pause. "Well, that was very specific," said Wynstead. Jaron had never thought about how precise he was with his order. It just seemed routine at this point.

"And for you?" asked MaKayla, pointing to Wilfred as she finished writing, a slight smile on her face.

"Wilfred will have a T-bone steak, medium rare, with a side of eggs. I will have a julienne salad, light dressing, with croutons on the side," replied Wynstead with an annoyed tone. It was as if he was irritated that MaKayla had asked Wilfred his order before she asked his or that she had asked him anything at all.

"Okay," said MaKayla as she collected the menus. "I'll put that right in and be back with your drinks."

*****

As MaKayla entered the back room and put their orders in, she looked for Liyah. She knew that this table might be a bit difficult just by the way they placed their orders. They seemed like they were doing business or something important. She felt her nerves begin to take over, and her mood began to change for the worse again. She tried to shake it off. She couldn't seem to find Liyah anywhere. Once the drinks were ready, she took a deep breath, gathered the drinks, and headed back to the table.

*****

Jaron found it curious that Wilfred did not order his own drink or food. He also noticed the annoyance that Wynstead displayed when MaKayla talked to Wilfred. He figured he had better get to the business at hand. He tried to focus and not think of MaKayla, but he was struggling. This was the moment that he had been waiting for, the first time she ever served him. It was his opportunity to talk to her, and he couldn't. *Maybe if all this goes well with Wynstead, I can talk to her a little before we leave or on the way out. Wishful thinking,* he thought, shaking his head, smiling. He pulled out his paper presentations and set one in front of Wilfred and one in front of Wynstead.

"Is there something that amuses you, Mr. Coleman?" asked Wynstead.

Hearing his voice and him saying his name in that way made Jaron feel like he was in trouble, like he was being called to the principal's office back in school. "Oh, nothing. It's nothing," he stammered. He began going through the presentation page by page. There was no response from Wynstead as they went through the first couple of pages, just audible moans and grunts.

Once Jaron reached page ten, MaKayla returned with their drinks. It had begun to rain outside. Jaron wondered if this was a sign, but once again, he tried to clear his mind of everything that wasn't the deal. MaKayla set down his lemonade and water, then Wynstead's cappuccino. Just as she went to set down Wilfred's tea, lightning struck, followed by a big boom of thunder. This startled MaKayla, and she wasted most of the tea on the proposal paper that was in front of Wynstead.

Wynstead immediately slid his chair back and stood up. "Are you kidding me? Are you serious right now?" he yelled.

"It's okay," said Jaron as he got up to help with the spill. "I have it on my laptop." "Good thinking," he imagined his father would say to him in a situation like this. That made him feel a little better.

"I am so sorry," said MaKayla. "I was just startled by the thunder."

Wilfred, Jaron, and MaKayla began grabbing napkins and wiping up the spilled tea. Jaron unconsciously placed his hand on hers. "It's okay," he said reassuringly. He stared into her eyes, and they drifted away while everything around them disappeared for just that brief moment.

"This is unacceptable," grunted Wynstead as he took his seat. This caused them to snap back to reality. Jaron slowly slid his hand from on top of hers. Their eyes were still locked, as if searching for something. MaKayla was swarming with emotions. Somehow, she felt comforted and calmer. *But I don't even know him,* she thought. "Who's afraid of thunder?" bellowed Wynstead, shaking his head, causing MaKayla's gaze to be drawn back to the spill, removing the feeling of comfort.

"Allow me to bring you a fresh one, on the house," said MaKayla, reaching for the teacup.

"No," said Wynstead sternly as he grabbed the teacup and set it back down. "That is quite all right. He can drink this one. Just hurry up with our food."

"Okay. I apologize once again," she replied as she walked away, going into the back room.

Jaron did not like the tone or manner in which Wynstead spoke to MaKayla. He figured he needed to hurry this meeting along before things somehow got worse. Jaron pulled out his laptop and pulled up the presentation. He handed Wynstead his paper packet. "Here you go. I'll just go off my laptop. See? No worries."

"Yeah, I suppose," said Wynstead as he sipped his cappuccino.

*****

MaKayla entered the back room in a panic, trying to shake off the nerves, but nothing was helping. Liyah walked in with a smile on her face. Then it immediately changed when she noticed the look on MaKayla's face.

"What's wrong? You look like you're freaking out."

"I am. I can't calm my nerves down. I just wasted tea all over this guy's business papers, and he was freaking out. It was an accident. The freaking thunder scared me. You know how thunderstorms are for me."

"It's okay. Don't worry. Just finish off the table with a positive mentality. You can't change what happened, but you can control what you do going forward."

"Thanks girl," said MaKayla as she took a deep breath.

"Are you okay?" asked Mr. Stacy as he entered the back room.

"Yeah. Just a rough table, but I'll handle it. I think the one guy is a regular, but I can't be sure. I'm pretty sure I've heard his order pretty often back here."

"You sure?"

"Yeah. But there's one guy at the table that's really a jerk."

"Okay. Well, I'll keep my eye on you anyway."

"Thanks, Mr. Stacy."

"Okay. Let me see their order to make sure we get it out to them as soon as possible."

MaKayla took a seat in a chair in the back room and placed her face into her hands. She sat there for a minute and collected her thoughts. Before she knew it, the order was ready to be taken to the table. She stood up, took a deep breath, grabbed the food, and proceeded to the table.

*****

Jaron had continued with his presentation, getting more than halfway done before MaKayla returned with their food. She gave them a moment, allowing them to remove their items from the table, an extra precaution to prevent the same mistake as last time. She began setting down their food one by one, starting with Jaron and ending with Wynstead.

"You've gotten our order wrong," scolded Wynstead. "Do you mean to insult me by giving me a salad?"

"No, sir, not at all," said MaKayla sincerely. "That is what you ordered. I have all your orders right here," she said, pulling out her notepad.

"So you're calling me a liar? I am a steak-eating man. Does Wilfred look like he eats steaks?"

"This is all a simple misunderstanding," said Jaron calmly in an attempt to quell the situation. "All we have to do is simply switch the meals and all is right."

But Wynstead would not have it. He seemed to become even more furious at the thought. "All is right, all is right?" he repeated in a shocked and heightened tone. "No, all is not right. I will not be called a liar! I will not be treated in such a way."

"Sir, I'm not calling you a liar. I'm simply saying, the way I served it is the way I wrote it down. I apologize if I got it wrong, but I don't think this is that big of a deal." MaKayla began to look overwhelmed, as if this was too much to take.

"You apologize; you apologize. Is that all you know how to do correctly? Apologize?" Wynstead said sternly.

MaKayla, with her eyes welling up and through a trembling voice, said, "Once again, I apologize." Then she turned and walked away.

*****

MaKayla entered the back room, and the tears began to stream down her face. Mr. Stacy, who had watched the entire thing, was immediately at her side. "It's okay," he said as he rubbed her back. "I saw the entire thing, and you handled it superbly. Liyah will take over the table for you. I want you to go home and get some rest, okay?"

"But what about today? I can't leave you guys like that."

"Look, things have already slowed down. I think we've made it through the rush, so we'll be fine."

"But I don't want to put more work on Liyah."

"We already talked about it," said Liyah. "And I'm fine with it. Hey, we'll split the tip," she said, smiling in an attempt to get her to smile.

MaKayla tried to push a smile out as she wiped her face. "Are you guys sure? I can handle it. I just need a moment to regroup."

"We're sure. You just go home and relax," said Mr. Stacy.

"Hey, think about it this way. Your vacation starts now," said Liyah as she threw her hands up in a very dramatic fashion.

MaKayla smiled. "Thanks you guys. I owe you one," she replied, hugging them.

*****

"Do you really think that was necessary?" asked Jaron. "It could have been easily resolved."

Before Wynstead could respond, another waitress appeared. "Hi. My name is Liyah, and I'll be taking over for MaKayla. Is there anything that I can get for you?"

"Yes, the check," said Wynstead in a very disgruntled voice.

Jaron turned and noticed MaKayla leaving the café, and with her went his one chance to get to know her. He wondered if she was okay, if she just needed someone to talk to. He hoped she hadn't gotten in trouble, especially seeing that it wasn't completely her fault.

His mind wasn't even on the deal or Wynstead or anything but her. A part of him wanted to get up and go after her, just like they always did in the movies, in a very dramatic fashion. *But this isn't the movies,* he thought. *And I don't even know her.* The realization of this thought disappointed him, but he figured he had better get his mind back on the task at hand. Wynstead, who seemed to be a more complicated task than he had initially planned for.

"Yes, can we get these things to go?" said Jaron. "We can finish this meeting back at my office." Wynstead got up and walked toward the door, Wilfred immediately behind him. "I'll take care of the check up front," said Jaron almost to himself since they were halfway to the door when he made the statement. He waited for the food and paid the bill, leaving a substantial tip for MaKayla. When Liyah came back with the food, he asked, "Is she okay?"

"Who, MaKayla? Yeah, she's just tired, that's all. She'll be fine. I do want to apologize on her behalf though. It's not like her to get orders wrong."

"Well, she actually didn't. He ordered wrong. She was very professional about the entire situation. There was no need for him to speak to her in that way. So I'd like to apologize for the way things went. I hope you have a great day."

There was so much more he wanted to say, so much more he wanted to ask, but there was no time. He had to finish this business with Wynstead, and he didn't want to make matters worse by having him waiting. In the car, he called ahead and had Tina prepare a conference room for them.

"I can't believe you eat at that place regularly. How can you possibly do it?"

"Well, it's really not that bad. I've never had an issue before."

Jaron tried to keep a smile on his face, although he was growing more and more annoyed and frustrated. The rain was really coming down, and the traffic had begun to back up, causing it to take longer than normal to get back.

"And that waitress, what a bumbling misfit. How did she even get that job?" said Wynstead disgustedly. Jaron sat quietly. He didn't agree, but this was no time for an argument.

Chapter 4

Once back in the conference room, Jaron attempted to begin the presentation again but was interrupted by Wynstead. "I understand that you worked hard on this presentation, but I'll assume everything is already in place, and for whatever aspects aren't, Wilfred here will fix them later. There's no need to continue." Jaron was appalled. He actually felt disrespected. He leaned back in his chair and thought, *Wow, that was unprofessional. He couldn't even let me finish.*

Wynstead looked at Wilfred and nodded. Wilfred opened a briefcase and actually began speaking. "We are prepared to offer you this plus the number at the bottom, which would be similar to a signing bonus, for a majority stake in your company," he said as he pointed to two separate numbers on the document that he slid in front of Jaron.

Jaron sat up and began to look the document over. The numbers on the paper were much higher than they had initially discussed or than he had anticipated. "You will still retain your title and some holdings in the company, as well as some input in business decisions. We will retain your staff for the most part in the beginning, as well as add others, as long as they can keep up with the changes."

"Wait. What changes?" asked Jaron as he looked up from the document curiously.

"I told you earlier that you have to make the people work for you, and I'm going to show you how. There's always some sacrifice in growing. Perhaps some of your workers will be the sacrifice, but I'm sure they'll be okay," Wynstead said through a sly grin.

Jaron sat staring at the numbers on the document and imagined all the good he could do with that amount of money. *Is the sacrifice worth the money?* he thought, suddenly feeling uneasy. He didn't trust

Wynstead, and the more he thought about it, the more he realized that he just wanted to own the company.

He thought about his dad, about his smile and the words and advice he always gave him, reminding him why they were doing this. He thought about the rude and inconsiderate remark Wynstead made in the car about lessons his father never taught him. Then his mind shifted to the café and MaKayla, her smile and how she had been disrespected by Wynstead and the tears in her eyes. That took his mind to all those people he watched outside his window in his office and the café. To the people he wanted to help. All his employees who worked so hard. How they deserved someone who appreciated them and their hard work. He could see their smiles in his mind.

Finally, he thought about Wynstead—the way he talked as if Jaron should have a driver or at least someone who brought his car for him. How he looked down on the people on the way to the café, how he looked at the café in disgust, and how he felt superior to these people, the same people whom Jaron wanted to help. *What's the deal with Wilfred? He treats him like he has no mind of his own. Will he treat me this way? This isn't what's best for us,* he thought, shaking his head and letting out a sigh of disappointment. He stood up and stretched out his hand.

"I knew you'd see how beneficial this would be for both of us," said Wynstead with a large grin on his face as he pushed his chair back from the table, preparing to stand up.

"Actually, I don't think this deal will be in the best interest of my company. I appreciate your time and offer, but this won't work for us."

"Us? What do you mean us? You have a business partner?" Wynstead asked, curious.

Jaron paused, somewhat caught off guard by the question. Just then, Tina's voice came to his mind. "We're a team, you know."

"Yes, actually, I do. I have multiple partners when it really comes down to it."

"Why haven't I heard about this before now? Why aren't they here? Better yet, who are they?" asked Wynstead in a furiously annoyed tone.

Jaron heard Tina's voice again: "Don't rush. You still have time." He simply smiled. He had a feeling that everything would be okay. "But you have met them. You've talked to Tina several different times and to that lovely young lady Krystal, who greeted you when you came in. You see, Mr. Wynstead, everyone in this building, all the vendors, consumers, and customers, we are all partners. We can't make it without each other."

Wynstead began laughing. "You're kidding me, right? Oh, wow, you actually had me going there for a minute," he said as he wiped his head in relief.

"No, I'm not kidding. I'm actually as serious as I can be," replied Jaron, still standing and smiling, but he had withdrawn his hand by now.

"Are you mad? I mean, that is a very substantial amount of money. Perhaps you should allow your accountants to look over the numbers before you are so quick to make your decision."

"I've made my decision. I really do appreciate such an offer, but it isn't in the best interest of our company, so I must decline."

"Why, I never!" Wynstead said. He was infuriated, his face beet red. He was mumbling, and his words were not clear. He stormed out of the conference room with Wilfred right behind him, trying to hurriedly grab the documents and close his briefcase as they made their way to the elevator.

Jaron stood at the elevator and allowed Wynstead to get on. "Have a good day," he said. After the door closed, he took the next elevator up to his floor. As he exited, he saw Tina smiling. He returned the smile and said, "Do me a favor. I want everyone in the first-floor lobby in fifteen minutes. I don't care what they're doing. I want them to drop it and be there."

"Sure thing," Tina said, smiling as if she knew something that no one else knew.

Jaron went into his office and closed the door behind him. He collapsed onto his couch. *What did I just do?* he thought. *That could've really made a difference for us. Did I just make that decision solely off of emotions? Maybe I should've brought in the accountants to see just what I*

SPRING SHOWERS—THE BLOOM

was dealing with. A million different thoughts were running through his mind. What would he tell all his employees now?

His eyes caught the picture of his dad. His thoughts calmed, and MaKayla's smile crept into his mind. He looked out of the window. The rain had stopped. *It must've been a sign,* he thought. He stood up and fixed himself in the mirror, then exited his office. It was quiet. Everyone was gone. Only he remained on the floor. He entered the elevator and prepared himself for everyone who would be waiting when he got off.

*****

MaKayla took the long way home. She was in no rush to get there. She thought about her day and how everything had transpired. "What could I have done differently?" she asked herself. "That just ended horribly, but that was really nice of Liyah and Mr. Stacy. I wonder if I messed up whatever business they were doing. That one guy didn't seem too happy at all about the situation. The other guy seemed a bit more understanding. I'm almost sure I've seen him in there before. I hope it all works out for the best. Lord knows I can only imagine how it must feel to be in his position. I'll be there one day, one day soon." With that thought, a smile crept across her face, and she began to feel better.

*****

Once the doors opened, there was an eruption of cheers and applause. Jaron made his way through the crowd and to the center. He smiled and put his hands up. The cheers and applause stopped. He looked at all those smiling faces, which awaited his words.

"I called this meeting because I wanted to formally address you all, not send this in an email. As you all know, today, Mr. Wynstead came to present me with a deal that would essentially merge our company with his. This deal would take us to that next level and open up a vast number of opportunities for our company.

"When I began as just a young boy, my goal was to change the world, to help fix it, through helping people. But there's no changing this world without changing the people in it. We can't do it without one another. We all need one another. I think that if you work here, you understand this and would like to help as well. Most, if not all, of you have heard me talk about this. The offer presented to me today was bigger than I anticipated. I'm talking two extra zeros bigger."

The applause and cheers began again. Jaron raised his hands, and silence fell upon them. "I turned down that offer," he said, looking at all those smiling faces. There was murmuring all throughout the crowd. The smiles turned to looks of confusion. "I turned it down because Wynstead offered that to me—not to us but to me—but what am I without you? He, doesn't see your value, but I know your value."

As he talked and turned, he saw Tina and her smile, and he felt more confident. "That is not what we want. He wanted majority control, and I cannot do that for any amount of money. We, all of us, are the majority. The control is in our hands. What would I be without you? A singular man with a great plan and an idea. You—we—make those plans and ideas into a reality.

"Now don't get me wrong, that amount of money could have taken us where we want to go, but I could not pay the price, or risk the sacrifice of any of you for that money. I did not start on this journey all those years ago with the hopes of getting rich. That wasn't and has never been my goal. So I promise you, right here, right now, that we will change the world, and we will do it the right way. I cannot do it alone. I'll need your help. We have an uphill battle, but the fist is stronger than the finger. If we work together, I know we can do it. Now are you with me?"

The applause and cheers began to grow until it was a loud roar. Jaron smiled, comforted by the approval of his employees, and he made his way to the elevator, followed by Tina and a few other employees. Everyone was shaking his hand and patting him on the back as he made his way there. Once he made it back upstairs, he and Tina went into his office.

"Oh, how I wish I had been there to see the look on his face when you turned him down," said Tina through a smile. "I bet he was pissed." She laughed and clapped her hands. "I'm proud of you, and I'm sure your dad is too," she said, hugging him tightly.

"I hope so. I mean, that was a lot of money I turned down."

"You aren't here for the money. Look out there," said Tina as she pointed out the window to the people below. "That is why you do it. Yeah, you may have been able to help them, but at what expense?"

"You're right. I really appreciate you being here and having my back like this."

"What did I tell you earlier? We're a team. I got you," she said, smiling, as she lightly punched him in the arm. "Now let me get back to work. That phone won't answer itself."

"Okay. Go ahead," he said through a smile.

After sitting on the couch for a while, Jaron got up and grabbed his phone. "No celebration tonight," he sent to Xavier. "I'll call you later with the details." About ten minutes later, Xavier responded, "Okay. Hope everything is cool. I'll talk to you then." Jaron sat back in his chair. *What's your move now?* he thought. *Where do I go from here?* He wasn't disappointed with his decision but hated that things turned out this way. It felt like he was starting from scratch. "So many people are looking to and counting on me. I have to do better," he told himself.

*****

Once MaKayla got home, she continued to finish the little bit of packing that she had left. Her flight would leave early in the morning, and she wanted to be ready. Her phone rang, and she answered. "Hey, Mom. How are you?"

"I'm good. How are you? Ready for this vacation?"

"I'm better now. I had a really rough day today. Between being up late to finish an assignment and a really bad customer at work, it's been hectic. Mr. Stacy let me leave early, and Liyah covered for me, so I've been able to relax and reset. I can't wait to get there. I miss you guys so much."

"Well baby, we miss you too. And it's good you have people like that in your corner, looking out for you. You won't find too many people like that nowadays."

"Yeah, I know. That's why I try to keep them as close as I can."

"That's the way you have to do it."

"Well, I'm done packing now. About to eat and relax before I head to the airport. What are you guys up to?"

"Well, your dad is still at the office. He wanted to get ahead so he wouldn't have to work so much once you get here. Me, I'm just sitting here, reading this book I've been reading for the past few days. Ironically, it reminds me of you."

"How's that?"

"It's a story about a young girl working her way through college and how determined she is to accomplish these goals that she's set for herself. She won't let anything stand in her way, and she's stubborn. She won't accept help even though it's right there for her."

"Mom," said MaKayla, "we're not going to start this again, are we?"

"I was just telling you what the book was about," said her mom as she laughed. "You asked."

"Yeah, yeah, yeah. Sure you were."

"You sure you're okay?"

"Yeah Mom, I'm okay, but I'll be even better when I get there."

"I hear that," said her mom, and they both laughed.

"Oh, Mom, I almost forgot to tell you. I got my new furniture the other day. This place is really starting to come together."

"Oh, the gray one you were telling me about?"

"Yeah. I'll take a picture and send it to you."

"Okay. I'm sure you'll need my expertise in really making it pop."

"Come on now Mom. You know I got this." They began to laugh again.

"Yeah. You must get that from me."

"Okay. Let me find something to eat, and I'll let you know when I get to the airport."

"Okay," her mom replied, and they hung up the phone.

What do I want to eat? Hmm, MaKayla thought as she looked around the kitchen. *No appetite, and I don't feel like cooking. Maybe I'll order pizza.* "Yeah, that should be fine. A little sausage and cheese should do me just right," she said out loud, nodding her head as if to agree with someone's statement. She smiled as she called in her order. "Guess I'll watch a little TV until it gets here."

*****

Jaron began going back over the past three months' numbers, looking for any potential profits that he might be able to use for growth. He sat there for hours, going over documents. Tina had left for the day, and before he knew it, the sun was going down. He hadn't made much progress. He was only seeing a little growth in certain areas, but he needed that to cover other areas. He looked at the clock. Eight o'clock was rapidly approaching. He picked up his phone. There were a few text messages—his sisters with just random messages and Xavier checking to see if he was okay.

"I better call it a night," he said. He gathered his things and made his way out of the building. Everyone was gone for the night, so he set the alarm as he left. He sat in his car and just exhaled, letting all the day out—the good, the bad, and all else that remained. He started his car and made his way toward his house. The streets were vibrant. There were a lot of cars and people. He had forgotten it was a Friday night. *I'd better call Xavier before he gets into whatever he's planning for the night.*

Jaron picked up the phone and called. Xavier answered and said in a relieved voice, "You good, man?"

"Yeah. You know, just one of those days. You know how it goes."

"Well, what happened with the deal?"

"Well, he had a great proposal, financially. It was at least ten times more than what we initially discussed and anticipated. I'm talking two extra zeros at the end."

"Well, that sounds great. What could be wrong with that?"

"He wanted majority control for one. Although he didn't say it, he was basically going to gut the company. It's like he just wanted it to be the complete opposite of what we've built, like he wanted to make it just like the rest of these other companies."

"Oh, wow, I'm sorry to hear that. I guess your dad was right, huh?"

"Yeah, but no need to be sorry. We'll still be okay. We're still going to make major moves. I just have to find the right outlet."

"Yeah, I hear you. You know if I can help, I will. Just let me know."

"Yeah, I know. But how's everything with you?"

"I'm good. I'm thinking about going to Cliché tonight. You should roll with me. It'll be good to clear your mind. Plus, you know all the beautiful women are going to be coming out because the weather's starting to break."

That made Jaron think of MaKayla all over again. He wondered if she would be going out tonight to help forget about the day she had. He shook his head. *What am I thinking?* he thought. "I'm sure they will," he said, laughing. "But not tonight man. I'm going to just chill at the crib. I'll probably turn in early."

"You sure? You know we can do it big."

"Yeah, I'm sure. You know I appreciate the offer. Have fun for me though."

"Okay. I'll talk to you a little later then."

"Okay. Cool. Be safe."

"Definitely. One."

"One," said Jaron as he hung up the phone. He thought about grabbing some food before going in, but then he remembered he had all that food from the café. When he got in, he just ate his sandwich and put the rest in the refrigerator. He sat on the couch and turned on SportsCenter. He watched most of the highlights until he finished eating. After he finished, he went into his room and laid across his bed.

His mind was still going over the events of the day, but now it was calmer. He kept replaying MaKayla's face and how it sounded when she said her name. "MaKayla," he said with a smile. *After all this time, that's her name. She probably thinks I'm a loser for being with someone like Wynstead, and I wouldn't blame her. I hope she's okay. I hope she didn't get down about him and his stupidity. MaKayla,* he thought as he drifted off.

*****

After eating, MaKayla's phone began ringing. It was Liyah.

"Hey. How was the rest of your shift?"

"It was good. We were really slow."

"Did that table give you any more trouble?"

"Nope. They actually took their food to go."

"Dang, was I that bad?"

"No. It wasn't even your fault."

"What do you mean?"

"The guy—"

"Which guy?"

Liyah laughed. "You know, the cute one. You know which one," she said, smiling.

"You're so crazy," replied MaKayla, laughing.

"Don't act like you didn't notice."

"Anyway," said MaKayla, smiling, "what did he say?"

"He just came to the front—after leaving a very nice tip, might I add—and asked about you, basically saying he hoped you didn't get in trouble and seeing if you were okay. He said it was the other guy's fault, because he actually ordered wrong. Mr. Stacy said he knew it the whole time when I talked to him about it. He said you never mess up orders no matter how tired you are."

"He really said all that?" asked MaKayla curiously.

"Who, Mr. Stacy or the guy?"

"The guy, Liyah, the guy."

"Oh yeah, he really did. And he looked all concerned and sincere too. He apologized, saying the other guy had no reason to treat you that way. He said you were very professional in how you handled it."

"Wow, that's interesting. I'm glad we have someone like Mr. Stacy as a boss. He really looks out for us and pays attention to us," said MaKayla, trying to quickly switch the subject. She wanted to ask Liyah if he was a regular or if she had seen him before, but she knew

Liyah wouldn't leave it alone once she started. She was sure she had seen him before. There was something about him that felt so familiar.

"Yeah. No other boss would've let you leave like that."

"Yeah, I know."

"Okay, so now that you're on vacation, you need to get up and get dressed."

"Get dressed for what?"

"We're going out tonight. You don't work tomorrow, and I don't have to go in until one."

"Um, my flight leaves at three in the morning, Liyah. I'm not going out," said MaKayla, laughing.

"Oh, shoot, I didn't even know that," replied Liyah, sounding disappointed. "Dang, you know there's going to be so many people at Cliché tonight. With the weather easing up and all, it's going to be nice. Plus, it'll help you forget about this crazy day you've just had. I mean, you can always sleep on the plane," joked Liyah.

"Yeah, I know, but I'm going to be in for the night. We're going to get to live it up next week when you come back home. Don't have too much fun without me, and make sure you're safe."

"You know I will. I love you. Let me know when you get to the airport."

"I love you too, and I will."

"Okay. Later," they said as they hung up.

MaKayla took a short nap and headed to the airport around one. She wanted to make sure she had enough time to check in before her flight was scheduled to leave. After checking in and waiting for her boarding call, she sat down in her window seat. She made sure she sent all the necessary messages before turning off her phone. She lay back and stared out the window. She began to think about the guy from the café. *He actually was pretty cute, and that was pretty nice of him to come and say that about me. I hope everything worked out with his business deal. I hope I didn't mess it up. Good people deserve good things to happen to them.* That was the last thought in her head before she drifted off to sleep.

Chapter 5

It was 4:17 a.m., and there lay Jaron, staring at the ceiling, a million thoughts running through his mind. He let out a deep, heavy sigh. *What I wouldn't give for just one night of good, refreshing sleep. I can't even remember what it feels like to sleep through an entire night and to wake up to the sun opposed to it being the other way around,* he thought. "Well Dad, it would seem, once again, you were right about Mr. Wynstead, but I think I handled that situation with class and dignity, wouldn't you say?" He paused as if waiting for a response, although he knew none was coming. He smiled and sighed again.

What am I going to do now? He tossed and turned, trying to find a comfortable position, one that would allow him to fall back to sleep. Nothing worked, but this didn't annoy him. It was a nightly occurrence. He had already taken a shower when he woke up a few hours earlier. That usually helped him fall back to sleep, but it made no sense to take another one. *I wonder if Mom has plans for tomorrow. Maybe we can go to breakfast or something. I'll call her in the morning to see.*

Jaron got up, went to the kitchen, and poured himself a glass of water, then walked to the window in the living room and stared out of it. His mind went to MaKayla—that smile that lit up his day, the way her voice sounded, the way she walked, everything. He smiled, but that changed immediately when he remembered how the day went and ended. How Wynstead treated her and how he probably ruined any chance he had of getting to know her.

He became concerned. *I wonder what happened to her. And why did she look like that when we first came in? Did she get in trouble because of Wynstead? That would be horrible, someone getting in trouble for someone who treats people that way. Even worse, what if she got fired?*

I mean, she didn't have the look of someone who'd just been fired when she was leaving, but maybe she was trying to hold it together.

Maybe I should've talked to the manager or something and let them know it wasn't her fault. I mean, I did tell that one girl, but I suppose I could've done more. I hope she's okay. What if she needed someone and no one was there to comfort her? He shook his head.

It is pointless for me to think of all of this and have no way of knowing. I'll drive myself crazy like this. No wonder I can never sleep. Always creating questions where I can't possibly know the answers. But maybe that's the beauty of it all, that I can make the answers whatever I want them to be. This thought made him feel a little better. He imagined that she was okay, just needed a break from everything. *That's why she looked so drained, but what is everything?* He laughed, shaking his head. *There you go again,* he thought.

He continued to drink his water and look out the window. He could tell it was cold by the condensation that had formed on the window. He looked at the random cars that drove down the street, wondering where they could be going or coming from at this time of the morning. Then he glanced up at the stars and the moon. It was a very clear night, and the sky seemed to glow a bit brighter.

Without even trying, he started to think of MaKayla again. *What if she's looking at the stars and the moon the same way I am? How cool would that be?* He realized his train of thought. "You truly are hopeless," he said out loud. "I'm going back to bed." He finished his water and placed the cup on the kitchen counter.

Wow, five already. Let me try to get a few more hours of sleep. He closed his eyes, and random images of his day flashed in his mind. He noticed one that he had almost forgotten about, and he held it there for a while. It was the moment he was helping MaKayla clean up the tea from the table, when he touched her hand and told her it was okay. In his mind, he could see her eyes so clearly. She had a look of concern and relief all in one, and just for a brief moment, she almost smiled. He wondered if this was because of him. *Nah,* he thought.

SPRING SHOWERS—THE BLOOM

There I go overthinking things again. But that would be nice. His mind went blank, and he was sleep.

*****

MaKayla woke up and stared out of the window for a minute, at the dark sky that seemed endless and the itty-bitty lights of the cities below. *What time is it?* she thought as she pulled out her phone, turning it on. *Five twelve? That's it,* she thought. *I guess I can try to get some more sleep before we land. I am pretty tired.* She turned off her phone and looked around the plane. The two ladies next to her were fast asleep. They didn't look like they were in the most comfortable positions. She figured their necks would hurt when they woke up.

There was a lady playing with her infant child, the baby's cooing sounding like the melody of angels. Then there was an old couple. They were asleep hand in hand, her head on his shoulder and his arm around her. They looked so happy and peaceful. She could only imagine the love they shared. *What's it like to be loved like that, for it to last that long or even as long as my parents'?* She smiled, shaking her head. *Those are things from movies, fairy tales, and the past. No one loves like that anymore, although I would if ever given the opportunity.*

These thoughts continued to dance in her head as she turned back to the window. It was a smooth flight—no turbulence, not noisy, just a good flight. *This will be good for me, getting away and getting a reset, getting to see Mom and Dad. I really have missed them a lot, and I know that they've missed me too. I really hope Dad's not too busy. I know how work can be for him. It'll be nice to just spend time together with no distractions like we used to when I was younger. I can't wait for Liyah to get here either. We have so much catching up to do. This is going to be good,* she thought as a smile arose on her face, and she drifted back to sleep.

*****

Jaron rolled over and looked at the clock, the sun seeping through the curtains. *Eight twelve? I don't even remember going to sleep.*

He lay there for a while, staring at his curtains. His mind was blank, minus the random thoughts that passed through. "Well, let me see if Mom is up," he said after a while, "although knowing her, I'm sure she is." After searching for his phone, which he found entangled in the covers—unsure of how it got there—he called.

"Hey baby," his mom said after answering the phone.

"Good morning Mom. How are you today?"

"I'm doing pretty good. What about yourself?"

"I'm good. No complaints."

"To what do I owe this call?"

He laughed. "I can't just call to check on you?"

"Of course you can, but I know you. So what's up?"

"Man, you've got ESP or something," he said, laughing.

"It's a mother's intuition. You wouldn't know anything about that," she replied, laughing.

"Well, I was going to see if you had any plans. Wanted to know if you'd like to go to breakfast or something."

"Nope, no plans. Well, other than my random errands, but there's no time frame on those. I was actually just about to make something to eat, but we can go to breakfast instead. Are you up and ready?"

"Nope. I'm lying here in the bed, nothing but boxers on."

"Well, I guess you'd better get on it. I expect you here in about an hour."

"Okay. Let me get up then."

"Okay. See you then," she said.

"Later," he replied as he hung up the phone.

Wait, he thought. *I invited her to breakfast, and she ended up giving me the orders like she invited me.* He smiled, shaking his head. "Have to love moms." He got up and took a shower, then got dressed. He did his routine walk around his house while drinking a glass of water, making sure all was where it needed to be. Once he left the house and stepped on his porch, he was immediately hit by a strong, brisk gust of wind. It made him shudder. "Maybe I should've dressed a little warmer. Eh, I'll be in the car, so it won't really matter."

The street was still. There was no movement at all. He attributed this to the fact that it was a chilly Saturday morning, figuring most people would be sleeping in. He got in his car and made his way to his mom's house. Traffic was light, so it didn't take him long.

*****

MaKayla's plane landed at nine fifteen. She turned on her phone and texted her mom to let her know that she had landed. She didn't receive a text back, so she made her way to baggage claim to pick up her luggage. She texted her dad as well as she walked. *That's weird,* she thought. *One of them should've replied by now.* To her surprise, as she reached baggage claim, there stood both her mom and dad, smiling at her. She couldn't hold back her smile and ran to give them a hug.

"Hey!" MaKayla said emphatically as she hugged them both at the same time. "I didn't expect you guys to meet me in here. You know I can carry my own bags, right?" They smiled.

"There she goes, still wanting to be independent," said her mom. "Come here. Let me have a look at you. Have you been eating like you're supposed to? You're looking a little thinner than I remember. What's it been, like, three years or so?" joked her mom, turning her back and forth, examining her like an outfit.

"Mom, stooopppppp!" grumbled MaKayla through clenched teeth while forcing a smile to her face. "You're embarrassing me."

"No one's paying us any attention." Her mom smiled as she let her go.

"Yeah, yeah, yeah," MaKayla said as they walked toward the conveyor belt from her flight. "You guys missed me that much, huh? You had to come all the way into baggage claim? Couldn't wait to see me?" she asked, a smile on her face.

"Well actually, we have a surprise for you," said her dad.

"Uh-oh. A good surprise, or a bad surprise?" MaKayla asked, looking back and forth at her mom and dad. They both just stood smiling in silence. "Dad, are you going on a business trip or something?"

"Well, something like that," he replied, smiling.

"But Dad, I just got back, and you've known I was coming for weeks now. This had to happen today? Couldn't you just spend time with me before you leave? I can't get a day? Mom, you can't just let him leave! You're not going to let him just leave, are you?" MaKayla folded her arms and began to pout. "I can't believe this. You got my hopes up just for you to leave?" Her mom and dad began laughing to the point where it became hard to catch their breaths. "I don't see what's funny," said MaKayla.

"Honey, you're overreacting. I'm not going on a business trip."

"But you said that—" MaKayla tried to explain her side before being cut off by her dad.

"I'm not going on a business trip. We all are going on a trip," he said, removing three plane tickets from his pocket, "to start your vacation off right."

MaKayla placed her hand over her mouth in shock and disbelief. "Are you serious right now?" she asked emphatically. "Mom, you knew this the whole time and didn't say anything? What if I don't have the right clothes? Why didn't you guys tell me?"

"We wanted it to be a surprise baby. You've been working really hard, and we are so proud of you. We wanted to show you just how proud we were. Plus, we know that you would've fought us had we told you," said her mom. "You deserve it, and even though you like to earn everything you get, to pay your own way, you've earned this. But we wanted to pay your way this time."

"I don't know what to say. I mean, thank you. You shouldn't have, but I'm so happy and surprised that you did. I don't know what to do."

"Well, how about you get your bags since you can carry them by yourself? Then we can go get something to eat before our flight leaves, because I'm starving," her dad said, smiling.

"Dad," said MaKayla, smiling.

"Okay. I'll get the bags, but I'm serious about this food. I'm starving."

"Well, I told you to eat before we left but no, you didn't want to listen, so now you're hungry," said her mom.

"Yeah, yeah, yeah. I know, I know," responded her dad as he grabbed the bags.

They went to the dining area after checking in as they waited for their flight, which boarded at ten fifteen. They talked about how her flight was and the past few days of work and school briefly while eating. She was just in such shock and disbelief. Her parents always did nice things, but this caught her off guard. She never saw it coming. Nevertheless, she loved it, a week's vacation with her parents—no work, no school, and no distractions. *This is going to be great,* she thought. They boarded their flight and prepared for takeoff.

"Hey Dad, so while we're on this vacation, there's not going to be any working, right?" asked MaKayla curiously.

"I already took care of everything that I needed to take care of for next week, rescheduled all my appointments, and the only reason the office is to call me is for extreme emergencies. No work, just me and my two favorite ladies."

"Okay. We're going to hold you to that," said MaKayla as she sat back in her chair, smiling.

*****

Once Jaron arrived, he called his mom to let her know that he was outside. "Okay. I'll be out in a minute," she said.

"All right," he replied. He waited for exactly one minute and began to blow the horn—not obnoxiously but just enough to get her attention. He knew she hated it when people blew the horn and even more to be rushed, but he found it hilarious.

She came steaming out of the house, all bundled up. He could see the annoyance on her face. He could barely hold in his laughter. She got into the car and immediately lit into him. "Now why would you do that? I told you that I'd be out in a minute."

"Well, it was past a minute Mom, and I was just holding you accountable for your words." He had a smirk on his face as he backed out of the driveway.

She continued to go off on him. "You could've woken someone up unnecessarily, out here, making all that noise. Don't make no kind of sense. You know I raised you better than that. You must have lost your mind or something. And wipe that grin off your face, because it's not funny, shoot."

He burst into laughter, no longer able to hold back. "Okay, okay, I'm sorry," he said as he wiped the tears from his eyes. "Oh man, that was funny. It never gets old."

"No, it's really not funny, Jaron."

"Okay, Mom. So where do you want to go eat?" he asked knowing that changing the subject would take her mind off it.

"Let's go to that new breakfast place they just opened."

"New breakfast place where? I don't think I've heard about it."

"Yes you have. We were talking about it the other day—you know, down the street from the Lakeview mall."

"Oh, you mean Pete's. That's not that new Mom."

"Well, it's new to me, so let's go there."

"Pete's it is," he replied, pulling off.

"So how'd you sleep?" she asked.

"Up and down. I probably woke up two or three times. Just couldn't stay asleep. What about you?"

"I slept good. Probably went to bed around ten or eleven and was up before six. Oh, when we leave Pete's, let's go to Lakeview so I can pick up a few things."

"Okay. That works. I want to see if they have this movie I've been looking for."

They arrived at Pete's shortly after and were seated in a small booth. After ordering their food, his mom asked, "So how did the meeting go?" She took a bite out of an apple that was brought by the waitress.

"Well, I got good news and bad news."

"Okay. What's the good news?"

"His offer was at least ten times more than we discussed or anticipated, like, two extra zeros at the end."

"Wow, that is good news. So what could be the bad news then?"

"I declined his offer."

"Why did you decide to do that?"

"He wasn't right for our company. He wanted a majority stake in the business."

"What?" exclaimed his mom. "Majority stake in the company? He's out of his mind!"

"Yeah, I know, and he was talking about gutting the company, basically bringing in all new people. Although he didn't come right out and say it, I could tell that's what he was actually planning to do. Then he was talking about how I'm not supposed to work for the people, how I'm supposed to make them work for me. Now you know that completely rubbed me the wrong way. He actually seemed to be taking little jabs at Dad, but I guess I could've been looking into it too much."

"Yeah, I can imagine. It sounds more like good news, good news, like you were going to sell your soul to the devil." They both laughed.

"You want to know what the kicker was?"

"What's that?" she asked, taking another bite out of her apple. "These are really good apples, by the way. You should try one. I wonder where they order them from."

"Mom," Jaron said, smiling.

"Oh yeah, sorry. You were saying?"

"I took him to the café that I always go to. He was a complete snob and so rude to MaKayla."

"Okay, wait," said his mom through a smile as she continued to chew. "Who is MaKayla?"

Jaron smiled a nervous smile. He remembered that he didn't know her name before that day, so neither did his mom. "She's the waitress I've been telling you about."

"Oh, so you two are on a first name basis now, huh?" Her smile grew wider.

"No Mom, it's not like that," he said shyly. "She just happened to be our waitress, so that's how I found out her name. What a day for that to happen, huh?"

"Why do you say that?"

"Because he was a complete and total jerk to her. They had to switch our waitress, and it looked like she was about to cry."

"Oh wow, that's horrible! What did she do to make him act like that?"

"That's just it. She didn't do anything. He ordered wrong and tried to blame it on her. After they switched our waitress, she left. I hope she didn't get fired."

"Well, did you say or do anything?"

"I told our new waitress before we left that it wasn't MaKayla's fault, that she handled the situation professionally. I felt rushed because I had Wynstead waiting in the car. I feel like I should've done more."

"Well, at least you did something. So what are you going to do next time you see her?"

"What do you mean the next time I see her?"

"I know you're going back up there, and I know you'll be looking for her, or at least you better. If you really like this girl, then you should consider formally apologizing to her for his actions, and we both know that you really like this girl. Maybe even talk to the manager, but that might be too much, or maybe not."

"You really think I should do that? You don't think I'll look—I don't know—crazy or something?"

"Does it matter? Since when did you become concerned about the way people view you or what they think about you?"

The waitress returned with their food and placed their plates in front of them. "Can I get you anything else?"

"Actually, I was wondering if you knew where you guys ordered your apples from."

"Seriously Mom?" said Jaron through a look of embarrassment.

"Actually, I don't, but I can try to find out for you."

"Thank you. That will be greatly appreciated," she said to the waitress. "Why do you look embarrassed?" asked his mom as the waitress walked away.

"You really had to ask her about the apples? Who asks those types of questions?" asked Jaron as he cut into his pancakes.

"It was a perfectly normal question," she said, smiling. "You don't like the way it feels, huh? Teach you to blow a horn at me."

SPRING SHOWERS—THE BLOOM

He couldn't help but smile as he ate his pancakes. She never forgot anything, and she played it so well. They ate and talked about random things, like the weather, shopping, her job, and their food, which both were enjoying. After finishing, they made their way to the register to pay.

"I got it," said Jaron.

"No, that's okay. I'll pay for it," responded his mom.

"No, really, Mom, it's okay. I got it."

"Look, you drove, and I'm paying, and that's final."

"Okay. Have it your way. You pay."

"That's more like it," she said.

The cashier was amused by the back-and-forth between Jaron and his mom, her head going back and forth between them to keep up with the conversation. After paying, they turned to leave.

"Oh miss, I almost forgot. Did you happen to find out about the apples?"

"Oh yeah, I actually did. I wrote down the name and location. I tend to forget things."

"Oh okay. Thanks. I'd almost forgotten as well," Jaron's mom said, turning toward him, smiling. He was already walking out the door, shaking his head. "That was really nice of her to write it all down for me, now wasn't it Jaron?"

"Yes Mom, it was nice." He remembered now why he rarely played jokes on his mom or did things to embarrass her. She was much better at it than he was, and he was so easily embarrassed.

"That really was a nice place. Plus, the food was good and reasonably priced," said his mom.

"Yeah. Me and a few of the guys came here a few weeks ago. They really liked it too."

"We're going to Lakeview now, right?"

"Yeah, that works."

"So what's next? What are you thinking of doing now?"

"What do you mean? As far as what?"

"I know you had a lot of plans and things riding on this Wynstead deal. So now that it's fallen through, what are you thinking of doing?"

"I really don't know Mom. I was going over numbers like crazy last night, but I couldn't find significant enough growth anywhere to be able to use. I mean, even when I did, I needed it to cover losses somewhere else. So I myself am at a loss right now."

"What about a different business partner? I know you had a long list of potential people."

"Now that you've said it, do you remember Mr. Thomas?"

"Yeah. He was pretty close to the top of your father's list of potentials, wasn't he? He just didn't have as much financial backing as Wynstead, right?"

"Yeah. He actually called me the other day, asking if I still wanted to get together to discuss a potential deal."

"What did you tell him?"

"I told him that I was already finalizing a deal with someone else on Friday. He told me that if anything fell through or didn't work out, I should give him a call back."

"See? There you go right there. You're worrying about something that's already taken care of."

"Yeah, there you go, right as usual. Thanks Mom. With the way things happened yesterday, I'd really forgotten all about him. I really don't know how, but I did."

"Doesn't matter now. All that matters is that you have solutions to work toward."

"Yeah, you're right."

"You know what? Let me call your sister Kelly. When I talked to her the other day, she was sick or had a bug or something."

"She and Shannon actually texted me yesterday. I forgot to reply."

"Hello? Hey baby, how are you? Are you still feeling sick? Oh okay. That's good. Glad you're feeling better. Maybe it was something that was going around that you caught the tail end of. I'm good and full. No, I'm with Jaron. He invited me to breakfast. Girl stop." His mom laughed. "Your sister is asking why we didn't invite her. Are you trying to ease your way into becoming my favorite?"

"Tell her I don't have to work at what I've already achieved. I simply have to do maintenance now." Jaron could hear his sister laughing through the phone.

"Y'all stop it." His mom smiled. "Why don't we all go out for dinner tomorrow?" she asked.

"I'm free," said Jaron. "But what about her and Shannon? They're always busy."

"Look who's talking," he heard Kelly's voice through the phone. "Ask him why he never texted me back from yesterday."

"My bad sis. I completely forgot. Long day."

"Yeah, now who's always busy?" She laughed along with her mom.

"Well, can you make it baby?" their mom asked. "Okay. Good. And you guys let me handle Shannon, okay?"

"Fine by me," said Jaron.

"Oh, and you can invite that guy friend of yours. What's his name again? Johnny? Justin? Jacob? Oh yeah, yeah, Jalin, Jalin. Yeah, invite him. Okay, well, I hope he can make it. Yeah, we're about to head to Lakeview for a little. What are you up to? Oh, I got all my cleaning done earlier, so I know that feeling. Okay, well, I'll let you get back to it. I'll talk to you later. Love you too," replied his mom as she hung up the phone. "It'll be good to have all of you together again. It's been a while. One of you is always missing."

"Yeah, I know. We have to do better, make sure we can all get together more frequently."

"I agree," she said as they pulled into the parking lot. "This is the closest entrance to where we both need to go."

They went into the mall and shopped for about an hour and a half, talking about everything under the sun, his mom making frequent references to apples, to make sure he remembered his lesson of the day.

*****

The flight was only two hours. They made use of the time by playing cards and Scrabble on the plane. Once they landed, they collected their luggage and got into their rental car, then drove to the hotel. The sun was beaming. *It has to be around eighty-five degrees,* thought MaKayla as she stepped out of the car, shielding her eyes. "I haven't felt the sun this warm in months," she said out loud. "This is going to be a good vacation. I can already feel it. Mom, you up for a jog? I didn't get mine in this morning, and I know that it would feel good down by the water."

"Sure. Let's get settled into our room first."

"Okay. And Dad, you're more than welcome to join us." MaKayla smiled.

"Better late than never, but I think I'll sit this one out. Maybe next time baby."

Their room was a double suite, and its beauty hit MaKayla immediately upon opening the doors. It had a beautiful ocean view with sliding glass doors, through which the sun was streaming in. There was a Jacuzzi bathtub and a waterfall shower. She had her own king-size bed with gorgeous white linen bedding with gold stitching and a flat-screen TV, which was mounted on the wall. There was also a kitchen area fully equipped with stove, sink, microwave, and dishes and a small living room area that had its own TV, white leather recliner couch, and two white single recliners on both sides of the couch.

MaKayla stood in the doorway in amazement. She couldn't believe her eyes. "Is this, like, a let-out couch or something?" she asked, pointing to the couch. "Because I call dibs on the bed."

"Yes, the couch does let out into a bed. Do you plan on having company or something?" asked her mom, smiling.

"No. Why did you ask that?"

"Well, this is your room, so who's going to sleep on the couch?"

"This is my room? All to myself?" asked MaKayla in a very excited and surprised tone. "Where is your room?"

"You see that door right there? You open it, and there's a passageway to our room next door."

"Are you serious?" asked MaKayla, her smile growing in size.

"Yes, we're serious," said her father as he stood smiling, relieved to see that his daughter was happy. She spent so much time trying to do everything herself and fighting those who tried to help. He felt good being able to do something that she accepted without any issues.

MaKayla dropped her bag, walked over, and wrapped her arms around her parents. She just hugged them, not speaking, the tightness of her grip saying everything that her mouth couldn't.

"You're welcome baby," said her mom. "Now go on, get unpacked so we can go take this run." MaKayla held on for a little while longer, then turned, ran, and jumped on the bed. "I'll be ready in twenty minutes," said her mom as she walked away, smiling.

MaKayla lay there for a while, staring out of the window, just thinking. *Wow, this is amazing. I can't believe this. Wait until I tell Liyah.* She walked to the sliding doors and slid them open, stepping out onto the balcony. She closed her eyes and allowed the sun to wash over her, its warm embrace bringing her closer.

She let out a sigh and opened her eyes, looked out at the water. It was so beautiful, so blue. There were people on their boats, and there were ones who were lying, walking, riding, and playing on the beach. *I wonder how many other people are here for spring break. How many of those people down there needed this as much as I need it?* She smiled. *I suppose they all do. Otherwise, they wouldn't be here.* She giggled a little as she turned and walked back into her room.

MaKayla began to unpack a few things she would need for her jog and then changed her clothes. She walked through the corridor and knocked on the door. When her dad opened it, it was like she was walking back into her room. It was a mirror image of hers.

"Look at you guys and your fancy little room," MaKayla said as if hers was not the exact same. They all laughed. "You ready to go Mom?"

"Yeah. Give me one minute and we can go."

They left and went jogging and walking up the beach, stopping periodically to take in the scenery. They didn't talk much. It was as if they both needed to clear their minds, to ensure they enjoyed themselves the best they could on this vacation. Occasionally, they would meet each other's glance and smile. No words were needed to be spoken. In those moments when they stopped and stared either at people or the water, they would exchange brief words about its beauty and innocence or the simple joys of life.

Once they made it back to the hotel, they saw her father stretched across the bed, taking a nap. "I'm going to finish unpacking, take a shower, and order some room service," said her mom.

"Then I'll do the same. We're having dinner later?"

"Yeah. I don't know where yet, but we will."

MaKayla returned to her room and began unpacking.

*****

After they got back to his mom's house, Jaron gave her a hug and a kiss before she got out of the car.

"I'll call you tomorrow afternoon with the details for dinner."

"Okay Mom. I love you."

"Love you too."

Jaron sat outside and watched to make sure she made it in the house before he pulled off, then he texted Xavier. "Hit my line when you get a free moment." His phone was ringing within five minutes. "Hello, man I didn't expect to hear from you so soon."

"Man, you just saved my life."

"Saved your life? What do you mean? What's up?"

"I was just about to get into it with Candace. I'm leaving her house right now."

"What are you two into it about?"

"About last night. Oh maaaaaaaan, it was soooo crazy. I told you that you should've come."

"Oh yeah, what happened?"

"Man, Troy got tore up. We trailed this fool home, and he was all over the road. I was worried he wasn't going to make it."

"What? Why didn't somebody take his keys?"

"That's just it. He tried to fight us every time we tried to. He was in Cliché, trying to get every girl to go home with him, asking them just outright if they wanted to have a threesome."

"Now y'all know he can't hold his liquor. He doesn't even drink like that."

"Yeah, I know, but he wasn't himself last night. It was like he was possessed." Xavier laughed.

"Why are you laughing? He could've hurt himself or, even worse, somebody else."

"Yeah, I know, but you had to be there to understand. Plus, he got home safe, and I didn't want him out there fighting any of the guys. I just tried to pick the lesser of two evils, you know?"

"Yeah, I can understand that. So why did you and Candace get into it?"

"She's really getting, like, real serious all of a sudden."

"I thought you guys were already serious?"

"Yeah, we are, but this is different. I can't explain it. She's talking about me not going out to clubs like that and making safer choices, talking about how she doesn't want to lose me, talking about how I need to stay away from these club girls because they don't mean me no good, how I need to think about what it would be like to raise a family and stuff. I don't know man. That type of talk scares me."

"I know it does." Jaron laughed. "But I've been telling you some of those same things for a while now."

"Yeah, but you're my boy, my ace. You know me well enough to hit me with that. Me and her only been together for six months, and you know that's a long time for me, but not that long, you know?"

"Yeah, it is. And nowadays, it's a long time period. Maybe it's just that time of the month and your crazy night just got to her."

"Yeah, I hope so. You know I don't track those things." Xavier laughed. "So you could be right. So what's up with you?"

"Just dropped off Moms. We went to breakfast and did a little shopping. She actually brought something to my attention as far as the next direction I may want to go with the company."

"Now that's what's up. Moms always comes through when you need her."

"Yeah, but I was texting to see if you guys wanted to come to my crib and watch the game tonight."

"You know I'm in. Everybody else will probably be down too—well, except Troy." Xavier laughed.

"All right. Cool. I'll call him right now and see what's good. Then I'll shoot a text to everyone when I finish."

"Okay. Cool. I'll talk to you then. One," he said as he hung up the phone.

"Man Troy," Jaron said, shaking his head as he called him.

"Hello," came a very somber voice from the other end of the phone.

"You busy bro?"

"Nah. What's up?"

"How are you feeling?"

Troy let out a deep sigh. "To be honest, I'm disappointed in myself. I don't even remember half of what happened last night. I know I tried to fight Will and Danny Boy. That's not cool man. I'm not even sick or have a hangover. I just know that I'm better than that."

"Don't sweat it. We've all been boys for years, and we've been through worse. We always came out on top before. This won't be any different."

"Yeah, it sounds good, but it doesn't feel that way."

"Okay. Well look man, I wanted to invite all you guys to my crib tonight to watch the game."

"I don't know about that. Nina's not too happy with me either right now, and after last night's debacle, that might not be happening."

"Where's she at?"

"In the front room. I think she's keeping her distance from me so she doesn't keep getting upset."

"You mind if I talk to her?"

"Sure. It's your funeral."

"Baby," Jaron heard Troy's voice come from the phone, and seconds later, he heard Nina.

"What do you want?"

"Phone's for you. It's Jaron."

After a few seconds of Jaron holding the phone in silence, actually nervous about what was about to happen, he heard an irritated voice come from the other end of the phone.

"Hello?"

"Hey Nina. How are you?"

"Irritated and annoyed, but I've felt worse. What's up?"

"Look, I know he messed up big time last night, and it's just as much the guys' fault as it is his."

"You don't understand Jaron. I woke up to his car parked on the lawn and him sleeping on the steps."

"Oh wow, I didn't know all of that." There was a brief silence as Jaron thought of what to say next. "All in all, you know Troy. He's a good dude. He doesn't do crazy stuff like this, and you know he would do anything to make you happy, so just take it a little easy on him."

"Is that why you called, to plead his case for him?"

"No, not at all," responded Jaron quickly. "I actually called to check on him. He told me how you were upset with him, so I was just trying to be a voice of reason." There was silence again, and Jaron figured this was as good a time if any to see if he could get Troy out of the house. "Plus, I wanted to know if…um—"

"If what?" she asked sharply.

"If he could…maybe…come watch the game at my house tonight," he said hesitantly.

"Are you serious right now? After the night he had, you want me to let him go out again?" came a very irritated and annoyed voice from the other end of the phone.

"Look, I understand that, but think back over all the years you've known me. Has he ever gotten into any trouble while he was with me?"

"No, but what does that matter?"

"We'll be at my house, and I'll even come get him. The best way for him to make it right is to show you. It won't help if you guys are just cooped up in the house, upset or annoyed, so why don't I come get him a little later and you go out with your girls? Then tomorrow, you guys can reset."

There was a long pause. "You're lucky I like you Jaron, unlike some of your other friends he hangs around, but you owe me."

"You know you're like a sister to me. Anything I can do, I got you."

"You better feel lucky you have a friend like him," Jaron heard a fading voice say.

"What did you tell her? I owe you big time."

"No biggie. You know you're my boy. Just be ready between six and six thirty. I'll come grab you."

"Okay cool. Thanks again bro."

"Definitely. One."

"One," he replied as he hung up the phone.

Jaron then went into the group text with all the guys, stating, "Let's watch the game at my house. We'll order pizza and wings. I'll grab drinks. Be there by seven thirty. You down?" One by one, the responses started to trickle in—"Most definitely," "Yep, yep," "7:30 it is," "Sure thing," "Bet." Jaron felt good. He had a great morning with his mom, who helped him figure out his next move with the company, he helped his friend avoid an argument, albeit unintentionally, he got his other friend out of a tight spot with his girl, and he had plans with the guys to watch the game in what he figured would be a great night.

Chapter 6

MaKayla woke up, somewhat startled. There was a loud sound that was coming from the TV. She wiped her eyes as she sat up in the bed, looking at the TV. There was an old black-and-white movie playing. *How did it even get on this channel?* she thought. She attempted to watch it, but it bored her, and her thoughts began to wander.

I wonder if everything is going okay at the café. I wonder if they could use my help. She smiled. *I've barely been gone a day and I'm over here worried. Guess that's the owner's mentality in me.* She pulled herself out of the bed. *Let's see what all this hotel has to offer.* She put on a pair of black shorts and a black-and-white tank top, then slipped on her flip-flops.

She roamed the halls, going to every floor just to see how it looked. She took pictures of the different paintings on the walls, of the different views she got from the different floors of the hotel, and even of the hotel itself. She even took a picture with some random people she met in the lobby. They noticed her taking pictures and struck up a conversation with her. Once they found out she was on vacation, they wanted to be a part of her experience, to really help her have some memories she wouldn't forget.

They took pictures in all types of poses—serious, goofy, elegant, model type, all girl, and some of her by herself. Although this was out of character for her since she had a very reserved, to-herself personality outside of work, she figured, "Hey, I'm on vacation. What the heck!" After they finished, she made her way to the pool area. Despite the beautiful day, there were still a lot of people in the pool. Some were working out, some were in the sauna, and some were in the hot tub.

She made her way back upstairs to see what her parents were up to. She knocked on the door, and her mom answered. "We were just talking about you. We thought that you were still sleeping."

"Nope. I've been checking out the hotel—you know, taking pictures and such. I met some pretty cool people in the lobby. We ended up taking a few pictures too."

"Wait. You took pictures with people you didn't even know? Now there's something you don't see every day," said her mom through a smile.

"We're on vacation. I figured, why not? Plus, they were really nice."

"Well, that's good baby," said her dad. "We're going to start getting ready to go eat in a few."

"All right. What do you think, between seven thirty and eight?" she replied

"Yeah, that should work."

"Okay. I'll go start getting ready," she replied as she walked through the door that led back to her room.

*****

Jaron got home about five minutes later, got in the shower, and changed clothes to prepare for the night. He was out of the house by five twenty-five and had made sure the house was in order before he left. He arrived at Troy's house at six ten, parked, and walked to the door. After ringing the doorbell a few times, Troy answered. "Come in for a minute. I'm almost ready," he said as he walked into the house.

"Where's Nina?" asked Jaron.

"She's sitting in the living room. She's still somewhat upset with me."

Jaron walked into the living room and saw Nina sitting on the couch, a frown on her face. He went and sat on the couch next to her, extremely close, to the point where they were rubbing shoulders. He nudged her a little but got no response. He nudged her again. "So you're not going to talk to me? That's rude," he said through a smile.

"Hi," she said with an annoyed voice.

"How are you? No change? Not even the slightest bit?"

"Nope, not at all."

SPRING SHOWERS—THE BLOOM

"What can I do to help?"

"Nothing at all. Be grateful that I'm letting him go," she said, folding her arms.

Jaron smiled. "I am grateful, but I don't want you sitting here all frowned up."

"I'll be fine," Nina said, still not looking at him.

"How about a joke?"

"I'm not in a laughing mood."

"Okay, well, you know I'm going to tell you anyway. Okay, so here's the next pickup line that I'm going to try on a girl. Let me know if you think it'll work. I need your assistance though, okay?"

She looked at him and shook her head. "All right, since I know you won't leave me alone otherwise," she said, sighing heavily.

"Okay. So I walk up and say, 'You dropped something,' and she says—"

"Dropped what?" asked Nina.

"Our conversation. So how about we pick it up right here?" said Jaron as he smiled.

Nina shook her head. "Prepare to be dismissed with that one."

"Okay, okay. How about this one? Kiss me if I'm wrong, but dinosaurs still exist." Nina shook her head, and Jaron noticed that she almost cracked a smile. "No?" he said. "What about, on a scale of one to ten, you're a nine. See, I'm the one you need." Her smile slowly began to show. "No still?" he said emphatically through a smile. "Okay. So what about, are you a ticket? Because girl you got fine written all over you." Nina burst out into laughter. "That's what I wanted to see," said Jaron, smiling.

"You are so slow," said Nina. "Those will never work on any girl. They are going to laugh at you."

"That's the point," said Jaron. "Once I get them laughing, then I can open up a real conversation, right?"

"Yeah, I guess that's a good plan."

Feeling relieved and somewhat accomplished by her opening up, Jaron asked, "What plans do you have for tonight?"

"The girls and I are going to go out for drinks a little later and maybe grab something to eat too."

"Cool." Just then, Troy walked in. "You ready to go?" asked Jaron.

"Yeah. You?"

"Let's get it," Jaron said, getting up off the couch. "Make sure you keep that smile on your face. And remember those pickup lines. Don't let anyone try to use them on you."

"Sure thing. And you make sure I don't regret this."

"You won't," said Troy.

"I was talking to Jaron," Nina said through an annoyed voice. "I'm still upset with you."

"Well, I love you, and I know I've got some making up to do, so making up is exactly what I'll do."

"Yeah, I know," she said, resisting the smile that was pushing at the corners of her lips. Troy walked over and gave her a kiss on the cheek, then he and Jaron left.

"How do you do it man?" asked Troy.

Jaron laughed. "Do what?"

"You got her in there laughing and not even mad anymore."

Jaron laughed again. "She wasn't ever mad, just disappointed. You know how crazy that girl is about you, and vice versa. I just took her mind off of what she was disappointed about, that's all. It was easy for me to do considering I wasn't involved."

"Yeah, I can understand that. I just hate when she's upset."

"She'll be fine after tonight. You know you guys don't hold on to these types of things. That's how you made it this far."

"You know what? You're right. Let me stop worrying so much."

"Cool. Now we have to make a stop at this store and grab some drinks and paper plates before we head to the crib."

*****

They stopped at the store and made it to Jaron's house around seven twenty. Xavier and Tony were already there, waiting in the car. "What took you so long?" yelled Xavier from the car. "We've been here for over five minutes."

Jaron shook his head. "Well, I'm pretty sure I said seven thirty. So while I appreciate you being early, I'm not late. And what's five minutes anyway?" They all started laughing as they walked up to the door.

"You good?" asked Xavier to Troy.

"Yeah man, I'm good. How are you guys?"

"I'm good."

"I'm good," said Tony and Xavier.

"How'd you even get to come out tonight? I was sure you'd be in some deep stuff for last night," said Tony.

"I am, or was, or I still am. You know what? I don't know. Ask Jaron. This is his doing." They all looked at Jaron.

Jaron just smiled. "Hey, I have my ways." They all laughed.

"Seriously though, you know Nina is like a sister to me. I just had to talk to her, that's all."

"Oh, so you just got it like that, huh?" said Xavier.

"What do you mean?" asked Jaron.

"You got me out of a bind earlier. Then you get him out of one too just a little while later."

Jaron laughed. "No, no, no. Yours was unintentional, but that's just one of the perks of having a friend that's cool with your girl, I guess. Plus, it helped that I wasn't there with you guys last night."

"Yeah, that makes sense," said Tony.

"Well, turn on that TV. The pregame should be on by now. I'm going to order pizza and wings."

Jaron walked into the kitchen and ordered the food. He came back with chips, ice, cups, shot glasses, paper towels, and paper plates. When he walked back in, Will and Daniel had arrived. He noticed a weird vibe and how Troy was on one side, seemingly alone, while everyone else was conversing on the other side.

"I ordered the food. It should be here in about thirty to forty minutes," said Jaron.

"What did you get?" asked William.

"Three meat lovers and fifty wings in a bunch of different flavors."

"That should be good. I'm starving," said Daniel.

"Yeah, we know. You're always hungry," said Tony.

"Okay, well, put the TV on mute for a minute. Everybody, grab a shot glass." Jaron grabbed the alcohol and filled everyone's glasses. "So let's get this out the way and over with."

Everyone looked around, and Xavier said, "Um, did I miss something? Get what over with?"

"Well, there are obviously things that need to be said about last night. I can feel the tension. We've been boys for way too long to let a drunk night mess that up, so man up and get whatever you have to say off your chest, and let's move forward." There was a slight pause, and everyone looked at one another. Jaron got ready to speak but was cut off by Troy.

"Okay, look man, I want to apologize for how I acted last night, especially to Will and Danny Boy. Y'all know I would never act like that in my right mind, but that doesn't matter, and it's no excuse. I appreciate you guys following me home to make sure I got there in one piece." After finishing, Troy lowered his head.

"There are a lot of things that we all could've done differently last night," said Will. "We know you don't drink like that, so we should've gotten to you or your keys before it got to that point. That's on all of us. No hard feelings here. We're all brothers. Through thick and thin, we got each other."

There was a pause, and Daniel burst out singing. "What can a brother do for me?" Everyone started laughing.

"Here's to drunk nights that make way for sober laughs," said Tony. They all raised their glasses and then threw the shot back.

"All right. Now let's get to this game," said Xavier.

"Wait. I just got one more question," said Jaron. "How did you guys let him park his car in his yard?"

"Wait. What?" said Xavier.

"See? I told you," said Danny Boy. "I told you that he got back in the car. His car was parked on the street when we left, and he was opening the door to his house."

"Oh yeah," said Troy. "For some reason, I thought I had a driveway. I figured it made more sense to park there than on the streets. I didn't want to get sideswiped by a drunk driver, so I went back to move it." Everyone paused and then began to laugh. "Hey, in my mind, I parked pretty well in that driveway."

*****

MaKayla had just finished getting ready when her parents came to her door.

"Hey, you ready?" asked her dad as she opened the door.

"I sure am," she replied as she looked around the room to ensure she had everything before she left.

The restaurant wasn't far, so they decided to walk. It would only take them about fifteen to twenty minutes. The weather was beautiful. The sun had just finished setting, and the temperature was around seventy-five degrees. There was a cool, gentle breeze coming in from the ocean that made MaKayla's hair gently lift up. She closed her eyes and embraced it every time it blew. The streets were vibrant and filled with laughter, people talking, dancing, and music. They walked and talked as they made their way to the restaurant.

They were seated and stayed there eating, talking, and laughing for almost three hours. The restaurant had an inviting ambiance, and all the patrons were in such a good mood. They were seated outside, by the beach, so there was a lot of activity. Everyone was dancing and polite. It was as if it was a family reunion or a party of sorts.

MaKayla was happy. She looked at her parents, at the smiles on their faces, and at the love they had in their eyes for each other. The laughter that came from their mouths made her smile even bigger. She often wondered how they were while she was gone. Were they happy? Was everything okay? This dinner told her all that she needed to know. It was just as it had always been. She could feel the love flowing from them.

*****

They watched the game, ate, drank, and laughed. After it went off, they started playing cards. Troy got a call and stepped out of the room. He came back about five minutes later, grabbed his drink, and downed it. Then he grabbed his coat. "Hey fellas, it's been real, but I'm about to get up out of here."

"Wait. How are you getting home? I picked you up."

"Oh, you know man, Nina's outside waiting on me."

"Well, you better get out of here then," said the guys, laughing as he did his goodbyes one by one.

"Hey Jaron, thanks again," said Troy.

"No biggie bro. Go have fun."

The night wound down, and the guys fell asleep one by one on the couch or in random chairs. Jaron straightened up a little before making his way upstairs, where he fell across his bed and was fast asleep in no time. He woke up around two fifteen and made his way downstairs. Daniel and William were still asleep, but Xavier was awake, putting on his coat.

"Where you headed this time of the morning? Home?" asked Jaron.

"Nah man. I'm going to imitate Troy."

"Oh, Candace. You have to go make up, right?"

"Yeah man. She just called, wondering where I was and upset because we haven't talked since earlier."

"Yeah, you better make that right. You good to drive?"

"Yeah, I'm cool. I'll shoot you a text when I get there."

"Okay cool. Good luck." Jaron laughed.

"You know I got skills. I don't need luck."

"Yeah, yeah, yeah. Hit me when you make it."

"All right bro. One."

"One," said Jaron as he closed the door. He got a cup of water and made his way back upstairs. He figured he would be back up in a couple of hours and dozed back off.

*****

After leaving the restaurant, they walked around for a while. It was such a beautiful night, and they just wanted to enjoy it. They talked about old vacations and new ones that would be fun to go on. You couldn't even tell it was late because the streets still thrived.

People were out as if it was close to nine instead of past midnight. They made it back to the hotel a little after two.

"Are we still going jogging in the morning?" MaKayla asked her mom. "I'm up for it if you are."

"Sounds like a plan."

They said their good nights and went to their rooms for the night. MaKayla changed into her nightclothes, brushed her teeth, and climbed into bed. *Today was a good day,* she thought. *I hope the rest of this vacation is just like this.* She considered watching TV but was fast asleep before she knew it.

*****

To Jaron's surprise, when he reopened his eyes, the sun was already streaming through his curtains. He lay there for a while, somewhat confused, wondering if it was a dream. He searched for his phone in his pocket and pulled it out. *Eight fourteen. Hmm, let me see if the guys are still down there,* he thought. He checked his messages as he walked down the stairs. There was one from Xavier from 2:48 a.m.: "I made it. Holla at you tomorrow" There was also one from Daniel from 3:47 a.m.: "We're leaving bro. Didn't want to wake you."

When he got to the bottom of the stairs, he noticed that everything was pretty much straightened up, but that didn't surprise him. He was surprised by the fact that he didn't wake up or hear anything. *I must have really been tired,* he thought. He grabbed a few slices of pizza and threw them in the microwave while running the dishwasher. There weren't many dishes, just the cups and glasses that they had used and a few pieces of silverware.

After eating and washing the dishes, he took a shower, then he laid back in the bed and watched random shows on TV. Around eleven, he got a text from Xavier.

"You good man?"

"Yeah, all good on my end. What about you and Candace?"

"You know me. I told you I got skills. We're good."

"That's what I like to hear."

"Well, I was just checking on you. I'll hit you up a little later."

"All right bro."

*****

MaKayla opened her eyes. Her room was still basically dark. Only a little light peeked through the curtains. *Did we oversleep? Why didn't Mom wake me up for the jog?* she thought. She grabbed her phone to call her mom, but she already had a few missed calls and a text message from her. "No run today. It's storming." MaKayla rolled out of bed and opened her curtain. Just as she did, there was a loud boom of thunder, which caused her to jump back several feet. *How did I sleep through all of this and those calls? What time is it?* She grabbed her phone again. *Eleven fifty-three? Man, I must have been really tired to have slept this long.*

She walked back to the window and stared out. The clouds were dark gray and fought the sun to keep it from showing. The waves rode in fast, foaming white, then crashed against the beach before receding back to the ocean. She stood there for several minutes, just watching that process repeat itself. It was mesmerizing.

She walked over and opened the door that went to her parents' room. She knocked a few times. "Come in," she heard a voice say. She opened the door to find her parents still lying in bed. She stretched as she walked through the door.

"Why are you guys still in bed? Have you even eaten yet?"

"Yes, we ate. And have you seen that storm out there? It's perfect for a lazy day."

"Well, you know what? I think I'll join you," said MaKayla as she lay across the foot of the bed. "Can you pass me the menu? I think I'll order some food."

"Why can't you go do that in your room?" asked her mom through a smile.

"So you're trying to kick me out? I just came in here, and you're trying to kick me out already? I thought this was a family vacation? Now you don't want to be around me?"

"Oh, don't be so dramatic. I'm trying to watch this movie, and you know how I hate interruptions."

"Oh, let her stay. She's not hurting anything or anyone. You can still watch your movie."

"Thanks Daddy," said MaKayla, smiling, as she turned her attention back to the menu. She ordered her food and went to take a shower. She came back just as her food arrived. After eating, she laid back across the foot of the bed and fell back to sleep.

*****

Jaron fell asleep and woke up to his phone ringing. It was his mom. "Hello," he said through a groggy voice.

"Are you still sleep at twelve forty-five in the afternoon? What's wrong with you? That's not like you at all," came his mom's voice from the other end of the phone.

Jaron cleared his throat. "I was up earlier, and I just fell asleep lying here, watching something on TV. I don't even remember what it was."

"Oh, I was about to say."

"How are you Mom?"

"I'm good. I just got off the phone with your sister Shannon."

"What did you talk about?"

"We were just discussing dinner tonight."

"Oh yeah, I almost forgot about that."

"Well, we're going to Jerry's Steakhouse at six."

"We're leaving at six, or everybody will be there at six?"

"Everybody will be there at six. I already talked to Shannon and Kelly. Kelly will bring Jalin, so it's all set."

"Okay, good. What time do you want me to come pick you up?"

"You don't have to. Shannon is going to come get me."

Jaron began laughing. "Are you sure Mom? You know Shannon drives crazy."

"Yeah, I know. She has a new car that she wants me to see, so I told her I'd ride with her."

"Okay. Well, I'll see you guys there. Let me know if anything changes."

"Okay. Love you. Later."

"Love you too," he said as he hung up the phone.

Jaron turned the channel, realizing there was a game on. He looked at his phone and noticed he had a missed message from Troy.

> "Man, I know I told you already, but thanks again for yesterday. I truly appreciate that. Definitely came through when I needed you to."
>
> "Like I told you yesterday, it's no biggie man. That's what we're here for. I know you'd do the same for me."

A few minutes later, his phone vibrated.

> "Yeah, I know man, but a lot of people talk about it. It's good to see it in action. Plus, I didn't know what I was going to do about Nina. You came through more than you know."
>
> "So you guys good again?"
>
> "Yeah. We talked on the way home, and then we TALKED when we got in the house."
>
> "Hey, what's understood doesn't have to be discussed. LOL. Glad I could help."
>
> "Cool bro. I'll catch up with you later. We're on our way into this movie."
>
> "Cool. Tell Nina I said what up too."
>
> "Alright."

Jaron watched the next two games that came on while getting ready for dinner. He left the house at five fifteen to make sure he wouldn't be late. He couldn't be sure how the roads would be. Traffic was somewhat heavy, and he made it to the restaurant at five fifty.

He texted both of his sisters to see where they were. Kelly responded three minutes later: "Parking now. Where are you?" He responded, "Parked by the front." She pulled in two spaces away from him. He got out of the car and walked toward his sister's. She got out and gave him a hug, a huge smile on her face.

"Hey, where's Jalin? I thought Mom said he was coming with you?"

"Yeah, he's on his way. Just running a little late. Got caught up at work."

"Oh okay. Have you talked to Mom or Shannon?" asked Jaron. "I texted Shannon, but she didn't respond."

"Yeah, me too. Let's wait by the front. We should see them pull in."

They stood there talking for about ten minutes before Jaron asked, "Do you think we should call? You know how Mom is about being on time."

"Yeah, but you also know how Shannon is. She's always late." They both laughed. About two more minutes passed, and a big black truck pulled up in front of them.

"Is that Jalin?" asked Jaron.

"Nope. He doesn't have a truck." Just then, the window rolled down. Inside sat their mom with Shannon in the driver's seat. "We should've known," said Kelly as she shook her head. "Always have to overcompensate. Go park so we can go eat." Shannon smiled and rolled up the window as she pulled off. She came back with her head up, strutting in a stuck-up, playful manner.

"Now why did you go get a monster truck knowing it's too big for a midget like you?" joked Jaron.

"Oh, you got jokes, huh? Well, I texted you the other day. I was going to have you go with me to pick it up, but you be too busy for us little folks."

"Stop playing and get over here and give me a hug," said Jaron, walking toward his sister with his arms outstretched. Kelly joined in, and she and Jaron squeezed Shannon tightly.

"Mom, tell them to let me go," said Shannon.

"Stop crying. We're just showing you love," said Jaron as he let go of his grip.

SEASONAL STORMS

"Stop playing now so we can go get a table," said their mom.

They walked into the restaurant and got a table for six. Shannon always made sure they got an extra seat whenever they went out to eat. She always said that their dad would never leave them and that they should make sure he had a seat when he got there.

"How far away did you say Jalin was?" asked their mom.

"Oh, he should be here in about twenty to thirty minutes," replied Kelly.

"Oh okay. Well, let's at least order drinks until he comes. So what's new? Don't all answer at once," asked their mom.

"Okay, well, I'll go first," immediately responded Shannon. "Last week, I got offered a new position. It'll just about double my pay. I'll be able to travel free of charge—for work, of course. I don't have a team that I manage, but there's like a group of people that I'll work with, like a fashion brain trust."

"Wow, congratulations," said Kelly.

"Yeah, congrats sis. I'm really happy for you."

"Well, baby I always knew that you'd get far, and now look at you. You really got your career off the ground," said their mom.

"What's your official job title?" asked Kelly.

"A fashion buyer."

"Oh, so you basically get to decide what the company will purchase?"

"Yeah, me and the group that I'll be working with. We get to go to all the fashion shows, and we'll have invites to parties—everything."

"So that's how you got the monster truck, huh?" asked Jaron.

"It's not a monster truck, bighead, but yeah. I got a sign-on bonus, which was quite substantial, I might add. Okay, so who's next?" asked Shannon excitedly.

"Well, seeing as you already went, we might as well keep the ladies first trend," said Jaron, looking at Kelly through a smirk.

Kelly took a drink of water. "Why are you always trying to put somebody on the spot?" She looked around nervously as if there was something she needed to say but didn't know how to. "Well, there's nothing new at work for me. It's same old, same—you know, hiring, trying not to fire anyone, paperwork, etc., etc., etc." Kelly was the head of human resources for an up-and-coming IT company. It wasn't a lifelong dream of hers or anything like how it was for Shannon or Jaron, but she enjoyed it all the same. "That's about all that's new in my life." She nervously smiled.

"What about you and Jalin? How's everything with you two? It's been, what like ten, eleven months? But who's keeping track?" said their mom with a smile.

"Eleven, Mom. Thanks for noticing. We're good. Nothing new, you know." Kelly lightly laughed and nervously drank some more water. "What about you, little brother?" she said as she playfully nudged her brother, attempting to quickly shift the attention off herself. Their mom looked at her suspiciously but turned her attention to Jaron once he began talking.

"Let me see. Where should I start? So much to say, so little time," said Jaron jokingly.

"Stop playing," said Shannon through a smile.

"Okay, okay. Well, work has been somewhat hectic. I had a major merger deal fall through Friday, hence my lack of communication," he said through a smile.

"Excuses, excuses," said Kelly, smiling. "But how did it fall through?"

"Well, I guess 'fall through' isn't the right term. But after our final meeting and seeing the true side of who I'd be going into business with, I realized that it wasn't in the best interest of the company. He wasn't the type of person that I wanted to be in business with. Although he never verbally said it, he didn't respect me or the way I thought, felt, or handled business. He turned out to be a real prick too, so"—Jaron shrugged—"it's just an aspect of the business side of what I do."

"So what are you going to do now?" asked Shannon.

"Well, after talking to Mom yesterday, I realized a silver lining in it all, and I plan on seeing where that can take me starting next week."

"In other words, he may have another potential business partner, who will probably be a better fit anyway," said their mom.

"I don't know why you always have to talk in riddles and try to have these deep metaphors anyway," said Shannon.

"He gets it from Dad. Remember how he used to talk like that and have some deep, underlying message in everything?" said Kelly. "I'd be like, 'Dad, I love how you make chicken breasts. Feel like making some?' Then he'd say something like, 'Well Kelly, if you give a man a fish, you feed him for a day. But if you teach a man to fish, he can feed himself for a lifetime.' I'd be like, 'So is that a no? You could've just said no Dad.' He'd say, 'No, I'm not saying no. What I'm saying is, we can make it together. That way, you'll always be able to have it with or without me.' So why didn't he just say that?" Kelly smiled. Everyone started laughing loudly.

"Yeah, that was your father for you, always trying to teach and get you guys to think deeper."

"I really miss him," said Shannon as she put her head down, looking at the empty seat.

"I'm sure he misses us too," said Jaron, sensing the change in the mood. He figured it was best to not stay on the subject. He looked at his mom and smiled. "So Mom, I guess that means you're up. What's new with you?"

Their mom smiled. "Now Jaron, I talk to you and your sisters all the time. There isn't anything new that you guys don't know."

"So you told them that you're going on that cruise?" Jaron smiled.

"What cruise, Mom?" asked Shannon. "I want to go. Where is it going to?"

Kelly cleared her throat loudly. "So you're holding out on us, huh?"

"I'm not holding out on anyone. I haven't decided if I'm going or not yet. It's a cruise with Tracy and some of the other ladies I talk to, and it's going to Jamaica. I don't know about going just yet."

"Mom," said Shannon, "you know I was just telling you that you needed to get away for a while and just relax. It'll be good for you, and it could help with your blood pressure."

"Really?" said Kelly, surprised. "I just had the same conversation with her too."

Jaron started laughing. "What's so funny?" his sisters asked.

"We have all been telling her the same thing, because that's the same thing I told her," said Jaron, smiling. "So it's decided. You can go Mom. You need it."

"Who's the parent here?" asked their mom.

"You are," they all said in unison, as if it had been rehearsed.

"Okay. So I'll tell you if I'm going anywhere."

Jaron leaned over to whisper to Kelly, "She's going, whether she knows it or not." They all laughed because he said it loud enough that their mom could hear it but acted like he was whispering.

Just then, the waitress returned with Jalin and their drinks. "What can I get you?" asked the waitress.

"I'll just have a water with lemon," said Jalin. He said his greetings to everyone and took a seat next to Kelly. "How are you feeling?" he asked her.

"I'm okay. I feel good."

Shannon began making kissing noises and faces. "Oh get a room you two," she said.

"Um, actually, we have an apartment, for your information," said Kelly through a smile as she rolled her eyes. "Everything good at work?" she asked.

"Yeah, just had a couple of the files mixed up. I had to sort that out before I left."

"Jalin, what is it that you do again?" asked their mom.

"I'm the chief financial advisor for Brickman & Schmidt, the law firm on Jefferson and Seventh."

"Oh, how do you like that?"

"It works for me. I like numbers. Plus, they handle a lot of pro bono cases, which makes my job that much more important. We have to make sure we can distribute the income evenly to be able to still handle those cases."

"Not many firms do that nowadays, huh?" asked their mom.

"No ma'am, not that I know of."

"Oh man, I like that, respectful, but I'm going to need to see your face a little more often."

"Yes ma'am. I'll make sure I get on that."

Kelly locked her arm with Jalin's and stuck her tongue out at Shannon. "Whatever," said Shannon through a smile. The waitress returned with Jalin's water and took their orders. They sat and continued talking and laughing until their meals came. "Man, this all looks good. I'm going to need to taste some of everyone's food," said Shannon.

"I will never understand how you eat so much and yet you're still so small," said Jaron.

"I'm not small. I'm simply compact," snapped Shannon. "I will never understand how you haven't broken your neck yet. I know that big old head has to hurt it, but at least we know where all your food goes."

"My head isn't even that big. But you know what they say, the bigger the head, the bigger the brain."

"Yeah, and the bigger the brain, the smaller the intellect."

"Well, I must be the exception to that rule, and you must be the reason they made it with that colossal noggin of yours."

"Mom," said Shannon in a whiny voice, "Jaron's talking about me again."

"Jaron, leave your sister alone," said their mom as she put mashed potatoes into her mouth.

"Now you know she started it Mom. If she can't take it, she shouldn't dish it out," said Jaron.

"I said leave her alone Jaron."

"Okay, but you're lucky Mom is sitting here. Otherwise…," said Jaron, smiling. After they finished eating, Kelly asked to be excused and rushed to the washroom. "What's wrong with her?" asked Jaron. "Maybe she's not over that bug just yet then, huh?"

"I'll go check on her," said Shannon as she got up and followed Kelly to the washroom. They returned several minutes later.

"Are you okay?" asked their mom worriedly.

"Yeah. I just need some water. I don't know where that came from. I was feeling fine, and then… I don't know."

"Well, let me take you home and maybe give you some more of that tea you had yesterday," said Jalin.

"Yeah, that's probably best," said their mom. They got up to leave, said their goodbyes, and left the restaurant.

"I hope she feels better," said Jaron. "I'll check in on her tomorrow." After paying the check, he and the rest of his family got up and left the restaurant. "Okay, I love you guys. Let me know when you make it in," he said after walking them to Shannon's truck.

"Okay, baby," replied their mom.

"Alright, bighead," said Shannon through a sneaky smile.

"See, Mom? You better get her."

"What did I say, Jaron? You better leave that girl alone."

Shannon stuck out her tongue. Jaron smiled as he closed the door. Walking back to his car, he felt good. He had a great time with his family. It made him miss how much time they used to spend together. *We have to do better,* he thought as he started his car.

His drive home was smooth. There was no traffic at all. His mind wandered in and out. He was trying to focus on what he had to do this upcoming week. As he walked into the house, he suddenly felt tired. *I'll take a shower, and then to bed I go. Maybe I'll sleep this whole night through,* he thought.

*****

The storm didn't let up the entire day, so MaKayla and her family just relaxed for the majority of it. They played board and card games for most of the time. MaKayla made her rounds again, this time taking pictures of the view of the storm. Even though the thunder frightened her, the storm was still so beautiful in her eyes. She had hoped to run into the people from the lobby again, but no luck. *They were pretty cool people,* she thought. *I wonder what they're doing today.*

She and her family picked a movie and found a restaurant that delivered to order from. They sat and ate as a family again as they watched the movie. After it ended, MaKayla went back to her room because her parents were falling asleep, and she didn't want to keep them awake.

She turned on her TV and flipped through the channels, hoping to find something that would capture her attention, but to no avail. She turned off the TV and got comfortable in the bed. She let her thoughts replay the day's events in her mind. *I could do this every day,* she thought. *But I have work I must finish. I'm so close I can feel it. Then I can relax. Well, I guess I can do that for the rest of this week too.* She smiled as her eyes closed, and she drifted off to sleep.

*****

After taking a shower and getting ready for bed, Jaron laid there in the darkness and allowed his thoughts to drift away. First, there was Kelly. *I hope she's okay and not coming down with something too bad.* Next, his thoughts floated to work and Mr. Thomas. He felt good about that possibility and where it could potentially take them. His mind stayed there for a little while but eventually took him to MaKayla. *I have to apologize and let her know that it wasn't her fault. What if she's upset with me because I didn't say something sooner? What if she got in trouble or had lost her job? I wonder what she's doing right now. Will she even remember me? What would it be like to take her to dinner with my family? Would she like them? Would they like her?*

His thoughts began to trail off, and soon, he was fast asleep. He woke a few times through the night to use the washroom and get water but didn't stay up longer than twenty minutes each time. He woke before his alarm, as usual, and was feeling very optimistic about the day. There was much to be taken care of, and he planned on getting to it all.

Chapter 7

MaKayla stretched and let out a yawn. She didn't even realize she had fallen asleep. She rolled over and stared out of the window as she lay across the bed. The sun was rising in the sky and was casting a beautiful orange light across the horizon. She looked at the water, the beautiful blue that mixed with the orange, the way the waves rode out in an attempt to meet the sun. She watched until they faded, then found another to follow. Her mind was empty. She felt at peace.

I could lie here forever, she thought as she let out a sigh. She replayed her thoughts from the night before, trying to remember what she was thinking about before she fell asleep. *Oh yeah, my future and how I'm almost done.* She smiled at the thought of accomplishing her goal. *I wonder what Mom and Dad are doing.* Just then her phone vibrated. It was her mom.

"Are you up?"
"Yes," MaKayla said.
"Okay. Get ready. We're going to breakfast in forty-five minutes."
"Okay," she replied.

She made her way out of the bed and into the bathroom to get ready. She stood underneath the shower, just letting the water run down her body. She listened to the music she had put on before getting in the shower and smiled.

Images of her danced in her head. She imagined herself acting out the lyrics of the song. She stopped trying to hold back and let the song's melodic words take hold of her. She began to softly hum as she swayed underneath the steamy downpour. The humming turned into soft singing and slowly rose in volume. Before she knew it, she was in full performance mode.

This continued for several songs and all the way through her shower, then into her room as she got dressed. She paused for a moment as she looked out of the window, catching a glimpse of a very old couple in a warm embrace. She noticed how the sun beamed upon them ever so brightly as if it beamed just for them as a beacon of their love. She remembered the couple from the plane who held each other as they slept and began to smile. *I bet they have that fairytale life—together forever, for better or for worse, and all those beautiful things. One day, I wonder if that'll happen for me,* she thought, then she laughed. "Wishful thinking," she said and went back to getting ready.

*****

MaKayla and her parents walked to a small restaurant two blocks from their hotel.

"I heard they have the best pancakes in town," said her mom to her dad.

"Well, I'll be the judge of that," he replied through a laugh.

The sun was so warm on MaKayla's face, and the cooling breeze took her to another place. She didn't even hear her parents' conversation. "You hungry baby?" asked her mom, but MaKayla didn't respond. Her eyes were fixed on the sky.

Her dad gave her a little nudge. "You okay?" he asked.

"Yeah." She smiled. "Why wouldn't I be?"

"You were just daydreaming or something. Your mom was talking to you, but you didn't say anything back."

"I was just looking at the sky. Do you ever just look at it and notice how amazingly beautiful it is? That gorgeous baby blue color, and there isn't even a cloud for as far as you can see."

"Yeah, today is definitely a beautiful day," replied her dad.

"This was a great idea. I'm really happy that you guys decided to do this. I really appreciate it. You don't know how much I've needed this."

Her mom smiled. "Actually, baby we did. That's why we did it."

MaKayla didn't respond. She just smiled and turned her attention back to the sky. It fit her mood perfectly—beautifully peaceful. Her parents went back to talking to each other as they walked into the restaurant. MaKayla requested to be seated by the window so she could continue to bask in the beauty of the sun. Of course, her parents didn't mind, so that was where they were seated.

*****

Once Jaron got to work, he said his customary greetings and hit the ground running. "Tina, I need you in my office right away," he said after they spoke.

"Ooooookkkkkaaaaayyyy," said Tina, getting up and walking into his office with a smile. "You seem to be pretty upbeat today," she said.

"I am. You know, mind over matter. So I think, so I am. So on and so forth," said Jaron as he set his things down and removed his coat, not even looking in Tina's direction. Tina stood smiling, awaiting his instructions. "Okay. First, I need you to get me Mr. Thomas's number. I need to talk to him immediately. After that, call Gerry and ask if he finished those last three reports. If he hasn't, tell him to just bring me what we have.

"Then set up an eleven thirty meeting with the heads of the finance department as well as Gerry, Charles, Adam, Lisa, Kathryn, and Don. They will need to have all necessary financial documents and files for the last six months as well as ideas for cost cutting and growth. That should be it for now, but I need that number ASAP," said Jaron hurriedly.

"I'll get right on it," replied Tina.

Gary, Charles, Adam, Lisa, Kathryn, and Don were all employees from different departments in the company. They had one thing in common, though: they were problem solvers. This was Jaron's own personal think tank. Whenever he couldn't find a way out, he would get them together and bounce ideas off them. It had always worked in the past, and he hoped it would come in handy today.

After about fifteen minutes, Tina appeared in the doorway. "I could not find Mr. Thomas's office number, but I did find his cell phone number. Would you like me to keep looking for the office number?"

"No. I'll just use that for now. It should be fine."

"Okay. Here you go," said Tina as she handed him the number. "Also, Gerry doesn't get in until nine thirty, but I did send him an email and left a message on his phone."

"Okay. Can you close the door on your way out?" said Jaron, still not looking up at Tina.

"Sure," said Tina as she turned and walked out the door. *Something is off,* she thought. Or perhaps she had read his mood incorrectly that morning. *Mr. Coleman seems rushed or frantic or something. I don't know. I'll give him some time and see if it wears off,* she thought.

Jaron made a call to a vendor whom he had received an email from earlier, inquiring about a new product. He handled the phone call rather quickly unlike his normal routine. After the phone call, he stared at the number for a while; and although there was a lot of noise from the employees, who were hard at work, everything seemed silent.

He could only hear his mom's voice: "He's already given you the tools. Now you just have to use them." He smiled, realizing that she was right and that he wasn't nervous at all about calling Mr. Thomas. It felt right, not like with Wynstead, where he felt like he was walking on eggshells when he talked with him.

He looked at his picture of his dad. "Thanks," he said softly through a smile. He dialed the number and sat back in his chair. It rang three times, and then there was an answer.

"Hello," came the voice from the other end of the phone.

"Hi, Mr. Thomas. This is Jaron, Jaron Coleman."

"Yes, I know who you are Jaron," said Mr. Thomas with a chuckle. "What can I do for you?"

"Well, if you recall, we had a conversation earlier last week about potentially doing business together."

"Yes, I remember. I thought you had another deal you were finalizing?"

"Well, after looking over the offer, I realized that it wasn't in the best interest of my company, so I removed myself from that conversation."

*****

"Dad, no business calls while we are on vacation. Remember, you promised," said MaKayla through a pouty face.

"Yes, I remember, but this wasn't planned honey. Just give me one minute," her dad replied, covering the mouthpiece with the palm of his hand.

"You have sixty seconds Dad." MaKayla looked at her mom, and they simultaneously looked at their watches.

"Okay, okay," he said.

"I'm sorry. Am I interrupting?" MaKayla heard the man on the phone ask. "I would have called your office, but I seemed to have misplaced the number."

"It's okay, but yes. I'm on vacation with my family. My daughter just came home for spring break, so I promised no work while we were here."

"I completely understand, and I apologize for calling on this number."

"No, no, it's okay. Of course I'm still interested. I'll be out of the office for the remainder of the week. I'll be back on Monday. I'll have my secretary email you all of my information. You send me your proposal. Monday, when I get in, I'll look over it and get back to you. How's that sound?"

"Perfect. And I truly appreciate the opportunity. I'll talk to you on Monday. Enjoy your vacation."

"Five, four, three," MaKayla and her mom counted down.

"Okay. I'll talk to you then. Goodbye," her dad said as he hung up the phone. "There. You see? Done, and in under a minute."

"Give me your phone," said MaKayla's mom.

"Why? It was just one time, and I didn't plan it."

"Ooooohhhhh, you're in trouble." MaKayla smiled. "You better do as she says if you want to enjoy this vacation, if you know what I mean," she said, winking.

Her dad handed the phone to her mom and shook his head, smiling. "You two are something else."

"Now you'll get it back after breakfast." Her mom smiled as she put the phone into her purse. "Now where were we?"

*****

Jaron hung up the phone and pumped his fist, but there was no time for celebration. There was much work to be done. He pulled up his proposal for Wynstead and began looking it over. He didn't want to present the exact same thing to Mr. Thomas. He began editing and updating the appropriate things. Before he knew it, about forty-five minutes had passed, and it was ten o'clock. There was a knock at the door. "Come in," said Jaron.

In walked Gerry with his laptop and a stack of files. "You wanted to see me, Mr. Coleman?"

"Yes, Gerry, come in, sit down, and close the door." Gerry pushed the door closed with his shoulder, as his hands were too full. "Were you able to complete those reports? I know I asked for them by tomorrow, but if you have them today, that'll be great."

"I finished all three, but I've only been able to fully review two of them. I still have a couple more sections to review in the third one, then create the comparative report," said Gerry as he set the items on the desk and took a seat.

"Okay, so here's the deal. I'm going to need you to work in here for the next hour. Is there anything that you need from your desk?"

"No, not right now."

"Okay. And you got the invite to the meeting, right?"

"Yes. Eleven thirty, right?"

"Yes. I'm going to help you, because I'm going to need these reports for that meeting. You get started on the comparative report, and I'll finish the review."

"Okay," said Gerry as he opened his laptop and passed several files to Jaron.

"While you're at it, try to think of as many growth and cost cutting ideas that you can. I don't care how unattainable they may seem."

"Alright," said Gerry. They worked in a feverish pace, not taking any breaks, and finished at eleven twenty.

"Email a copy of the comparative report to everyone on the meeting invite. Grab what you need and meet me in there in ten."

"Okay," said Gerry as he grabbed his things and walked out of the office.

"Tina," called Jaron as he rushed around the office, grabbing everything that he thought he might need for the meeting.

"Yes," said Tina as she walked into the office.

"I don't know how long this meeting will last, so just take messages for any calls. I don't want to be bothered unless it's an emergency."

"Okay," she said as she turned and walked out the door.

*****

After eating breakfast, MaKayla and her family decided to take a walk along the beach. *This couldn't be more perfect,* thought MaKayla as they walked. There was so much laughter everywhere, from children, to women, to men, old and young. It was beautiful and she smiled thinking the music that the ocean made as the waves crashed onshore and the people dove in, was like something from one of those CDs, sounds of serenity, or something like that.

She lagged behind, giving her parents space enough to enjoy the scenery alone, but not too much that they weren't all together. She watched the couples holding hands, the children building castles and digging in the sand, and the parents who helped them. The children down by the water raced the waves back to shore but lost with laughter as the water tickled their feet. This was something out of a movie, not real life. It was simply too perfect.

*****

Jaron arrived at the meeting. Everyone was already there, patiently waiting. The meeting lasted for over two and a half hours. There was an enormous number of ideas for helping to further the company. Some would be very risky, and some might cause some serious sacrifice. Jaron was happy with the results. He had known he had the right people in the meeting.

He was, however, mentally drained, and physically, he felt somewhat weak. He went back to his office and lay across his couch. *I need to rest for a moment,* he thought, *to allow my mind time to regroup.* As he lay there and thought about the tasks at hand, he suddenly realized that he hadn't eaten anything. *I'll go to the cafeteria when I get up,* he thought.

*****

When they got back to the hotel, they decided to do a little shopping. First, her father wasn't going to go, but he needed to pick up a few things, so he decided to accompany them. It had been quite a long time since they all went shopping together. Someone was always too busy or tired to go.

MaKayla couldn't remember the last time she had felt so happy and at peace with how things were in her life or even had a moment to appreciate them. What was supposed to be just a regular, relaxing vacation back home had turned into the perfect reboot, one that she didn't even know she needed. Her smile hadn't faded since she got in the shower, and she could feel the happiness within herself.

*****

SPRING SHOWERS—THE BLOOM

Before he knew it, there was a knock on the door. Jaron had fallen asleep. "Come in," he said as he sat up. In walked Tina. "What can I help you with?" he asked, wiping his eyes and stretching.

"What's going on with you?" asked Tina in a worried tone.

Jaron looked at her curiously, her tone and question catching him off guard. "What do you mean?" he asked, getting up and walking to his desk.

"You haven't really been yourself. You came in this morning and was somewhat rude, to be honest. You've been short all day, not really courteous, and pretty commanding, not your normal cordial, polite self. I know you have a lot on your plate with the Wynstead deal falling through and trying to find the next step to take with everything, but we are still a team, and we should act accordingly."

The words took him by surprise. He hadn't paid much attention to how he had conducted himself that day. His focus had solely been on accomplishing the tasks in his mind. It would seem that he had forgotten about the way he wanted to go about getting things done, ensuring that everyone knew they were in this together. His stomach tightened a bit as he thought about the meeting, wondering if he had treated them the same. His relationship with Tina allowed her to approach him in that manner. The other employees wouldn't feel as comfortable.

"I apologize. The bad thing is that I haven't even noticed it. My mind has been all over the place today, trying to get focused and—you're right—trying to find the next course of action. Here, have a seat," said Jaron as he pulled out a chair for her. Then he walked back to his chair behind the desk. "You know how much I need you, right? I mean, just like you're doing right now, you help keep me grounded and focused. I don't know how I'd be able to hold it together if you aren't here. I just came in today so focused and stressed at the same time. I suppose it got the best of me. I apologize if I was rude and giving off a negative vibe. You know what? Have you eaten yet?"

"Yeah, a little sandwich and some chips earlier. Why?"

"Well, I'm starved. I haven't eaten since breakfast. How about we head down to the cafeteria and see what Art and Mary have left?

My treat. Then I can fill you in on everything that happened today and discuss my preliminary plans with you."

"Well, I guess I'll let you make it up to me. Plus, you know I'm not going to turn down food."

They walked to the elevator after setting their phones with the appropriate messages in case any calls came through. They sat, ate, and laughed while discussing the meeting he had today and the Mr. Thomas deal. After they finished, they returned to their floor and checked for any messages. No one had called, and Tina was all caught up for the day, so they both got ready to leave.

*****

MaKayla didn't buy much—a few shirts, a pair of flip-flops, and two pairs of shorts—but being with her family the entire time made the trip more than worth it. Plus, she and her mom planned on going to another shopping center later on in the week without her dad. They didn't want to put him through the hours of shopping they planned on doing.

They ate lunch in the hotel restaurant, and after relaxing in the room and talking, they went to the fitness center and got in the pool. They stayed down there for hours, playfully working out, swimming, challenging one another to contests, and talking with the other guests.

*****

Once he stepped outside, into the warm sun, Jaron realized how he hadn't gone to the café today. Panic raced through him, followed by feelings of concern. He calmed his thoughts and tried to think of the best possible outcomes, like, *"Maybe she was off today anyway. Maybe she worked later. Maybe she would've been too busy to talk anyway. I'm sure she doesn't even remember me."*

His thoughts calmed as he drove home, but he couldn't get her off his mind. He just wanted to see her smile and hear her laugh. That would be enough to tell him that everything was okay. He promised himself that he would make time to go see her tomorrow regardless of what was going on at work.

Next, his thoughts shifted to his dad. He wondered what he thought of his current predicament. He would have the perfect words and metaphor for the situation, something that would tell him exactly what he needed to do without telling him anything at all. "Man, I wish you were here," he said softly. Somber emotions began to take hold of him as he thought of how much he really missed his dad. He began to think of how it didn't feel like so much time had passed.

It was like just yesterday that they were taking lunch breaks together, having family functions, going to sporting events, or just sitting and talking—about life and all the deep meanings that lie unfound, untouched, undiscovered, and not thought of by people. He missed those talks more than anything. With him, he could truly be himself without any reservations. That was where he drew his confidence, in knowing that no matter what, his dad was there.

*****

They relaxed in the sauna and then the hot tub before going back upstairs. They ordered pizza and had it delivered to the room. They all took showers and changed their clothes before the food arrived, then found a movie to watch as they ate. MaKayla's parents fell asleep once they finished eating, and she was up watching the movie by herself, although she wasn't really watching the movie. Her eyes were on the TV, but her mind was elsewhere.

When the movie went off, she quietly went back to her room, hoping not to wake her parents. Her curtains were still open from earlier that day, and the moon mesmerized her. She slowly walked toward the sliding doors, completely captivated by the moon's size, its color, and its light. It appeared bigger than she could ever remember seeing it before. Its reflection cast far across the ocean. She stared and smiled.

It was as if she heard music coming from the moon, music of the sky. She took a few steps back and noticed a figure in the glass.

The sight slightly startled her, but she quickly recognized herself. She noticed how she was smiling and realized she couldn't remember the last time she did and was unaware as to why.

She kept backing up, making sure she kept her eyes fixed on the moon. Once she made it to the bed, she slowly sat down and laid back, staring at the ceiling in the darkness. The only light coming in was that of the moon, but it was more than enough to light up the ceiling. She began to hear the music again and started to see herself, her face smiling down on her from up above.

*****

Jaron had been driving around for hours, just thinking about everything, but now he had arrived home. He sighed as he got out of the car and made his way into the house. Once he was in the house and had put his things away, he sat on the couch and turned on the TV. He scanned the channels until he fell asleep. He awoke at twelve sixteen and went to get in bed. He tossed and turned for a while before he was able to fall back to sleep. The next morning, he awoke, as usual, before his alarm went off and prepared for his upcoming day.

The day was a gloomy one, and it was storming as he drove in to work. He smiled because this made him think of MaKayla, how she was frightened of thunder. *I'd protect her,* he thought, then shook his head. *There you go again. You haven't even talked to her, and you're already protecting her from evil monsters? Ready to storm the castle and slay the dragon, huh?* This made him smile even more, although it was true. *I'll make sure to go see her today,* he thought, smiling even more. He made it to work a little later than usual due to the extra traffic.

Chapter 8

MaKayla awoke to the sun in her face. She was in bed and under the covers but didn't remember when she got there. She rolled out of bed and slightly pulled back the curtains, enough so that she could see out but not be blinded by the sun. The sun had company on this day, as the clouds were making their way slowly across the sky, frequently playing peekaboo with the sun.

She grabbed her phone to check the time. *Eleven ten? Wow, I've really been sleeping late these past couple of days. Talk about catching up,* she thought. She walked over to her parents' room and knocked on the door. Her mom immediately opened it as if she had been anticipating her arrival the entire time.

"Well, good morning, sleepyhead," her mom said as she opened the door.

"Good morning," said MaKayla as she walked through the door, stretching. "Did you guys eat already?"

"Your dad just finished breakfast, but I haven't yet. What do you say you go get dressed and we go to lunch?"

"What about Dad?"

"I'll be fine. That big breakfast requires this bed and I to have a meeting in a little while," he said, laughing.

"Okay," said MaKayla, smiling. "I'll be ready by twelve. Is that good?"

"Sounds good to me," replied her mom.

"What are you in the mood for?" asked MaKayla.

"I can really go for a good burger and fries."

"Oooohhhhh, that sounds good. Let me hurry up. You got my stomach talking to me now."

*****

Jaron went about his normal schedule, still working on and through the potential ideas he had for company growth. At around eleven thirty, he got ready to go to lunch, informed Tina that he would be back in about an hour, and left the building. The rain was still coming down pretty steadily. He would not be walking today. As he drove, he noticed that there weren't a lot of people out, and he wondered if the rain was a bad omen.

"Maybe I should wait to talk to MaKayla. Perhaps today isn't the day. Okay, okay, let me stop thinking like that," he said to himself. *"Maybe this will be even better. Perhaps the café will have less people, which will give me the time and opportunity to talk to her."*

He arrived at the café, parked, and entered. Although the weather was bad, the café was rather packed. He was seated in his normal place and placed his order. *I don't see her,* he thought. A feeling of concern came over him. *Just calm down,* he thought. *It's not like she was here every day before.* Just then, Liyah came from the back room, plates in each hand and on her arms as well. *Maybe I can ask her if I don't see MaKayla before I leave.*

For some reason, Jaron felt relieved to see Liyah—a glimmer of hope, perhaps. It was probably because of the fact that he would be too nervous to talk to MaKayla if he saw her anyway, so this was the easy way out. He sat and ate, watching the rain as it hit the window and rolled down, combining with the other water droplets to form puddles at the base of the window. It was something so important, so necessary to everything, yet so small and unappreciated. He imagined the puddles having a party for every water droplet that made its way down to join them, welcoming them home like they had completed their rite of passage.

He finished eating, and still, there was no sign of MaKayla. *I'll ask Liyah about her,* he thought. He went to the front and paid his bill, then stood there for a while in hopes of getting Liyah's attention. It was rather difficult with the café being so busy. Then came the moment when she came from the back room empty-handed, and their eyes met.

"Can I talk to you if you have a moment?" asked Jaron.

"Um, okay. It'll have to be quick. It's crazy in here today," responded Liyah, curiously looking at him. She wondered what he wanted to talk to her about. Hopefully, it wasn't some negative carryover from his last visit. She pushed the thoughts aside. "How can I help you?"

"I don't know if you remember me, but I was here Friday. You switched out with MaKayla."

"Oh yeah, I remember," responded Liyah as if it had just come back to her.

"Well, I was just wondering if she still works here, if she got into any trouble because of that," said Jaron, somewhat stammering. "I know I told you it wasn't her fault. I just hope that I didn't cause her to get into any trouble, and if so, maybe there is something I could do to fix it. Maybe I can talk to the owner or something."

Just then, Mr. Stacy's voice came from the back. "Liyah, I got two tables ready for pickup. Let's go, let's go, let's go."

"I'm sorry. I have to get back to work. Give me a minute." Liyah rushed back into the room and came back out, hands and arms full once again.

Jaron waited around for another fifteen to twenty minutes, but the traffic into the café was only picking up, so he left, figuring he would try again another day. On his short ride back to work, his mind ran crazy. *She must have gotten fired or something. Otherwise, Liyah would've just said so, right? Don't be so quick to jump to conclusions. She could've just as easily said that yes, she was fired. You won't know until you know, so stop assuming and overthinking. I hope she's okay. Man, if I could just see her and know that she is okay, then everything would be fine*, he thought. *I guess I'm just going to have to come back and find out, then.*

*****

MaKayla and her mom found a small burger restaurant four blocks from the hotel, went in, and were seated. It was about half full, and a lot of conversations were going on. They looked over the menu for a few minutes, and then the waiter came with water. "Are you ladies ready to order?" he asked.

"Yes. I'll have a double cheeseburger with everything, a small fry, and a medium Dr Pepper, light ice," replied her mom.

"And you?" the waiter asked, turning to MaKayla with a smile.

"I'll have a triple cheeseburger with everything and bacon, large fries, cheese on the side, and a large strawberry lemonade."

"That's a lot of food for a little lady. You sure you can eat all of that? Our patties are pretty big."

MaKayla smiled, shaking her head. "Yeah, I'm sure. Don't let my size fool you."

"Okay. If you say so," replied the waiter, smiling, as he took the menus. "I'll put that in right away for you ladies."

"You know, you definitely have an appetite unlike anyone else's. I remember when you were just a baby. You would eat constantly and then throw a fit if we stopped you or wouldn't give you more. You were a chubby little thing, just as cute as you wanted to be, and those cheeks were to die for. We thought something was wrong, but the doctors kept telling us that your metabolism was just fast and more advanced than your body. Now it's still the same and hasn't slowed down a bit."

"Yeah, I love food. What can I say?" MaKayla smiled.

"So what's new? What's been going on? We don't really get to talk like we used to," said her mom, taking a sip of her water.

"Everything is pretty much the same, just a lot of work and school, but I'm managing pretty well."

"What about a boy? I know there has to be someone who has caught your eye by now."

"Nope, no boy, just books, a lot of books." MaKayla giggled. "No time for all that right now. I have to stay focused on what's most important and not get sidetracked by temporary things." Once the last word slid out of her mouth, an image of Jaron slid into her mind. It caught her off guard, but she liked that he popped into her mind. Then her mom's words pulled her back to their conversation.

"Hmm," murmured her mom. "Okay. Well, how's Liyah?"

"You know Liyah. Still as crazy as she's always been. We don't talk or see each other as much now—you know, with us having our own places and our different schedules. She took off next week though, and is going to come back home. We'll catch up then." MaKayla felt her stomach slightly cringe. What she had told her mom was a version of the truth, but she left out how she was the one who had distanced herself from Liyah, albeit unconsciously. It was still something she knew she should have been more aware of.

"Hmm," murmured her mom again. "That's new. You two used to be inseparable, always going on and on about each other. Wherever one went, the other was sure to follow, and you guys wouldn't have it any other way."

MaKayla smiled, although it was not a genuine smile, and turned to look out the window. She began to go over the things her mom had said, most of which she had been thinking herself for months, but she couldn't really give in to the thoughts. There were too many other things to attend to. Her face began to show her concern despite her efforts to cover it up.

"What's wrong baby? You can talk to me, you know?"

MaKayla let out a sigh. She sat silently staring out the window. "What am I supposed to do Mom?" she finally said in a somewhat hopeless tone.

"Do about what? What's wrong?"

"It's not that it's wrong. It's just not right, if that makes sense. I mean, I'm working really hard and doing everything necessary to get to where I'm trying to go, but..."

"But what? What's on your mind?"

"What if I'm making a mistake? What if I'm taking the wrong road?"

Her mom grabbed her hand and looked into her eyes. "Baby," she said, "it's okay to make mistakes, to take the wrong road. Most of the time, that's the only way to really get to where you want to go. You just have to realize that it's okay to stop and enjoy what's around you along the way. You don't have to rush to get to where you think you need to be. Just travel in the direction where you think you want to go. But keep your eyes open. Learn, experience, and enjoy along the way. Then you'll see which way to go and if your destination is really where you want to be."

"I just don't want to fail or let anyone down."

"The only way you'll fail is if you don't try, and your father and I are already extremely proud of you. You're already successful to us, and I'm sure anyone else who is of importance to you feels the same way."

"I just have to finish this, and then I'll be able to relax and enjoy."

Her mom chuckled. "Don't allow yourself to get caught up in that mindset. It could be your downfall. You think you'll be satisfied with just graduating with no help? Nope, not you. Next, you'll want to *just* open your own business with no help. Then you'll want to *just* make it profitable with no help. Before you know it, years have passed, and you've alienated all who love and care about you, and for what?

"Is it really worth it? How much of life will you miss out on just to get to where you're trying to go without any help? Don't get so caught up in making a living that you forget to leave time to make a life. Tomorrow isn't promised baby. We really learned that the hard way."

There was a pause as her mom collected herself. She grabbed her hand tighter. "All we have is here and now. Before you know it, it'll be gone. And I'm sorry to tell you, but there's truly no getting it back. All you'll have to fall back on are the memories of what was. Don't be so focused on where you're going that you miss out on the beauty of how you get there."

MaKayla sighed. "How did you do it?"

"Do what?"

"Give up everything."

Her mom laughed. "Baby, I didn't give up everything. I gained it all. Your father, you, your…your brother, our life—I wouldn't trade it for anything."

"But how did you know that you were making the right choice?"

"I don't know. I just did. There comes a point where you realize, 'I could have everything and it could mean nothing, or I can have

SPRING SHOWERS—THE BLOOM

nothing and it could mean more than everything else.' I chose the latter and would never think to do it any other way."

"So your family is nothing to you?"

Her mom smiled again. "No baby, they are more than everything else. When I was young, I was ambitious just like you. Then I met your father, who was just as ambitious, but he…he had something more, like compassion, a sense of purpose, a sense of what it was all for. He rubbed off on me in that way. I didn't give up my ambitions. What I was ambitious about just changed. Everything that your father and I did was for our family, so you guys wouldn't want for anything but still be able to understand the value of hard work, so that we could spend time together, real valuable time, and not have to worry about what it would affect.

"Even though you don't realize it, look at you, independent despite our constant attempts to help you. You could just relax, not work or want for anything and just go to school, but you chose to do it on your own. I'd say that what we attempted to achieve and teach you has been well-received, so we've accomplished what we set out to do. Look at us now, in this beautiful city, those beautiful rooms, and your father and I able to take off a whole week of work without it affecting anything."

MaKayla looked at her mom with a sense of reassurance, but still, curiosity roamed through her eyes. "Don't spend your whole life trying to be successful and to accomplish these goals without having someone to share it with. Now, I'm not saying go run off and get married or have a boatload of kids. I'm just saying, slow down. You'll never know what life has to offer if you're only looking for one thing. Don't close your eyes to your dreams and goals, but open them to everything that may be presented along the way. Who knows how much better your dream can become?"

MaKayla smiled. She fully grasped what her mom was saying, and she was right. She had never talked to her mom about this before, but it was perfect timing, just what she needed to hear. "I've never thought of it that way, and it really makes sense the way you put it. I want what you and Dad have. It seems so genuine and real.

SEASONAL STORMS

I'm really happy that you guys are my parents and have placed the perfect example right in front of me."

Her mom smiled. "It isn't always going to be easy, but I can guarantee you that it will be worth it—with the right person, of course. That person that can calm the storms as they rage all around and within you, the one who can make the moon seem like it draws closer just to shine on you two—it's an amazing feeling baby, and I can't wait until you fully experience it."

They continued to talk, even after their food was brought. They hadn't talked this much, just the two of them, in a really long time, and MaKayla fully embraced it. They sat there for about two hours, just talking. They ordered ice cream after they finished their food and made sure to get some to go for her dad. He was wide awake when they returned, already in his beach gear. "Get ready ladies. It's time to go enjoy this sandy beach." MaKayla was excited to go. She had a new bathing suit and couldn't wait to put it on.

*****

Jaron returned to work and finished up his ordinary workload, then did some more work on the potential growth projects for the company. He stayed later than usual, feeling that he wouldn't be able to have everything ready by the time he needed it. He sent out an email before he left, another meeting invite to the same people. They had to have a final draft of the proposal by Friday, because no one worked on the weekends, and it needed to be there by Monday. Plus, they had to weed out the other potential growth projects that weren't feasible.

*****

They stayed at the beach for hours, playing volleyball, building sandcastles, lounging around, talking to random people, swimming, and just enjoying the weather. The sun began to set, and it was a sight to behold. The clouds in the sky stood still just to observe it, the fire-orange sphere slowly pushing its way into the horizon, spilling its orangish-red shadow into the ocean.

The ocean itself sat there calmly as the sun set, barely moving. Only the smallest waves came to shore but quickly ran back into the ocean, as a child would do when playing in the water. MaKayla noticed a couple with their two kids, a boy and a girl. They were sitting at the water's edge, the waves barely touching their feet. They looked out at the sunset, the four of them, barely talking, just basking in its beauty.

Just then, her mom's words replayed in her head: "Don't spend your whole life trying to be successful and to accomplish these goals without having someone to share it with." She smiled and turned to see her parents sitting on a blanket, hand in hand, enjoying the sunset too.

They sat out there for a few more hours, talking, reminiscing, joking, and enjoying the weather. Then they went back into the hotel and ordered room service and showered before the food arrived. They played a few board games and called it a night. MaKayla walked around the hotel a little before going to her room. It was quiet. No one was out of their rooms or roaming the halls aimlessly, as she was.

Her mind was still on the conversation that she and her mom had earlier. She knew she had to get back to where she used to be with Liyah. She was her best friend, her sister, and she hated that things had gotten to the place that they were now. "Sticky fingers," she said softly through a smile. *I'll fix it,* she thought. *I have to.* She made her way back up to her room and lay in bed until she fell asleep.

*****

Jaron picked up food on his way home and fell asleep on the couch to the TV again after eating. His night went similar to the night before, and his Wednesday workday went past before he knew it. They had ordered food for the meeting, so once again, he missed out on the opportunity to go see and talk to MaKayla.

He made a promise to himself again to ensure that he went the next day. *I must really be busy to have to make promises in order to see her,* he thought. *Plus, I haven't talked to Mom, Kelly, Shannon, or any of the guys. I'm tripping, but I'll get back on it.* He picked up his phone and called Kelly. "Hello," she said in a rather upbeat voice.

"Hey sis. I meant to call and check up on you earlier this week, but I've really been swamped at work."

"Yeah, I know. You're trying to work on a new deal and all. No biggie."

"So how are you feeling? Finally got rid of that bug? You sound good."

"I sure am. Well, for the most part, I'm doing really good. Can't complain about a thing." She sounded happier than usual, but Jaron thought nothing of it. *I mean, who wouldn't be happy if they weren't sick anymore?*

"Well, that's what I like to hear. Everything good at work?"

"Yeah, you know, same old, same. Nothing new on that front for me."

"Well, I'm not going to hold you sis. Glad you're feeling better."

"Okay. And it's good to hear from you too. Don't stress over work. It'll work out. It always does."

"Wise words from a wise woman. I love you sis. Talk to you later."

"Later," she said, chuckling as she hung up.

Jaron was pulling up in front of his house when he realized how tired and drained he felt. When he made it in, he went right into his room, took off his clothes, and laid across his bed. MaKayla popped into his head—her smooth hand and the way their eyes met for that ever so brief moment that he wished was an eternity. "MaKayla," he said, smiling, as he drifted off to sleep with that vision of her replaying constantly in his head.

*****

MaKayla's day had been a blur from start to pretty much the end. She had breakfast with her parents, followed by a trip to the aquarium. After that, they ate lunch, then dropped her dad back off at the hotel while she and her mom went back shopping. They ended up being out for almost five hours.

Her dad was quite pleased that they had left him out of that adventure. They picked up dinner on the way back and relaxed while showing him all the items they had purchased. MaKayla and her mom hadn't gone shopping, just the two of them in years—well, at least not like that—so her dad had figured they had some making up to do.

MaKayla and her mom agreed to go jogging in the morning once again if the storm that was supposed to hit didn't come. She went back to her room and stared out the window for a moment. *I wonder what Liyah is doing. I haven't really talked to her since I got here.* She picked up the phone and called her. Liyah answered on the first ring.

MaKayla smiled. "Awwwwww, you were patiently awaiting my call, huh?" They laughed.

"I was actually about to text you to see how you were doing. How are things back home?"

"I'm not there." MaKayla smiled.

"You're not home? Where are you then?"

"You won't believe what happened," responded MaKayla excitedly. "Mom and Dad met me at the airport with more plane tickets, and we all came on vacation."

"So you're not going to be there when I get there?" asked Liyah in a disappointed tone.

"Yeah, I will. We are only here for the week, so I'll be coming back the same day you're coming in. It is so beautiful here, and you wouldn't believe the room that I have all to myself. I took a bunch of pictures. I'll show you when we both get home." They both laughed again. "The beach is so beautiful, and the people are so friendly."

"Hmm, tell me about these friendly people," said Liyah in a sly tone.

"What do you mean?"

"You know what I mean. I know you've met a bunch of cute guys, and I want to hear all about it."

MaKayla laughed. "I really haven't even thought about it or thought about guys since I've been here. I've really just been relaxing."

"Oh, speaking of not thinking about cute guys, that guy came in looking for you again."

"What guy came looking for me?"

"Don't act like you don't know who I'm talking about. The cute one from Friday."

"Why did he come looking for me? What did he say?" MaKayla felt a slight flutter, almost like butterflies, in her stomach. She couldn't tell if she was nervous or excited.

"I'm not completely sure, because we were swamped, and I had to get back to my tables before I could finish talking to him. He seemed to be concerned if you still worked there. He even asked if you got in trouble and if he could do something to make it better," said Liyah hurriedly.

"Liyah, stop playing. That's not even funny. Nobody would come and do that, especially days later. When was this anyway?"

Liyah laughed. "So you think I'm joking, but you ask when it was? He came in yesterday, and I'm not joking. I'm serious. He was really concerned. He even stood there for a while, waiting for me to get a free moment to talk. But once things slowed down, he was gone. He probably had to go back to work or something."

"That's crazy. I wonder why he's so concerned about me. Why would he be looking for me?"

"Maybe he's just one of those types of guys, you know, a nice guy." There was a brief pause, and then they both started laughing.

"A nice guy? I haven't seen one of them in a very long time. If he is one, then we have to find out where he's been hiding." Although MaKayla played down the idea to Liyah, inside, there was a sense of hope. She was suddenly intrigued by this situation.

They continued to talk for about an hour—not about Jaron but about the café, school, MaKayla's vacation, and things they would do when they got back home. MaKayla felt good about having such a long, in-depth conversation with her. It had been far too long since they did.

Once they finally got off the phone, MaKayla quickly dozed off, fast asleep, but it didn't last long. She became somewhat restless, and although her body told her that she was tired, her mind was far

SPRING SHOWERS—THE BLOOM

too busy for her to sleep. She got out of bed and took a walk around the hotel, then outside, in front of the hotel.

It was a very muggy night, and the storm clouds slowly began to make their way across the sky. There was a fountain in front of the hotel. MaKayla sat there and lightly brushed her hand back and forth through the water. A gentle breeze slowly making its way in from the ocean cooled the humid air that sat stagnant. She stared at the clouds and how they came together, covering the moon, then slowly drifted past.

She began to think about the café and how she missed it—the regulars whom she knew so well, the people she worked with, and especially Mr. Stacy. A smile curled up in the corner of her face as she pictured him hustling and bustling through the kitchen. Then her thoughts went to Liyah and how she loved her and how she was grateful for her sister. *I don't tell her that enough,* she thought. She chuckled, thinking about the fun times they had had, then got a little sad that things had changed so much. Her thoughts flowed to her parents—the much-needed talk she had with her mother, her dad's smile, and all they had done to make this vacation what it was.

The clouds had completely covered the sky. You could no longer see the moon, only its light trying to peer through them. Then came the lightning, which began to light up the clouds, but no thunder ensued. *I'd better get back in before the storm comes in completely,* she thought, getting up from the fountain, shaking off her hand. The wind had begun to pick up, and her hair was being thrown around. She went back into her room and snuggled herself back into bed, completely closing the curtains before she did. Her mind was a lot calmer, and she slowly began to drift away.

There was a big flash of lightning, and it caused her to jump. "I thought I closed the curtains," she said out loud. She rolled out of bed and began to walk toward the doors. Then came the thunder with a vicious boom. She jumped but was caught by a set of arms, which were gently wrapped around her but tight enough that she felt safe. "It's okay. I won't let it hurt you," said the voice from behind her.

She wasn't sure who it was, but the voice felt vaguely familiar. The hands, the arms, its comfort felt like home. However, she wasn't startled. Instead, she turned and embraced the hug. His chest, warm and soft, his arms, holding her just right. His cologne filling her mind, pulling her in closer to him, causing her to want to hold him tighter to smell more.

A flash of lightning lit up the room. She looked up, and there was Jaron, smiling back at her. She flashed a smile back and closed her eyes as her lips moved toward his. Then came another crash of thunder. It sounded as if it would shake the clouds from the sky.

She jumped again and opened her eyes. There she was, back in bed, alone. It was all a dream. She wiped her eyes as if in disbelief. The curtains were still closed, but she could hear the rain falling outside of her window. *I can't believe I really just had a dream about a man I don't even know. Where did that even come from? I wasn't even thinking about him,* she thought.

A smile moved across her face as she replayed the dream in her head—his arms, his chest, his smile, and that smell. "Mmm," she said as she wrapped her arms around the pillow and covers and began to squeeze them. *That was a good dream, though,* she thought with a smile.

She rolled over and looked at her phone. *Four sixteen. Let me try to go back to sleep.* She lay there for a while, thinking about Jaron, how he looked at her in the café when their hands touched, how she felt safe and comfortable in that ever so brief moment. *I wonder why he's been looking for me. Maybe he just wants to apologize and make sure I'm okay. It's probably nothing more than that.* She shook her head. *Let me not allow my thoughts to get the best of me,* she thought with a smile. She closed her eyes and allowed the dream to replay in her mind until she fell asleep.

Chapter 9

The next morning arrived rather quickly, and Jaron could only remember waking up once the whole night. "Now that's progress," he said to himself as he got out of bed and prepared for the day. He was in a really good mood despite the gloomy-looking weather outside. "At least it's not storming again. Last time I got soaked." He made his way in to work, a bright smile on his face and a mentality to really get work done.

As he exited the elevator, Tina spotted his demeanor. "Uh-oh, what's her name?" she asked sarcastically from her desk.

"Ha-ha, very funny," he said. "And good morning to you too."

"Well, you're in a rather upbeat mood. To what do we attribute this?"

"I'm not really sure. I just have a good feeling about today, you know? It's just one of those things that you wake up with."

"Yeah, I know what you mean. I'm glad you're in that mood, because I've already gotten four calls this morning from disgruntled suppliers and vendors. They want you to call as soon as you can."

"No sweat. I'll handle it. Just leave it up to me," said Jaron, smiling, as he walked into his office. Tina followed with a handful of papers.

"Here are the calls and messages for you as well as two files that were on my desk this morning."

"What's in the files?" asked Jaron curiously.

"Don't know. They had your name on it, and they were sealed, so I didn't open them to see."

Jaron sat down as he took the items from Tina. "Can you remind me when eleven thirty gets here? Just in case I forget. I plan on taking my lunch around that time."

"Yeah, I know it's around that time you always take your lunch when you're going to the café."

Jaron smiled as he opened the files. He read through them and noticed they were the preliminary drafts for the proposal for Mr. Thomas, as well as the other projects he had his team working on. He smiled. His team was always on top of things, and he loved them for it. He knew that he could depend on them for just about anything. He simply needed to ask. *Today is going to be a great day,* he thought, leaning back in his chair.

He began making the calls to the vendors and suppliers, smoothing over the issues that had arisen while reassuring them that business would continue as usual. After his calls, he leaned back in his chair and turned to stare out of the window. The day looked gloomy, and the dark-gray clouds floated around effortlessly through the sky, covering the sun, not allowing it to show itself, yet you could still tell it was there.

Its brightness is fighting through the clouds to still be recognized, saying, "I'm still here. Even in the dark days, I'm still here. That is us," he thought. *That's this company. We will not go without a fight. Even when things get rough, we still fight. They still fight. We are still here.* This put a smile on his face. He turned back toward his desk and was met by the smiling picture of his dad. "We are still here Dad. We're not going without a fight."

Jaron turned his attention to emails, trying to get to them all before he took his lunch break. This was somewhat of a difficult task, because they continuously came. Eleven forty came, and he knew he wouldn't finish, so he just left the ones that were there for later. He grabbed his jacket and went to open the door.

As the door swung open, there was Tina, arm raised, fist clenched, and she smiled. "I was just about to come and get you."

"Uh-huh. Sure you were." He smiled. "I'll be back—"

"In about an hour. Yes, I know," she said, smiling, as she walked back to her desk.

He got onto the elevator and walked outside, stretched his arms, and paused for a minute. *It's really not that bad out. Maybe I should just walk. Nah, I got a lot of work to catch up on, and the more time I have, the better. Plus, if it starts raining, I don't want to get caught in that.* He walked to his car and made his way to the café. Today was much different from Tuesday, when he last went. There were a lot of people walking the streets outside, but when he got to the café, it was almost empty. *This will be perfect,* he thought. *Now when I see MaKayla or Liyah, I can talk to them. They won't be too busy with customers or work.* He asked to be seated at his usual seat, ordered his food, and waited.

*****

MaKayla woke up in a very good mood, but once again, she had slept in. *Eleven thirty-seven? Man, how do I keep sleeping so late? Oh well, guess that is the purpose of a vacation.* She could still hear the rain coming down outside. She went to the doors and pulled back the curtains. The sky was still cloudy but was painted light gray now. It sporadically lit up from the flashes of lightning, but the thunder was a lot calmer than it had been the night before.

The ocean, however, raged against the storm. Waves of all sizes covered with white foam smashed into one another and then crashed along the beach. *It's a battle royal.* She smiled to herself before turning away from the doors. She picked up her phone. There were no missed calls, but there were two messages, both from her mom. The first read, "No jogging today. Storm hasn't let up." The next said, "We're going to the spa. We'll be back to get you around one so we can go to the spa appointment your father is making for us."

"Cool!" MaKayla said emphatically. "That gives me enough time to eat and get ready before they get back." She did her usual, ordered room service, and got into the shower before it arrived. She ate and watched a movie before picking clothes out for the day.

*****

Jaron waited and waited, but no MaKayla came, and even worse, this time, there was no Liyah either. He began to get worried, and all sorts of negative thoughts ran through his mind. *This is the second time I've been here this week, and no MaKayla. I usually see her two, sometimes three, times a week. Something isn't right. Something must be wrong.* He continued to think as he ate.

Let me calm down. I'm overthinking things again. I have to stop thinking the worst, but I just can't help it. I haven't seen her in what seems like years. Where could she be? Why isn't she here? What if she quit because of what happened? Now I'll never get to see her again. He felt his mood begin to drastically change, and that happy, upbeat feeling that he had all day, he felt it begin to drift away.

He checked the time and realized that he had been there longer than he had anticipated and needed to get back to work. "There's always tomorrow," he told himself. "Things will work out." He paid for his food and made his way back to work.

The sky seemed darker and much gloomier than earlier. It was harder to see the sun behind the clouds, as if its will to fight through was fading. He made it back and immediately went to work on his emails. Tina had several messages for him when he returned as well. The email flow died down, and he was able to get through the rest of them rather quickly.

*****

MaKayla's parents arrived at twelve fifty, big smiles on their faces. "What have you two been up to? Why are you smiling like that?" she asked curiously.

"We haven't been doing anything," said her mom through a smile. "You ready to go?"

"I sure am. How far is the spa?"

"It's like a twenty-minute drive, and man is it beautiful there."

"What all will we be doing?"

"Full-body massage with hot oil and hot stones, manicure, pedicure, and skin revitalization treatment."

"Ooh, that sounds good, like I'm definitely going to be refreshed when I get out."

"My thoughts exactly." Her mom laughed. They left and made their way to the spa.

"Despite the weather, today is going to be a good day," said MaKayla.

*****

He tried to work as much as possible to keep his mind from drifting back to MaKayla, as it often did. Once he responded to messages that he had received earlier, he turned his attention back to the files of proposals. He noticed several issues and discrepancies that he would need to discuss with the team. He paused for a moment, realizing that scheduling another meeting for tomorrow would affect his going back to the café.

He let out a sigh. "Business before pleasure. Do what I have to do now so that I can do what I want to do later. Yeah, yeah, I know Dad," he said out loud as if his father was there, talking to him. He sent out the meeting invite to the team, placing it as high priority. They only had tomorrow to complete the Thomas proposal, and it needed to be perfect before he sent it out.

He felt like he needed to do more, but his mind said otherwise. He was beat. He looked at the clock and realized that he had put in yet another long day, so he prepared to leave. *There's no need to push it today when I'm already tired and still have tomorrow.*

Once he made it to his car and was on the road, he called his mom. She didn't answer at first, which was weird. *I hope everything is okay,* he thought. *I'll give it some time and try back.* But she beat him to it. Five minutes later, his phone rang, and he smiled as he looked at her face smiling back at him. He felt a sense of relief, looking at her smile.

"Hey Mom. How are you?" Jaron asked, smiling.

"I'm good. How are you?"

"Tired Mom. I'm beat. It's been a long week. But wait, why didn't you answer when I first called you?"

"Oh, I was in the washroom, washing my hands. Didn't want to get the phone wet."

"Oh, okay."

"Well, if you're tired, that must mean you've been pretty productive this week then, huh?"

"Yeah, I'm trying to be. I do have some good news, though."

"What's that?" asked his mom curiously.

"I talked with Mr. Thomas, and he's still open to doing business. We've been working on the new proposal all week, making sure it's ready to be sent to him by tomorrow so that he can read it over on Monday."

"Well, that really is good news. See? I told you things would work out."

"Yes you did Mom. Oh, and I talked to Kelly yesterday. She sounded so much better. I guess she got over that bug she had."

"Yeah, we've talked a few times this week. She's been in a really good mood. It's probably the weather changing. You know, good weather helps people have good moods."

"Yeah, I noticed the same thing when I talked to her. So how have you been? Have you been relaxing, or do I even want to know the answer?"

"I actually have been relaxing. I haven't had much work to do around the house lately."

"How's work?"

"Work is work. You know there's no change there. Just the regular, day-to-day activities."

"Well, I'm happy to hear that. I really am," said Jaron excitedly. "What about that trip? Did you decide on it yet? I know you guys should be booking and putting down payments here soon, right?"

"No, I haven't decided yet, but I am considering it a little more now."

"Well, that's even better. I knew I'd change your mind. Just needed some time."

"You haven't changed my mind Jaron," she said through laughter. "I just simply said that I was considering it more now."

"Yeah, okay. Call it what you want, Mom, and I'll call it what it is." They both laughed loudly. "Okay, well, I was just checking in on you. I didn't really want anything."

"Um, don't you have something else that you're supposed to be telling me about?"

Jaron knew she meant MaKayla but played as if he didn't. "What do you mean something else?" he asked with a smile on his face.

"Don't act like you don't know what I mean. What happened with you and the waitress? Oh, wait, what was her name again? Mackenzie? McKinley?"

"It's MaKayla, and nothing happened."

"What do you mean nothing? You didn't go down there and talk to her like we discussed?"

"Well, yes, and no."

"Okay. I see you want to play games today. You remember what happened last time you tried that, don't you? Or do I need to remind you about the apples?"

"Okay Mom. Dang, you don't have to take it there. Well, I went down there Tuesday and today, but I didn't see her there either day. I talked to her coworker briefly on Tuesday, but even she wasn't there today. She was extremely busy when I did talk to her Tuesday, so I didn't get to find out anything before she had to get back to work. I'm really trying not to worry Mom, but it's hard, to be honest. What if she actually did get fired or even quit because of what happened? I'd feel horrible."

"Well, you could always go back down there tomorrow."

"No, I can't. I have a meeting at work that'll probably last majority of the day. We have to finalize the proposal and make sure everything is right, so I won't be able to leave. We usually just order out for lunch and have it delivered. So you see, I won't be able to go back this week."

"Well Jaron, you still have next week. There's no rush baby. You just have to not overthink these things. Wait until you know for sure before you go drawing conclusions and developing how you feel. The only thing that will lead to is more stress, and for what? For all you know, you could be completely wrong."

"I hear you Mom. That's what I've been trying to tell myself, but you know how my mind wanders and does its own thing."

"Yes baby, I do know, but it's your mind. If you feel it drifting offtrack, then pull it back."

SEASONAL STORMS

"I suppose you're right Mom. It's just something I'm going to have to work at, though."

"Over time, you'll get the hang of it," said his mom, going back to her comforting voice as opposed to the more forceful one she had been using.

"I love you Mom," said Jaron. "I really appreciate you."

"I love you too baby, and I appreciate who you are and who you are working to become. Now go get some rest. Make sure you're focused tomorrow."

"I will Mom. I'll talk to you later."

"Later baby," she said as they hung up.

*****

MaKayla and her parents spent almost four hours at the spa, enjoying all they had to offer. They partook in a few snack delicacies here and there as well. They returned to the hotel to change their clothes for dinner. They felt so refreshed and relaxed that they wanted to go to sleep, but since they were all hungry, they went out for food instead. The storm had died down, and all that was left were small versions of the huge thunderclouds from earlier.

The streets had livened up and were once again teeming with people and cars and filled with music. They made it something quick so they wouldn't be out long even though it had turned into a beautiful night. After eating, they returned to the hotel and went to their respective rooms. MaKayla didn't even change her clothes. She just laid across the bed and was asleep in no time.

*****

Jaron had been sitting outside for some of the conversation, and now that happy, upbeat mood had been restored. "Thanks Mom," he whispered as he got out of the car. When he got into the house, he went into the kitchen and looked for something to eat. He threw a pizza in the oven and went to change his clothes. After eating and getting in the shower, he was asleep in no time at all.

The week was getting the best of him, so falling asleep had become easier. On this night, however, it was staying asleep that seemed to be the issue. He awoke countless times, seemingly every hour. Thoughts of the proposal, of his dad, and of MaKayla—everything seemed to be running through his mind that night. Every time he wound his mind down from one group of thoughts, another one revved it right back up again.

When he finally awoke for the day, he felt as if he hadn't really slept much, and his body seemed more tired than when he went to sleep. He was frustrated but realized that he had an important day ahead of him and needed to get focused. He showered twice as long this morning, making sure to collect and organize his thoughts so everything wasn't so jumbled. He made himself a big breakfast and took his time to eat. He knew he would need the energy for the day.

As he walked outside, the sun beamed down on him. He didn't realize that the sun was out or that the clouds had passed. He smiled, remembering how he felt seeing the sun have its battle with the clouds, how it wouldn't give up. Now there it was, beaming in victory. It didn't give up; it won. "That must be a sign for the day," he said as he stood smiling outside of his car.

*****

MaKayla and her mom woke with the sun, finally getting to go jogging again. The sun had returned with a vengeance, and there were no clouds in the sky to shield from its fury.

"It has to be, like ninety-five degrees," said her mom as she wiped the sweat from her forehead.

"Yeah, it's really hot out here today. I won't complain though."

"Let's finish up so we can go enjoy our last day here. With this beautiful weather, I'm sure it'll be a good one."

They continued their jog and made their way back to the hotel to prepare for the day.

*****

Jaron made his way to work without any issues, no real traffic, and he was there before he knew it.

"Good morning, Mr. Coleman," greeted Krystal as he entered the building. "You're looking rather, um, how do you say—"

"Amazing?" joked Jaron. "Yes, I'm in a great mood despite a somewhat tumultuous night."

"Oh, what happened?"

"Nothing out of the ordinary. I just couldn't really sleep. How are you today? Everything good?"

"I'm doing pretty good. It's a beautiful day, and it's Friday. Who could ask for more?"

"I hear you on that. Glad to hear you're doing good. Enjoy the rest of your day," said Jaron as he walked to the elevator. He arrived at his floor, and the doors opened to his employees all hard at work. It seemed more like the day was halfway over instead of just beginning. "Good morning Tina. Any messages for me?"

"Good morning to you too, and no messages. I guess you took care of those yesterday."

"I would suppose so, but no news—"

"Is good news." Tina laughed. "You're in a good mood again, I see."

"Yeah. Blame it on the weather."

Jaron was smiling as he walked into his office. Once he put his things down, he took a moment to just pause and look at the outside world, to get that last bit of motivation that he needed to have a productive day. He smiled while looking at the busyness of the streets down below. He imagined that the people were all in a good mood. *I mean, it is Friday and a beautiful day indeed. Who could ask for more, as Krystal said?*

He immediately turned his attention to his laptop, making sure everyone had confirmed his invitation to the meeting later that day. Next, he made sure to check and reply to all the new emails that were in his inbox. "I guess my taking care of yesterday's overflow helped cut down today's, just like with the messages." He continued working through the emails until they were all completed.

After finishing, he turned his attention to the proposal, which would be the main focus of the day. He just scanned through to ensure that he had documented all the key points that he needed to touch on and revised them before having it sent out. Upon completing his morning tasks, he made his way to the meeting room, where, once again, everyone sat patiently waiting for him.

He stood in the doorway for a moment, smiling. They were such a dedicated group of people, and he loved working with them. Into the room he went, and they immediately got down to business. Although the proposal was completed, minus the alterations that needed to be made, the meeting lasted the majority of the day. There were brief pauses here and there, but they stayed in that room, ensuring the proposal would be perfect. He also had them working on the other projects as well.

Jaron was overcome with a feeling of confidence once they left that room. He knew they would accomplish what they had set out to do. Now he just hoped Mr. Thomas would be receptive to it as well. He wasn't that worried, though. They had other plans in the works as well.

He saw the error in his initial plan with Wynstead of putting all his eggs in the same basket, so once the proposal fell through and the basket was gone, so were all his eggs. Now he had a plan in place that they would initiate whether the Thomas deal worked out or not. The company would move forward, and he was determined to ensure that happened. The outlook was good, and they came out of that room just as the sun came out that day—brightly shining.

*****

MaKayla and her family ordered room service and discussed what they would do on that day, trying to see what they could fit in before the vacation ended. She didn't really care. She just wanted them to spend as much time together as possible, so they would do everything together. After eating and planning out the day, they each showered and got dressed. First on their list would be some final sightseeing and picture taking, something MaKayla had looked forward to since they got there.

*****

Jaron returned to his office and tried his best to catch up on the emails and messages that awaited him. To his surprise, it wasn't much. He emailed the proposal to Mr. Thomas, giving a glance to his dad as he did. *This should make you proud,* he thought, pressing send. He sat back and spun to look out the window. The streets were vibrant. There was so much life happening right below him. People were laughing, and radios were playing. The weather was changing, and people were embracing it.

I wonder how MaKayla's doing, he randomly thought. *Where did that come from? I mean, I haven't really thought about her all day. And just out of the blue, there she is.* He smiled as he spun back to face his desk. It made him happy that she could come into his mind without him trying to force it. "You can come and go as you please," he said out loud through a smile.

*****

They took pictures everywhere and with everything that caught their eye—random people, famous monuments, different ocean views, and the city skyline view as well. They laughed and talked the entire time. *It's the perfect way to start off our last day,* thought MaKayla.

They got lunch on the go, picking up small items at random restaurants. They wanted to get a full taste of the city before leaving. There was an ice cream parlor that her mom made very clear they would have to go to, and she got no argument from them. The heat was intense, so ice cream was a welcome relief. After their sightseeing, they went to pick up a few souvenirs and made their way back to the hotel to get ready for dinner.

*****

SPRING SHOWERS—THE BLOOM

Everyone had left for the day, and Jaron was alone in the building. *I guess I've done enough for one week,* he thought. He packed up his things and got ready to leave for the day, giving a quick glance around his office to ensure it was in order. The sun was already setting once he made it to his car, and his body began to remind him that he hadn't really slept the night before. *Man, I'm really tired all of a sudden,* he thought as he let out a yawn. His phone began to vibrate in his pocket. He took it out and read the message. It was from Xavier: "What's up man? Haven't heard from you all week. You good?" Jaron called Xavier and it went to voice mail. "Hit me back when you get this, bro," he said before hanging up.

Ten minutes later, Xavier called back. "Man, where you been? You good?" he asked as Jaron answered the phone.

"Yeah, I'm good man. Just been going extra hard at work this week, trying to get this proposal together for Monday."

"Oh, okay. I feel you but man, shoot yo boy a text or something. Let me know you're still living."

Jaron laughed. "I hear you. My bad."

"See, that's what I love about you. You took that hit on Friday, and you're right back in there, swinging all this week. Got to respect that."

"Yeah, well you know, if I don't do it, then who will?"

"I hear that. So what's the move for tonight? You want to hit Cliché or what?"

"Man, I'd love to go out, but I'm beat. I was just thinking of how tired I was before you texted me. I didn't get much sleep last night, and like I said, this week has been hectic."

"I understand that. Don't overdo it man. Definitely rest up."

"Anyway, you sure that isn't going to cause any problems, you going out tonight? I mean, you know what happened last week."

"Come on now. You know me. I'm a man. Nobody is going to tell me what I can and can't do." Xavier laughed. "Plus, I've been chilling with her all week. She's been a little sick, but she's okay now."

"Yeah? So was Kelly, but she's good too."

"Well, you tell Kelly that if she needs anything, anything at all, she only needs to give me a call."

Jaron laughed, shaking his head. "I'm sure, I'm sure."

"Alright man, I'm not going to hold you. Just hit me up sometime tomorrow and see if we can't get into something."

"Alright cool. That's if Candace don't have you on lockdown."

"Me? Lockdown? Never." They both laughed. "Alright man. One."

"One," said Jaron as he hung up.

I wish I had somebody who had me on lockdown, someone to come home to after these long days, someone that will help me sleep through the night and make waking up that much better. Although his mind was tired, MaKayla still made her way in. *I wonder what that would be like with her.* He made it to his house and went inside, MaKayla still running through his mind.

I wonder if she's going out tonight. Maybe she had a long week and needs the relief, he thought as he lay across his bed. *Probably not. She's probably someone who enjoys staying in the house. We'd order food and watch movies until we fell asleep or just listen to music and talk. Maybe we'd just dance the night away until we were too tired to do anything but sleep.* He smiled and began to imagine what it would be like to lie on her chest, listening to her heartbeat, her caressing his head as he fell asleep. In no time at all, he was fast asleep.

*****

After getting dressed, they walked about seven or eight blocks to La Cinco, or what everyone else called the Five. It was a small Hispanic restaurant, but it was extremely nice. This capped off the night for MaKayla. *Tacos and other Hispanic food—what could be better?* she thought.

Once again, they were seated along the beach, and the cool ocean breeze did battle with the leftover heat from the day. The music was vibrant, and people were dancing in the restaurant and on the beach. MaKayla and her family even got up to join in a few songs, dancing with one another and the occasional stranger. The night was a perfect way to end their vacation.

SPRING SHOWERS—THE BLOOM

When they left La Cinco, they walked along the beach back to their hotel, taking in the breeze and the sounds of the night. MaKayla gazed out at the ocean and at the small, gentle waves that rode in to shore, softly crashing against the sand, making the most beautiful music nature could compose.

She smiled as she looked at her parents a little ways away, hand in hand, cuddled up. *What could be better?* she thought. She was happy, and everything went the way she needed it to even though she hadn't planned any of it. *Maybe this is exactly what Mom was talking about the other day,* she thought. After a few minutes of standing along the beach, they went inside the hotel.

"Make sure you have everything together baby. We leave for the airport at nine," said her dad.

"I will. It's all basically packed already, but I'll double-check anyway."

"Okay. Good night. See you when the sun is up."

"Good night." She smiled as they went into their room, and the door closed behind them.

She went into her room and made sure she had all her things packed and ready to go. She pulled open the curtains and crawled into bed, the moon painting her room with its light. She gazed out at it all—the moon, the ocean, the people, and a couple's silhouette off in the distance, hand in hand. It was perfect.

I wonder what he's doing, she thought. A smile crept onto her face. *Where did that come from? I don't even know his name.* Her eyes returned to the couple as they moved farther away from her sight. Shaking her head, she went to sleep.

Chapter 10

Jaron was accompanied by another sleepless night. He tossed and turned every which way after waking up around two. He tried everything that he could think of—from drinking water, to listening to music, and watching TV—but nothing helped. He laid there, the TV watching him more than he was watching it, and just let his mind go. He thought of his dad.

If he were there, what would they be doing that weekend? How much better off would the company be if he were there to work with him? He tried to change his thought pattern, but it just kept going. He felt that he should be doing more to show his dad that he had listened, that he had taught him well, and that he wouldn't let him down.

He began to stare at the ceiling, trying to create storylines for the shadows, anything that would take his mind somewhere else. It worked for a moment, allowing his mind to rest just enough for him to fall asleep, but two hours later, he was up again.

His thoughts now focused on MaKayla. He felt somewhat bad, like he was obsessed or something with someone he hadn't even held a conversation with. He couldn't stop himself from thinking about her—how she looked, how she smiled, and how she talked. Any memory of her continuously replayed in his mind.

I wonder what she's doing right now, he thought. *I wonder if she would even remember me if she saw me again.* He began to smile, shaking his head. *You would swear I've known her for years or something as much as I think about her.* He rearranged himself in his bed, and after a few minutes, he fell asleep, this time for the remainder of the night.

*****

MaKayla woke up with the sun streaming in and her mom standing by her bed.

"Come on. Get up. We have to get ready to go," said her mom.

"What time is it?" asked MaKayla through a yawn.

"It's eight, and we have to be out by nine."

MaKayla threw her legs out of the bed and stretched. "Why didn't you wake me up earlier?" she asked through a long yawn.

Her mom laughed. "I've been texting and calling you since seven. You have to be really tired. You've been sleeping in."

"Yeah, I guess my body just had to recuperate. Plus, that spa was amazing."

"Girl that was like, two days ago."

"Still, it matters," said MaKayla, smiling. "All I have to do is get in the shower and get dressed. I'm already packed. My bags are by the door."

"Okay. Well, I'll tell your dad so he can take them to the car."

After MaKayla finished getting ready, she took one last look out of the big sliding doors and at the beauty that stood before her. The sun was rising to its glory in the sky but was not yet at its peak. The ocean was covered in its pretty blue color, only rivaled by the blue sky with white clouds randomly placed about.

The beach was already somewhat busy for it to be so early. Since it was such a nice day and a Friday, she figured it made sense. She allowed her eyes its final farewell to the scene and made her way down to the car. They drove to the airport, which was about twenty-five minutes away. After checking in and checking their bags, they went to the dining area and got some food, awaiting their boarding call.

They boarded the flight and took their seats, all three in a row—MaKayla by the window, her dad by the aisle, and her mom in the middle. She leaned back in her chair and stared out, looking up at the sky, as the flight attendant went through her routine. Once they were up in the air and all she could see was the blue sky for miles and miles, she closed her eyes and fell asleep.

*****

SEASONAL STORMS

The flight was only two hours, and MaKayla was awakened by the vibrations of the plane as it made its descent. They caught a cab home since her parents didn't drive to the airport. Their luggage barely fit. Luckily, the cab was a van.

Once she got in the house, she took her luggage to her room and just stood there for a while. It had been almost two years since she was home and saw her room. It looked exactly the same. She put her bags down and walked around her room, picking up random things, pausing and then smiling as if each item was transporting her somewhere in the past, to some happy place.

She turned to find her mom staring at her from the doorway, smiling. "This room has missed you as much as you've missed it," said her mom.

"I can see that," said MaKayla, returning the smile. "It feels the same as the last time I was here, like nothing has changed."

"It hasn't. Your father and I come in here from time to time, but we don't bother or move anything. It's just our little piece of you."

"I've missed you guys just as much, if not more, all the time. That's why I'm glad we took all those pictures. It'll give me something to have when I'm not with you guys." Her mom smiled. MaKayla knew that smile. Her mom didn't need to say what was on her mind. MaKayla knew it was bittersweet for her to hear those words.

"Alright, well, I'm going to go help your dad unpack. You know where we are if you need anything. You do remember?" asked her mom in a playful tone.

"Of course I remember Mom," said MaKayla, smiling, as her mom walked away.

MaKayla began unpacking a few things but decided not to unpack it all since she would have to put it all back when Friday came around. She picked up her phone and texted Liyah: "What time does your flight get in?" She put her phone down and laid across her bed, staring at the walls. She felt tired but didn't know where it came from. *Maybe my body is getting used to resting. It's going to be pretty upset once this week is over,* she thought, smiling. She laid there for a while, not thinking about anything in particular, and fell asleep before she knew it.

*****

Jaron awoke a little after twelve, and he just laid in the bed for a while, trying to think of the things he needed to do for the day. He had errands that he had to run—pay a few bills and pick up a few items for around the house—but nothing major. He got up, took a shower, and got dressed to go handle the things he needed to take care of. He grabbed a granola bar and headed out. He wasn't very hungry and figured he would get something while he was out.

He received a group text around four: "Let's go watch the game. Get food and drinks. Meet up around seven." He replied, "I'm in. Where are we meeting?" More confirmations flowed in, followed by potential meeting places, which was finally set to William's house between seven fifteen and seven thirty.

He finished his errands and went back home to get ready for his night. His mom called just for a little small talk and to say that they wouldn't be getting together for dinner until the following Sunday. That was fine with him. He figured the night might be a long one with the guys. He would need to recuperate before work on Monday, especially since he anticipated hearing back from Mr. Thomas then. After getting dressed, he made his way to William's house, which was a twenty-minute drive from his own in good traffic.

He arrived at seven eighteen. The guys who were already there were standing outside in a circle, talking. He stepped out of his car and walked toward them, still singing the song he was listening to in the car. Daniel walked toward him, bobbing his head and laughing.

"You trying to get yourself a deal, huh?"

Jaron just smiled, shaking his head. "That's just my song. You know how it be Danny Boy."

"Yeah, I do."

"Who else are we waiting for?" asked Jaron as they walked closer.

"Just Troy and Xavier. Tony came with William, and I just pulled up maybe five minutes ago."

"Okay, cool, because I'm starving. Haven't really eaten anything all day."

"And they say I'm the one who's always hungry." Daniel smiled.

They walked up to the other guys, and five minutes later, Xavier pulled up, music blasting. He was bobbing his head as he sat in the middle of the street, just staring at the guys. "Go park," they said, waving him to move down the street. He and Troy walked up, and the guys figured out the driving situation. They chose William's house because it was the closest distance to the bar and grill, so even if they all drank, they wouldn't be driving far to get back to the rest of the cars. When they arrived at the bar, it took a while for them to be seated due to the large number of people who were already there.

*****

MaKayla didn't do much all day after receiving Liyah's text around six that her plane had just gotten in. She would just be chilling with her parents for the night. She decided to just relax. She laid around just snacking on things and watching TV. She truly felt at home. It was like she never left. Her parents followed suit and just relaxed with her.

They all just sat on the couch or on the variety of beanbags that were spread around the living room, something that her father had a deep affection for. They popped popcorn, ate ice cream with fudge and strawberries, and just lounged. She and her mom planned to make a big dinner the next day. She hadn't had one of those meals in ages, and her body longed for it.

*****

They were seated, and Jaron immediately began ordering food before the waiter could even get their drinks. The guys didn't complain; they just followed suit, putting in their food and drink orders as well. They didn't need time to look over the menu, because they came so often that they pretty much knew it by heart. The game was already on, and there was a lot of cheering, talking, and just overall noise. Xavier gave Jaron a nod, asking him to take a walk with him. They got up, walked outside, and stood in front of the doors but far enough away that they weren't in the way.

"What's up man? You good?" asked Xavier.

"Yeah, I've just been working pretty hard, why? Everything good with you? I know we haven't talked that much, but are you cool?"

"Yeah man. I've just been stressing more than usual lately."

"Stressing about what? What's bothering you?"

"This whole thing with Candace man. She's so bipolar lately and all on my back for no reason. It's like one minute, she's mad at me, then the next minute wants to be all lovey-dovey. I'm starting to think she's crazy for real."

"How long has it been this way? Things aren't getting any better?"

"I mean, it's back and forth, up and down. One minute, she loves me. And the next, she hates me. You know I don't get like this over women. Usually, I don't care. But there's something different about her. Like, seriously man." Xavier let out a sigh. "She's special, not like the other women I've talked to in the past. I really care about this girl. Quiet as kept, I didn't even go out last night. I went to chill with her. She didn't even ask me to. I wanted to. I just don't know what's going on with her. It's really starting to frustrate me."

"So you've talked to her about this, I'm assuming?"

"No, not really. Like, what am I supposed to say? 'Hey, you know, you've been acting crazy lately. Why?'"

"No, man." Jaron laughed and placed his hand on his shoulder. "You have to let her know that you realize that something's wrong, that you care that something is bothering her. For all you know, the reason she's like this is because she doesn't know if you care or she's fighting with herself about if you care or not. If she's as special as you say, then you have to let that be known to her. Let her know that you're there to support her and she can count on you. I mean, when it's all said and done, that's what women want, love and support."

"I still don't know man." Xavier shook his head and looked at the ground. "She should already know that. I mean, I'm here, aren't I?"

"True, but it's nothing like hearing it and seeing it put into action."

Xavier sighed again. "I guess that makes sense. You could have a point."

"Trust me man, and don't mess this up. I like Candace, and I can see that she really makes you happy."

"You like everybody. That's your tragic flaw. But she does make me happy. Oh, and she does this thing with her tongue—"

"That's enough. I don't need to hear no more," said Jaron as he threw his hands up and began walking toward the door.

"What? Why are you walking away?" Xavier asked, laughing. "You're my boy. I thought I could tell you anything."

They made it back to the table and found the other guys in a friendly yet heated debate.

"What's all the fuss about?" asked Xavier.

"Tony really thinks he can beat me in basketball—one-on-one or him, William, and Danny Boy against me and any other two people I pick," said Troy emphatically. "Can you believe this dude? He must have fallen and bumped his head."

"You're not that nice man. Plus, my defense is not to be messed with," replied Tony.

"Okay, well let's settle it then," said Xavier.

"Man it's like nine o'clock. How are we going to settle anything?" asked Tony.

"Next Saturday, we hit the park—me, Jaron, and Troy against you, William, and Danny Boy. After we finish destroying you guys, because we are going to destroy you, then you guys can play one-on-one to settle it once and for all."

"Now we're talking," said Troy, rubbing his hands together and shaking his head with a devilish grin on his face.

"Y'all not destroying nothing over here," said William, waving his hands, laughing.

The waiter returned with two other servers, countless plates and drinks on their trays. The guys continued the discussion while watching the game, eating, and drinking. They stayed until closing time and then went back to William's house for more drinks. Jaron took Troy and Tony home before he went home himself, making it in around four. Both his body and mind were exhausted, so he crawled right into bed and fell asleep.

*****

MaKayla awoke the next day around ten and went down to see what that enticing aroma was. Her dad had made breakfast—buttermilk pancakes, French toast, eggs, grits, sausage links, ham, and sliced fruit.

"Good morning baby. I hope you're hungry, because it's some good eats over here," said her father, taking a bite of his sausage.

"Man, I didn't expect to wake up to this, but I'm going to guarantee you that it won't go to waste," she said, grabbing a plate from the cabinet. "You know what? Let me get two plates, because one just won't do."

"Yep, that's the same thing I said when I first started eating," replied her father as he shoved a forkful of pancakes into his mouth.

MaKayla made her plates, sat down, and began eating. She and her mom planned out the menu for the night and what they needed to get from the store. After eating, she took a shower, and they went grocery shopping.

*****

Jaron awoke and looked at his phone. "Ten thirty-seven? Oh man, I overslept," he said as he threw back the covers and jumped out of bed. He grabbed his towel and rushed into the bathroom, turning on the shower.

He called his office to let Tina know that he was on his way, that he was running late, but it went to voice mail after several rings. After listening to the voice mail, it dawned on him. "It's Sunday, not Monday," he said, laughing and hanging up the phone. He went back and sat on the bed to allow his body to calm down. *Well, I'm up now. Might as well get in the shower,* he thought.

After getting out of the shower and getting dressed, he went to the kitchen and made himself breakfast—eggs, grits, bacon, and French toast. He took his food into the living room and ate while watching SportsCenter. After he ate, he cleaned the kitchen and went back to his bedroom.

He threw himself across the bed and stared at the blank TV screen, contemplating his day. *I think I'll just lie around today. I've got a big week coming up, and I need to be prepared for it. I'll call Mom in a few and see how she's doing. Plus, I want to find out when the next time we all will get together.* His mind continued to wander, and he set no boundaries, allowing it to go wherever it wanted. His eyes began to feel heavy, and he figured he would rest them for a little while.

*****

Once they returned from the store, MaKayla and her mother immediately began cooking. Her father sat in the front room, watching TV, randomly throwing comments into their conversation. It was these simple things that MaKayla missed the most—cooking with her family, the random conversations, and the jokes, just the simple things.

MaKayla texted Liyah, telling her that they were making a big dinner and that she was more than welcome to come over if she liked. Ironically, Liyah and her family were doing the same thing, so she and MaKayla randomly exchanged pictures of the meals they were preparing.

*****

Jaron awoke again, this time not as abruptly but still in shock. It was now six thirty-seven, and he had slept most of the day away. "I can't believe I was even that tired," he said as he scrolled through the messages and missed calls he had accumulated while in his slumber. Two missed calls were from his mom, and they were several hours apart, and there were two text messages. He also had a group message from the guys, getting the trash-talking started early for next weekend's game.

He called his mom back and talked with her for several minutes. It was nothing of importance. She just wanted to check on him and make sure he was doing okay. They figured that they would wait until the middle of the week to choose a time for Sunday, although they did decide that it would be this upcoming Sunday. His stomach seemed empty, as if he hadn't eaten all day. He had a taste for pizza and wings. He called and placed an order when he got off the phone with his mom. He considered going to pick it up since he hadn't really been up all day but decided against it.

*****

When the food was done being prepared, MaKayla helped her mom set the table. They had an amazingly beautiful array of food, and it appeared as if there would be more than just three people eating. They spent about fifteen minutes debating with her father about sitting down and having a family-style dinner or sitting in front of the TV, eating. He was outnumbered. Plus, it was his two favorite girls. There was no way he would win, but he put up his fight anyway.

They sat at the dining room table, eating, laughing, and talking. Her dad discussed business propositions with her to get her opinion, against her mother's better judgment. She didn't like when they discussed business during dinner, but this was the one sticking point that her father would not be moved on during their debate.

*****

When Jaron's food arrived, he once again sat in the living room. This time, he had a few movies he pulled out to watch. The food really hit the spot, and he laid across the couch rubbing his stomach when he was done. "I'm not going to fall asleep on this couch," he told himself. "As soon as this movie goes off, I'm going upstairs and getting in bed."

SEASONAL STORMS

He didn't make it through the movie before he dozed off and was fast asleep, waking several hours later with the movie back at the title screen. He smiled and shook his head as he got off the couch. He turned off the TV and DVD player, finished off his cup of water, and headed upstairs.

"Wow, I can't believe I haven't thought about MaKayla all day," he said, laughing, then thought,. *It's not like I'm obligated to, but I do enjoy when she graces my presence and strolls through my mind.* He climbed into bed and pictured her walking by, face glowing with that beautiful and innocent smile. He shivered with delight. *That's the way to end the day,* he thought as she faded into the distance, and he faded into his sleep.

*****

After dinner and after her mom's self-proclaimed world-famous peach cobbler and vanilla ice cream, MaKayla and her mom cleared the table and cleaned the kitchen together. Her dad offered to help, but they told him he would just be in the way. He decided to accept their decision and not debate this situation. He went back to watching TV in the living room.

This time, there wasn't much conversation, just more of taking care of the business at hand, getting the kitchen cleaned. Although they didn't talk much, it seemed as if they were because of the way they worked so well together. The day had come and gone, and MaKayla and her mom were drained from the cooking and cleaning. Once they were finished, they both sat in chairs and stared at each other for a few seconds, then simultaneously burst into laughter.

MaKayla went to her room and laid in bed, letting out a sigh as she stared at the ceiling. *That was good,* she thought. *The whole thing—conversation, food, laughing, just being with them—it was all good. I wonder if Liyah enjoyed her meal as much as I enjoyed mine. I better go get in the shower before I fall asleep lying here.*

She rolled out of bed and got her things for the shower, found a few songs she wanted to hear, set them up in the playlist, and got in. It was just what she needed. "I know I'm going to sleep good tonight.

That food and that shower—perfect combination," she said, climbing into bed and falling asleep before she knew it.

*****

Jaron woke up in a somewhat confused mood, like he was in limbo and didn't know whether to be happy or worried, although he wasn't sure why. Well, he did expect to hear from Mr. Thomas, which gave him some cause for concern, but this felt like something more, like it was more than just work. He couldn't put his finger on it though. Maybe it was because he couldn't really sleep again, but that had never made him feel like this before.

He went about his morning routine nonetheless and made his way into work. He didn't notice the things that he normally did on his way to work. It was as if he was in a trance, as if he was just going about his routine.

Tina greeted him with a huge smile and an extremely upbeat tone in her voice. "What's got you in such a good mood?" he asked.

"I don't know, to be honest. I just woke up feeling really good. Did you see how beautiful it is outside? I love spring."

"You sure that's it? Because I've never seen you like this over the weather."

"I just feel like today is going to be a good day, like this whole week, something good is going to happen."

"For who?"

"I don't know, but I don't think it matters either. Just the fact that it's going to happen is good enough."

"I'm glad you feel that way, because I woke up teetering between feeling worried, concerned, and happy."

"Anything wrong or bothering you? What do you have to be concerned about?"

"I guess just thinking about Mr. Thomas and the proposal, hoping he likes it. I don't know. I didn't sleep too well last night."

"Well, that's normal for you." She smiled. "Don't worry about Mr. Thomas. I'm sure it'll all work out for the best."

He returned her smile. "You sure? Because I want to know if you know something I don't."

"Yes, I'm sure, and I only know what you know—that you're a very hardworking, dedicated, intelligent businessman. If you combine that with all of your other skills, there's no way things won't work out for you."

"You know that your review doesn't come up for another three months. I'm pretty sure it'll be a great review already, so why are you trying to flatter me?"

She shook her head, softly laughing. "I'm just being honest—nothing more, nothing less."

"Well, it is greatly appreciated and much needed on days like this. It's those types of things that tip the scale in the positive direction."

She handed him a piece of paper with two messages. "Oh, and did you call here yesterday?"

"Yes." He laughed. "Had my days mixed up. I thought I was running late."

She laughed. "Yeah, that happens to the best of us."

Jaron walked into his office and put his things down while looking at the piece of paper that Tina had given him. He called back the numbers and went about the routine of the day. It was the best way to get his mind back on track. He worked until eleven thirty and then left to take his routine lunch. It was a fairly nice day, but he didn't want to walk, so he drove his car instead. *Okay. Today's the day. I'm sure I'll see her today,* he thought.

*****

MaKayla lay in bed, awake but still tired. She didn't feel like getting up, and since she was still on vacation, she didn't have to. She was in the house alone. Her parents went back to work that morning, each coming in to say their goodbyes to her as they left. *There's no need to get up. I don't have anything to do,* she thought. Her phone began ringing. She looked at it, and she saw that it was Liyah.

"Hello," she said in a groggy voice as she answered the phone.

"Are you still asleep?"

"Mentally, yes. Physically, I'm just lying here. What are you doing?"

"I'm getting dressed, the same thing you should be doing."

"And why would I be doing that?"

"Well, I'll be there to get you in about forty-five minutes. I'm starving, and since you're still in bed, I know you haven't eaten either. I know you're hungry. You're always hungry." There was a pause. "Hello? You still there?" inquired Liyah.

"Why, or how is it possible, for you to talk so fast this early in the morning? That takes energy. Where do you get it from?"

Liyah laughed. "It's not early. It's after eleven. And I don't know where it comes from. Maybe it's excitement from thinking about food or maybe the fact that we're on vacation and we get to hang out like we used to," she exclaimed excitedly.

"Yeah, yeah, yeah," said MaKayla, yawning.

"Besides, I've been up since like eight, on the phone with Darrell. It's the first time we've been apart for so long. But anyhoo, get up and get ready. I'll be there in a little while."

"Okay, okay. I'm getting up."

"Okay. Good. I'll honk when I'm outside."

MaKayla laid in bed for a little while longer after she and Liyah hung up. She really didn't want to move, but she had to. Hearing Liyah talk about Darrell made her think about Jaron for some strange reason. She smiled and shook her head, then literally rolled out of bed and lazily walked to the bathroom.

She turned on the shower and then lazily walked back to her room. She grabbed her towel and other items she would need while she was in the shower, then moped her way into the washroom, dragging her feet as she walked. When she finished her shower, she felt more energized, not as tired as she was before. She picked out clothes and got dressed.

It wasn't long before Liyah was outside, honking her horn. MaKayla texted her mom and dad to let them know that she was leaving and went to get in the car with Liyah.

"You don't look tired to me. I guess you woke up, huh?"

SEASONAL STORMS

"The wonders of a hot shower. It's guaranteed to wake you up and put a little pep in your step," joked MaKayla as she swung her fist through the air in a playful manner.

"Let's go to Mary's pancake house. I've had a taste for those pancakes for a while now."

"That's fine with me. I'm just hungry period."

MaKayla's mind was still on Jaron. Even the talk of food hadn't shifted it. She wondered if she should tell Liyah but was apprehensive about it. *What if it's just a passing thought and feeling? But it has been coming up more and more. Besides, we're supposed to talk about everything anyway. What better way to start getting back to us than this?*

"You know, the craziest thing happened last week," said MaKayla in an almost curious tone.

"You mean when you were on vacation, living the lavish life?" Liyah laughed.

"Ha-ha, real funny. No, I'm serious."

"Okay, okay. What happened?"

"You remember the night we talked on the phone?"

"Yeah. That was, like, Wednesday or something."

"Yeah. So it was storming. I promise I don't remember going to sleep, but I ended up dreaming about the storm."

"Well, that's not really that crazy. It actually makes sense," said Liyah through a smile. "Maybe you shouldn't take vacations, because I think it has killed your brain cells. I mean, it was storming, and you dreamed about it. What's crazy about that?"

"Ha ha! But that's not it. That guy was in my dream."

"What guy? You had a dream about a guy? Ooohhh, I want all the details. What did he have on? Where were you? What did you have on?"

"Um, Liyah," said MaKayla, cutting Liyah's statements about the details, "can I finish telling you about my dream?" She smiled.

"Oh yeah, sorry. I just got excited. You know me." Liyah smiled, almost embarrassed.

"Yeah, I do," replied MaKayla, smiling and shaking her head. "It was the guy from the café. He was in the dream."

Liyah was quiet and somewhat surprised. Then she began smiling. "Ooohhh, what kind of dream did you have?" She smiled slyly. MaKayla gave her a look out of the corner of her eye. "Okay, okay. I'm sorry. Finish your dream, man." Liyah smiled.

"Thank you. Now it wasn't like that. He was just holding and comforting me, and it felt so good and real. I wasn't shocked or surprised he was there. I was actually relieved and happy."

"So wait, you're telling me that this guy that you've never really even talked to or know, for that matter, comforted you in your dream, and you were okay with that?"

"Yeah. And the crazy thing is, when I woke up, I was looking for him. Like, I still wanted him to be there. That's crazy, isn't it?"

"I don't know what to say. I'm shocked. That's not like you at all. So do you like him or something?"

"I don't know. I mean, I don't know him. How can I like him, right? He has just been popping into my mind. Nothing major. I've just been thinking about him and what he's doing or things like that."

"I think you've got a crush on him. You should've told me. Then I could've said something when he came in last time."

"Well, I hadn't had this dream or had even thought about him like this back then. Plus, you're crazy. Who knows what you would have said to him?"

"You're my girl. I wouldn't do you wrong. I got you."

"Even still, I don't know why all of this is even coming up. I really don't have time for a relationship right now, not with all that's going on in my life."

Liyah laughed. "You'd be surprised what we make time for when it's what we really want. Plus, you always say that, but you're always stressed out, and maybe that's why, if you know what I mean," she said, winking at MaKayla.

"Yes, I know exactly what you mean, Liyah," said MaKayla, smiling and shaking her head. "I already told you that I go jogging to relieve stress, and it works out just fine, thank you."

"It may work out fine for now until you find someone to work you out," said Liyah, holding back her smile in an attempt to look serious. A few seconds of silence went past, and they both burst into laughter.

"You see what I mean? You're so crazy," said MaKayla, still laughing. Liyah just smiled and turned up the radio, and she began to sing along.

MaKayla knew Liyah was right. The fact that she actually told Liyah about the dream meant that this was a lot more serious than she was saying it was. She had begun to desire more, especially after her conversation with her mom and that vacation, but she couldn't get ahead of herself. *Who knows where this will go, if anywhere?* she thought. They pulled into the parking lot and got out of the car. They walked into the restaurant, neither speaking. MaKayla was still in her zone, and Liyah was still half mumbling, half singing the last song she heard on the radio.

*****

Jaron walked into the café, got his usual seat, and made his usual order. He sat there in somewhat of a trance, staring off into the distance. His mind wasn't all over the place as usual. No, he was focused. *When I see her, what should I say? Or should I even say anything? I'll see if she notices me before I say anything. If not, then I'll approach her.*

All his thoughts ran like a flowing river into one direction: MaKayla. He still, after all this time, could not place his finger on the reason why he was so captivated by her, this woman whom he knew nothing about aside from where she worked and how she looked. And still, after all this time, he felt as if he had known her forever. But more than that, he wanted to know her. He wanted to know more than just how she looked. He wanted to know her soul, her mind, and the essence of her.

The waitress returned with his food, temporarily breaking his thought pattern. He began to eat, and his thoughts flowed back to her. He did not remove his gaze from the front-back area where the employees came and went, not even to enjoy the beauties of the outside world, as he so often did. He was afraid that he might miss her and that his chance would be gone once again.

Time passed, and he finished his food. He lingered at his table for a while, finding the most minute things to do so he wouldn't have to leave. Still, time went past, and he could not stay much longer. He had already been there for an hour, and there was no sign of her or Liyah. He let out a sigh and made his way to the cashier to pay for his food. "I guess today isn't the day," he mumbled to himself.

He got back into his car and sat there for a while, just staring up at the sky. It was a very light blue with streaks of white from the dissipating clouds. It looked like the canvas of a painter, one that was being turned blue but the white would not fade away. It simply mixed with the blue, which was why it remained.

He smiled. For once, not seeing her didn't make him feel sad or down but only gave him more hope. He didn't really understand why, but that was the way he felt nonetheless. Perhaps it was simply what he must endure to get what he desired. Somehow, he knew that he would see her. *Somehow, we have to meet,* he thought as he drove back to the office.

*****

They sat there eating, laughing and planning out their vacation days. "Just chill today. We'll just chill," said Liyah. "Tomorrow, we'll go shopping. We haven't gone shopping in a long time together. It's a need of ours." She laughed. "You know, my parents have been asking about you. You should come by one of these days."

"I know. When they heard that we were both going to be in town, they set up that dinner with everyone this Friday." MaKayla laughed.

"Don't sound so excited. They're just parents who miss their children and want to see things the way they used to be."

"Yeah, I guess you're right."

"Which reminds me, we're going out Friday night."

"Wait. How? We got the dinner."

"Yeah, but that's at six thirty. We'll be done in time enough to go out."

"You haven't been out with me in what feels like years."

"It's the first time we both have absolutely nothing to do the day of or after. I know when we get back, we're both going to be busy trying to finish the semester strong, so we have to take advantage of the time we have."

"But right after dinner? You take forever to get ready. You're really sure that we're going to have enough time? Plus, our flight leaves extra early in the morning. We're going to be dead tired."

"Yes, really. Trust me. We'll have more than enough time, and it's going to be fun."

"We're going to be stuffed and tired from eating so much. Plus, you didn't mention anything about you taking forever to get ready or leaving early in the morning."

Liyah smiled. "Our parents are going to drive us to the airport, and we have a long flight, so we can sleep on the plane if we're really that tired. As far as me getting dressed, um, well, we're going, and that's that."

"Okay." MaKayla sighed, shaking her head. She couldn't help but smile. She knew that once Liyah set her mind to something, it was hard to change it. "But I didn't bring any going-out clothes," she said as one last attempt to get out of it.

"Even better. We're going shopping, remember? Gives us one more thing to look for."

"You had this in your mind the whole time, didn't you?" MaKayla asked, realizing there was nothing she could do. She was going out with Liyah.

"I sure did ever since Mr. Stacy gave me the time off and, well, you turning me down last Friday helped me finalize my decision as well."

MaKayla just smiled, shaking her head. They continued eating and planning where they would go, what they would wear, and things of that nature. MaKayla felt happy. She felt like she was getting her best friend back, and the look on Liyah's face, so excited, so happy, she missed that look, and she was glad that it was back.

*****

SPRING SHOWERS—THE BLOOM

When Jaron returned to the office, he was greeted by Tina with a handful of messages. He took them and went directly into his office and began to work on them. The other plans that he and his team were working on had begun to come to fruition. It only further proved to him that his team was doing their part. Now he must do his as well. This was what the rest of his day consisted of; but there was no call, email, or even message from Mr. Thomas. By the end of the day, before Jaron got ready to leave, he checked again. Still, there was nothing. A part of him wanted to worry. "But it's only Monday," he told himself. "We still have time."

*****

Liyah had plans with her mother later that afternoon, so she dropped MaKayla off back at home after their lunch. "I'll be here at ten thirty. Are you going to be ready?"

"Why so early? Why not, like, one thirty?" MaKayla laughed. "Of course I'll be ready. Just text me when you're on your way."

The remainder of the day was chill and quiet for MaKayla. Her mom brought home Chinese. "Your dad's working late. Some new proposal he got today," said her mom as MaKayla came downstairs to greet her.

"Just like the good old days, huh?" MaKayla smiled. "Just me and you."

"Yep, just me and you," replied her mom.

They ate and watched TV. Her mom went to bed early, and MaKayla followed not long after, although she didn't fall right to sleep. She laid there for a while, just daydreaming, until she fell asleep.

Chapter 11

Tuesday came and went for Jaron, but there was still no sign of MaKayla or Liyah, and once again, there was no word from Mr. Thomas. The calls and messages were at a very high volume, however, and it was enough to keep him busy and his mind off the other things. He still felt hopeful about meeting MaKayla, and although he was a little more worried about the deal with Mr. Thomas, he didn't allow that to get the best of him. "These things take time. It's not something that can happen overnight. I have to be patient," he kept telling himself. "Slow and steady wins the race."

*****

MaKayla woke a little before nine and caught her parents before they left. She let them know what her plan was for the day and made herself a small breakfast. This was the first time she had woken up so early without her alarm since she was on vacation. The added bonus was that she didn't feel tired. She was in an upbeat mood and excited to be spending the day with Liyah. She had missed these times.

After eating, she got in the shower and got dressed, making sure she had everything she would need for the day. Liyah texted her to let her know she was on the way and was outside honking by ten thirty-eight.

"You hungry?" asked Liyah as she pulled off from MaKayla's house.

"I ate a little breakfast earlier, but you know me—"

"You can always eat," interrupted Liyah. They both smiled. "I'm not that hungry, but I haven't eaten anything, and I know that I need to. So let's just grab something to go on our way to the mall."

"Or we can just grab something from the food court at the mall."

"Yeah, well, I guess if we pass something that catches our eye, we'll stop. If not, food court it is."

They ended up stopping at a small carryout-only restaurant and eating on their way to the mall. They stayed at the mall for close to four hours, going from store to store, browsing, trying things on, and taking pictures so they could have references. The mall was somewhat busy but not too crowded. They figured that most people were either at work or at school seeing as the schools there weren't on break yet, not to mention that it was a Tuesday.

They both had seven bags as they walked out of the mall to go get food on what they called their lunch break. Then it was off to another mall. MaKayla had a smile on her face the entire time, and her stomach hurt from laughing so hard. She had forgotten just how silly Liyah could be, but she was definitely remembering now. They went to a burger and fry place for lunch and sat down to eat. Their meals were the exact opposite. Liyah just had a regular cheeseburger, small fry, and drink. But MaKayla had a triple cheeseburger with bacon, large fry, and a large strawberry milkshake.

"I don't know how your parents did it or even still do it." Liyah smiled, then took a bite of her burger.

"Do what?" asked MaKayla as she swallowed a mouthful of fries.

"Have any money left. I'm surprised they could feed you and still make ends meet." They both started laughing. "And look how little you are, still, after all these years of eating like this. You don't gain any weight. How is that possible?"

"I think it all goes to my brain, which is why I'm so smart," said MaKayla, smiling, as she pointed to her head several times.

"Well, I don't know how you're going to own your own restaurant one day and you eat this much."

"Why? What's wrong with that?"

"Remember, don't get high off your own supply." They both began to laugh uncontrollably.

"I'll be fine. I don't have to eat all the time. You see, I don't eat up everything when we're at work, now do I?"

"I guess you have a point there."

They made their way to the next mall, which was between thirty and forty-five minutes away but took them almost an hour due to rush hour traffic, but they didn't mind. It just meant more time for them to sing and perform to the music that was coming out of the radio. Their windows were let down since the weather was beginning to warm up, and their heads were periodically out the window with invisible microphones in their hands as they performed.

The next mall was a lot busier than the previous one, but it didn't bother them one bit. They just went about their business without any concern or interest of who else was there. They hadn't found anything to wear for when they planned on going out, so that was their focus in each store they went to. They shopped for at least four hours and left the mall just before closing time. They laughed when they talked about being at the malls from almost open to almost close.

"Talk about getting your fix," said Liyah.

"Tell me about it. I haven't had one of these since we got ready to leave to go to school." Although they didn't go into nearly as many stores as they had in the previous mall, they came out with just as many bags, just smaller ones this time. They made their way to an Italian restaurant, where they would eat dinner. It was the perfect mix between elegant and chill, fancy and rowdy. It was also Liyah's favorite place to eat at back home.

"You know what I just realized?" said MaKayla, smiling, as they took their seats.

"What's that?"

"We were supposed to be shopping to decorate our places. We've been out shopping all day, and neither one of us has bought a thing for them."

"See? That's why I didn't plan anything for tomorrow or Thursday. You never know what you'll need extra time for," said Liyah, pointing to her head several times. "I'm smart." They paused, and then both began laughing. "So I guess tomorrow or Thursday, we can make that happen then," she said. "Well, let's shoot for Thursday just in case. Something tells me that it'll be an all-day affair again." Liyah smiled.

"I think you're right. Plus, I think my mom wanted to go." MaKayla started laughing.

"Mine too. I'd forgotten all about that. She told me that before I came back here."

"Well, I guess we should probably invite them too, huh?"

"Yeah. But if we go early and have them meet up with us, then we can at least get some or most of the stuff we want without having to worry about hurting their feelings. You know they won't like what we pick."

"Not a doubt in my mind, but they'll really like it if we invite them. We just have to bite the bullet and deal with it." They both smiled and ordered their food.

They stayed for a while, drinking wine and eating, reminiscing about the times they had come there before they went away to school—the double dates, the birthday celebrations, and even just the random times. This was the place where MaKayla always brought Liyah when she needed a pick-me-up. For some reason, it always made her feel better and happy.

*****

MaKayla made it home a little before twelve, and her dad was still awake. "Why aren't you asleep? Were you waiting up for me?" She smiled as she trudged through the house with all her bags.

"Did they have anything left?" asked her father, smiling.

"Yeah, and Liyah got the rest." They both laughed. "Let me take these upstairs, and I'll be right back."

She took the bags into her room and set them in a corner. She took off her coat and pulled out some pajamas. She came back down in them and sat by her dad. He placed his arm around her, and she nestled in close to him.

"You got any plans for tomorrow evening?" he asked.

"Nope, not really. Liyah and I were considering going shopping, but it can wait until Thursday. Hopefully, Mom can come with us. Liyah's going to invite her mom too," said MaKayla through a yawn. She didn't realize how tired she was. They had been going all day, and she was beat.

"Wait. Shopping again? Can't you guys let them restock the shelves and racks first?"

"Not that type of shopping Dad. It's for both of our places."

"Oh, okay. I was going to say, but yeah, can you put it off until Thursday? I want to take you and your mom out to eat tomorrow."

"Sure Dad. Anything for you," she said as she drifted off to sleep underneath her father's arm.

*****

Jaron arrived at the office fairly early. It was his attempt to get ahead of the messages and calls for the day. The weather was very gloomy, and it rained off and on for the majority of the morning. The morning went as he had planned, and he finally got a handle on the calls, emails, and messages. He received a call around eleven o'clock from Mr. Thomas.

"Hello, Mr. Thomas. How are you?"

"I'm doing pretty good. Can't complain. How about yourself?"

"Well, we've been pretty busy lately, but that's nothing to complain about."

"I have to agree with that. Well, let's get right down to it."

"Alright. I hope that our proposal was received well."

"You know, Jaron, your father bragged about you and your brilliant mind. He went on and on about your knack for business at such a young age. You've definitely done him justice with this proposal. I see why he felt the way he did about you."

"Thank you sir, but I can't take all the credit. I have an amazingly hardworking and intuitive team. I wouldn't have been able to do it without them."

"And humble too. I love that quality in a business partner. I know it's short notice, but can you get your team together in, say, an hour and a half, around twelve thirty your time?"

"Yes. I don't think that would be a problem."

"Okay. I'll get my team together as well, and we'll call in on a conference number, if that suits you, to discuss some of the details and the thought that goes into it."

"That sounds like a plan to me. I'll get on it right away and have my assistant send you our conference number."

"Now, Jaron, we won't be discussing monetary numbers. I'd like to keep those details between you and me until the proposal is agreed upon on both sides."

"That works for me as well."

"Alright. I'll talk to you then, later."

"Okay. Later."

A smile rose on Jaron's face, and he sat back in his chair and stared at his father's picture. *Even when you aren't physically here, you're still here, helping me out, and that's why I love you,* he thought. He sat there staring for a few more minutes, then grabbed his laptop but paused. "I'd better call everyone myself. Tina," he yelled from his desk. She came in seconds later.

"Yes? Is everything okay?"

"Yes. It's better than okay. We're back in the game. I need you to send Mr. Thomas's office our conference call numbers. We have an emergency meeting in about an hour, so I won't be taking any other calls until I'm done."

"Would you like me to call or send out the necessary invites to the meeting?"

"No, thank you. I'm going to start calling everyone now."

Jaron picked up the phone as Tina walked out of his office, and he called each person who helped on the proposal one by one, informing them to bring everything they needed and to be in the conference room by twelve fifteen. After his calls, he grabbed all that he felt he would need, double- and triple-checked everything, and made his way to the conference room to set up. One by one, the team members trickled in until they were all there.

He took a moment to talk to them and bring them in more to his thought process and what they were trying to accomplish with the meeting so they would be better equipped to handle questions and everyone would be on the same page. He thanked them for their hard work up to that point and praised them for the work they had already done on the other business opportunities, as they were already starting to see return from them. The phone began ringing at twelve twenty, and by twelve thirty, everyone was in on the conference call.

The meeting lasted until four thirty. They covered every portion of the proposal and discussed the necessary changes and the pros and cons. The finalization of the deal was set for a month from that day. Jaron would fly out to meet with Mr. Thomas in person. That would be when all documents would be signed. They had until then to get everything in order and to agree on what to take out and what else to put in.

Jaron was so pleased with his team members that he gave them Friday off with pay. They were to come in and get to work tomorrow but not overdo it. They would rest up with those three days so they could hit it hard going forward. He knew he had been riding them hard from the proposal to the other business opportunities. He didn't want to burn them out.

*****

MaKayla had been in chill mode for the majority of the day. She was actually still a little worn out from all the shopping from the day before. Her mom came in around three thirty to find her asleep on the couch. MaKayla woke up as her mom came to sit down beside her.

"I didn't even know that I'd fallen asleep. I was watching a good movie. Can't remember what it was called though."

"You mean that movie was watching you, right?"

"Ha-ha, real funny Mom," said MaKayla, smiling. "How was work?"

"It was okay. Nothing special. A lot of work to get done though. How was your day?"

"I just relaxed for the most part, ate a little something earlier, but that's about it."

"How did your day go with Liyah yesterday?"

"I had a ball Mom. She is so crazy and had me crying-laughing the majority of the day."

"Yeah, she always has been a character."

"Oh yeah, that reminds me. What time do you plan on getting off tomorrow?"

"I don't know. Maybe four or four thirty. Why?"

"Well, you said you wanted to go furniture shopping with me. Liyah and I were thinking of going tomorrow. I was wondering if you wanted to come."

"Well, you know I'm a busy woman, so I'll see if I can move some things around to fit you in," her mom said, smiling.

"Yeah, yeah, yeah." MaKayla smiled back. "We'll meet you at the store. What time is Dad supposed to be picking us up for dinner?"

"He told me to be ready by sixty thirty, so I'm assuming he'll be here by six."

"Okay. Good. I still have time before I have to get up and start getting ready."

"I'm going to go take a nap before I start getting ready too," said her mom as she made her way up the stairs.

MaKayla picked up the remote and began channel surfing, then texted Liyah to let her know that her mom was in for tomorrow. Liyah replied fifteen minutes later: "So is mine." They continued texting, planning out their day for tomorrow. After watching the end of one of her favorite movies, she made her way upstairs to find something to wear to dinner knowing her dad would be there in about an hour.

*****

Jaron packed up his things and got ready to leave after what he felt was a successful day. He had a stack of messages that Tina had handed him when he got back to his office. They would have to wait until tomorrow. On his way home, he called his mom to tell her the good news.

"Hey Mom. How are you?"

"I'm okay. I'm trying to hurry up and get out of this rain. How are you?"

"Oh, I'm doing really good. I got that call back from Mr. Thomas today."

"So I'm assuming that everything is working out the way you want and need it to?"

"They are definitely coming together. We had a four-hour conference call to iron out all the details that need to be updated. We'll sign the final draft in a month. I'll fly out there to see him."

"Well, that sounds great baby. I'm happy that things are coming together. Now is that the only thing that you've been working on, or do you have some other good news for me?"

Jaron knew that his mom was talking about MaKayla. Ironically, this was the first time he had thought about her the entire day. "No, Mom," he said. "I'm working on it, but no progress yet."

"Well, how long does it take you? Do you need me to come hold your hand or do it for you?"

"Mom, it's not that serious. I said I'm working on it. You know you can't rush perfection."

"Okay. We'll see how much progress toward perfection you've made when I see you Sunday."

"Mom, that's like, two more days realistically. You're kidding, right?" Jaron laughed.

"We will see come Sunday."

"Okay Mom. Have you made it home yet?"

"Yeah. I'm walking into the house now, so I'll talk to you later. I'm going to get out of these wet clothes."

"Okay. I love you. I'll talk to you later."

"I love you too. Later."

Jaron's mind instantly went to MaKayla when he hung up the phone. He had been so caught up in work that he didn't think about her at all that day. For some reason, this made him feel bad. Although he knew it wasn't his obligation, he didn't want to let her slip away.

Due to the traffic caused by the weather, not to mention him stopping to pick up a few groceries, it took him longer than normal to get to his house. He got home and immediately went to the kitchen. He was feeling better than the two previous days and really felt like cooking. He made baked chicken breast, macaroni and cheese, string beans, baby carrots, and sweet potatoes.

After he finished eating, he looked at the amount of food he had made and laughed. *Oh well, I guess I have lunch for tomorrow.* He texted Tina: "Don't bring lunch tomorrow. It's on me." She replied, "Okay." He packed up lunch in Tupperware bowls for both of them and then went about cleaning the kitchen. He had his favorite playlist going, and it helped him get through with his cleaning faster. Then he went to take a shower and laid down after to get ready for tomorrow. He knew it would be a long day, remembering the stack of messages he had left on his desk. His eyes closed, and he drifted off to sleep.

*****

Their dinner went very well. MaKayla's dad told them some of the details about the new proposal that he had received and his excitement on working in the medical field with this promising young businessman. This came as a shock to MaKayla and her mom.

"You rarely speak so highly of a young business associate," said her mom.

"I actually can't remember any that you have either," chimed in MaKayla.

"I know, but this one is different. He's like a game changer. He's the one who called while we were on vacation."

"Oh," said MaKayla, eagerly wanting more details so that she herself could further break down the deal.

"Enough of the business talk," said her mom, realizing where the conversation was headed.

"But Mom," said MaKayla, disappointed.

"You can talk to your dad about it later or tomorrow or something, but for now, it's family time."

"Don't worry baby, I'll bring you up to speed," said her dad, giving her a wink.

They sat there for hours, eating, laughing, reminiscing, and just talking about any and everything they could think of. They talked about the upcoming dinner with Liyah and her family and how excited they all were to be doing things like they used to.

She could tell her parents had really missed her and how things used to be. Although they wouldn't come right out and say it, she could feel it. She wondered if they knew how much she had missed them, but instead of waiting, she just blurted out, "I really missed you guys," in the middle of her dad talking. It caught them off guard. They paused and looked at each other and then simultaneously replied, "Aww, we've missed you too."

"Where did that come from?" asked her dad.

"I don't know, just being here, sitting here thinking about everything. This whole vacation has been much needed. I feel revitalized, and it's like you guys just helped rejuvenate me, mentally, physically, and emotionally. That spa helped too," she said, and they all began laughing. "I think about you guys a lot. I'm just so busy. I never get time to pause and check on you."

Her mom smiled. "We think about and talk about you every day. We've definitely missed you too. We are really just so proud of you for standing on your own and making your own way the way you are. That vacation was something we all needed. I'm glad you're almost at the end of this part of your journey. Soon, your hard work will all pay off. I'm so eager to see where your life will take you. I know there are great things in store for you."

MaKayla started to tear up and smile. She was at a loss for words. It seemed like everyone was until her dad chimed in. "Yeah, what she said." They all started laughing hysterically, drawing attention from the other guests at the restaurant, who also just smiled.

They paid the bill and left the restaurant. The car ride home was a quiet one. Her dad had the radio on low—just enough for them to hear but not loud enough to disturb their thoughts. She was happy to have the support of her parents, because she had turned down so many other things they had offered her. They still had much to give. Even if it wasn't physical, it was still necessary and vital to her success.

She stared out the window as they drove, her eyes following clouds and taking in the moonlight. They arrived home and gave their hugs and kisses, then went their own separate ways. It was an interesting way to end such a great night. It was as if they knew things were ending, but no one wanted to address them. Some things were better left unsaid, and this was one of those times.

*****

Thursday seemed to come and go without Jaron really getting any real grasp on it. He was all over the place the entire day, only stopping to eat lunch with Tina. She was happy that he had brought cooked food and was surprised that he had cooked it all by himself.

"Mr. Thomas needs to call you every day if this is the result," she said, laughing.

"Hey, I can cook. I just choose not to, or I just don't cook enough to bring leftovers."

"I see. I learn something new about you every day, it would seem."

The messages, emails, and calls were coming in at what seemed to be an even faster rate today. Everyone is probably trying to get this stuff done before Friday so they can relax for the weekend, he thought. *Whatever the reason is, I'm in for a long couple of days.*

*****

MaKayla woke up early that day for some reason. She couldn't sleep the night before. She wasn't tired, and her thoughts didn't seem to bother her too much. She figured it was her body preparing for her vacation to be over. She even thought about Jaron. She wondered if he still came in and looked for her. She wondered what she would do if he came in while she was at work. Even more, what if he spoke to her? What would she say?

A part of her got excited at the thought while another part seemed overly nervous to imagine being in such a compromising position. She laid there for what seemed to be hours, just thinking about what she had to do when she got back and how she had to finish out the year strong. In no time, she was up and dressed, ready for the day, waiting for Liyah to come, who arrived shortly after.

"You look tired," said MaKayla.

"I am," Liyah said, smiling through a yawn. "But that's not going to get in the way of our day of shopping."

"Well, why are you so tired?"

"Darrell didn't want to get off the phone last night, talking about how much he misses me and can't wait until I get back."

MaKayla looked at her with a smirk on her face. "You're saying that like you don't like it."

Liyah was quiet. Then a smile crept onto her face. They both began to laugh. "I can't lie. I love that he's like that—annoying, irritating, and all lovey-dovey just because he misses me. It makes me feel special."

"That would be because you are special. You deserve this. Embrace it and take it all in." MaKayla smiled. "I'm so happy for you."

"We didn't get off the phone until like five something." Liyah smiled.

"I guess you two are getting pretty serious, huh?"

"I would have to say we are. We've talked about moving in together."

"Wait, wait, wait. Already? Don't you think you're moving a little too fast?" Liyah burst out into laughter. "What's so funny? I'm serious."

"I know, but we aren't talking about now. Like, when we finish school, you know, graduate and everything. We've talked about how it would be to come home to each other every night, cook with and for each other, just everything."

"Oh, I was about to say."

"Look at you, always so cautious, always so protective."

"It's only because I love you and don't want you to get hurt."

"I know. That's why I love you the way I do. I know you'll always have my back. Let's get something to eat. I'm starving," Liyah blurted out, causing them both to laugh.

"Yeah, I'm with you on that," said MaKayla, shaking her head. "You're something else."

After eating breakfast, they headed to Monica's Masterpiece, an art store that carried everything from art supplies, to paintings, and rugs. They followed that by going to Larry's Linens, looking for sheets and comforters for their bedrooms. Time went quickly.

Before they knew it, they were meeting their moms at the mall. After their brief greetings, they went into the mall, which was a lot busier than when Liyah and MaKayla went shopping. They made their way from store to store, debating with their parents on the way certain items would look in their places and the type of feel they were going for. They didn't buy much due to the disagreements. Had they not started out earlier, they wouldn't have gotten much of anything for their places.

The last store they went in, they managed to find items that all of them agreed upon, but the items would be too big to carry back on the plane, so they would have to be shipped back. They packed the items in MaKayla's mom's truck to take back to her house. Then they would add the other items they bought and have everything shipped to MaKayla's place by Saturday. They wanted their places decorated by the time they went back to school and planned on resting up on Sunday for the coming week.

Although they argued most of the time, they could tell that their moms were just happy to be there with them. The way they laughed, smiled, and talked was something that they had been missing out on while they were at school. So they too, were just as happy, although they wouldn't say it. The day had been long and tiring, and now both Liyah and MaKayla were drained.

"Don't be up all late on that phone again," said MaKayla, smiling.

"Why not? We're not going to eat until after six, so I have all day to sleep," Liyah replied, laughing. "While you're talking, you make sure you don't have any more dreams about storms."

MaKayla just shook her head, smiling. She knew that Liyah was referring to her dream about Jaron. It gave her a warm feeling on the inside, although she wasn't really sure why. "I'll see you guys tomorrow for dinner," she replied, waving as Liyah and her mom walked toward her car.

*****

MaKayla's dad was sitting on the couch when they came in. "Don't you feel like going with us to UPS?" she said, smiling.

"Sure. Anything for you baby. It can't be that much anyway," he said, rising and walking out the door to the truck. He stopped with his mouth open when he saw how full it was. "Are you serious right now? There's no way your place will fit all this stuff. Do you have a mansion and just didn't tell us?"

MaKayla smiled. "It's not all mine. It's Liyah's too. We're going to ship it all back to my place from here. Plus, Mom bought a few things too."

"I bought two little vases that are on the floor in the front. Don't try to put this on me." Her mom smiled.

They got into the truck and went to UPS to send their things. They discussed their day while driving. After leaving, they stopped and got food. MaKayla ate in the car and went right to bed when she got back home.

Chapter 12

The next day was very similar to the day before for Jaron, except for the food aspect. He worked past twelve and didn't remember eating anything, so he took a break and decided to go to the café. He knew he wouldn't be able to stay long due to his workload. He would just get his usual to go and hope that he was lucky enough to see MaKayla. He didn't have time to walk, so he drove, although it was the perfect weather for a walk.

The sun was shining, not a cloud in the sky. There was a light breeze, so it was not too hot. The birds were chirping, and nature was blooming all around him. Still, he had so much work to attend to before the day was out, so he had to go and come right back. When he arrived at the café, he noticed how busy they were. This put somewhat of a damper on his spirits, because he knew that even if he saw one of the girls, neither of them would really have time to talk.

He placed his order and began to wait, his head on a constant swivel in hopes of seeing MaKayla despite the circumstances, but he had no such luck, he figured, and turned his attention to the people walking up and down the street and how happy they were. Everyone was out enjoying the weather.

Just then, he heard it. "MaKayla, your order is ready for tables 2 and 7." He turned with intense excitement. Huge butterflies soared through his stomach, and his pulse heightened. "My name is McKinley, not MaKayla, for the last time," he heard the voice say as she exited the back room with plates in both hands. It wasn't her. He could do nothing but smile and shake his head. How excited he had been for nothing. He chuckled. Then his order number was called.

Jaron got back to the office and sat down to eat while checking his emails. They had slowed down a little from the morning, but he still had a lot of work to get done before the day was over. There was a knock at his door.

"Come in," he said through a mouthful of food.

"You had three calls while you were out. Plus, the numbers from last month were dropped off by Ashley."

"Okay. Thank you. How's your day going?" he asked as he took another bite of his sandwich.

"It's been pretty good. Busy as usual, but you know that just helps the day go by a little faster."

"I would have to agree with you on that."

"How about you?" she asked.

"Mine has been about the same, working to keep up with these emails and calls, but all in all, it's a good day."

"Okay. I'm about to go to lunch, if that's okay with you."

"Sounds like a plan. I'll be here when you get back."

He finished his lunch and went back to work, focused and determined to get ahead of the calls and emails. The next time he looked up, it was already three o'clock. He couldn't believe that he had been in such a zone, but he was happy that he was. There were only a few more emails to check and he would be caught up with all messages and calls.

The rest of the day breezed past, and he left the office at four thirty. He thought about calling his mom, but seeing how there was no movement on the MaKayla front, he changed his mind. He made his way home, went in, and stretched out across his bed. The week had gotten the best of him, and he was tired.

*****

MaKayla lounged around all day. She did not actually get out of the bed until three. She figured she didn't want to still be lying in bed when her mom got home. She wouldn't hear the end of it. She got in the shower and threw on some chill clothes, then went to sit on the porch. It was a beautiful day, and the flowers were starting to bloom. The wind began to gently blow, and she closed her eyes to

SPRING SHOWERS—THE BLOOM

just embrace the entire moment. She smiled when she opened them and saw her mother pulling into the driveway.

"Why are you sitting out here all by your lonesome?" asked her mom as she came and sat on the porch beside her.

"I just came out here not too long ago. It's a beautiful day. I figured I'd take it in seeing as I'm leaving in the morning."

"Yeah. It went too fast for my liking, but I'm happy that you were here. Can't say I wasn't. What have you been doing all day? I hope you didn't stay in that bed the entire time."

"Now Mom, come on. You know me." MaKayla smiled.

"I'll take that as a yes then." There was a brief pause, and they both began to laugh.

"Let's go for a walk before we have to get ready for dinner."

"Oh, so you can stay in bed all day, and then after I've had a full day of work, you want me to go walk with you?"

MaKayla just smiled. "Well, I am leaving in the morning Mom."

"You're lucky I love you. Let me go change and put my stuff up."

"Okay. Thank you," she said playfully.

Her mom came back out, and they went for a walk around the neighborhood, talking and reminiscing on how things were when she was younger. They came across the park where Marcus was hit by the truck. They both became silent, neither saying anything. Knowing the significance of the place and the sadness it had brought their family, now wasn't the time to bring it up. They just kept walking.

When they got back home, her dad was already there, sitting on the porch, right where she had been. "And where were you two?" he asked, smiling.

"We just went for a walk, trying to enjoy this beautiful day."

"How was it?"

"It was good. Not much has changed since I was here, but still, it feels different seeing it all again, like an eerie case of déjà vu or something."

They sat on the porch and talked for a while, then went to get ready for dinner and left. They got to the restaurant about ten minutes before Liyah and her family did, so they got a table for them all.

They sat and ordered drinks, and within minutes, in walked Liyah and her parents. The way MaKayla was sitting allowed her to see the door, so she called to them as they entered the restaurant. They all greeted one another with hugs and handshakes for the few men, who now realized they were outnumbered. It was somewhat nostalgic having them all together again, and MaKayla loved it.

"I heard you women took the liberty of doing some spring cleaning," said Liyah's dad as they took their seats.

MaKayla looked confused. "I haven't done any cleaning," she replied in a confused tone.

Liyah laughed. "He's referring to our shopping."

"Ooohhh, I get it now," said MaKayla, throwing a wink his way. "We just picked up a few things, that's all. Nothing major."

"Just a few things, huh? Well, from what I heard, those few things cost almost twelve hundred dollars to ship."

MaKayla and her mom looked at her dad with a scowl on their faces. "Why are you guys looking at me like that? What did I do?" her dad asked.

"Well, you were the only one who was with us when we shipped the things. Plus, you paid, so I wonder who told him how much it cost?"

"Hey, now wait a minute. Your mom was there—okay, yes, I told him. What's so wrong with that? We were just talking, and…" The scowl returned to their faces. "Okay, okay. I called him to tell him. There. Are you happy now? Where's the drink menu? I'm going to need a few drinks for tonight, I see," said her father as he picked up the menu to cover his face.

"Don't feel bad. My girls do me the same way. Always being so secretive. It's like they have their own little club and we're not invited." Liyah and her mom turned their attention toward him. "You know what? After you finish with the menu, let me see it. I think I'm going to need one too." There was a slight pause, then an eruption of laughter from the table. The waitress returned and took their drink and appetizer orders. Liyah's dad turned to them. "So ladies, have you guys met anyone who's caught your attention?"

"Dad, do you really think this is something we want to talk to you guys about?" responded Liyah.

"Now Liyah, be nice to your dad. He's just asking. Besides, we're all curious."

Liyah shook her head. "Seriously Mom? Not you too."

"Hey, we're all adults here. And if some little boy is talking to our little girls, I think we have a right to know."

"Yeah," chimed in MaKayla's dad.

"Well, first of all, Mom, we're grown women now, and we don't talk to little boys. We talk to grown men."

"Oh, well, excuse me for getting the terminology wrong. But no matter how old you are, you'll still be our little girls." They all began to laugh.

Liyah attempted to switch the subject. "So what do you guys have planned for after dinner?"

"Now Liyah, you know you're not getting off the hook that easy."

Knowing they weren't going to just drop the subject, MaKayla figured she would go ahead and get it out of the way. "Well, I've been way too busy with trying to manage and maintain everything to have time for a guy," she responded through a smirk.

"Seriously MaKayla? Now don't just be telling me anything, because you know I'll know."

"Dead serious Mrs. Jones," replied MaKayla. She raised her right hand as if being sworn in to testify. "Plus, I would never lie to you. I don't have the time to even *think* about a guy." She emphasized the word *think* as she smiled and looked at Liyah out of the corner of her eye.

Liyah stared at MaKayla through a look of shock and disbelief. She smiled. "Is that so? Don't even have the time to *think* about them, huh? Not enough time to even *think* about one?" She made sure to emphasize the word *think* as well. Their parents bounced their eyes back and forth between the girls as they dropped their hints.

"That's right, not even one," said MaKayla as she put her head down, smiling, and took another sip of her water. At that moment, Jaron popped into her head. She went back to when they were in the café and he held her hand for that brief moment, and a huge smile crept onto her face.

"So what about you honey?" asked Mr. Jones. "Are you too busy too?"

Liyah rolled her eyes and shook her head at MaKayla in a playful manner. "No, and yes, if that makes sense."

"Nope, it doesn't. Are you saying no, you're not too busy and yes, there is someone?" Liyah's dad asked, and MaKayla stared at her curiously to see what her response would be.

"Okay. If I answer this question, can we move on? There are plenty of other things to talk about."

"Sure. I promise. I just want to know," replied her dad.

"Yes, there is someone, but it's not that serious."

"Really? How does he look? What's his name? Where's he from? Does he go to school with you? How long have you been talking? What does 'not that serious' mean?" asked Liyah's mom in a very excited tone. MaKayla laughed, remembering where Liyah got her fast talking from.

"Mom, Dad promised we would move on."

"I know, but I didn't. That was his promise, not mine."

"True, but you always tell me that you two are one. You make decisions together and live with the consequences together."

"She has a point there. We do say that."

"Oh okay, but we'll be finishing this conversation later. I can't believe you didn't tell me."

"So, Mr. and Mrs. Thomas, how have you been? It's been a long time," asked Liyah hurriedly to avoid more interrogation from her mom.

"Yes, it has been a very long time—too long, if you ask me," MaKayla's mom replied.

Liyah playfully sank into herself. "Sorry," she said softly while bashfully smiling. They all let out a soft chuckle. "Well, we're almost done. Then we'll have more free time to be around more."

"So how are you guys liking the way your majors are shaping out? I haven't really had the time to sit and talk with MaKayla like I want to. You know this is a vacation, and I didn't really want her thinking about school that much since she was taking a break from it," said MaKayla's dad.

"It's been an adventure, to say the least. I mean, I expected a lot of work, but it's been more than I anticipated," replied Liyah. "I say that knowing that I have help and have utilized it." She turned to MaKayla, smiling in a teasing manner. "So I know that it's been even more on MaKayla."

MaKayla smiled. "It has been a lot of work, and sometimes, I wonder what I've gotten myself into. But I know when we finish, it's going to be the biggest satisfaction and relief. I can't wait to see where all of this leads us."

"Well, there's no doubt in my mind that both of you will be successful in your respective careers. Who knows? They may even cross paths at some point. I know that there have been more than a few times that your parents have helped us out with work things and vice versa. That's the beauty of having friends and not just business associates, so make sure you maintain those relationships that have helped you get to where you are and nurture the ones that will help you to get even further."

"Okay Dad, you're getting a little deep, aren't you? We didn't just graduate out of high school." They all laughed.

"Okay, okay. You're right. I'm just imparting some of the knowledge that I've gained over my years."

"It's greatly appreciated, Mr. Thomas." Liyah smiled.

"Now I don't know if this is some big secret or if Liyah even realizes it," said MaKayla as the attention turned to her. "But our paths will definitely be intertwined. The first business deal that I have, she'll be right there with me and in every deal that follows. Well, at least she'll be in the loop. I'm sure she'll have endeavors of her own to tend to, but who better to make sure the financial aspects of my business are in order than my sister? I'd never have to be concerned about someone taking from me or if the person handling my finances is trustworthy. She maybe a little crazy, but when you get down to it, I think we all are." She smiled at Liyah.

"Now you're trying to make me cry in front of them. That's not okay," said Liyah, giving MaKayla a hug.

"This time off and us being close again has helped me realize that I don't and shouldn't be trying to do it all on my own. Nor do I want to. Oh, and Mom, you helped a little." They laughed. "We've come so far together. I can't see myself taking those steps and not having you by my side."

"Well, I'm glad you've seen the error of your ways and how phenomenal I am," said Liyah, putting her head up in a playfully saditty manner. "You know that I'm here whenever and however you need me."

Their parents just looked on in adoration. "We did a good job with these two," Mr. Jones said, acknowledging their piece of the moment.

"Yeah, yeah, yeah. You guys aren't half bad," said Liyah, smiling.

"Okay. I'm ready to order so we can eat. We all know those appetizers aren't going to be enough for us," said MaKayla.

"You mean enough for you, don't you, MaKayla?" Liyah smiled.

"You know what I mean," MaKayla replied through a smile.

She was happy, and it was not just a brief moment of happiness like you would get from watching a funny movie or hearing a good joke but really true and genuine happiness. She needed that to help rejuvenate her to make it through the home stretch of her journey. The thoughts of how her future would unfold once again danced around in her head.

They ordered and continued conversing throughout dinner. Their parents attempted to catch up on every single detail of their lives, and although Liyah's dad promised, her mom continued to attempt to get information on Liyah's love interest—to no avail, though.

*****

Jaron felt his phone vibrating and rolled over to an incoming call from Xavier. He checked the time. It was seven thirty-eight. *Man, I don't even remember falling asleep. I had to have been really tired,* he thought. He answered the phone and attempted to clear his throat so as not to sound asleep.

"Were you seriously asleep at seven thirty on a Friday night? You have to be kidding me," greeted Xavier.

"I wasn't really sleep. I just dozed off for a minute, that's all."

"Man no you didn't. I've called and texted you at least three or four times apiece since six o'clock. You were out."

"Okay, okay. I was sleep man, but I've been tired, and it just caught up to me. I'm up now, so what's good?"

"Man, I need to talk to you about some real serious stuff."

"Is everybody okay? Nobody's hurt, right?"

"Yeah, physically, everybody's cool. Just get dressed. I'll be there in about twenty-five minutes, and we're going for a ride."

"Alright. Just hit me when you get outside." Jaron hung up and began to worry. Xavier rarely talked like that, so he knew it was something very serious. He changed his clothes and put on something more relaxed. Before he knew it, his phone was ringing again. "On my way out," he said as he answered the phone.

He grabbed his jacket, turned off the lights, and walked out the door. He threw on his hood and sprinted toward the car. The rain was coming down pretty hard. *Probably why I slept so long,* he thought. He instantly recognized the concern on Xavier's face as he got into the car.

"Man, what's up? I don't think I've ever seen you look like that before," Jaron asked as he shook off the water from his sleeves. Xavier was silent, just looking forward, shaking his head. Jaron could feel the concern rising inside himself. He tried reading Xavier's expression and demeanor. *What could he have possibly done so wrong? Why isn't he talking?*

"X, man, you have to talk to me. I've known you for a long time, but I don't know what you're thinking on this one," said Jaron, trying to keep his voice and tone as calm as possible. Xavier closed his eyes and exhaled deeply, still shaking his head. "What is it X? What's going on bro?"

"I don't know what I'm supposed to do man. I never in a million years saw this coming."

"Wait. Is this about you and Candace?"

"Yeah man. I…" He just started shaking his head. His mouth was open, but no words came out.

"You what? I know this isn't you being afraid of what you feel for her or how deeply you're falling for her."

"I know I really care about this girl, you know? It's different, like I was telling you about the other night. Yeah, there's a part of me that doesn't know how to navigate these emotional waters, but it's deeper than that."

"What more could there be? You don't know how to tell me you're—"

Xavier cut him off. "She's pregnant man. I'm about to be a father."

Jaron paused. He could not speak. His thoughts were confused. He was almost envious of Xavier. Then he caught himself. *But wait,* he thought, *not Xavier. I can't believe this.* "Wait, what? Are you serious?" Jaron finally bellowed. "I thought you were protecting yourself to avoid this specific situation. I know you are more careful than to keep going when one breaks, so how did this happen?"

Xavier let out a sigh, then shook his head. "We haven't been using protection for the last, like, two months. You know I'm not good with those dates, but it's somewhere around there."

"Whoa, you really just stopped strapping up?"

"I told you man, it's different. Like, I trust her. I know she's not messing around on me or anything like that, so I wasn't worried about catching anything."

"Well, did this scenario ever come up in a discussion?"

"Yeah, of course, the first time we didn't use anything, but I never thought it was going to happen, especially not this soon."

Jaron began to laugh. Xavier looked at him in disbelief. "I'm sorry, I'm sorry, but how did you think that this wouldn't happen?"

"I don't know man. I just didn't. I know it sounds crazy and stupid on some levels, but that's why I needed to talk to you."

"Okay," said Jaron, letting out a sigh. "So how does she feel about being pregnant?"

"She told me she doesn't know how to feel. She doesn't know if I'm ready or if it's what I really want. She wants the baby, and she said she wouldn't even consider not having it."

"Okay. So what did you say after she told you that?"

"I didn't say anything man. I just sat there in shock. Then I got up and left."

"You did what? Why would you leave her like that and not say anything?"

"I didn't know what to say. I've never been in a situation like this, so that's why I called you."

"I told you last time we talked that you needed to reassure her, to let her know that you're there for her and she's not in this alone, so you take that advice and you walk out on her after she tells you that she's pregnant, not like with someone else's child but with the child you created with her?" replied Jaron, shaking his head.

"I know man. I be tripping, but I don't know what to do."

Jaron shook his head. "When you drop me off after this talk, the first thing you're going to do is call and apologize to her regardless of what comes out of this conversation."

"But I—"

Jaron cut him off. "I don't care if you have to call one hundred times to get her to answer. That's what you're going to do, because you don't do that to someone you love, let alone the woman carrying your child. Alright?"

"Alright man, dang."

"Okay, so first things first. How do you feel about her being pregnant, you being a father, and her being the mother of your child?"

"To be honest, I'm afraid."

"Afraid? Afraid of what?"

"What if I'm not a good father or provider or I can't be what they need me to be? What if I fail them? Even worse, what if I have a little girl?"

"What's wrong with having a little girl, X?"

"I'm what's wrong, me and a million other guys out there just like me. This really got me to thinking about everything wrong I've ever done to a woman. What if my daughter pays for that? I don't want any guy out here using, abusing, or taking advantage of my daughter." Jaron smiled and chuckled a bit. "I'm serious man. Why are you laughing?"

"I'm smiling because you just answered your own questions. Don't you hear the passion and emotion you're speaking with? What would make you think you aren't ready? You don't want those things to happen to your daughter. Then who better than you to help school her to the ways of the world so she knows what to look out for?

"Plus, we're all like brothers, and you know we're not going to let anyone do her or him—let's not get too ahead of ourselves—wrong. That child automatically will have five more overprotective and caring uncles. Plus, you'd be the first to start the next generation. That child will be fine. Now answer the rest of my question. What was the first thing that popped into your mind when she told you?"

"The first thing that popped into my mind when she told me, before the concern and negativity took over, was that I'm the luckiest man on earth. I know you know Candace, but you don't know her like I do. She has everything a great mother would need and then some. I mean, the first thing she said was that she wouldn't even consider not having it. That right there shows me that she's already willing to do anything for our child. Why are you smiling now man?"

"You said 'our child,' X. You've already made up your mind that you want to have this child. You just needed to talk to someone to get all the negativity out of the way."

"I don't know man. I'm still worried. I mean, a child is a huge deal and a huge responsibility. You're now responsible for someone else's life, and that's not something to take lightly, or you can screw up. You know what I mean?"

"Look, you already said that the child having Candace as a mother is the best thing that could happen, and she chose you to be the father of her child. That means she sees that you're capable of being responsible for that life, that she believes in you as much as you believe in her. I mean, let's think about it like this. We've been boys since grammar school, right?"

"Yeah," said Xavier.

"If I call, would you come?"

"Of course, no matter the situation."

"Who came and stayed at my house for a month straight after my pops passed—no parties, no clubs, would just sit in silence, and let me cry without judgment?"

"Me. I mean, you're my best friend. We might as well be brothers. That's what aces do."

"You know what? You're 100 percent right. Now you're going to be that child's ace, and all that I know you'd do for me, you're going to be willing to do for that child and then some. You're more than capable. I mean, sure, you're crazy, but you gotta be crazy when raising a child nowadays.

"You're concerned that you won't be a good father? Then be a great father. You don't want to be a bad provider? Good. Then get on your grind even harder. You have at least two more reasons to do so. You said what if you can't be what they need you to be. Now you already know we don't use that word, for one. Two, the mere fact that you're thinking about these concerns, immediately after finding out, says you're ready to do what's necessary to be what they need. Stop overthinking and embrace the most beautiful thing that could ever happen to you."

"I guess you're right."

"You guess? No, I am right. That's why you called me, because you knew I'd give you honest and true advice. If I didn't think you could handle it, then that would have been the way this conversation went, but it's not, and you know I'd never steer you wrong."

"You're right, you're right, but what do I tell her when I call her?"

"I honestly think you should go talk to her face-to-face. Trust me. It'll make her feel a lot better and a lot more secure."

"That's going to take a lot man. I know she's pissed."

"Well, good. You get to show her that she picked the right man and you're ready to step up to the plate. You can start right now by showing her how responsible you can be in this situation."

Xavier sat quietly for a while, just thinking. Jaron just sat as well, not wanting to interrupt his thought process. He watched as the raindrops streamed down the windshield, attempting to make it to the bottom before being wiped away by the wiper blades. This reminded Jaron of life, of the conversation they were having.

Just like those raindrops hitting that windshield, we were brought into this life. We had lights shining on us, just like those streetlights were doing. Then we flowed and moved, trying to find our way to something. We didn't know what it was, but we went that way anyway. And every now and then, we met up with another drop, and they helped us move a little faster toward our destination. He instantly thought of MaKayla. He wanted her to be his raindrop, the one who would help him move faster. Xavier's voice came in, bringing him back to the conversation.

"Alright, but let's just cruise for a little while longer before I drop you back off."

"That's cool. We need to have a game plan for tomorrow anyway."

"Man, I almost forgot with everything that's going on. We're going to crush them." Xavier smiled.

They drove around for about another hour before Xavier dropped Jaron off. The moment he walked into his bedroom, his mind was flooded with thoughts. He laid in his bed and allowed his thoughts to roam free. He was happy for Xavier and the fact that he came to him to talk about it, but there was a small part of him that envied him. He thought back to their conversation at the bar and grill, about him having someone to help build the Coleman empire.

He smiled and thought of MaKayla. "Don't get too far ahead of yourself. You haven't even talked to her," he told himself. Still, he couldn't help but imagine how things would be if he were in that situation with her. He tried to shake it off and put his focus elsewhere, but once he started thinking about her, he couldn't take his mind off her. He began to feel sad. *I wish I didn't have to think about her and I could actually call or text her. Man, this is frustrating.*

He just laid in bed with the lights off, and only the moonlight shining in. He stared up at the ceiling and just allowed his mind to drift, to fully imagine a life with her. He smiled as he felt his eyes grow heavier. *She helps me go to sleep every time,* he thought as he rolled over, making himself more comfortable in bed. "Who knows what the future holds," he whispered softly. He allowed his eyes to close, and the images in his head faded to darkness, and he was sleep.

Chapter 13

"Okay. We need to get going, because we need to go change our clothes," said Liyah as she finished off her drink.

"You guys have to leave already?" replied Liyah's mother with a fake frown on her face.

"I think we should. You know how long she takes to get ready, and I don't want her rushing me," said MaKayla through a smile.

"Oh okay," replied Liyah's mom. They all got up and exchanged hugs and kisses.

"You guys got the bill, right?" said Liyah jokingly. Their parents just smiled.

"You guys have a good time, and be safe. Text us when you make it where you're going," said Liyah's mom.

"Okay Mom. We know the drill. We're adults, remember? We're not teenagers anymore," replied Liyah.

"I know, I know. I'm just saying," replied her mom.

"Well, you guys have a good time, and don't stay out too late," said MaKayla jokingly to break the slight tension. They waved and walked out the door.

"Man, why is she always so overprotective? I mean, we live hundreds of miles away. I think we can handle ourselves at a club," said Liyah in an annoyed tone.

"Don't let that get to you. We're lucky they even care. They're just lonely without us, and they want us to be safe," said MaKayla.

"Yeah, I guess you're right. It just gets to me sometimes," replied Liyah.

"We just have to appreciate all this while we have it. I mean, in a few months, all of this is going to change," said MaKayla through a somber tone. "We'll be completely on our own, living our own lives and building our own careers, our own futures."

"Yeah, that's a little scary when you think about it, so let's not think about it and just enjoy this night."

"Okay," said MaKayla, smiling, as Liyah pulled off.

They went to MaKayla's house to get dressed. They had planned on leaving from there in the morning since it was closer to the airport than Liyah's house. It took Liyah an hour and a half to get ready while MaKayla, on the other hand, was ready in forty-five minutes.

"I have no idea why it takes you so long to get ready," said MaKayla as they walked down the stairs to the car.

"Wait, wait, wait. Take another picture of me on the stairs," said Liyah.

"Seriously, Liyah? Haven't we taken enough pictures?"

"Just one more. You know I have to have an array of pictures to choose from. I want to send Darrell the best ones."

"Okay. Stand still."

The night was beautiful. There were no clouds in the sky, just a multitude of stars and a huge, beautiful moon. It was about seventy-three degrees, and the wind blew ever so lightly as MaKayla snapped the picture, causing Liyah's hair to flow at the perfect angle.

"Oh my God, I love this picture. Skip opening up your own café. You should be a photographer."

"Stop playing." MaKayla smiled. "One picture doesn't make you a photographer."

"I know, I know. I was just playing. Come on, because I know it's going to be crowded, and these heels were made for dancing, not standing in line."

"You're so silly," said MaKayla as she got into the car.

The club was a twenty-five-minute drive, and they listened to party music all the way there. They had the windows down and the music all the way up, and they danced as if they were already in the club. When they hit the street that the club was on, they noticed how long the line was.

"Do you see this line? I told you they were going to be crowded," said Liyah.

"Want to go somewhere else?" asked MaKayla.

"No, not really. I really had my heart set on coming here."

"Okay. I guess we'll be waiting in line then."

"Well, I'm going to let them valet the car. That should save us some time."

"Alright. Fine with me. I'll pay for parking since you drove." MaKayla exited the car and paid the valet worker. They walked past the entrance and began to walk to the end of the line.

"MaKayla, is that you?" came a voice from the entrance of the club. MaKayla and Liyah stopped and turned around. Out of the entrance came a man. He was six-two with short, waved hair, fresh lining with thin sideburns, mustache, and goatee. He was muscularly built and had a nice smile.

"Kevin? Kevin Lewis?"

"Yeah. How have you been? I haven't seen you since high school."

"I've been good. I've been away at college, and I'm just back for spring break. You remember Liyah, don't you?"

"How could I forget? You two have always been joined at the hip. How are you?"

"I'm good. Do you work here or something?"

"Oh yeah, yeah. I'm kind of like a bouncer slash promoter, among other things. My uncle owns this place, so I work with him."

"Oh, is that so?" said Liyah sneakily.

"Oh, don't even worry. Y'all don't have to stand in line or pay. Come on. They're with me," said Kevin to two other men who stood at the front door.

MaKayla looked at Liyah, who seemed to be excited about the situation. Although MaKayla was feeling a bit apprehensive, she shrugged her shoulders and figured, why not? Kevin escorted them through the club to the VIP section.

"Are you sure this is going to be okay?" asked MaKayla nervously.

"Of course. I told you, this is my uncle's spot, and I work with him. It's just good to see you," said Kevin as he leaned in for a hug. MaKayla leaned the rest of the way, although she did it hesitantly. "I'll be right back, and I'll send a waitress over to get you guys some drinks. Don't worry about paying. It's on the house."

SEASONAL STORMS

"You don't have to do that," said MaKayla.

"I know, but I want to."

"Yes, he wants to," said Liyah, grabbing MaKayla's arm and pulling her down to have a seat. "Thank you Kevin," she said. "What are you doing?" whispered Liyah as Kevin walked away.

"What do you mean what am I doing? What are you doing?"

"He's clearly into you, and we get to benefit from that, so why turn it away?"

"He's into me? You really think so? That's just Kevin being Kevin. You know how he used to be in school."

"Yes, I do, but he never looked at you the way he looked at you tonight. Plus, he never looked like he looked tonight."

"You are so silly. I think you're reading too much into it. He was just being nice."

"All that knowledge, you better put it to work and see it for what it is."

"I already told you that I don't have time for anyone. Plus, he stays way out here."

"Oh, but you have time to be having dreams about a certain someone, don't you? Talking about you don't have time to think about anyone," said Liyah jokingly.

"You know it's not even like that. It was just one dream."

"I know, but I'm just saying, don't stop things before you know what can come of it."

"I hear what you're saying, but let's just enjoy being here with each other. I'm not concerned about that."

"Okay. I can get with that."

Right on schedule, the waitress appeared. MaKayla and Liyah ordered drinks and then made their way to the dance floor. Although MaKayla appeared to be enjoying herself, laughing, dancing, and joking with Liyah, for some reason, their previous conversation had her thinking about Jaron. She noticed a few couples in the club and wondered if Jaron liked going out, if he liked dancing, or if he even could and how fun it would be to teach him if he couldn't. Then she began to wonder about what he was doing and if he had been back to look for her after Liyah left.

Why was he looking for her? Surely a businessman of his caliber wouldn't be interested in someone like me, she thought. As her thoughts changed and became somewhat negative, so did her mood. She figured it was time to take a break and go back to their section for a while. On their way back, they each ordered another drink. They sat down for a while, neither of them saying anything.

Liyah was still bobbing her head and rocking to the music. "You okay?" she finally asked, breaking their silence. "You just kind of drifted off out there on me."

MaKayla paused, wondering if she should tell Liyah about her thoughts. *Is it really that serious for me to have to tell her? I mean, either way, she is my best friend, so why not?* she thought. She opened her mouth to start telling her, and at that moment, Kevin walked up, carrying their drinks.

"Are you beautiful ladies enjoying yourselves?" he asked, handing them each a drink. Since they both ordered the same thing, he didn't have to figure out whose drink was whose.

"Yeah. This DJ is on point with his mixes and how he's covering so many different genres, mixing the old with the new," exclaimed Liyah.

"Yeah, Devin is definitely the best in town. He works at the radio stations from time to time, but he's usually busy here or working a party. You don't remember him? He was two years ahead of us. He went to Central and used to throw those really dope house parties."

"Now that you've mentioned it, I do remember him. He was good back then, but he's definitely gotten better," replied Liyah.

"What about you? You enjoying yourself?" asked Kevin, directing his attention to MaKayla.

"Yeah, it's nice—good music, nice crowd, good drinks. I like it."

"Well, I'm glad to hear that you guys are enjoying yourselves." Kevin sat and talked with them for about thirty more minutes, discussing school and how they liked it and things he was doing in his own life. The majority of his attention and conversation was focused on MaKayla.

"Come on. Let's go back to this dance floor. I think we've rested enough, and you know I love this song," said Liyah.

"Okay, okay. I'm coming."

"I would love to come join you guys, but you know I need to make sure everything else is going good, but I'll be around."

They headed back to the dance floor and began to dance, Liyah looking curiously at MaKayla. "Why are you looking at me like that?" asked MaKayla.

"You know why. Don't try to downplay it."

"Downplay what? What are you talking about?" asked MaKayla curiously.

"I know you saw how he was looking at you, how he kept directing his attention to you."

"That was nothing. You're looking into it too much."

"I'm telling you that he's into you, but anyway, what were you going to say before he came and sat down? You were going to tell me something."

"Oh yeah, it was nothing. Don't worry about it." MaKayla smiled.

"Don't look at me like that. Tell me what you were going to say."

MaKayla sighed. "Okay. I just kept thinking about the guy from the café while we were on the dance floor the last time. I don't know where it came from, but it was like my mind was flooded. I even got sad thinking about not being enough for him." Liyah stopped dancing, her mouth just dropped, and a smile rolled across her face. "What? Why are you smiling like that?"

"I should've known that's what it was just by the way you looked."

"Oh hush. But I'm being serious. I don't know why I'm thinking about him like this."

"Wait. What do you mean not being enough for him? Any man would be lucky to have you by their side, and whoever is blessed enough to call you their own will be the second luckiest man in the world."

MaKayla smiled, then stopped. "Wait. Why only the second? Who will be the luckiest man then?"

"My husband, of course." Liyah smiled as she went back to dancing. They both burst into laughter and fell into each other's arms, hugging each other tightly.

"That's why I love you," said MaKayla. They released each other and continued laughing.

Kevin walked up, smiling. "What's so funny?" he asked.

"Oh nothing. It's just something between us girls," replied Liyah.

"Oh, I understand. No problem here," Kevin replied, raising his hands as if he was trying to calm a heated situation.

Just then, the DJ changed the music, and a slow song came on. It wasn't just any song; it was MaKayla's favorite. Liyah looked at her in excitement, awaiting her reaction to the song. Ironically, she didn't look excited. She was more tense than anything.

"You mind if I dance with your friend?" Kevin asked Liyah.

"Well, that's really up to her."

He turned to face MaKayla, who was clearly nervous and looking for an escape route, but it was too late. "You want to dance?"

MaKayla opened her mouth to protest, but all that came out was, "Um."

"Oh come on. I love this song. I'm not going to bite unless you want me to." Kevin smiled as he pulled her close to him.

Liyah stood close by, pretending to be dancing on her own but paying enough attention that if she needed to step in, she could do so. MaKayla was tense and barely moving. She was trying not to think so much, to actually let go a little more. *What's wrong with me? I love dancing, and I love this song,* she thought. *Maybe it's because he pulled me in close to him without allowing it to just happen. Maybe it's because I feel like he's trying to control this. Maybe I'm overthinking it. I mean, he seems to be a nice enough guy.*

No matter what MaKayla thought, she wasn't comfortable with him. She couldn't let go. He continued to try, rubbing her shoulders and her back, attempting to comfort her, but it wasn't working. Every stroke just made her more and more tense.

Liyah noticed and slowly made her way closer. She was finally right next to them. "You mind if I cut in?" she asked, then pulled MaKayla away from Kevin. He moved by himself and watched them as they danced close by.

"Thank you," whispered MaKayla. "I don't know how much longer I could've stood there."

"I know, and now I have to make it look good, so give me a second." Liyah let go of MaKayla and began dancing with Kevin. This took his attention off MaKayla, and he focused on Liyah.

MaKayla continued to dance and slowly felt the tension remove itself. She soon forgot where she was and allowed herself to be lost in the music. It was like no one else was there, just her and the music, and she felt everything else drift away. After a few minutes, the song changed, and she was back to reality.

Kevin was staring at her with an intrigued look. "Why didn't you dance like that with me?" He smiled.

"I don't know. Some songs, I just prefer to dance alone. It helps me to let go and be free."

"I can understand that. I love a woman who knows how to move, and you definitely know how to move," he replied as his eyes surveyed her body.

Liyah grabbed MaKayla's hand. "Want to go sit back down? I'm a little tired."

"Sure. Let's go." Kevin followed but at a far enough distance that he could not hear their conversation. "Did you see how he was looking at you? It was like he wanted to eat you," said Liyah as she burst out into laughter.

"Yes, I did but I don't think that's funny, Liyah. Him undressing me with his eyes like that, it's actually somewhat creepy."

"Okay, okay. You're right. Let's just go sit back down and have another drink."

"Nah, no more for me. I mean, one of us has to drive back, right? Plus, we have an early start tomorrow, and I don't want to be fighting with a headache all day."

"See? That's how I know you love me. Look at you volunteering to be the designated driver and all."

"I can't stand you," said MaKayla as she began to smile and laugh.

"You love me," replied Liyah as she sat down. The waitress came, and Liyah ordered a drink. Kevin ordered a drink too, and MaKayla ordered a bottle of water.

"Why aren't you having another drink? Is it because I'm here? Do you feel you have to be on your best behavior?" asked Kevin.

"No." MaKayla smiled. "I'm driving us home, so I don't want to drink anymore."

"Oh, well, I could take you guys home if that's the issue. That way, you could enjoy yourself."

"No, that's all right. I don't need to drink to enjoy myself, but thanks for the offer though."

"No problem."

They sat and talked for another thirty minutes before the girls decided they were ready to go. "Well, it was nice seeing you again," said the girls as they got up to leave.

"It was good seeing you guys again too. Maybe I can come out and visit you one of these weekends."

They stopped and looked at each other. "No offense, but that probably won't work. It's the end of the semester—you know, that final push. Plus, we both have internships and jobs. It'll be this way until the end of the school year," said MaKayla.

"I understand, but, I mean, you guys must get a day off." They both broke out laughing. "What? What did I say?"

"What's a day off? I've never experienced one of those."

"Me neither. Perhaps we should inquire about that when we get back," the girls joked.

"No, we rarely, if ever, have a day when there isn't work, school, or internship. And on the rare occasion when we do, it's never at the same time. So usually, those days include a lot of rest. Well, for me at least. I can't speak for Liyah."

"Same here," Liyah said as they reached the door, and she handed the valet her ticket.

"Well, maybe I can come just chill with you guys or something."

"Maybe when we come back," said Liyah as she walked toward the car, which had just pulled up. She got in and sat down.

MaKayla began to walk toward the driver's side, but Kevin grabbed her arm. "Hold on for a second. Look, I know you have a lot going on right now and you're really busy, but I really enjoyed spending time with you tonight."

Wait. I didn't know we were spending time together, she thought. *I thought I was spending time with Liyah.*

"I was thinking maybe we could exchange numbers and get to know each other better. Who knows where it'll go from there?"

"I don't even want to waste your time with false or empty promises. I just don't have the time for that right now, and it wouldn't be fair to you if I were to do that. Plus, I'm not saying you're going to bring stress, but I know when people exchange numbers, there are expectations. And when the expectations aren't met, it causes issues. I know I can't meet the expectations, and I don't have the time to deal with what comes from not meeting them. I hope you understand what I'm saying."

"Yeah, it's cool. It was nice seeing you again. Too bad we couldn't have built on it."

"Okay," MaKayla said as she tipped the valet. She gave Kevin a hug and said goodbye.

Liyah pretty much slept on the car ride home. MaKayla didn't mind since it wasn't far and since she had a lot on her mind, primarily Jaron. She couldn't shake her thoughts. *I wonder why I lied to Kevin. I know if that were the guy from the café, the conversation probably would've been different. We would have each other's numbers. I can't believe I'm thinking about this guy like this. What's wrong with me? But I'm so intrigued by the mere thought of him and curious as to how things might be.*

I have to be crazy to be thinking about a man who has only said a few words to me, and I don't even know if he looks at me that way. You know what? Let me stop thinking so hard on this. I can't do anything about it even if I wanted to. I mean, I don't even know his first name.

She just smiled and turned up the music a little louder and began to sing. She figured that if she was singing, then she wouldn't be thinking about him. She made it to her house several minutes later. It was two twelve when they made it in. MaKayla made sure to set her alarm, and although she had to tell Liyah several times, she made her set hers too. "Five thirty seems about right. We have to be at the airport by seven," she told Liyah although she was already fast asleep. "Good night," she said even though she knew Liyah couldn't hear her, turned off the lamp, and fell asleep.

*****

SPRING SHOWERS—THE BLOOM

The next day didn't come fast enough for Jaron. He was up and down all night, his brain all over the place. He rose with the sun and started his day. He had already eaten, showered, gotten dressed, packed his bag for when they went to play basketball, and picked out what he was going to wear when they went out later that night. It was ten twenty-seven, and he had just finished doing the dishes when his phone began to vibrate.

The guys were waking up and were discussing the ride situations and what time they would meet at the park. Jaron was going to pick up Tony and Xavier, and they would meet at the park at one. He was glad that he was already ready, because he had to leave soon to pick up the guys and get to the park on time. He finished the kitchen and went to watch a little TV before he left.

He left his house at eleven forty-five, went to get Tony, and then picked up Xavier, because his house was on the way to the park. Tony did a lot of trash-talking in the car. Jaron and Xavier, on the other hand, just sat there laughing and acting like they couldn't hear him.

"It's okay. Ignore me if you want, but you won't be able to ignore the game on the court," said Tony.

"Should I tell him?" Jaron asked Xavier.

"Man, somebody needs to," replied Xavier, laughing.

"Tell me what? What can you possibly have to tell me?"

"Look man, you're doing a lot of talking. But at the end of the day, that's all it is, just talk. Seems like you're trying to compensate for something. Your skills, perhaps? You know how the saying goes. What's understood doesn't have to be explained. I guess you know we don't understand your skill set, so that's why you're trying to explain so diligently right now, huh?"

Tony didn't reply. He only shook his head and repeated, "Okay. We will see. Don't understand my skill set? I'll show them."

They arrived at the park at twelve forty-five, and the others came about ten minutes later. It was a perfect day to play basketball. It was about seventy-two degrees. There were very few clouds in the sky, and a nice breeze blew every so often. They all went through their stretching routines and the rules for the games. They agreed to play three games to twenty-one, and the best out of the three would be declared the winner. In between each game and after the last game, if they needed one, Tony and Troy would play one-on-one to eleven. The best out of the three games would win and have bragging rights. The trash-talking intensified once the rules were settled.

*****

MaKayla woke up to the sun in her eyes. "Oh my God, we've overslept," she yelled out, nearly falling out of the bed. "Liyah, wake up," she said emphatically as she shook Liyah.

"What? What? Why are you shaking me like that? What's wrong?"

"We're going to be late. We overslept," said MaKayla.

Liyah grabbed her phone and squinted through one eye. "My phone says five twenty-four, so how did we oversleep?" she asked as she yawned and stretched.

"Oh, mine too," MaKayla replied as she looked at her phone. "I'm sorry. I just saw the sun and thought—"

"You tripping? We could still be asleep. You of all people know how valuable every second is."

"Yeah, I know. Sorry. I guess I was just worried about being late. We're up now. We might as well start getting ready."

"Let me know when you're out of the shower," said Liyah as she let her body fall back to the bed and pulled the covers over her face.

"Sleepyhead," said MaKayla as she picked up a pillow and threw it on Liyah, but she didn't move, just let out a low noise that sounded like a moan.

*****

It was really hectic for them once they actually got up and started going—making sure they had all their stuff, dealing with the random questions and comments as they tried to get everything together, and trying to grab something small to put in their stomachs. Well, that was mostly Liyah, who didn't want the effects of the night before to catch up to her in a bad way. Their parents decided that they would all go to the airport. That way, they could all see them off, and they wouldn't have to do so much maneuvering of their luggage.

They made it to the airport at six fifty, which gave them enough time to say their goodbyes and get their things and head into the airport. Both of their mothers cried as if they were leaving for the first time, so their hugs and words lasted longer than their fathers'.

"Now you know you're too old to be crying like this Mom. It's not like we're little girls and have never been away from home before. Dad, can you come get her? I think she needs a hug from you or something."

"Just hold her tightly and let her know that you love her. She'll be okay," he replied.

MaKayla's interaction was quite the opposite of Liyah's. She herself had to fight back tears when she hugged her parents. She really enjoyed her vacation and was just getting used to being around them again. Now it was back to reality. There was a part of her that didn't want to leave, that just wanted to stay, a part of her that was tired of working and studying so hard, of all the pressure she had placed on herself. She wanted to be done already.

"We're so proud of you, and we can't wait to come down there and see you walk across that stage, to see all that hard work pay off," said her mom.

Hearing those words put her mind back on track and reminded her what she was doing and why she was doing it. She smiled and let go, wiped the tears from her mom's cheeks, and gave her a kiss and one last strong embrace. "I love you guys so much. Don't go getting into trouble while I'm gone." Her parents laughed, and she walked to Liyah's parents and hugged them.

The girls then turned and walked together into the airport. They checked in and made their way through security to wait for their boarding call. Their plane began boarding fifteen minutes later, at seven forty-five. Somehow, Liyah had arranged it so they would be seated next to each other. MaKayla didn't say anything. She just smiled and shook her head. Liyah always did things like that. She was spoiled in that way and liked everything the way she wanted.

SEASONAL STORMS

MaKayla had the window seat, and Liyah was seated next to her. Their flight took off at exactly eight, and both texted their parents before turning off their phones as the plane prepared for takeoff. Liyah was fast asleep five minutes after the plane leveled off, head resting comfortably on a pillow that she had placed against MaKayla's shoulder. MaKayla just smiled and made herself comfortable as she stared out the window.

She thought back over the last two weeks, everything she had done, all the laughs with her parents and Liyah, the pictures she had taken. Then she thought, *Are you ready? Home stretch now. It's almost over.* She smiled. "I'm ready," she lightly whispered. *I'm tired. I guess I can get some sleep too.* She lowered the shade, placed her pillow against the window, and fell asleep.

*****

Their descent woke MaKayla up. She looked over. Liyah was still fast asleep. She raised the shade, and the city came into view. She smiled to herself, then nudged Liyah. "We're back."

"Huh?" said Liyah. "What happened?"

"I said we're back. Look."

"No way. I just closed my eyes. That was, like, six minutes." MaKayla just laughed and turned to look out the window. "Well, at least it looks like a nice day outside—not too many clouds and sunny."

"Yeah. I hope it feels as good as it looks. You know this weather can be deceiving," replied MaKayla.

They landed several minutes later and exited the plane. They turned on their phones and texted their parents to let them know they had arrived.

"One fifty-eight," said Liyah. "What time are they supposed to deliver our things?"

"They said they would be there between four and four thirty, but I haven't tracked them since we left to see if they are still on schedule."

"Okay. Let's get our stuff and head to the car. I'm going to call my brother to see if he has painted my place."

They walked to the luggage pickup and got their bags. It took them about twenty minutes before they got all their things from the conveyor belt.

"You remember where you parked, right?" asked MaKayla.

"Of course I do. It's right over there. You know I wasn't parking far from the door." Liyah laughed. They made it to the car and put their bags in. "I've called him three times already, and he hasn't picked up. It's two thirty, so I know he's not asleep. So what is he doing?" said Liyah as she started the car. "He probably hasn't painted my place and doesn't want to tell me," she said as she dialed the number again.

Chapter 14

Jaron, Xavier, and Troy won the first two games. The first was 21–9, and the second was 21–15. They only agreed to play the third because Tony said the first one was only a warm-up, so the third game would really tell all. Troy also beat Tony the first two games of their one-on-ones, and Tony had the same excuse as to why he lost them as well.

William's phone rang. "Hold on guys. Let me see who this is. They keep calling."

"Hurry up. Don't be trying to get no rest on the side," said Xavier.

"Hello. No, I can't talk right now. I'm at Wright Park, playing basketball. I'll call you back when I'm done," he said as he hung up and ran back to the court. "Sorry. That was my sister calling. Now let's get back to it."

*****

"He just hung up on me. We're going up to that park. I can't believe he hung up on me."

"It still says the same thing on the tracker, between four and four thirty."

"Good, so we'll have more than enough time to go by there and still make it to your place in time."

"Sounds like a plan to me," replied MaKayla.

They made it to the park twenty minutes later.

"There he is, sitting on those bleachers. Come on, he's not even playing."

"Just chill," said MaKayla, laughing. "He's probably tired. He looks sweaty, so he had to have done something. I'll be right over. Let me just check this voice mail."

"Okay," replied Liyah.

William and the guys walked off the court as Liyah walked toward them. William noticed her and walked ahead, the other guys still discussing the games. "I told you that I was going to call you back," he said. "But I guess you just couldn't wait, huh?"

"Nope, I couldn't. Plus, you were rude, hanging up on me like that."

"I told you I was in the middle of a game. You're just so impatient. What did you want anyway?" he asked as he gave her a hug.

"You're all sweaty. You're lucky I love you," Liyah said, embracing him. "Did you paint my place like we talked about?"

"That's really what you came over here for, to ask me that?"

"Yes it is. So did you?"

"You could've just gone home and saved us both the hassle."

"If you hadn't hung up on me, then we wouldn't be here. So again, I ask, did you?"

William shook his head, smiling. "Of course I did. I told you I was going to. Why wouldn't I?"

Liyah's face lit up. "Is it really nice now? I know it looks good. Doesn't it?" Just then, MaKayla walked up.

"Oh my God, MaKayla, it's been forever. Come give me a hug," exclaimed William.

"Be careful. He's sweaty," said Liyah.

"Oh hush," said William, hugging MaKayla.

The guys were right behind William, and their conversation had died down for the most part. Jaron heard William say MaKayla's name and immediately turned to see if it was her.

"I know. I was just telling Liyah that I haven't seen you in forever," MaKayla said as she hugged him back. She let go and noticed the other guys standing behind William, whose attention was now fixed on her.

"Oh, I'm sorry. This is Tony, Troy, Danny Boy, Xavier, and Jaron. You guys remember Liyah, my little sister, and her best friend, basically my other little sister, MaKayla."

The guys all spoke a variety of "How are you doing?" and "Hey, what's up?" all but Jaron. He said nothing; he just stared. He couldn't believe it was her. After all this time, there she was.

"How are you guys doing?" replied Liyah.

MaKayla's eyes ran across them and stopped as she got to Jaron. *It's him,* she thought excitedly. A feeling rapidly rose inside of her that she hadn't felt in years. She allowed her eyes to take in his physical appearance. There he stood, glowing, as if the sun chose to highlight his presence, but she soon realized it was the way the sun reflected off his sweaty body. The silhouette from her dream now had all its features.

He had to be between six and six-two. She imagined hugging him and her head resting comfortably on his chest, his chest that protruded from his shirt perfectly, the shirt that was snuggly attached to his body. She wasn't sure if it just fit that way or if the sweat acted as an adhesive. She figured it was the perfect combination of the two. The shirt allowed her to see the slight indentation of his abs, and she allowed her eyes to roll down each set until they rested at the top of his shorts.

She slowly lifted her eyes, following the path his veins and muscles made back up his arms, up to his shoulders, where several of his dreads lay at rest. The others were pulled back in what she assumed was a ponytail based on how they all flowed. She followed his neck up to his face. She wanted to see his smile, that smile that made her comfortable in her dream. Instead, when she got there, his expression set off the alarms inside of her.

He didn't look happy. He looked more confused and apprehensive. *Perhaps he's surprised to see me,* she thought, but those thoughts were quickly washed away with fear and doubt. This wasn't good. She had found herself in a most uncomfortable situation.

MaKayla looked at Liyah, a look that told Liyah that she was nervous. Liyah turned to face the guys again and recognized Jaron. Her face lit up once again, and she turned back to MaKayla, but MaKayla's expression had not changed. Her mind was racing, and she didn't know what to do.

It's one thing to think and imagine talking to him, but now that he's here right in front of me, what do I do? she thought. *My hair isn't done, and my clothes aren't matching. I look a mess. I can't believe this is happening.* She felt the anxiety build, and she became more and more nervous.

Jaron was no better. He too was trying to make sense of all his thoughts, to control them, but he was failing miserably. *I can't believe I never put that together. William is always talking about his sister, Liyah. How did I not think about that? I've been sitting here looking for her and MaKayla this whole time, and now she's right here. Of all the days, this had to be the day. I mean, I'm all sweaty, and all the guys are here. I know how they get around women, let alone one of us talking to one of them. Talking to them? Who am I kidding? What would I say? Am I supposed to bring up the café? That would make me look dumb right now. Maybe she doesn't even notice me. But by the way she's looking and the way Liyah just looked right at me, I'm sure they know it's me.*

"Thanks Will. I knew I could count on you," said Liyah, quickly realizing the enormity of the situation and how uncomfortable MaKayla was.

"You're leaving already? Wait," said William as he followed behind her.

"Yeah. We have to get to her house. There's a delivery coming that we have to be there to receive."

"Oh okay. But how were Mom and Dad?"

"You know, same as usual. Mom was really overdramatic, crying and stuff, when we got ready to get on the plane. We really need to go. We don't want to miss the delivery. I'll call you later and bring you up to speed."

"Okay. Well, I'll talk to you later. It was good seeing you again MaKayla, and stop being a stranger."

"Good seeing you too," MaKayla replied nervously. "I'll try."

The girls got into the car as William turned to walk away. He gave one last wave that they returned and went to rejoin the guys.

"Okay. Now I'm really confused," said Liyah. "Tell me what's going on."

"What do you mean? Why are you confused?"

"Well, first of all, I think it is pretty funny that he and my brother are friends and we've never met him. Plus, today of all days, we happen to meet him. Just crazy," said Liyah, shaking her head and smiling. MaKayla didn't respond. She just sat there, her mind going a million miles an hour.

"So explain to me how just yesterday, you were talking about how you couldn't get him off your mind—not even completely yesterday but less than twelve hours ago. Now today, he was right in front of you, and not only did you not say anything. You looked worse than you did while dancing with Kevin last night. How is that possible?"

MaKayla still didn't respond. She heard Liyah, but her mouth wasn't moving. She was stuck. Finally, after several seconds of silence, she muttered, "I don't know."

"What did you say? I couldn't hear you."

"I don't know," she said, dropping her head. "I mean, sure, in theory, this is all amusing and nice. But in reality, it's not funny at all. Look at me. I'm not even matching. My hair's all over my head. And on top of that, what was I supposed to say, 'Hey, I heard you were looking for me'? That wouldn't have worked at all. I would've looked dumb. Plus, all of those guys were there, so that made me even more uncomfortable. You know how I get when I'm uncomfortable.

"I don't even know why he was looking for me. Maybe he just wanted to make sure I didn't lose my job and I'm overthinking it. Plus, what makes you think that he doesn't even have a girlfriend? I mean, a good-looking guy like that who is also clearly intelligent, because he came to the café for a business meeting, and he doesn't have a girlfriend? Highly unlikely.

"I mean, what exactly was he supposed to do, just come in and whisk me off my feet?" Liyah didn't say anything. She just sat there smiling and staring at MaKayla. "Why are you smiling Liyah? This is serious. It's not funny."

"I was just making sure that you got it all out. You clearly had a lot to say."

"I'm done. I just don't know. It all just happened out of the blue, and I wasn't ready at all."

"For starters, who cares how you look? No offense, but he's seen you at work, and you know we rarely come dressed to impress there."

"That's different, and you know it." Just then, Liyah's face lit up. "Why are you looking like that?" asked MaKayla nervously.

"I have a great idea."

MaKayla exhaled. "Not one of your crazy plans, Liyah."

"No, hear me out. This is a good one."

"Okay. What is it Liyah?"

"I'm thinking, next weekend we go out, and we have William meet us with his friends. That way, you can be dressed up, looking how you want, and you're not caught off guard by him being there. You'll be able to ease your way into talking to him, because there will be other people around. You know it's easier to break the ice in a group."

MaKayla sat quietly, actually contemplating Liyah's idea. "That's not a bad idea, but I don't want to do that," she finally said.

"Why not? It could work!" exclaimed Liyah.

"Well, for starters, I don't want to pull Will into this like that. It's not fair to him. Plus, I don't want you and him attempting to play matchmaker. If anything goes wrong, he'll feel responsible. I mean, that is his friend. Besides, he could still have a girlfriend. Do you know how embarrassing that would be? He didn't even say anything. He probably just came to the café to make sure I was okay." She paused for a moment. "I just wish I'd known he was going to be there. I could've been prepared for what to do."

"Well, you always tell me that sometimes, the best things in your life come when you're completely unprepared for them. Who knows? Maybe he's one of those things. Just relax. It's over now, and we have some decorating to do. That should help clear your mind. Plus, at least now we know his name, and we can stop referring to him as the guy from the café. We can discuss it more while we're working on our places."

"Okay," said MaKayla as she leaned in and hugged Liyah. "Thank you," she whispered.

"Thanks for what?" asked Liyah as she hugged MaKayla back.

"For knowing me. You saw how uncomfortable I was and got me out of there, even with your brother trying to talk to you. I know how much you two love to talk."

"Oh, that's nothing. You would do the same for me. And William will be fine. I can talk to him anytime." They smiled as Liyah started up the car and pulled off.

*****

Jaron just stood there, stunned, disappointed, confused, and swarming with emotions, not knowing what to feel. *She was right there, and I let her slip away. I didn't say one single word. I think about her every day. Most of the time, I can't go to sleep without thinking about her, and I didn't even say hi. I've waited so long for that opportunity, and I wasted it. I don't even know if she still works there anymore.*

The other guys' conversation had picked back up as William made his way back toward them. Tony stopped going back and forth with Troy.

"Man, Will you didn't tell me that your sister looked that good. And who was that with her? You said like a sister, which means she really isn't, huh?"

"Hey, that's my little sister man. Don't talk about her like that."

"Hey, I'm just saying what we all were thinking. I'm not trying to be disrespectful, but those were two beautiful women."

"Don't you guys remember that party I had late last year? My sister was there. I thought I introduced you guys. The only person who wasn't there was Jaron. He was outta town on business."

"Oh, I do remember," they all said together.

"Don't mind him," Troy chimed in. "He's just trying to change the subject and get the spotlight off him. We destroyed you guys, and I put in work on him." The guys all broke out into laughter and made their way to the cars.

Jaron lagged behind, feeling somewhat relieved that Troy had switched the subject. He didn't want to hear the guys talk about how beautiful MaKayla was. She didn't belong to him, but he didn't want anyone else thinking about her in that way.

Xavier slowed down until Jaron was next to him. "You all right man? You look like you just lost your best friend. I don't know if you've noticed, but I'm still right here."

Jaron tried to quickly change his expression in an attempt to throw Xavier off. "Yeah, yeah, I'm good. I just had a couple thoughts on my mind. Nothing major."

"You sure? Because you know I'm here if you need to talk."

"Yeah, I'm good man. And I know you got me if I need you."

They stood by the cars for about twenty minutes longer, discussing the games and planning out the night, before they all got in and drove off. They agreed to meet up at the bar and grill at seven, which gave them around three and a half hours to get ready and meet up there. Tony and Troy would drive to Jaron's house and ride with him, and they would pick up Xavier on the way.

The car ride back was quiet. There was a little conversation here and there but nothing extensive. Jaron was in another world, his mind completely fixated on MaKayla and his lost opportunity. He was on autopilot, just driving but not really thinking, at least not about where he was going. He replayed the situation several times in his mind, coming up with different things he could have said or things he could have done to get a better outcome.

He hadn't even really realized it, but he was driving down his block and close to his house. He shook it off, realizing he had dropped the other guys off and was now in the car by himself. *Well, at least I got to see her again. Man, she's so beautiful, even though she looked really nervous. I wonder why she was so nervous or looked that way,* he thought as he made his way into his house.

He immediately undressed and made his way into the bathroom. He stood under the shower, not moving, just allowing the water to run from his head down his body. His thoughts were flowing through his mind, and the water seemed to steady them, to put things into perspective, everything in its proper place. He thought about how at least now he knew that Liyah was William's sister. Even though he didn't want that to be the route that he took, at least he had a route outside of the café. It was a positive, but it wasn't enough to lift his spirits.

He stayed in the shower for an hour and fifteen minutes. It was five o'clock when he got out. He was starting to get dressed when he got a call from his mom. He thought about not answering. *Maybe she can sense what happened with MaKayla,* he thought. "Nah," he finally said. "Hey Mom," he said, answering the phone in an upbeat tone. They talked for about fifteen minutes, and she never mentioned MaKayla. They just talked about their days and about tomorrow since they were going to have a late lunch, or an early dinner, with everyone at three.

When they finally got off the phone, he just smiled and shook his head. *It's Saturday. Why would she call about MaKayla today? She knows that I only get to see her during the week at the café, so she has no reason to ask about her today. I wish I had told her about it though. She would've known exactly what to say to get my head back in the game. Maybe I'll talk to her about it tomorrow and try to get my mind off of it all tonight.*

*****

MaKayla and Liyah made it to MaKayla's place about fifteen minutes before the delivery truck arrived. They didn't talk much on the ride, just listened to the radio and randomly sang. MaKayla did all that she could to keep her mind off Jaron and the situation that had just happened, but it wasn't really working. *What's wrong with me?* she thought, shaking her head. *I'm never like this about any guy, so why am I like this about him? I mean, sure, he looked good standing there all sweaty and stuff, and Liyah's right, at least now I know his name. Jaron,* she thought.

She noticed Liyah looking at her out the corner of her eye, smiling. "Why are you smiling at me?" she asked Liyah curiously.

"What were you just thinking about?" responded Liyah.

"I wasn't thinking about nothing. Why?"

"Well, that nothing must have made you feel pretty good. I don't know if you've noticed or not, but you were just smiling."

"No I wasn't," MaKayla said, smiling. "I wasn't even thinking about anything to make me smile."

"I know. You were thinking about *nothing*." Liyah smiled, making sure to emphasize the word *nothing*. They both laughed as she pulled up in front of her place.

They talked and decorated until MaKayla got everything where she wanted them to go. Then she stood back, feeling accomplished, and smiled as she looked at everything and how it all came together. "I really like it. I mean, I liked it before, but now I really like it." They both laughed.

"Well, we're not done. We have a whole other place to decorate, remember?"

"How could I forget? You've talked about and planned the entire time we were doing mine."

"I know. I'm just excited. Plus, I want to see how the paint job came out, to see the finished product of it all."

"Okay. Let's go then. We can grab something to eat on the way over. I'm pretty hungry," said MaKayla.

"How do tacos sound?" asked Liyah with a smile on her face.

"It sounds like you're speaking the language of love via food." They both laughed as they walked out of the apartment.

*****

Troy arrived at six, and Tony got there fifteen minutes later. They instantly started talking about the game, who did what and why. Jaron just sat there, smiling. He really enjoyed being with the guys and the relationship they all had. They were like a band of brothers. They argued, fought, and looked out for one another just like brothers would.

They left at six thirty and went to get Xavier. He appeared to be in a real good mood, which made Jaron feel even better. When he got in the car, Tony asked, "Why are you so happy?"

"Why not? I mean, what's not to be happy about? Oh, well, I guess if I got whooped like you did today, I wouldn't be too happy either."

All the guys started laughing, except Tony. "Hey man, skip all that. Am I the only one who didn't know William was holding out like that?" The guys got quiet, and Jaron felt himself tense up.

"You're going to keep trying to go back to girls when you can't face the fact that you got whooped, huh?" said Troy.

Troy and Tony started going back and forth again, but Jaron didn't say anything. He just sat quietly. Xavier noticed Jaron's mood change but didn't say anything. He just sat back and pretended to get involved in the trash-talking. They made it to the bar and grill several minutes later. William and Daniel were already there, and Jaron pulled in next to them. The guys all got out and shook one another's hands as they walked toward the front doors.

"Hey Jaron, slow up man. Let me talk to you for a minute," said Xavier. "Hey, guys, go ahead and just order us the usual. We'll be there in a minute."

"Okay cool. Hurry up though. You know we have to wait for everybody before we can eat the food," replied Daniel.

"Okay. I know you're hungry, as usual." The guys all laughed and walked into the bar and grill.

Jaron waited for the guys to be inside before he asked, "So how'd everything go with Candace?" He assumed that was what he wanted to talk about.

"It went good. Thanks for that. But that's not what I wanted to talk to you about."

"Oh, I just figured, you know, because of last night and all. My bad. What's going on then?"

"That's exactly what I'm wondering. What's going on with you? And don't tell me it's nothing. Now if you don't want to talk about it, that's fine, but don't tell me it's nothing, because I can clearly see that it's something. You were fine until after we finished playing ball. Then next thing you know, you're off in your own world. You didn't even say anything when I got out the car. Then on the way here, I could see it all on your face. Maybe the other guys don't notice or you can fool them, but I've known you too long for you to be able to fool me."

Jaron sighed and leaned against his car. It was a beautiful night. The temperature hadn't dropped any, and the breeze was really light and consistent. He looked up at the sky. The clouds were moving slowly through the air. It was very clear, so there appeared to be stars everywhere.

Then there was the moon, and although it was glowing, it was alone. It sat there in the sky, close to all those stars, but not close enough to touch any of them. He figured that he was the moon and MaKayla was the stars. She was close, but he still couldn't touch her. He felt a gentle breeze blow across his face, and he closed his eyes and embraced it.

"Come on Jaron. Tell me something man. You're starting to get me worried."

"It's a long story man. No simple way to tell you."

"Well, it's a Saturday night, and neither one of us works tomorrow, so all we have is time. So what's up?"

Jaron sat there for a minute and finally let out a sigh. "Okay. It's about a girl. No one knows about her except my mom."

Xavier's concerned look turned into a smile. "A girl, huh?" he said.

"Yeah. I'm beyond infatuated with her. She works at the café. You know the one not far from my job that I always go to?"

"Yeah. It's like ten minutes away, right in the middle of the street."

"Yeah, that one. Well, anyway, the first time I saw her, I was stunned, like, speechless. It was crazy. This was months ago. I talked to my mom, and you know her. She's been on me about talking to her ever since that day—"

"Wait, wait, wait," said Xavier, cutting in. "You're telling me you saw this girl months ago and you've never said anything to her? It's been this whole time, and I'm just now hearing about her? What are you waiting for?"

"I don't know. The timing is never right. She's never been my waitress, and whenever I'm leaving, either she's busy or I'm in a rush. Well, except for two weeks ago—"

"Oh, okay. So you finally talked to her then?" Xavier stopped talking when he noticed the look that Jaron was giving him.

"Let me finish."

"Okay, okay. Go ahead."

"Well, two weeks ago, that Friday that I met with Mr. Wynstead, we went to the café for the business meeting, and she was our waitress. I couldn't believe that I had waited for that opportunity all that time. Then of all days, it happened when I was on a business meeting with him. So anyway, things went bad, and he ended up yelling at her and being completely disrespectful to the point where she walked off crying, then left like five minutes later, and we had a different waitress. I tried to explain that it wasn't her fault before I left, but you know I was with Wynstead, and I had to hurry up. That was why I didn't want to go to Cliché with you guys that night."

Xavier started to pull everything together in his mind. He still stood quietly and attentively, just listening and nodding when appropriate. He let out audible groans and moans when things clicked in his head or he was surprised.

"I went back the next week, looking for her to apologize for Wynstead and make sure she didn't get in trouble, but she was never there. The waitress that replaced her, however, was there. They appeared to be good friends, so I asked her about her, but she couldn't tell me too much because she was busy and I was in a rush. Then the next few days and last week, neither one of them was there.

"I went back three or four times last week, and neither of them was there. I think about this girl all the time. Most of the time, I wake up in the middle of the night, and all I can think about is her. It's the only thing that'll help me go back to sleep. I don't know if she is in a relationship, if she even looks at me in that way or anything, but I can't get her off my mind man."

"Okay, okay, okay. I'm following you, but what I don't understand is, what brought it out so much today?"

"Well, here's the crazy part. The waitress that replaced her, her name was Liyah." Xavier's mouth dropped, and he stood in shock. "She's William's sister, and this whole time, I never knew that while I was searching high and low for her."

"Get out of here. What a small world, huh? But wait, how did you not know that? William talks about her all the time, and she was at that party Will had last year," said Xavier.

"Well, if you remember, I didn't go to the party. I was out of town on business. Plus, Will goes back and forth between saying Liyah and Aaliyah, so it just never clicked."

"Ah, that's true. Makes sense," replied Xavier.

"Oh, wait. It gets better. The girl, the waitress that's got me losing my mind, well, her name's MaKayla. She's Liyah's best friend." Xavier stood silently, and a look of shock once again rolled across his face. Then out of nowhere, he started laughing hysterically. "Please tell me what is so funny about all of this, because I don't see it."

"Man, this is unreal. If I didn't know you the way I do, I'd be sure you were lying. This is, like something off of a soap opera or one of those ridiculous TV shows."

"Yeah, except that it's real, not TV."

"Okay. So the girl of your dreams and her best friend are William's sisters."

"Yes. How crazy is that?"

"So, wait, why didn't you say anything today when you saw her?"

"Okay, think about it man. What was I going to say? Plus, I was all sweaty, not to mention that all the guys were there. You know how the guys get when we're all together and girls come around, let alone someone trying to talk to one of them."

"Yeah, you're right. Probably best you didn't say anything. Well, maybe they didn't notice you."

"They definitely noticed me. I saw Liyah look at me, but I can't be sure about MaKayla. Then did you see how quickly they went to leave? I feel like I blew my one opportunity. I mean, of all days, why did it have to be today?"

"You know, that's the second time I've heard you say that during this conversation. You expect the clouds to open up, the stars to align, and things to fall perfectly in place? Nah, that's not you, not the Jaron I know, not the 'Where there's a will, there's a way' Jaron. You talk about how much you feel she could mean for you, but you're concerned about waiting on a perfect opportunity.

"You know how the saying goes. Nothing comes to those who wait but dreams or they miss the worm or something like that. You know how it goes." They both began laughing, and it helped Jaron feel ten times better. He understood exactly what Xavier was trying to say. "So was that what happened in the car on the way here? You started thinking about a missed opportunity?"

"Well, not really. It was more so the fact that Tony was talking about her the way that he was."

"Aw, I understand now," Xavier replied, shaking his head. "Man, don't worry about him. You know how Tony is."

"Yeah, but it's the fact that I can't say, 'Don't talk about her like that.' She doesn't belong to me, but I still don't want anyone talking about her or looking at her that way."

"I understand, but you know, if you say she's off-limits, then it's going to be respected."

"Yeah, you're right. I'm just not ready for all the questions and stuff, you know?"

"Yeah, but don't let this get you down. I mean, if anything, you should be happy about what happened today. It puts you closer to her in the grand scheme of things."

"Yeah, I know, but that doesn't mean it's going to be for the best."

"All you can do is what you can do, and let the chips fall where they may." Jaron dropped his head and let out a sigh. "It's not that bad man. Don't look like that," said Xavier.

"It's not that. Well, not exactly."

"What is it then?"

"You know when you told me about Candace being pregnant? A part of me was jealous, envious, of you."

"Really? Why would you have to be jealous of me?"

"I want that, you know, the support you get from her, a woman who has your back and looks out for what's best for you, a woman who wants to build a family with you. You told me that, and as soon as you dropped me off, I thought about having all of that with MaKayla. I envisioned me being in that situation with her. That's crazy, right?"

"It's funny because if it weren't for you, I don't know where I would be right now."

"What do you mean?"

"Man, I talked to Candace like you told me to, and I couldn't have made a better choice. She was glowing when I talked to her. Not only that, but she asked me what happened that brought this out of me. I told her that I talked to you. She lit up even more and was all excited, something about her being happy that I told someone about it, because that meant I was really all in. Then the fact that it was you and you supported us made her even happier.

"You being jealous of me is definitely crazy. I am only where I am because of you. You know it's going to come for you too all in due time. And as far as envisioning those things with her, that's far from crazy. You have to see the goal before you can ever work toward it. Anything that you can imagine, you can make reality. Seeing is believing. If a man cannot see his destination, he is bound to get lost.

"Now if you really feel this way, then you need to do something about it. It's like I was telling you earlier. It's all good that you envision these things, but vision without action is merely a dream. Now if you combine some actions with this vision, now that, that, my brother, will change your whole world. And if you're lucky, it'll create the world just the way you want to live in it." Xavier paused and looked somewhat concerned.

"What's wrong?" asked Jaron nervously.

"Did you just hear that?"

"Hear what?" Jaron asked as he cautiously looked around to see if he could see or hear anything out of the ordinary.

"All that knowledge I just dropped for you. It's like we switched roles or something. I think I should be a philosophy teacher. I mean, clearly, I'm just a wealth of knowledge. Someone should benefit from this—aside from you, of course. I know you may not be sure sometimes, but I do listen when you talk, and you know how your dad always talked to us. That man was always dropping knowledge. I guess it rubbed off, and it's my turn to repay the favor. You know, it would seem that the student has become the teacher."

Jaron began laughing and shaking his head. "Yeah, you did just really give me a better sense of things, and I appreciate that. So, Professor X, if you're done with tonight's lesson, let's go eat, because I'm starving."

"Wait. I got some more. Don't stop me now. I'm on a roll, and it feels good. They're just flowing from me. Someone should write all these down." They laughed as they walked to the front doors, then into the bar and grill to join the rest of the guys.

Chapter 15

It was ten o'clock when they finished Liyah's place, and MaKayla was tired. "I thought we would never finish. You had to change everything like ten times."

"I know, but I just want it to be perfect, you know?"

"Yeah, I can understand that," MaKayla said, taking a seat on the couch. She let out a sigh. "Man am I tired. You have any plans for tomorrow?" she asked Liyah.

"I'm supposed to be spending the day with Darrell. I don't know what we're doing, but he's been complaining that he hasn't been able to spend enough time with me over my break. He's actually supposed to be coming over tonight. Well, maybe. I told him I didn't know if I'd be too tired or not."

"Ah, now I see why everything had to be perfect. You know you're not tired. You've been bouncing around here like the energizer bunny since we came through the door." Liyah just laughed. "What time is he supposed to be coming?"

"I don't know. He's out with some of his friends now, so afterward, I guess. What about you? What do you have up for tomorrow?"

"Relaxation. It's the last day of my vacation, and I'm not doing anything but lounging. I may get up and go for a jog depending on how I feel, but other than that, I'll be lying around all day."

"I'm not surprised at all. You want something else to drink?" asked Liyah as she walked into the kitchen.

"No, I'm fine, but we can get ready to go if you're ready. I'm beat, and I know you have to get ready for tonight." MaKayla laughed.

"Now you know you're welcome here as long as you want. If you want, we can have a girls' night. I'll tell him that he'll just have to come in the morning."

"No, don't do that. I'll just fall asleep on you," said MaKayla as she stretched and yawned. "Besides, he's right, you two really haven't been able to spend a lot of time together. I know if I had someone, you'd be out the door in a heartbeat to give me my space."

Liyah laughed. "You will have someone sooner than you know. Who knows? His name might start with a *J*, and I'll be the one fighting to get some of your time."

"Yeah, sure. That sounds like that's precisely what will happen," said MaKayla sarcastically through a laugh. "But let's go. I don't want you to have to drive back too late."

"Okay," said Liyah as she took the last swallow of her juice and grabbed her car keys.

They discussed how they had to be back at work and school in just a day. They were both dreading it but looking forward to it at the same time. "Home stretch," MaKayla kept saying. "We're in the home stretch."

They arrived at her house. "Call or text me tomorrow if you aren't too busy," she said to Liyah as she got out the car and waved while walking into her front door. She took a quick shower and laid down. The day had gotten the best of her, and she found herself exhausted as she laid there. Her mind, however, was still up and running, going back over the events of the day.

She tried not to focus on Jaron, because she figured it might lead to another dream, so instead, she thought about how much she enjoyed spending the day with Liyah, how it put a nice cap on her time with her. *I look forward to us getting back to how we were. This will be the beginning of our great comeback.* MaKayla laughed, as she could hear Liyah saying those words. She laid there a little while longer, smiling, before she dozed off and went to sleep.

*****

The guys stayed at the bar and grill until it closed at 2:00 a.m. Jaron only had two drinks, so he was good to drive. He made it home a little after three and sat in his car for a little while, smiling. He was thinking about how much fun he had with the guys and how it had taken his mind off everything else.

He got out of his car and walked up to his front door, but before he went in, he turned and looked up and down the street for no particular reason. He just wanted to take it all in—the silence, the calm, the gentle breeze, and the beauty of the night. He turned and walked into the door with a smile on his face. "Today actually turned out to be a good day," he said as he put his keys down.

He took a shower and went through what he needed to do tomorrow. He wanted to have things ready for work before he left to go meet up with his mom and sisters. Also, he had a little cleaning and rearranging to get to before he left. He got out, dried off, and threw on some shorts to sleep in. He laid there for a while and felt sleep creep up on him, tugging at his eyelids. He didn't fight it. He just allowed sleep to take over and drifted away.

*****

MaKayla woke up around nine. The sun was streaming in through her window, and she could hear the birds chirping outside. She laid in bed for a while. She didn't feel tired but wanted to just rest everything—her mind and body. She knew this would be the last time she would be able to do this for a while, and she planned on taking full advantage of it. She planned out her day as she laid there—what she would eat for breakfast, taking a jog, and getting things ready for work and school tomorrow, along with a few other things.

After lying there for about twenty minutes, she got up and got dressed to go for her jog. She stepped outside and was immediately greeted by the sun. It was really warm but refreshing as well. She couldn't help but smile as she made her way to the sidewalk and began her route.

The streets were very busy. People were everywhere, talking, walking, laughing, and jogging. She took her new route through the park. She thought it might be a little clearer, but it was quite the opposite. There were people jogging on the trail, blankets for picnics were set up on the grass, and kids were all over—some with balls, others with kites, and some just running with bubbles.

She could see people setting up their grills, preparing to barbecue, with coolers close by. She couldn't help but smile. It reminded her of her vacation with her family and walking up and down the beach. She kept jogging until she was out of the park and back on the streets, heading toward her house.

Once she got back home, she took a nice, long shower, threw on some lounging-around clothes, and just sat down for a few minutes. "Eleven twelve. I guess I'll make some breakfast now," she said as she got up and made her way to the kitchen.

*****

Jaron had a very peaceful night, only waking up three times and only for very brief moments. Then he was sleep again. When morning finally arrived, he got up full of energy, ready to take on the day. He made a small breakfast and sat and watched a little TV while he ate. After eating, he picked out his clothes for the day as well as what he planned to wear tomorrow. Time seemed to be moving a lot faster than he had originally anticipated. It was already after eleven o'clock.

He started the projects that he had created for himself around the house, which weren't anything major—usual cleaning of the kitchen, minor rearrangements in the living room and bedroom, and changing the bathroom decor. It only took him about an hour and forty-five minutes to finish it all. He got his things together to take a shower and texted his mom and sisters before he got in to make sure everyone was still moving on schedule.

He got out of the shower thirty minutes later and had received several messages from them. They were all on schedule, and they all planned to meet up there. He responded, letting them know that he too, was on schedule and asked if anyone needed a ride. His sisters replied first, both stating no, followed by his mom, who wasn't even at home, so she, too would drive. *Looks like I'll be riding solo,* he thought with a smile after replying to them. He got dressed and turned on some music as he prepared his things for tomorrow.

He wanted to get a jump-start on the week and planned on going in early. *Considering the amount of work I had last week, this next week will probably be even busier. I need to keep on top of everything for the Thomas deal as well as keep up with the new projects that we're working on,* he thought as he continued to organize his briefcase. He began to smile as he thought of his work, because it made him think of the company and his father and of how much he felt he owed to them both and how much they kept him going.

Just a little further and we'll reach our goal, Dad. It's amazing that you saw this happening so long ago. All the encouragement and motivation, I don't know where I would be without it, he thought, shaking his head. *I just wish you were here to reach it with me.* He felt his mood begin to shift, and he began to feel sad. He sat on his bed and stared at the picture of him and his dad that was hanging on his wall.

"That was a good day, wasn't it?" he said softly, smiling at the picture. "I still remember us talking that day, the advice you gave me." He could hear his dad's voice in his head. "'We should never regret the things we do, only the things that we never did.'" He sighed. "That's just it. I feel like there's so much that we never did," he said, shaking his head.

He got up and walked downstairs. He stood looking out the window, trying to find something to get his mind out of its negative state. It was truly a beautiful day. There were flowers just beginning to bloom, the sun was out in full force, and people were everywhere. "There are hardly ever this many people on this block," he said out loud as he walked to the door. As he opened it, he instantly felt his mood change. He smiled. "Thanks Dad," he said as he stretched in the sun.

"Just remember one thing," his dad would always say. "You're my son, and that will always be a constant. It'll always be there and never go away." His dad had a funny way of creating metaphors, which were still relevant for him now. He usually had to ask his dad to explain. Sometimes, he would; but other times, he would simply say, "You understand. You just don't know you do. Trust me."

His dad was right. At that very moment, Jaron realized why his dad always told him that he was his son. It was for a moment just like this, when he needed his dad but he couldn't see or feel him. The sun reminded him of what he would always say. His dad was telling him that he would always be there and that there was no way to change it, just like the sun would always be there.

*****

MaKayla finished eating and began getting her things ready for the next day, making sure to have everything in order so she wouldn't have to rush in the morning. She planned to go for a jog, then to class, followed by work, which didn't start until twelve. She did a little cleaning up since the place was a little out of sorts from the night before, then sat on the couch to relax. "What will I eat tonight?" she asked herself. "I'll probably order out a little later and turn in early to make sure I'm well-rested to start this week off right."

She smiled while thinking about everything she and Liyah had discussed while decorating her place. *I'm really happy that we did this together. Now those memories will be stored here for me to always look back on. I think I'll watch a movie,* she thought, grabbing one from the entertainment stand and putting it into the DVD player. She let out a sigh of relief and sat back on the couch.

*****

Jaron went back upstairs and finished organizing his things for work. His mood was a lot better, and his thoughts had shifted to more positive things. After he finished, he made his customary walk through the house and left to go to the restaurant.

It's a good thing I left as early as I did, because this traffic is crazy, he thought as he sat at a red light. The streets were teeming. People were everywhere. The weather had really started to be nice on a consistent basis. It was clear that people were taking advantage of it.

He made it to the restaurant at two fifty. He decided not to wait in his car and to sit on the bench at the front of the restaurant. There were already people standing outside—some smoking, some just talking. *I guess they're busy today. These people are probably all wait-*

ing for a table, he thought. *I wonder if we have a reservation. Let me text them and see.*

Before Jaron could finish the text, his mom walked up. "Why are you sitting here by your lonesome?" she asked, smiling.

"Hey Mom," he said, returning the smile and getting up to hug her. "I didn't want to sit in the car on such a nice day, so I figured I'd sit up here."

"Yeah, it is a really beautiful day, but you were in your own world. You didn't even see me pull in, did you?"

Jaron smiled. "No, I actually didn't. Did you see me?"

"Yeah. I pulled in just as you walked to the bench to sit down. There sure are a lot of people out here waiting," said his mom as she looked around.

"I know. I was just about to ask you guys if we have a reservation."

"Yeah, Kelly made one for us. There they are now," said his mom, waving as his sister's car pulled into the driveway. Kelly and Jalin walked up five minutes later.

"Man, looking for a parking spot is like finding a needle in a haystack," said Jalin as he greeted their mom with a hug.

Jaron hugged Kelly, then shook Jalin's hand. "How are you doing man?" he asked.

"Everything good on my end. I can't complain."

"That's good to hear. I hope my sister's been treating you right," Jaron said jokingly as he nudged Kelly.

"I couldn't be happier," Jalin replied as he and Kelly looked at each other, smiling.

"Mom, your daughter is late as usual. It's already three ten," said Kelly.

"Let's just go in and get seated. I'll call her and tell her to just come straight in when she gets here," said Jaron.

"Okay," his mom replied, and they all walked toward the door. They made it to their seats a few minutes later.

"She said she'll be here in five minutes, so we should see her by the time we finish eating," joked Jaron.

"Leave your sister alone when she's not here to defend herself," replied his mom.

"Okay, but you know she's always late. We were all just talking a few hours ago. We were all on schedule. Now she's late."

"Well, it was a lot of traffic, and you know her. She probably left with just enough time to make it here at three."

"I bet you're right Mom. Sounds like something she would do. Hey Jalin, did you catch that game last night?" asked Jaron, attempting to quickly switch the subject after noticing the look on his mom's face. They discussed the game and other aspects of sports while looking over the menu. They had ordered drinks and were discussing appetizers when Shannon walked in.

"That had to be the longest five minutes I've ever experienced," said Jaron sarcastically. "I'm willing to bet that you're late to work all the time, aren't you?" Jaron looked at his mom and noticed the look on her face. "Now Mom, you clearly said, leave my sister alone when she's not here to defend herself, and viola, she's here."

His mom's expression didn't change. She just looked at him. "Okay, okay. I'll leave her alone for now, but when you leave, I'm going to be bothering her again." They all began to laugh. Shannon went around and gave everyone hugs, saving Jaron for last and making sure to pinch him as she hugged him. "Now Mom, tell me you saw that," said Jaron as he jumped back from Shannon's pinch.

"Well, you shouldn't have been bothering her." Jaron stood with his mouth open and with a slight smile on his face. "Oh, close your mouth before something flies in it and have a seat," said his mom, smiling.

They sat down and talked about work and the things going on in their lives. They ordered and ate. Jaron and Shannon constantly bothered each other, eating each other's food and poking fun at each other. It didn't help that they were sitting next to each other.

When everyone was just about done eating, mostly just finishing up drinks and his mom finishing her dessert, Kelly said, "I have some big news." Her face lit up as she grabbed Jalin's hand, and he smiled at her. They all looked at her, excited to hear what her big news was. "Well, I'm—I mean, we…we're going to have a baby."

There was silence for about ten seconds, and everyone sat in shock. Kelly eagerly awaited their response. "Are you serious?" asked their mom as she dropped her fork and stood up to give them a hug.

"Oh my God, you really are serious," said Shannon with a huge smile on her face. "I'm going to be an aunt. This is crazy. I'm so excited."

Everyone stopped when they realized that Jaron was still sitting in his chair, not moving or talking, just in shock. "Are you okay?" asked Kelly worriedly.

Jaron finally snapped back to reality. "Yeah, yeah, yeah," he said. "It's just the craziest thing for you to come and tell me this. Just Friday night, Xavier told me the same thing. Ironic, huh?"

"Xavier is going to have a baby?" asked his mom with a look of shock on her face.

"Yeah, I know. Crazy right? Come here sis. I'm so happy for you. Now I know why you were sick the other day. This was what that bug was," said Jaron, making quotation marks with his fingers. "Congrats Jalin. I can see the excitement all over your face. I'm really happy for both of you."

"Thanks, man. But to be honest, I was just as shocked as you were when she first told me. That shock quickly turned into happiness. Now I just look forward to being here with her through this whole process. It's scary and exciting at the same time," Jalin said as he rubbed Kelly's stomach.

"Okay, so when do we get to go baby clothes shopping?" asked Shannon excitedly.

"Slow down Shannon. I don't even know the sex of the baby yet."

"Well can you hurry that up? Because I'm ready to have my niece's or nephew's wardrobe on point. Ooh, what if it's two or even three? How cool would that be, getting a niece and a nephew or two at the same time?"

Kelly sat quietly, and Jalin quickly stepped in. "Let's just focus on having one for now, Shannon." Everyone began laughing.

"Yeah, you just hush and make sure you're on point for work, or should I say on time," said Jaron.

Shannon punched him in the arm. "Oh be quiet."

"Hey, hey now," said their mom. "So Xavier is really having a baby too, huh? Is it by that girl you were telling me about?"

SPRING SHOWERS—THE BLOOM

"Yeah, she's the one."

"Is he excited or what?" asked his mom, taking another bite of her dessert.

"At first, he was nervous, all over the place. But after we talked about it, he couldn't be happier."

"Well, that's good. Maybe that's what he needs to help calm his crazy self down." His mom smiled.

"So Jalin, what are you hoping for, a boy or a girl?" asked Shannon, her voice drifting off as Jaron went into a world of his own.

They stayed for another forty-five minutes before leaving. They discussed the baby and their excitement. They talked about how they were raised and the things they hoped to do with the baby, but throughout all the conversation, Jaron was physically there but mentally elsewhere.

He would occasionally smile, nod, or laugh if he noticed everyone else laughing; but his mind wasn't there anymore. He had so much going through his head. He was bombarded with so many different emotions that it made him tired, sad, and frustrated at the same time. His emotions were a huge melting pot of happiness, excitement, sadness, frustration, hopelessness, and loneliness; and then finally, he felt nothing. He was just numb to it all.

As they left, they all said their goodbyes, giving their hugs and kisses. Even more now, their mom was adamant about them having weekly get-togethers. She insisted that they make them happen more often.

"Come walk me to my car Jaron," his mom said after they hugged and kissed Kelly goodbye.

"Okay. Where did you park?"

"I'm just over here," she said, pressing her alarm button, causing the horn to go off. "So what's bothering you?" she asked as they walked to her car.

Jaron considered letting it all out, everything that was on his mind and that he had been stressing about, and telling her about MaKayla, Xavier, Kelly, and his envy of it all. But he thought better of it, and finally after a short pause, he said, "Nothing's bothering me. Why would you ask that?"

"Because I know you, and I know when something's wrong. You stopped talking and interacting once your sister made her announcement. It was obvious to anyone who was paying attention. Plus, you didn't even have any smart remarks toward your sister when she left. We both know that's not you."

Jaron smiled as he thought about how much he enjoyed bothering Shannon. "To be honest Mom, I don't know what's wrong. I feel like I'm being pulled in a million different directions emotionally. It's crazy. The last time I remember feeling like this was…was…"

"Was when?"

"The first day I went back to work after Dad died." His mom stood silently, as if she were searching for the right words, yet trying to get it all out. "I don't know Mom. I just have a lot on my mind, and I need to clear it out—well, better yet, sort it out."

"I understand," replied his mom as she gestured for him to come in to give her a hug.

"I'll come get you after I get off tomorrow. We'll talk about it all. Maybe we can go somewhere for dinner to talk."

"I'd like that," replied his mom as she hugged him tighter. That was the one thing that he loved and respected about his mother, the fact that she never pushed too hard for him to talk and allowed him space. She always put him in a position to figure things out on his own, but she also knew exactly what to say and when to say it. It seemed like it always came just in time.

"Okay. I'll see you tomorrow," he said, waving, as he walked away from her car and toward his.

The sun was starting to set, but it was still a beautiful day. Jaron sat in his car for a while, just staring and thinking, trying to get things together in his head. "I know what I need," he said as he started the car and made his way out of the parking lot. He drove for about thirty-five minutes before reaching the lakefront.

He parked his car and got out, beginning to walk toward the bike, walk, skate, and jog path. There were people everywhere. He could hear kids laughing and playing, dogs barking, bike bells ringing, and riders saying, "On your left," or, "On your right." He walked down the path for a while, taking it all in, trying not to think, just letting everything be.

*****

MaKayla had ordered pizza, which she knew would be there shortly, so she decided to stand outside and enjoy some of the beautiful weather while she waited. She looked at the sky and smiled at how beautiful it was, then closed her eyes as a gentle gust of wind blew across her face. It took her back to her vacation once again, and she could do nothing but smile as nostalgia brought the memories flowing back into her mind.

Her phone vibrated in her pocket, bringing her back to reality. It was Liyah: "Hey, I hope you're enjoying your last day of vacation before we go back to the grind. Darrell and I are on our way into the movies. Text you when I get out." She replied, "No need to. I'll probably be sleep. And if not, you should be giving him your undivided attention. LOL. But seriously, spend as much time with him as you can. I love you, and I'll talk to you later."

Her pizza came, and she went in and ate while watching another movie. Afterward, she took a shower and went to lie down in her bed. *Well, tomorrow, I'm right back at it again,* she thought. *Man, it would be nice to talk to Jaron or even see him again. Where did that even come from?* The thoughts broke off. She smiled and shook her head, then snuggled in comfortably into her bed. "Wishful thinking, I guess," she said, shrugging, and was off to sleep.

*****

The water was a beautiful blue. It looked as if it was the mirror image of the sky. He looked up as a skater whizzed by him and let out a sigh. *There's so much beauty here, so much elegance, so much happening, and all of it is oblivious to any negativity.* He made his way to the pier and walked toward the edge, the wind whipping up and becoming stronger as he reached the edge.

SEASONAL STORMS

This was the place where he came when his life became overwhelming, when he needed clarity and couldn't find it anywhere else. He could only remember his dad bringing him one time to watch the sunrise, but that one time was all he needed to remember. This place made him feel closer to his father than anywhere else.

He just stood for a while, listening to the waves, watching the boats, both close and far away, smelling the air, and feeling the wind on his skin. He sat down and looked at the sky, which was beginning to turn an orangish-red color as the sun began to set. "What do I do?" he asked softly as he felt the sadness swelling up inside of him. "Why am I so envious of the ones that I love the most? Why can't I just be happy for them? Dad, I need to talk to you. I need your advice more than ever now." He dropped his head, and a few tears streamed down his cheeks. He didn't wipe them away. He just let them roll until they jumped from his chin and onto the ground.

"Dad, is it possible to love someone if you've never talked to them? I mean, I know it sounds crazy," he said, laughing lightly, wiping his face. "But this girl is..." There was a long silence as he thought of the right words. "She's everything," he finally said. "And everything that I envy them for, I want it with her. I don't know why, and I don't know how, but I do. She means everything to me, and I can't even explain why."

Jaron was silent for a while, occasionally shaking his head and wiping his face, although the tears had stopped. "Then there's the whole Mr. Thomas deal and the company. It's a lot Dad. I mean, it's what I want and feel we need, but it's a lot of work. I want my life to matter and to make a difference, but I don't want it to be all work. I want someone to share my life with, forever. I miss you Dad, more than you could possibly know. I think we all do, but I know I do."

Time flowed by, and he sat there quietly, just staring off into the darkness, which had now covered the sky. Only small dots of light could be seen on the horizon from the boats out there. He thought about all that he had said and all that he felt, and he remembered talking to his dad after he lost in a championship basketball game in high school. He and his dad were sitting on the steps of their porch on a night much like this one.

"Hold your head up son," his dad said as he gently lifted Jaron's head by his chin. "It's not about winning every battle. It's more important to win the war. You're so young son, and you have so much life in front of you. Just remember that as long as you're alive, as long as you're still standing, you can succeed. As long as you have those two things, there's hope.

"There is no such thing as a failure, only an opportunity to learn, an opportunity to become better. Even when your whole world seems to be crashing down all around you, let the dust settle, take a step back, and realize something that maybe you can't see because you're standing among what appears to be so much, so much loss and devastation.

"See, many lose sight of the forest when standing in the middle of the trees. But when you take that step back, you'll realize something very important. You're still standing son. There's still hope. There's still a chance. That's what tomorrows are here for. You have to keep going. Difficult roads lead to the most beautiful destinations. And nothing, son—and I do mean nothing—worth truly having, ever comes easy."

Jaron heard the all-too-familiar words again. "Sometimes, it's okay to make decisions with your heart and not your head, because your heart cares more. Your head is always worried, cautious, and sometimes afraid." A smile rolled across Jaron's face as he remembered his dad's words, as if he had come and spoken directly to him. "I love you Dad. Thanks," he said as he stared out into the darkness for a little while longer.

I have to make my world what I want it to be. It's all right here for me to do. I just have to do it. Nothing is permanent in this world, not even our troubles. Jaron turned and walked back down the pier and got in his car. He sat there for a while longer, watching the waves roll in and the happiness on the people's faces as they rode or walked by. He let out a sigh of relief, started his car, and drove home happy and excited to see what the future would bring.

Chapter 16

MaKayla awoke to her alarm clock blaring. She slowly rolled over and turned it off, then sat up and stretched, letting out a long and fulfilling yawn. *I feel like I haven't slept in days, and this is coming after a long, well-rested vacation,* she thought. *I'd better get up and get my day started. I have to get myself back in the routine of things.* She went to the front door and opened it but immediately closed it as a gust of cold air blew its way in, leaving her shivering. *Man, so much for nice weather. Even still, I'm going for a jog.*

She began to get dressed and plan out her day in her head, then stepped onto her front stoop and bent down to tie up her shoes. The sun was out but completely covered by clouds—not rain clouds, just gloomy light-gray clouds that seemed to mope around the sky like their world was coming to an end. She stretched once more and began her jog. She didn't check the temperature before she left, but the way it felt plus the fact that she could see her breath, she figured it was in the mid to low forties.

There weren't many people out jogging, walking, or driving. She attributed that to it being a Monday morning. She took the new route through the park, but even there, things were gloomy. Not even the animals were out, and there were no people on the trail. She made it back home in about twenty-five minutes and felt like she was fully energized. "Just what the doctor ordered," she said through a smile as she walked through the front door.

It's 8:07. There's more than enough time to make some good things happen, she thought. "No class until ten and no work until twelve. I can get some good studying in today," she said as she walked to the kitchen and put her teapot on the stove. She loved drinking tea but hated for it to be too hot, so she would let the teapot get extremely hot, then make her tea, get in the shower, and let it cool down.

*****

Jaron sat on the edge of his bed and followed the few rays of sun that crept through the curtains, staining the wall as they spread further and further toward the ceiling. He had been up since six, and no matter what he did, he couldn't get back to sleep. However, he wasn't tired. On the contrary, he was wide awake and energized. There was something new that he was feeling, something he couldn't quite put his finger on. He had a very optimistic feeling, a new motivation, so he was extremely excited to get his day going.

He turned off his alarm a minute before it began going off. *Seven forty-four. This will be the beginning of something good,* he thought as he stood up and stretched. He gathered what he needed and made his way to the shower. He had a million different thoughts flowing through his head, and he did his best to organize them, although the more he organized them, the more they came. *This is a good problem to have,* he thought as he stood in the mirror, brushing his teeth.

He quickly made two sausage patties and some eggs. He used that and cheese and the croissants he had to make two sandwiches for breakfast. "Ah, that hit the spot," he said as he finished off the last of his glass of orange juice. He got dressed and did his regular routine of making sure everything was in order before heading out the door. He went back in to grab his peacoat, because the weather was a bit chilly.

He drove to work in silence as he further attempted to organize the thoughts that were running loose through his mind. Once he made it to work, it was as if a switch flipped and turned everything off. All his thoughts were together, and he had a clear idea and focus for the day. This only raised his motivated feeling from earlier that day.

"Good morning Mr. Coleman," came Krystal's voice from behind the desk. "You look, um—I don't know—like you're on a mission. Is everything okay? If it's something bad, I didn't do it," she said through a smile in an attempt to lighten the mood.

"Good morning Krystal. Yes, everything is fine. Actually, better than fine. They're great. But if anything goes wrong, I'm coming to look for you, because by denying nothing, I'd say you're guilty of something," he said, laughing. "You were correct in your assessment of my mood. I definitely feel motivated, like a man on a mission."

"Well, I'm glad everything is great, and I really hope you accomplish that mission that you're on."

"I'll do my best," he said as he entered the elevator, and they both laughed.

*****

After getting out of the shower, MaKayla made herself a bowl of oatmeal and cut up some strawberries to go in it. She sat eating her breakfast and drinking her tea while listening to music. She had her motivation playlist on to prepare for the day and get her back in the groove of things. She cleaned her dishes and made sure she had everything that she needed for the day. *Wouldn't want to have to rush back because I forgot something,* she thought while smiling, then made her way out the door.

Her phone vibrated as she made her way into her classroom. It was Liyah. "Good morning. Just a few more weeks and we'll have this semester in the bag. I work at three today. See you there." She ended it with a kissy-face emoji, which put a smile on MaKayla's face. "Good morning. Yes, let's make some good things happen these last few weeks, and I'll definitely see you there." The text message gave her a heightened sense of motivation, but she didn't really know why. *Oh well, I'll just take it in stride,* she thought as she took her seat.

This was her only class for the day and was scheduled for an hour and a half but usually let out about fifteen to twenty minutes early. The time seemed to fly by, and before she knew it, the teacher was dismissing them. MaKayla looked down at her notebook and noticed how many notes filled the paper, and a smile washed across her face. *Right back in the groove of things. Haven't missed a beat,* she thought as she packed up her things.

"Ms. Thomas, can I speak to you for a moment?" came her teacher's voice from the front of the classroom.

A chill went up her spine, and her smile disappeared. *Am I in trouble? Did I not do something?* she thought as she walked to the teacher's desk. "Is everything okay, Mrs. Simmons?" she asked nervously.

"Of course it is. Why wouldn't it be?" replied her teacher as she looked up from a paper she was reading. "I just wanted to make sure everything was good with you. I enjoyed that final assignment that you turned in before break. You cut it somewhat close to the time deadline."

"Oh yeah, to be honest, it slipped my mind in my excitement and rush to prepare for my vacation. I'm glad that you enjoyed it though. I was worried that by rushing, it wouldn't be my best work."

"Well, no worries. You did great. But let me know if you need anything or things are becoming too much. I don't want you to get overwhelmed. I know I'm not supposed to say this, but you're my favorite student, and I really think that you'll do great things in the future. You know what I was curious about?"

"What's that?" responded MaKayla curiously. The teacher's previous statements had added a boost to her already high morale.

"Have you ever considered doing something in the field of social work? I know it's different from owning your own restaurant, but from reading your paper, I got the idea that it's as much, if not more, about helping and serving people as it is about the food. I mean, you even plan on having a program where the homeless eat for free. There isn't anything like that around here, and I definitely think it'll be vital."

"Wow, I never thought about social work. It does seem like a different end of the spectrum to me. I mean, it's mostly working with people with some sort of issue, and I don't mean that in a bad way. I'm just saying."

"No, no, you're right, but I know that you have a heart of gold and that you're always trying to help people. Plus, you love children, and they're a large percentage of the population that you'd be working with. I'm not trying to change your career goals. I'm just wondering if it's something that you've ever thought about or perhaps something you could consider incorporating into them."

"That actually sounds like a good idea and definitely something to give thought to. Maybe I could do some sort of food program or something like that. Thanks Mrs. Simmons. And between you and me, you're my favorite teacher too, but shh," said MaKayla as she placed her finger to her lips. "Wouldn't want that cat getting out of the bag." They both began laughing. "It's definitely something I'll give some thought to, but I have to get to work. I'll see you next week?"

"Sure thing. And I need to be heading to my other class too."

*****

As soon as the elevator doors opened, Jaron was pleasantly surprised when he saw that the office was already in midday form. It caught him off guard, and he stood staring until the elevator doors began to close. Then he hurriedly exited the elevator.

Tina sat at her desk, smiling. "Why do you look shocked and surprised?"

"I don't know, to be honest. It's just weird. I woke up with this huge feeling of motivation, and it would seem that the rest of the office did too."

"Well, that's good, because you'll need it."

"What do you mean?" asked Jaron, looking somewhat concerned.

Tina pulled out a stack of papers. "Well, there are twenty messages for you already, five of which are complaints. It's something about them being overcharged for their orders."

"Oh, get me Keith from sales. I'll have to make sure we've changed all the prices in our systems to match the new promotion. More than likely, that's the issue with those. Also, can you have Tim come to my office? No rush, but as soon as he gets a free moment. You know what? On second thought, I'll call Tim."

"Okay. Whatever you say. Oh, and I forgot to write one down, but Mr. Thomas called too. He said something about wanting to discuss numbers with you."

"Okay. Thanks Tina. I don't know if I say it enough, but I truly appreciate all that you do."

"As you should. I mean, I'm the best," Tina joked. They both laughed.

As Jaron entered his office, his mind started going full speed even though he had barely crossed the threshold. He put his things away while opening up his laptop. As if she had some form of ESP, Tina shouted, "Don't forget to call Mr. Thomas."

He just smiled. "Thanks Tina." He had forgotten just that quickly, so he grabbed a Post-it and made himself a note. Within fifteen minutes, there was a knock at his door. "Come in," he answered. In walked Keith, a rather big Hispanic man. He stood over six feet four inches and weighed close to 280 pounds. "Keith, I need you to run a price change check through your entire department."

"Is something wrong?" asked Keith.

"I have five messages from this morning from clients claiming that they were overcharged on their orders. I know we just rolled out that promotion, so can you make sure all the necessary changes were made?"

"Sure. I'll get right on it."

"Oh, and here are the order numbers of the clients who claim to have been overcharged. After you do the price checks, look up their orders and see if the prices they were charged match ours or if they were charged incorrectly. Then shoot me an email with what you find."

"Okay. No problem," said Keith as he grabbed the paper and exited the office.

After checking a few emails and responding to them, Jaron called Tim and asked him to come to his office as soon as he had a free moment. From the conversation, Jaron figured it would take Tim at least thirty minutes before he had the time to come, so he decided to call Mr. Thomas. He couldn't figure out why, but he felt nervous, as if this was his first time talking with Mr. Thomas. But once he heard the first ring, the nerves were gone.

"Hello. Mr. Thomas's office," came the voice on the other end of the phone.

"Yes, this is Jaron Coleman. He requested me to give him a call. Is he available?"

"One moment please."

"Hey, Jaron, how are you?" came Mr. Thomas's voice from the other end. It startled Jaron for a moment.

"I'm doing pretty good. How about yourself?"

"I'm doing good. Can't complain, and even if I could, I still wouldn't. What good would that do?"

"I couldn't have said it better myself." They both laughed briefly.

"So let's talk numbers just me and you before we get everyone else involved. I don't look at this as just a business relationship. I feel like what you're attempting to build completely embodies my values and views for the future, so I don't want you to think that I'm just doing this for simple monetary gain. I believe we can benefit so much more from this partnership than just financially.

"To be honest, there may be a point in the immediate future where we break even or may even have to take a loss financially, but it'll benefit us long-term for the vision." Jaron was speechless. He sat there quietly for a moment until Mr. Thomas's voice brought him back. "You still there Jaron?"

"Yeah, yeah, I'm here. That just caught me off guard."

"I know, I know. None of us goes into business to lose money, and no one wants to lose money, but sometimes, you have to lose a few battles in order to win the war."

Once again, Jaron was quiet; but this time, he caught himself before Mr. Thomas had the opportunity to say anything. "I apologize for my long pauses, but now I know exactly why you were so high on my father's list of partners. You sound just like him. We had so many conversations where he said the exact same things to me. I mean, we built this company on those fundamental beliefs. Wow."

"Your father was a phenomenal man, and I was looking forward to being in business with such an honorable person."

"Thank you. I truly appreciate that."

"I can't see how this wouldn't be a strong, successful relationship for both of us. I just want you to know, first and foremost, that you will not be selling or giving me a majority portion or even a large portion of your company per the terms of our deal. Your ownership stakes will remain the way they are."

"That's good to hear, but to be honest, I wasn't even concerned about you having a portion of the company."

"Okay. Well, what is the main reason you're looking to do this deal?"

"Well, I believe 100 percent in the method in which I conduct my company, and I believe that it's the most beneficial to the people we serve. I just cannot shoulder the full financial load of expanding our services throughout the entire country—well, not initially, at least."

"What do you mean initially?"

"Well, from my financial department's information, if we expand as is, we could be looking at eighteen months at the least before we break even, and that's with our prices remaining the same, no promotions or anything. I have been trying to create an account that would allow this company to weather such a financial lull, but with the way my business has been going thus far, it hasn't been going so well."

"Hmm," said Mr. Thomas. "That is a steep hill to climb, so I can see where the issue comes in."

"I don't want to jeopardize the integrity that we've spent so long building or the great relationship we have with our clients. I think that would work against the main goal. I also don't want it to negatively affect my employees. They work so hard and deserve to be rewarded for their efforts. I don't want to have to put a freeze on raises or even decrease pay. If anything, I'd like to increase it. I guess you could say it's a case of wanting my cake and eating it too."

Mr. Thomas erupted into laughter. "I never understood that saying. I mean, if it's your cake, why shouldn't you be able to eat it?"

Jaron began laughing. "Yeah, I know what you mean."

"So how much do you think this partnership will benefit you—financially, that is?"

"Well, if you're referring to me, as in my company, then it would benefit us greatly to help carry us over that financial lull without having to worry so much about money and focus on supplying the best product and service that we can, not to mention the knowledge and expertise you have to offer for traversing the different business landscapes. Now if you mean personally, it wouldn't financially benefit me at least for two to three years. I plan to put a freeze on my income for that time period to ensure that the company is stable before I consider a raise or a bonus."

"Are you serious?" exclaimed Mr. Thomas. "You don't want to freeze your employees' income, but you'll freeze your own?"

"Of course. Why not? I mean, it's not like I'm going to starve. Seeing the company flourish and the people who have been here so long get much-deserved promotions is more than enough payment for me."

"Your father was right, you're almost too good to be true."

Jaron sat there staring at his dad's picture and began smiling. He started to let his mind drift. His dad's smile came into focus, and even though he didn't say anything, he could feel his presence. "I learned from the best, so I guess we have him to thank for that."

"To be honest, I've never met anyone like you, especially not so young. I mean your father, sure, but there's a uniqueness about you. This gives me even more confidence and excitement for us to get started, so let's get down to the numbers, if you don't mind."

"I can't begin to explain to you how excited I am about this and our future together either, so let's get to it."

"Okay. So I don't have a round figure to give you yet. This is just to make sure that we are in the same ballpark, numbers-wise. After doing some research and running the numbers, we're willing to offer you two-thirds of your company's worth. In addition, we will front the necessary funds for all upstart operations for future facilities, personnel, and necessary materials and equipment for the next three years. There are other aspects of this deal that would need to be hashed out, of course, but I figured that this would be enough for a starting point. How do you feel about my initial offer? Am I way off or close or what?"

Jaron did not respond. He was shocked. He couldn't believe that he could more than double his company's worth with this deal, not to mention the upstart cash that he would no longer have to worry about.

"Did I lose you? Hello? Hello?"

"I'm... I'm still here. I... I just don't know what to say."

"I apologize if I'm off by that much, but I honestly felt like that was a quite substantial offer."

"Substantial? That is more than substantial. I can't believe what you just told me. It seems impossible. I know business details are kept private, but you more than doubled my last offer, and that didn't include the start-up cash. On top of that, you're not even asking for a majority stake in my company. This is a once-in-a-lifetime situation. I know deals like this don't come along very often, especially having the opportunity to work with someone like you. I don't know what to say other than thank you."

Mr. Thomas chuckled a little bit. "You had me worried there for a moment when you didn't respond."

"Sorry about that. I was just taken aback by your offer and didn't know how to respond. It caught me off guard."

"Well, I'm glad that you agree with my offer. That's a great sign. We didn't even have to negotiate. That's not to say the details don't still need to be hashed out, but I'd say we're off to a great start. So I'll get this over to financial and have them draw up a more precise, detailed plan and have it sent to you in the next week or two so that it can be finalized when you come down here next month."

"That sounds like a plan to me. I look forward to our meeting," said Jaron elatedly.

"All right. Well, you have a good, productive day, and if you need anything, don't hesitate to call."

"You do the same, and I'll make sure to do that." After hanging up, Jaron just leaned back in his chair and began staring at the ceiling. A smile slowly crept across his face, and an unfamiliar feeling of elation washed over him.

"Must be good news."

Jaron sat up quickly, brought back to reality by the voice. In his doorway stood Tim, a very small man, no more than five feet in height and weighing about 110 pounds. He had a full, thick beard but looked rather young in his facial features.

"Nope, it was great news, the best I've had in a really long time."

"Well, that's what I love to hear. Really the best way to start off the work week," replied Tim as he took a seat. "So what new idea will we be discussing today?"

Tim was in charge of production and new product concepts. Jaron would bounce all his ideas off him. Tim was whom Jaron liked to call his mad scientist. Regardless of how impossible they seemed, he would bring them to Tim and see what it would take to make them possible. This would be the topic of discussion once again.

Jaron had two new ideas he had been bouncing around inside his head since the night before. He was sure that with Tim's help, he could make them into real products, not just ideas. Jaron walked to his door and told Tina that he would be in a meeting and to hold all calls unless it was an emergency. He knew that any distractions could be the difference between success and a waste of time.

"Sure thing, Mr. Coleman. I'll be going on my break in about fifteen minutes. Will that be an issue?"

"No. Just forward the calls to me until you get back. We'll just hope that no one calls."

They all laughed as he closed the door.

*****

MaKayla decided to walk to work since the temperature had climbed to the low seventies and there was a nice breeze. She began thinking about what her teacher had just told her and how she could really see herself making a difference in that way. *I wonder what Dad would say. He's not just all business and profits. He likes to make a difference too. I'll give him a call sometime this week and run it past him to see what he thinks,* she thought as she stared up at a passing cloud.

The streets had become a lot busier since morning, when she took her run. Now there were people everywhere, cars constantly flowed up and down the streets, and animals were all over the place. She allowed her eyes to follow four birds as they flew to and from the trees. She imagined they were playing an elaborate game of tag or whatever version they had created for themselves. She thought back to the days of her playing with her brother and how he would always let her win. She never thought about it back then, but now that she was older, she knew that was what he did.

She smiled and let out a soft chuckle while shaking her head. He was such a good, sweet person, not tainted by the ugliness of this world. *He was pure and genuine,* she thought as she lost sight of the birds through some trees. *Man, I really miss him.* How could she miss him the way that she did when she was so young and so much time had passed since it all happened? She often thought about this. Did she really even miss him or just the idea of what he could have been?

Okay, it's time to stop thinking about this before I start to get sad. It's time to think about something more positive. For whatever reason, the first thing that came to her mind was Jaron and his hand on hers that day at the café when she wasted the tea. She smiled once again and shook her head as she opened the door and entered the café. For some strange reason, she wasn't bothered anymore by him coming through her mind like she was in the beginning. She had come to rather enjoy his visits and actually looked forward to it.

Although she kept denying it to herself, she hoped that he would come into the café that day just for the opportunity to see him once again. It was fairly empty when she walked in, which surprised her considering how busy the streets had been. *It'll probably pick up a little later,* she thought.

"Well, welcome back. I hope you enjoyed yourself while you were gone. Didn't miss us too much now, did you?" came Mr. Stacy's voice as he exited the back room.

A smile immediately came across MaKayla's face. "Actually, the answer to both of your questions is yes. I did enjoy myself, but I also missed you all a lot. I actually was wondering how things were going here while I was gone."

"Oh, you didn't think we could manage without you, huh?"

MaKayla smiled again. "You know that's not what I mean. You know how I am."

"Yeah, I do, and I know what you mean. I'm just messing with you. Things have been okay. A few of your regulars were looking for you though, and this place missed you just as much as you missed it."

"Well, I'm back now, so no need for me to be missed." They both smiled and walked into the back room.

*****

Just as MaKayla figured the café got busy about an hour later, she was already back in her groove, running four tables at a time and not missing a beat. It actually made her happy that she could get right back into the swing of things. She noticed Mr. Stacy smiling at her several times as she exited the back room with trays of food in both hands, maneuvering her way through the café like a ballerina in her prime. Before she knew it, in walked Liyah, who stopped and smiled at her as she entered the back room.

"Why are you smiling like that?" asked MaKayla as she arranged plates of food on the next set of trays scheduled to go out.

"Home sweet home, huh?" replied Liyah, making a rather dramatic spin and gesture with her hands and arms. They both laughed.

"You're so crazy, but I'm definitely glad to see you. We've been swamped these past few hours. It's like we're the only place open or something."

"Well, that's a good thing," said Mr. Stacy as he came out of his office. "Welcome back, Aaliyah. It would seem that the terrible twosome is back together," he said sarcastically through a smile.

"We prefer the dynamic duo, and I know you missed me. You don't have to hold it in. I understand," said Liyah as she put on her apron and flashed a smile.

MaKayla began laughing. "I don't know what you're going to do with her, but whatever it is, make sure it involves taking care of some of these customers."

"Oh, I'm on it. Don't you worry," he said as MaKayla exited the back room, hands and arms filled with trays of food once again.

She didn't have time to say it, but she was happy to see Liyah—not just because they were busy but because she missed her, even if it had only been a day since she last saw her. She was getting used to the idea of things going back to the way they used to be, and she planned on fully embracing it.

Chapter 17

Jaron and Tim found themselves sitting in his office for hours, discussing the multitude of methods for bringing to life the ideas that were swimming around his head. They ordered pizza for lunch so that they wouldn't have to stop working. By the time they were finished, it was five minutes to three.

"Wow, I can't believe we spent the whole day on this," said Tim, surprised.

"Yeah, me neither, but I feel like we got a lot accomplished, which is a definite plus."

"I would agree. So I'll try to formulate a sounder plan and get back to you on what we'll need to make these things happen."

"Okay. And once you do that aspect, I'll schedule another meeting, not just pull you from work like I did today." They both laughed.

"You can pull me from work to talk about new ideas whenever you want to." Tim collected his things and began to walk out the door. "Would you like this door open or closed?"

"Open. And can you ask Tina to come in here please," replied Jaron as he opened his email.

"You wanted to see me?" asked Tina as she walked in with a handful of papers.

"How did the day go? Anything of importance that I should know about?" He never looked up at her when he spoke. He was too busy looking through his emails.

"No, I wouldn't say that there was anything of urgency, but you do have a nice amount of messages here. There are quite a few of these that are about issues with invoices, clients feeling like they've been overcharged." He finally looked up as she finished talking, and she handed him the stack of messages. "I separated them for you.

The invoice issues are on blue paper, and the rest are on white. I figured they might be of a higher priority and you'd want to handle those first."

"Thanks. I appreciate that. And you were right in thinking that way." His eyes went back to his laptop as he placed the notes on his desk. "I'm trying to see if Keith has emailed me his results yet about the price change checks I asked him to do. It should give me a better idea of how to approach these other clients if he has."

"I would think he has, because he was up here a few hours ago, coming to see you, but I told him you were in a meeting. One of those messages in there is about him, so I figured he probably emailed you about whatever he was coming to talk to you about."

"You're right once again. He did email me. It looks like he found several items that had been overlooked or missed when we ran the promotion."

"So what would you do in a situation like this? Just refund what we overcharged them?" asked Tina curiously.

"Well, I'll definitely refund them what we overcharged and probably give them a credit of 10 percent of the value of their order. Just have to run it past financial and inform Keith in sales so there's no discrepancies again or any more confusion."

"Wait. If you're the…in charge"—Tina smiled, catching herself before she called him boss—"then why do you need to run anything past anyone?"

Jaron smiled, realizing that she was about to call him boss again. "Because we're a team, and even though I may be in charge, I can't make all the decisions myself, especially when it will affect someone's job. Plus, I don't know all the numbers and how my one decision could affect something else down the road. There's no point in having such a capable staff if I don't allow them to do their job. One of the main things I've learned from my dad is to not try to do it all myself. It'll only make things worse."

"That makes sense. Good to keep everyone in the loop."

"How did your day go?" Jaron asked as he sat back in his chair, smiling.

"I just told you. Remember when I first came in?"

Jaron smiled a little more. "No, you told me how the day went as far as messages for me, not how it went for you or how you're doing."

"Oh," she replied emphatically. "I'm doing pretty good. Got a positive feeling. I can see some good things happening this week."

"I would have to agree with that prediction. Actually, some good things have already happened, but I'll fill you in more once I get things finalized."

"Now you know that you can't do me like that. I'm going to want to know." She smiled.

"My apologies, but I don't want to jinx anything, and once I get it finalized, I'll have all the details to give you instead of bits and pieces."

"Okay, okay. I'll wait, then," she said, playfully pouting.

"How much longer do you plan on being here today?"

"I'm almost done, so probably about an hour, maybe a little longer. What about you?"

"I'll probably stay until around five, then cut out. Me and my mom are going out to dinner, so I'll just leave here and head right over there."

"Oh, okay. Where are you guys going?"

"I don't know. I haven't really thought about it yet."

"Just leave it up to your mom. She has good taste."

"Oh, so does that mean that I don't?" Jaron smiled.

"I plead the fifth. Hey, is that my phone ringing? Oh, sorry. Gotta go," she said, laughing, and she walked out the door.

"Yeah, sure, you plead the fifth. And I don't hear anything," Jaron said, smiling.

He texted his mom, "Are we still on for tonight?" Then he set his phone down and turned his chair toward the window. The sun had come out and was shining brightly. From the way the people who were now filling the streets were dressed, he could tell that the temperature was warmer.

He noticed a couple walking hand in hand, and a smile crept across his face, but it quickly went away as he realized that he didn't make it to the café today. *What would I even do if I see her? I wouldn't even know what to say.* He attempted to change his thoughts as he realized they were making a turn toward the negative.

Just then, his phone vibrated. It was his mom. "I'm glad you texted me, because I almost forgot. Been a hectic day at work. What time will you get to the house?" He smiled as he thought about his mom and how she must have looked when she remembered they were having dinner today. "I'll be there at six at the latest." She replied, "Sounds like a plan to me. See you then."

He set his phone back down and turned his attention back to the street. The day had been a productive one, and the thought of what was to come made him happy. He let out a deep, satisfying sigh. "It won't be long now," he said. "It won't be long now." He spun back around to his desk and began working on his laptop. He lost himself in the work, and by the time he looked up again, it was already five minutes to five.

"Oh shoot, I'd better get out of here, because I know how my mom hates when I'm late," he said as he closed down his laptop and rushed around his office, attempting to make sure all was right before he left. He gave one last look over everything, closed the door and made his way to the elevator in a somewhat rushed fashion. His floor was empty, but there were still a few people working in the office. The silence gave him a weird feeling of satisfaction, of accomplishment and completion.

*****

The day stayed busy until around seven o'clock. That was the first time MaKayla actually got to take a break and sit down. Before long, Liyah was sitting right next to her. It took a little nudge to bring MaKayla back to reality. She had drifted off into her own world again and didn't even notice.

"Oh, when did you get here? I didn't even see you sit down."

"I've been here. You were just staring off into the ceiling. I tried to see what you were looking at, but my eyes don't see what your eyes see."

"Well, that's because I wasn't looking with my eyes. I was looking with my brain." There was a slight pause, and they both began laughing.

SPRING SHOWERS—THE BLOOM

"The funny thing is, I believe you."

MaKayla playfully nudged Liyah. "Hey, you better watch it. But I really was," she said, flashing a smile. "It's been a long day, and I'm glad it's dying down out there. Oh yeah, so how did it go with Darrell? Did he like the makeover we gave your place?"

Liyah smiled nervously and began to fidget with her hands a little. "Um, it was good. Um, you know, nothing special, just normal. And he really liked the changes." She flashed a fake smile after a nervous little chuckle.

MaKayla turned to face Liyah. Curiosity flooded across her face, and her eyes squinted as if she was looking for something that was hard to see. Liyah was still looking away, and the fidgeting increased. It almost looked as if she was in pain. "What aren't you telling me?"

"What? What do you mean? I told you, it was just normal. Oh yeah, and he liked the way the place was set up and the things that were added."

MaKayla sat back in her chair and crossed her legs, letting out a soft chuckle. "You said that already."

"I did? I must've forgotten."

"So we're going to play this game, huh?" she asked sternly with a playful grin on her face.

"I don't know what you're talking about," replied Liyah, looking down at her hands. The fidgeting increased.

"Okay. I'll play along, but being that I'm your best friend and I know you better than you know yourself, I must say, I don't think it'll be fair." Liyah didn't respond and wouldn't make eye contact, but a slight grin slid across her face. "Okay, so stop me when this sounds familiar. Remember Travis—"

"Okay, okay, okay, yes, you know I remember Travis. He was my first, and I tried to keep it from you, but you knew anyway."

MaKayla just smiled. "Continue," she said as her grin grew.

"You're lucky I love you and I suck at keeping things from you, but…" Liyah let out a sigh. "So me and Darrell went out last night, as you know, but when we got back to my place, it was already really late. Plus, we'd been drinking, so we figured that it would be best if he just spent the night." Liyah stopped talking and looked at MaKayla, smiling.

"I know that's not all, because you two have spent the night together before, so what else?"

Liyah's smile turned back into a nervous grin. "Okay, so we took a shower…" MaKayla inhaled dramatically. "No, separately, not together."

"Oh, I was about to say." MaKayla smiled.

"Right. Get your mind out the gutter," said Liyah, still nervously smiling. "Then we laid down and talked until we fell asleep. This wasn't like any other time we spent the night together. I mean, it felt perfect just lying in his arms and being held. He was warm, but we weren't hot, and it was so comfortable. Now"—Liyah paused—"I don't know who or how it started, but at some point during the night, one of us woke up and started kissing the other one—"

"Wait, wait, wait. What do you mean one of you? Who started kissing who?"

"I honestly don't know, because I thought it was him, but he thinks it was me, and neither one of us remembers for sure."

MaKayla just shook her head and began smiling. "Okay. Continue."

"Well, you know, one thing led to another, and the kissing turned to rubbing and touching and more and more. I thought about stopping, but I didn't want to. I had wanted him to show me that he wanted me like that for so long, and I was happy that it was happening."

"Are you serious Liyah?" asked MaKayla with her mouth open, shocked. "You never said you felt like that. You've been downplaying how you feel this whole time. Why?"

"I don't know. I guess I was afraid to actually accept it, but I didn't want to hold back anymore. So you know, one thing led to another, but it wasn't sex. It was way more intimate and sensual than anything that I've experienced before. I think we made love."

"What do you mean you think? Please tell me that you used protection."

"I knew what was happening, but at the same time, it just felt so surreal. His arms pulled me closer, and his hands caressed me in ways I never thought imaginable. He wasn't just trying to have sex with me. He was meticulously trying to please me."

"So you're telling me that you didn't use protection? Liyah, where is this coming from? This isn't like you at all," MaKayla replied curiously, smiling.

"I know, but we were just in the moment, not thinking, just reacting. There wasn't a point when we stopped to even consider what was happening. I know it sounds crazy, but I honestly don't regret one single thing. I haven't thought anything negatively about what we did because I've never had someone tend and cater to my body the way he did. After it was all over, I was just lying in his arms again, in complete bliss and contentment. He kissed me and told me that he loved me."

"Oh my God, are you serious? What did you say?"

"I… I… I said it back to him."

MaKayla gasped. "You told him that you love him? You know that those words haven't come out of your mouth for a guy since Travis, right?"

"Yes, I know," replied Liyah. Her nervousness had disappeared, and she looked full of joy and excitement.

"Hey, ladies, anyone want to help these people?" came Mr. Stacy's voice from the front of the café. They were so wrapped up in the conversation that they didn't realize someone had come in.

"We're going to finish this conversation," said MaKayla as she got up to go greet the guests.

*****

Jaron pulled into his mom's driveway at six ten and sent her a text to let her know that he was there. She didn't respond, but instead, she was out the door a few seconds before he set his phone down. She was rather nicely dressed in spring colors—cool-blue and yellow scarf, knee-high brown boots, crème pants, and a multicolored blouse with a white camisole underneath.

"Do I need to go change my clothes?" he asked jokingly as she entered the car.

"Oh hush. I knew you'd be late. That's why I didn't make our reservation until seven."

"Reservation? Where are we going?"

"I haven't been anywhere really nice in a while, so I figured we could go to Manny's Steakhouse—you know, over by the Riverwalk."

"Of course I know where it's at Mom," he replied, smiling.

It only took about twenty-five minutes to get there, probably because most of the traffic was gone. They went to check in, and his mom told him about her day as they waited at the bar. For some reason, she was really excited and upbeat about her day. It had been a while since he had seen her like this over work. He attributed it to the glass of wine she had almost finished in that short time. She wasn't a big drinker, but she did love her wine.

"Perhaps we should eat before you have another glass," he said jokingly.

"Maybe you're right," she replied, smiling. "I think the bartender spiked my drink."

"Well, wine is alcohol. You do know that, right?" They both started laughing. Then the greeter approached them and took them to their table.

"Okay. Enough about me. What's going on with you? How was your day, and what was on your mind yesterday?"

"Well, that's a lot you want to know. How about we order first?" he said nervously, attempting to shift the attention.

She realized what he was trying to do but played along all the same. "Well, considering we're at a steakhouse, I think I'll have the porterhouse. That looks so good," his mom replied.

"That's a lot of food that comes with it. You sure you can handle all of that?" he asked timidly. "Never mind," he quickly said, throwing his hands up, after seeing the look she gave him. "I think I'll have the grilled chicken breast and half slab of ribs."

"Oh, is that going to be too much food for you?" asked his mom in a high-pitched, whiny voice. Jaron just smiled and shook his head.

"So now that we know what we're going to eat, care to enlighten me about how you're doing?" his mom said through a smile.

"Okay. Well, if you must know, I actually had a phenomenal day," he said, using exaggerated mannerisms.

"Wow, phenomenal, huh? That's a very positive word," replied his mom in a sarcastic tone.

The waitress returned, bringing them water and buttered rolls. "Are you ready to order?" she asked.

"Yes, we are. I'll have the twelve-ounce porterhouse, steamed broccoli, loaded baked potato, and garden salad."

"How would you like your steak?"

"Well done, no pink."

"And for you?"

"I'll have the half slab and grilled chicken breast with asparagus, Jasmine rice, and steamed carrots. Can you have them lightly salt the asparagus and carrots? Plus, butter on the side for the rice. Oh, and can we have an order of pot stickers as an appetizer?" replied Jaron.

"Can I get a bottle of Patricia Green Olenik Pinot Noir please?" added his mom.

"Sure. Will that be all for you guys?"

Jaron smiled, shaking his head. "A lemonade for me."

"Okay. I'll put that in and bring the appetizer as soon as it comes up. Shouldn't be more than ten or fifteen minutes."

"Why were you shaking your head?" asked his mom, smiling.

"Oh nothing." Jaron smiled as he took a sip of water. "Now where were we? Oh yeah, how my day was."

"Yes, you had a phenomenal day," said his mom in a very exaggerated tone with a smile on her face.

"Yes. I spoke with Mr. Thomas today, and what he told me caught me off guard in the best way possible."

"That must mean that you guys had a good conversation."

"Better than good. It literally left me speechless. I mean, I just sat there in pleasant disbelief."

"Wow, that good, huh?" replied his mom after swallowing a mouthful of bread.

The waitress returned, bringing the wine, lemonade, and appetizer. "Anything else I can get for you guys right now?"

"No, that'll be all," replied his mom as she poured a glass of wine. "Thank you."

"He's offering me two-thirds of the company's current value. In addition, he will front the necessary funds for all upstart operations for future facilities, personnel, and necessary materials and equipment for the next three years. I can more than double the company's worth with this deal, and you know what the best part of it all is?" asked Jaron, excitement racing through his eyes.

"No, I don't, but I'm sure you're going to tell me," his mom replied through a smile.

"He's not even asking for a majority stake in the company. This is ten times better than the previous deal with Wynstead, not to mention he's a great person too. The way he talked about Dad and why he wanted to work with me was exactly what I've been looking for. I know why he was at the top of Dad's list. I'm so lucky to be put in this position." His mom didn't say anything. She just smiled and took another bite. "What? Why are you looking like that?" Jaron asked curiously.

"I have this eerie feeling that I told you this was going to happen."

"When? I don't remember having that conversation."

"Let's see. We were in the kitchen. You were talking about how you didn't want your dad to be disappointed in you—"

"Okay, okay. I remember," said Jaron before she could finish. "I do listen, you know. Dad gave me all the tools I needed. I just had to use them," he said through a smile.

"Exactly. And it seems to me that you're figuring out how to use them. I had this conversation with your father a bunch of times. To be honest, it was always your father who knew you'd get to this point this soon. I knew that you'd get here. I just anticipated a lot more bumps in the road, but your dad would always shake his head. 'Nah, not my boy. He's only sixteen, but he already acts like a seasoned vet.'"

The thought of his dad having such confidence in him didn't shock Jaron. It was an added bonus on the day that he was already having. His smile continually grew until he felt almost overwhelmed with emotion. "I think I'll have a glass of wine too."

"I knew you'd come around sooner or later," his mom said, grabbing his glass.

Jaron smiled. "What if I didn't?"

"Oh, trust me, the bottle wouldn't have gone to waste." Jaron just laughed, shaking his head. "So was that the entirety of your day?"

"Well, that was actually just the morning. Afterward, I had a pretty productive meeting with Tim."

"That's the mad scientist and creative guy, right?"

Jaron laughed again, shaking his head. "Yeah. He helps develop the ideas I have, you know, kind of turns my thoughts into tangible items that we can produce. Then just a small bit of problem-solving, and bada bing, bada boom, that was my day."

"That does sound like a good day, but I didn't hear anything about MaKayla."

Jaron took a sip of his wine. "I didn't get to go to the café. We got caught up in the meeting, so we ordered pizza for lunch."

"Oh okay. There's always tomorrow, right?"

"Or the next, or the one after," replied Jaron through a phony smile. "You know Mom, I've been thinking. Maybe it would be better for me to just focus completely on work, you know, with the impending deal and these new products we're working on."

His mother chuckled sarcastically. "So what's really going on?" Her face was still and serious at this point. "Does this have something to do with what was bothering you yesterday?"

Jaron let out a sigh and sat silently for a moment. "Yeah, it does."

The waitress returned with their food, and the aroma of the meals made Jaron feel better. There was a feeling of nostalgia working its way through his body. He didn't know where it was coming from, but he liked it.

"Can you cut into your steak to make sure it's cooked to your liking?"

The knife slid through the steak with ease, and the juices began to run around the plate. "Yes, this is perfect," his mom replied.

"Great. Is there anything else I can get you?"

"Not just at this moment, but I have a feeling we'll be needing another bottle of wine here soon." A smile rose on her face.

"Okay. I'll be around. Just give me a sign when you're ready."

"Sounds like a plan to me," his mom said, still cutting her steak.

The waitress walked away, and Jaron too, began smiling. "You and your wine," he replied.

She smiled. "You may need it more than me seeing as how tense you got when I brought up yesterday."

"It wasn't tension. I am a little nervous about discussing it because it's so uncharacteristic of me, and I don't want to seem selfish." His mom didn't respond. She just began eating and looked on, patiently awaiting his response. He let out another sigh and smiled, then took a bite of his chicken. "Well, the thing is, I've always wanted a family, but you already know that, but the desire has been really strong lately. I try to work a lot more or hang out with the guys to get my mind off of it, but that rarely works."

"So where do you think this increase is coming from?"

"I think it's coming from Dad, his death."

His mom looked up, startled, and she even paused chewing for a minute. She swallowed hard. "What does your father's passing have to do with this?"

"I've just been thinking about how short life is and how you never know when it can be over. There's so much I want to experience, so much I want to do. Most of all, I want someone to share it with. I love being able to help and accomplish all the things that we're doing with the company, but sometimes, I start thinking, is it worth it if I'll never have anyone to share and experience it with?

"You know how much we love Dad, how much you two mean to us. I… I want that too. I know I mean a lot to the people that I'm helping, but that's not intimate or personal. I want what you guys had—I mean have, because I know that even if or when you get ready to let someone else into your life in that way, they'll never be to you what Dad is.

"I want to mean the world to someone and for them to mean the world to me, to have someone to come home to after a long, hard day's work and just seeing them makes the stress, frustration, and negativity melt away. I want to come home to warm embraces and problems that only a dad can fix. You know the ones that seem as if the world is ending to the child, but to a parent, it's an easy fix, the ones that make you look like a superhero just because you are able to fix the dollhouse just right or put the piece on the Lego set that they just couldn't get to fit? I think about it more and more, and I wonder if Dad really knew how important he was and still is to us."

His mom was still eating and smiling and sipping her wine. "He knows Jaron. He always knew. There's not a day that went by that he wasn't reminded by at least one of you, and if by the slightest chance one of you didn't, then there was always me. He talked about how much you guys meant to him. His family was his world, and nothing would change that."

"You see what I mean Mom? I want that. I want that feeling."

"So is this about your sister being pregnant?"

Jaron lowered his head, almost in a shameful bow. "Yeah, partly, but it's more than that."

"So what else is it?" she asked curiously.

"You know I told you that Xavier has a new girlfriend and that he just found out that she's pregnant too, right? He came and got me when he first found out, not because he was excited but because he was afraid and didn't know what to do. Can you believe that? He has exactly what I'm sitting here desiring and doesn't even know what to do. I envy them. I want that, and it's frustrating that it's not happening for me. There's this beautiful girl, and I can't even bring myself to go talk to her. I just go there day after day, ordering food. Don't get me wrong, the food is good, but it's like I'm waiting for this perfect situation to present itself, but I know it's not going to happen.

"What am I not doing right? I mean, I'm a good person. I look out for everyone. I don't hurt or take advantage of anyone. I'm intelligent, or at least I'd like to think so. I have a good job. I'm responsible. Am I unattractive or something? But even that doesn't matter to some people, so why isn't it happening for me?"

His mom put her fork down, folded her hands, and smiled. "So how exactly are you expecting this to go for you? What exactly were or are you expecting to happen?"

"I don't know. I don't have any expectations for this."

"Of course you do," she said, "because if you didn't, then you wouldn't be envious and feeling the way you're feeling. So you think you can just be a good guy, and miraculously, good things will come to you, that just everything you want will be yours because you're good? It doesn't work like that. If you want something, then you have to put the effort in to make it happen. Otherwise, we'll be sitting here having this conversation.

"Do you know how hard your father worked to get me to just go out with him, then how much harder he worked to keep me happy, because somewhere in that amazing brain of his, he figured that he would be letting me down if he didn't do more than what he did to get me, to keep me? On top of that, he kept you and your sisters happy, established himself in the business world, built a strong foundation for your company that you're building off of today, and was there for you guys in every way possible. And the crazy part is, he made it look so effortless."

She shook her head. In the midst of the conversation, she had begun staring off into the ceiling as if she could see his father doing all those things. They both sat silently. She stared at him, but Jaron couldn't bring himself to meet her eyes. He was ashamed. He felt he had disappointed her and himself by letting his wants overpower his will to fight for them.

"Now I refuse to sit here and listen or watch you beat yourself up. You and I both know that nothing ever comes easy in this life and that you have to work and fight for every detail of everything you want, and if you don't, you can't complain that you don't have it. Your father set a phenomenal example for you of what a strong man is and looks like. I see you attempt to model yourself after him and aspire to be the man he was, but that is not what you need to do.

"I'm sorry, but you will never be him. You are and will always be Jaron, and I'll be the first to tell you that you're more than enough just as who you are. You're a fighter, and you've been a fighter all your life. Where you get thrown off is that you're also a very deep thinker. It's a gift and a curse, depending on how you use it. So stop thinking so much on what you don't have, but instead, apply that energy to how to attain those things.

"You've already accomplished so much, but you put too much pressure on yourself—unnecessary pressure Jaron. These things take time, and just like a good bottle of wine, it gets better over time. You have to allow things to naturally develop and mature to get the best possible outcome. When it's rushed, it's unstable, not completely developed or thought out, and that's not the way you want things to be.

"If you're tired of just going to get food, then talk to her. I know it may be the scariest thing in the world, because she could say no, she could be involved with someone else, or she could not be anything like this illusion you've created in your mind. Then you'll have to face that reality. You'll have to face rejection, and those fantasies in your mind will be gone. That's a very likely outcome. It could be even worse when you think about it."

Jaron looked shocked, like he couldn't believe what she was saying, but he was curious to try to follow what exactly she was trying to get across to him. "But," she said, a smile rising on her face, "what if she's thinking the exact same thing? What if she's just as nervous about talking to you as you are or even more? What if she's waiting for you to make the first move? What if she's everything you're expecting and more? What if she sits up at night thinking about you or can't get you off her mind throughout the day?

"The crazy thing is that you'll never know which of those possibilities is the case until you find out. Until then, you'll just wonder and torture yourself with never-ending possibilities that can never be confirmed or denied. I don't know. Maybe I'm wrong and you've changed," she said, shrugging her shoulders. "But that's not the Jaron I know."

A smile rose on his face, and he realized that she had just presented him with the ultimate challenge and test. She was testing who he was, if he still was the resilient person he had always been. It was the ace she had always had up her sleeve, and she had been holding it to play it at this particular time. He raised his glass in a toasting gesture, and his mom raised hers.

"Thanks Mom," he said as they touched glasses. He didn't have to say it, but the challenge had been accepted, and he planned on rising to the occasion.

Chapter 18

The next morning, MaKayla woke up to the soft pitter-patter of raindrops against her window. She laid there for a while, just listening to the rain. Her alarm hadn't gone off yet, so she figured that she had some extra time. She could tell that it was going to be a dreary day. The sun was barely making its way through the clouds, so it appeared to be more night than day.

She closed her eyes and allowed her thoughts to roam—thoughts of the day, of Liyah, and of Jaron. She smiled as she threw the covers back. "Let me get this day started," she said through a yawn while stretching. "Let's see how bad it is. Maybe I can still get in a jog," she said as she made her way to the front door. There was a light drizzle, almost a mist, but nothing too heavy. "Yeah, I can get a little jog in," she said, closing the door.

She got dressed and went outside to stretch. The sky was dark, and the clouds appeared to be thick and heavy, almost like they were ready to explode. "I better make this quick. I don't want to get caught in a storm," she said as she took off down the street. She only ran about halfway through her normal route and turned back because the sky had begun an all-too-frequent light show, which seemed to be followed by the explosion of some enormous cannons in the sky. It seemed like there was a storm brewing, and MaKayla didn't plan on being a part of the mix.

She went through her normal routine for getting ready for the day. Everything was the same, but for some reason, she felt different. She couldn't put her finger on it and attributed it to not getting a full jog in. *I'm sure it'll pass*, she thought as she sprinted to the cab. The rain was now falling at a steady pace, so walking wasn't an option. She only had one class that morning, so she would just head to work after class. She figured it would be quiet because of the weather and time of day, so she could grab a snack and get some studying done before work.

*****

Jaron lay in bed, angled so he was facing the window. He was watching the sky. Little flashes slowly flowed through the clouds. They were just bright enough to show the lining of the clouds, but not enough to light up the entire sky. The rain brought comfort. *It's refreshing, like a cleansing or a new start,* thought Jaron. He felt around the bed until he found his remote and turned on the TV. SportsCenter was already on. He moved to the edge of the bed, stretched, and made his way to the bathroom.

He turned on the shower and stood facing the mirror. Although he was staring at himself, he wasn't looking at himself. It was like he was looking through himself. A smile crept across his face, and he shook his head. "One day, one day," he said. After getting dressed, he made his way to the kitchen. *I'll just grab something small. I'm not that hungry,* he thought.

*****

The drive to work took longer than usual, as people were driving slowly due to the rain that had begun to steadily fall. Jaron walked through the door and was greeted by Krystal's big smile. "Good morning, Mr. Coleman," she exclaimed.

"Someone's in a good mood. Any particular reason for that smile?" he asked.

"I honestly don't know. I just woke up and felt like today was going to be a good day. I don't know why, but it's like I can feel it. Has that ever happened to you?" she asked.

"Actually, it has, plenty of times," he responded.

"And did it turn out to be a good day?" she asked excitedly.

"Of course it did. Every day's a good day. It's all in how you view it," he responded as the elevator door closed.

A few moments later, the elevator door opened with Keith standing with a file in hand. "Ah, just the man that I was coming to see," he said, entering the elevator. "Just getting in, I assume?"

"Yes sir. So what do you have there?" Jaron asked, pointing to the file.

"The numbers from the accounts that were wrongfully billed. They have been corrected and credited the 10 percent, as you requested. Plus, I ran it by Lance in financial already. The numbers will work," stated Keith.

"Thanks Keith. I definitely appreciate it. Doing more than what's required was how we got to where we are and how we'll get to where we want to go," said Jaron as he scanned the documents. "Walk with me to my office—if you have time, that is."

"Of course. Something on your mind?" asked Keith.

"Always, always," Jaron replied as the elevator door opened. "Good morning, Tina. How are we looking so far?" he asked as he approached her desk.

"Fairly quiet so far, no messages. Eric is out. His wife went into labor last night. And Louis's son is sick, so he called in too," she replied.

"Hmm, two down from special projects, in one day. Okay," Jaron said, shaking his head as if agreeing to something. "Well, make sure you check in on them around midday to see how things are going and if they need anything," he said, entering his office.

"Hi Tina."

"Good morning Keith. Hope you're not in trouble," she replied jokingly with a smile.

"That makes two of us."

Jaron put his laptop on the desk and hung up his coat while placing his umbrella in the corner. "Have a seat," he said to Keith, motioning to the chairs. "Oh Tina, can you or Emily put together or purchase a care or congratulations package, and have it sent over to the hospital for Eric and his family, care of the company? You can put it on my personal expense account," he said as he walked to the door.

"Sure thing. I'll get right on it. You know I love things like that," she said, smiling.

"Okay. And ask Karla to come to my office when she gets a free moment, please. I'll be in here with Keith for a while," he said, smiling, as he pulled up the door.

"Ooh, Keith, you are in trouble," she said jokingly.

"How? Or I guess more importantly, why do you do it?" asked Keith abruptly.

Jaron was caught off guard and somewhat taken aback. "Did I miss something? What did I do?" he asked nervously.

"Just how you are—not just being on top of company business but also staying in tune with your employees on a more personal level. The amount of concern you show for us all individually, why? I mean, even listening to your speech the other day, seeing that you left a lot of money on the table for yourself, for us, I mean, trust me, it's greatly appreciated, but what makes you do it?"

Jaron sat back, relieved, and a smile crept across his face as he released a small sigh. "You had me worried there for a minute. It's actually not hard. I just understand your worth and value. For instance, I didn't ask you to run the numbers by financial. You stepped up and took that responsibility into your own hands, which allows me to know that I can trust you and count on you. That deserves to be rewarded.

"You all probably spend as much, if not more, time here at work than you do with your families, so I feel that you're my family, and I'm going to treat you as such. I know that I couldn't have made it this far without you guys, and I wouldn't be able to maintain it without you. I want you guys to wake up every day excited to come in here and help make a difference in what we do. Me getting money is really my last priority. I'm doing pretty good for myself, so to retain valuable assets, I don't mind putting money in your pockets opposed to my own. We're a company, a team. It's not just me."

"See? That's what I mean. I've never worked anywhere or with anyone at the top who thought that way, or at least they never expressed it." said Keith.

"So that's how you know you're in the right place." Jaron smiled.

"Makes sense," replied Keith, nodding his head in agreement.

"And my speech was pretty good, huh?"

"Yeah, it was all right." They both laughed.

"Now to the matter at hand," replied Jaron as he sat up and slid his chair closer to the desk. He pulled up a document on his laptop and slid around so that he and Keith could view it together. "So I know we discussed prospective locations when we started the discussion for expansion. I've revised it and went a little more in-depth to ensure that we have all the bases covered. I've already sent this to you, as I'd like for you to head this up for us. I'd like for you to research these markets, and let me know what would be the benefits and drawbacks to building in these areas."

"Pull in whoever you think you'll need, and delegate as you see fit, but keep me in the loop," said Jaron as he scrolled through the document. "If you have any other things you're working on, delegate them to your team. If you need anything, don't hesitate to let me know. What do you think?" he asked as he slid the laptop closer to Keith, who was scrolling through the slides himself now.

"What time frame are you looking at? I only ask so that I know who I need to pull and what time frame I need to put on the project for them."

"Does one month sound doable?"

"We can make that work. I'll make sure to have an update by the end of the week," said Keith.

"Sounds like a plan to me," said Jaron as he walked back around to the other side of the desk.

Jaron and Keith stayed in the office for a few hours, discussing their thoughts and opinions on the locations, such as what would make the most sense, which way to approach the research, and what they felt were the most important and key components.

"Be sure to add all immediate supervisors of anyone that you select to be a part of the team with you. Set up an initial meeting with them all before getting started. You can leave the door open," said Jaron as Keith made his way out the door. In an almost seamless transition, as if planned, in walked a tall, slender woman. Her short hair was in curls, and she was wearing a two-piece business suit, all black with a white blouse, and small, thin glasses.

"How's it going, Mr. Coleman? You needed to see me?"

"Karla, that was fast. You must have already been coming to see me," said Jaron, smiling.

"Nope, I can't say that I was. Plus, I don't know if you're being sarcastic or not, but that was a few hours ago that you requested my presence," she replied, smiling, as she took a seat, crossing her legs. "But since I'm here now, what can I do for you?"

"Well actually, I just wanted to make sure there was nothing that I can do for you," replied Jaron. Karla looked a little confused, but she didn't speak. She just sat there with a curious smile on her face. "Tina told me that Eric and Louis are out today. That's two down from special projects. I know you guys are already working pretty hard down there with this impending deal and the new promotion we just rolled out, not to mention whatever other projects you guys are putting together. So I'm just making sure you don't need anything to help cover the holes," said Jaron as he shrugged his shoulders, smiling.

"Well, now that you've mentioned it, I could really use a personal masseuse, one of those personal fans, you know, where a muscular guy stands there fanning me. Oh, and someone to feed me strawberries and grapes too. I do like my fruits," replied Karla, smiling and staring off into the ceiling.

"That's it?" replied Jaron, smiling. "I thought you were going to make some requests that were over-the-top or completely outlandish."

"Now why would I do that? You asked me what would be helpful, so I should approach that seriously," she replied, smiling.

"A simple no would've sufficed. I'm just trying to help, that's all," said Jaron, smiling.

"Yeah I know, but I keep telling you, we got this. Just relax. You know I'll let you know if we need something," she replied, returning the smile.

"I thought we included me. I must have been mistaken," he said, putting on a fake disappointed face.

"Oh stop it. You know what I mean. Wipe that fake look off your face," she said, laughing lightly, as she stood up. "But to answer your question directly, we're good for now. I'll let you know if that changes," said Karla as she walked to the door.

"Yeah, yeah, yeah. Pull my door up on your way out. Tina will check in with you a little later," he replied.

"Sure thing, you big baby." They both laughed as she closed the door.

Jaron spun around slowly in his chair and leaned back until his chair was against his desk. He stared out the window, trying to peer through the thickness that had grown. The rain had subsided and was replaced by a very thick fog. He could barely see two feet in front of him. He allowed his mind to roam, floating along with the mist. The thickness seemed to captivate while mesmerizing him. He was brought back to reality by a knock on the door.

"Come in," Jaron said, spinning around in his chair.

"I'm going to grab something to eat. Do you want anything, or are you going out?" asked Tina.

It was the first time he had thought about MaKayla all day, and he realized that he actually had the opportunity to see her today. "Um, I'll go to the café a little later, but thanks anyway," he replied as he turned his face to his laptop.

"Okay. I'll be back. Calls are forwarded to you. You want the door open or closed?" she asked, swinging the door back and forth.

"You can leave it open, at least until you get back," he replied.

"Hey, did it start raining again?" came Tina's voice from outside the door.

"Nope, nope, nope, but you should take an umbrella just in case," he called back to her.

"Okay. Be back in a minute."

Jaron didn't respond this time. He was already engulfed in his thoughts—some of excitement and some of nervousness. *What if she's there today and I get to see her? What will I say? What will I do?* A countless number of thoughts swarmed his mind. He tried to focus his thoughts and not overthink the situation. He achieved some success, but he couldn't completely stop thinking about her.

He directed his attention to his work, going through several different emails that required his response. One was from Keith. He had already put together a preliminary list for the group and was getting the approval before inviting everyone. Jaron smiled in approval of the list and the speed at which Keith was already working. *I knew he was the right person for the job,* he thought as he responded to the email.

After checking and responding to a few more emails, his door opened as Tina tried to talk through a mouthful of the sandwich she was eating. "I get it, I get it. You're back. Leave the calls forwarded to me until you're back off of lunch," he said, smiling, but never fully looked up. She gave him a thumbs-up and walked out of the office.

He enjoyed having Tina as his assistant. It was like working with his sister. It made him feel as if they were more of a family than a business. That was something his father always emphasized, treating people not only the way you wanted to be treated but also the way you would treat your brother or sister.

"When you work with people, a team, and you depend greatly on them to succeed, you have to maintain a healthy and strong bond. It shouldn't feel like work. It should be like a regular day." He smiled again, hearing his father's voice and thinking about how influential his father was in his day-to-day life.

About thirty minutes passed, and Tina walked back in. "I'm back. That was really good. I can't believe how hungry I was," she said, taking a sip of her tea.

"You definitely were. I couldn't even talk because you were too busy stuffing your mouth," said Jaron, laughing.

"Oh hush. You knew what I was saying," she replied, smiling and shaking her head. "I'm almost done with the care package, by the way. Emily had some pretty good ideas that I'm going to incorporate. I'll send you an email of what it looks like when I'm done."

"That works. I'm really happy for them. I know it's been something they've wanted for a long time. Good to see it's finally coming through," said Jaron, smiling. "So when are you going to drop a couple of little ones? You can't keep treating that dog like he's your son, you know," he asked, shaking his head.

"Ha! Who me? First, I'd have to find a guy worth my time, and we both know they're few and far between. Then the whole dating process and meeting the family and—nope, I'll pass on all that. It's just too much. Me and Trouble are just fine by ourselves. Plus, could you picture me with children? I mean, that would be crazy, don't you think?" Tina asked, staring off into the sky.

"Poor dog," said Jaron as he stood up and grabbed his coat.

"Why are you trying to rush greatness? You know perfection isn't made. It's one of those things that just happens." They both paused and looked at each other and then began laughing.

"I'm going to lunch. You're a trip. Can't rush greatness." He smiled, shaking his head.

"You know I'm right," she said, making her way around her desk.

Jaron didn't look at her. He just continued to smile as he headed toward the elevator. "I'll be back in a few," he said as the elevator opened. She just began overdramatically smiling and gave a thumbs-up again.

Jaron exited the elevator to find Krystal smiling. "You were right," she exclaimed excitedly.

Jaron smiled. "Okay. What exactly was I right about?" he asked curiously.

"Well, this morning, I told you that I felt like it would be a good day, and you told me I was right. I received an email a little while ago informing me that I got this apartment that I've been wanting for some months now. I actually had forgotten about it and assumed that I didn't get it since it took them so long to respond to me. I guess I was wrong. And it's even better because I didn't see it coming. I'm so excited. The apartment is perfect, and it just looks amazing. I can't wait to move in and start decorating."

Jaron just stood there, smiling. He enjoyed hearing people's happiness and excitement about the things going on in their lives and appreciated that she wanted to share it with him.

"Oh, I'm sorry. I'm just going on and on," she said, smiling, as her cheeks began to redden.

"It's perfectly fine. I'm happy for you. Sometimes, the best things are things we have to wait a while to receive."

Krystal smiled. "I'm sure you're right, just like this morning."

Jaron walked outside and looked up at the sky. Although the fog had lightened up, the clouds seemed to have darkened. He figured he would drive since he didn't want to chance getting caught in the rain despite the temperature being almost what he felt to be perfect.

*****

MaKayla entered the café and spoke to Mr. Stacy.

"You're here early, aren't you? I thought you didn't start for another hour or so."

"I don't, but I was done with my classes and didn't have anything else that I needed to do. So I figured it would be slow, and I could get a snack and study before my shift. I didn't want to wait and get stuck in the rain trying to get here."

"That's smart thinking," replied Mr. Stacy, tapping the side of his head with his index finger.

MaKayla smiled and grabbed a chocolate chip muffin, an apple, and a bottle of green tea. "I try to use my brains when I can," she replied.

MaKayla walked into the dining area. She took a seat and pulled out her laptop and notebook. Looking out the window, she could see the clouds darkening. *I'm sure it'll rain again soon,* she thought.

Chapter 19

There was a small drizzle as Jaron got out of his car. He put on his hood and grabbed his umbrella even though the rain was light. He entered the café and requested to be seated at his normal seat. He didn't think to look for MaKayla even though his waitress was McKinley. He didn't even think of the connection. He was still thinking about how excited Krystal was, how happy something so simple had made her. *It's the little things,* he thought. *That's what makes everything else worthwhile.* He followed the waitress toward his table.

There was a flash of lightning, followed by a loud crash of thunder. MaKayla jumped as the thunder crashed, causing her to bump the table, knocking over her bottle of green tea. Jaron bent to pick the bottle up without consciously realizing what he was doing. The thunder had just brought him out of his previous thought process. He paused as he placed the bottle on the table, realizing that MaKayla was sitting right across from his table.

She sat there quietly, looking at him, not knowing what to say or do. They were both stuck, caught off guard by each other's presence, unsure of what to do but not thinking about it either. Neither even breathed.

"It's a good thing that the top was on," came McKinley's voice, snapping both of them out of their trance.

"Thanks," said MaKayla nervously, turning back into her chair and facing her laptop.

"You're welcome," replied Jaron, speaking unconsciously, still in shock as he sat down.

"Is there anything I can get you right now, or do you need some time to look over the menu?" asked McKinley. Jaron sat quietly, still in disbelief at the situation that he was now in. "I can come back if you need a moment," said McKinley after Jaron didn't reply for some time.

"Oh, I apologize. My mind was somewhere else. But I know what I'd like," replied Jaron. MaKayla laughed lightly, hoping that it was seeing her that had an effect on him. Jaron smiled and placed his usual order.

"Okay. I'll be right back with your drinks and bring your food as soon as it's ready," she said, taking the menu from the table.

"Thank you," he replied as she walked away. He turned his attention to the window, afraid to look in MaKayla's direction.

What is he thinking? she thought. *What do I say if he says something to me? I mean, I'm sure he won't. I look like a mess. My hair isn't done, I have on work clothes, and I probably look tired. I have to just focus on studying. I don't know why I'm even thinking about him like this. This has to be Liyah's fault. She put all these crazy thoughts in my mind. But that's my girl, and I love her.* MaKayla's thoughts were all over the place and moving at a hectic pace, but all the while, a happy and inviting smile covered her face.

I guess this is my chance. I mean, I've asked for an opportunity like this, and here it is. What am I going to do with it? She looks like she's studying though. It would be rude of me to interrupt her. She clearly wants to have some peace, and I'd be interrupting that. I don't know why I'm so nervous. I mean sure, she's beautiful, and those deep-brown eyes are mesmerizing, and the way that one loc of hair falls over her face, just barely covering her eye, and her smile—man, her smile—the way her voice sounded when she said thank you... Did she hold my gaze, or am I thinking too much into it? Jaron thought as he watched the rain fall, which had started to pick up.

"Here you go," said McKinley, setting his drinks down. "I'll be right back with your food when it comes up."

"Thank you," he replied, taking a sip of the lemonade. Jaron let out a sigh. He had decided that it was now or never. He didn't want to let the opportunity to talk to her pass. He had done that already. He knew that if he did it again, he would regret it. He turned from the window and slid a little closer toward the end of the table, then took a deep breath and closed his eyes. *Here goes nothing,* he thought.

"Excuse me," Jaron said, looking in MaKayla's direction. "Your name's MaKayla, right?" he asked despite knowing the answer to the question. He had replayed it in his mind more times than he could count at this point, replaying the sound of her voice saying her own name and the gentle smile that resided on her face as she said it. That was her name. There was not a doubt in his mind. But he figured it was the best way to get a conversation started.

MaKayla looked up from her laptop. The hair that was covering her eye, she gently brushed back. She nodded her head yes, afraid to open her mouth to speak, because she didn't know if words would actually come out. He was beautiful to her. She had seen him before, several times, in the café and recently at the park, but this was different.

There was a childish innocence mixed into the manly structure of his face. His smile was amazing, eyes that peered into her soul. She loved it, the way he looked at her, the way he looked, and the way she felt, she loved it all. He wasn't just handsome, he was beautiful, like a perfectly worded poem, whose words you could feel coursing through your veins. The mere thought of him calmed her nerves.

"I'm sorry to bother you. I can see that you're studying. My name is Jaron, Jaron Coleman. I don't know if you remember, but a few weeks ago, I was in here with a few business associates, and you were our waitress."

"Yes, I remember," she said softly. Sadness began to fill her face as the memories began to replay in her mind. "I apologize if I messed up any business that you guys were conducting. I'm not normally like that. I'm really good at my job. I don't mix up orders or spill…"

MaKayla was talking very fast. She was extremely nervous, and the more she talked, the worse she felt. She didn't want him to think less of her. She just had to explain the situation, and he would understand. But before she could finish, there was another flash of lightning and a huge boom of thunder, which startled her, stopping her midsentence.

"Hey, it's okay. I actually wanted to apologize to you," said Jaron.

"Why would you apologize to me?" asked MaKayla curiously. "I didn't feel like you wronged me in any way."

"Well, I feel I need to apologize because you had to go through that. He had no right to treat you that way. And you didn't mess up the orders. He placed them wrong. I mean, sure, you wasted a little tea. But, but, but," he said, raising his hands as he saw the look on her face begin to turn somber, "that didn't matter. We cleaned it up quickly. And it's not like you did it on purpose."

"I just hope you guys were still able to conduct your business," she said, letting out a heavy sigh.

"Well actually, we won't be doing any business," said Jaron, smiling.

"I'm sorry, but why are you smiling? That's a horrible thing. Did he change his mind because of me?" she asked with raised panic in her voice.

"No, actually, I did," said Jaron, a feeling of pride flowing through him.

"Wait. What do you mean?" she asked.

"Well, after seeing how he treated you, among the other issues I saw with him, I decided it wouldn't be in the best interest of my company to do business with him. It was for the best, and an even better opportunity opened up for us, so it all worked out pretty well."

MaKayla didn't say anything. She just turned her head and smiled. *Wow, he took offense to how his potential business partner treated me. He doesn't even know me,* she thought.

"I was taught as a child, that if I see something or someone doing wrong, not to stand by and do nothing, especially if I have the ability to speak or act against it. I didn't speak or act quickly enough, and for that, I apologize. I tried come in a few times to apologize to you for what happened, but I guess we just missed each other or our days were off."

"Yeah, Liyah told me, but I was actually out of town. I went home for spring break." Jaron laughed. "Why are you laughing?" she asked.

"Because that would explain it. I didn't think of that. I thought of a lot of possibilities, but not that one. I was concerned that you quit or, even worse, were fired. I'm glad that you're still here," he said it before he could stop himself. "I mean, you know, that you still have your job despite that guy," he quickly and nervously said.

She just smiled. "Yeah, me too."

"I'm sorry that I didn't say anything when I saw you the other day at the park. To be honest, I didn't know what to say. I was just shocked. I mean, the whole time I was looking for you, and you're one of my closest friends' sisters of sorts."

"Yeah, it's a small world," she said, her face showing more curiosity now.

"Did I say something wrong?" he asked.

"Just curious. You said you were looking for me?"

"Oh," he said. He hadn't realized it, and although it was true, he felt like he shouldn't have said that part. "Well, yeah, you know, to apologize and make sure you were okay."

"That's very nice and caring of you. I appreciate it," she said, smiling.

"I'll let you get back to your studying. Sorry to have interrupted," said Jaron as McKinley brought his food and placed it on the table.

"No worries. It was a more than welcome break from the bookwork," she said, smiling.

"Hey MaKayla," came Liyah's voice as she made her way toward MaKayla's table. She slowed her pace as she noticed Jaron sitting next to her. Liyah didn't say anything but began making extravagant head gestures in Jaron's direction to MaKayla.

"You remember Liyah, don't you Jaron?" said MaKayla as Liyah sat down.

"Yes, I remember her. It's nice to see you again," he replied, taking a bite of his sandwich.

"Nice to see you too. I guess you two finally got to talk, huh?" said Liyah, smiling.

"Jaron was just explaining to me what happened with his business deal the other day, that's all. Come on Liyah. I have to go get ready to start my shift."

"But we don't start for another—"

"AA-Li-Yah, come on," said MaKayla sternly.

"Oh okay," replied Liyah with puppy dog eyes.

"It was nice talking to you Jaron," said MaKayla as she ushered Liyah down the walkway.

"Nice talking to you too," said Jaron, smiling, as they walked away.

As they entered the back room, Liyah burst into questions. "So I want to know everything. I can't believe that you were just sitting there talking like it wasn't a big deal. Okay, so when are you guys going to hang out? What's his number? Did you discuss favorite colors? Nah, it's probably too soon for that, huh? Where does he live? How old is he? Wait. He isn't like, super old is he? I mean to each his own, but I don't know about you dating a really old guy. I'm not sure how I feel about that. Where does he work?"

"I'm assuming he isn't involved with anyone. I mean, you did ask that, right? Because some guys have that 'I'm not going to tell what you don't ask' mentality.' So what are you going to wear when you go out? We'll have to go shopping for something together, and I can do your hair really nice, or are you guys doing something more low-key? Not too fancy in the beginning, right? Right," responded Liyah to her own question.

"Liyah," said MaKayla, who was just standing there, waiting quietly and calmly.

"Maybe we should do a double date. That way, if he's like crazy or something, I'll be there to get you out of it."

"Liyah," responded MaKayla, but Liyah still didn't respond. MaKayla began waving her hands in front of Liyah's face and gently repeated her name. Liyah finally stopped and began hugging MaKayla.

"Oh, I'm sorry. It's just that I'm so happy for you."

"Liyah," replied MaKayla, pulling Liyah off her, "none of that happened. It was just a simple conversation. He just wanted to apologize for what happened the other week." She held Liyah's arms with her hands and stared at her face. She let her go and stepped back. "Yes, he seemed really nice and thoughtful, but he wasn't trying to ask me out, or get my number, or date me. He just wanted to apologize and make sure I was okay, that's all, and that's okay. It's good to see there are still good guys like that out here."

"Wait Why? But—no, that doesn't make sense, MaKayla. He was looking for you this whole time, and that's all he wanted? People aren't like that. Are you messing with me? You didn't give him your number?"

"I'm serious. I didn't give him my number. We just had a nice conversation, that's all." Liyah was speechless. She opened her mouth, but nothing came out. MaKayla walked up and hugged her. "It's okay," she said, smiling. "The world hasn't come to an end."

"I know, but it just seemed perfect, you know, like something out of those romantic books. You deserve that. I'm going to go talk to him. He doesn't know what he's missing."

"You're not going to talk to anyone," said MaKayla, laughing. "Yeah, to be honest, despite what I've been saying and telling myself, that would've been nice, but it was also nice just to talk to him, to not have some guy only trying to get with you but who was genuinely concerned for you."

Liyah sighed. "I know. You're right. But you have to admit. He is pretty cute."

"Yeah, he's alright," replied MaKayla, then burst out laughing.

Jaron sat there smiling, eating, and watching the rain fall. It was starting to lighten up again. *I guess I can tell Mom I talked to her,* he thought. *Maybe I'll get another opportunity now that we've somewhat broken the ice. Who knows where this can go?* He did his best not to look too deeply, to overanalyze the situation. He was satisfied with just talking to her. He could be grateful for just that.

MaKayla was at the register when Jaron went to leave. "I hope everything was to your liking," she said, smiling, as she rang him up.

"It always is. Thanks for asking." Liyah walked out of the back room and stood beside MaKayla, but she didn't say anything. She just stood there, smiling. "It was nice talking to you, and I hope you were able to finish the studying you were trying to do. I hope I didn't disturb you too much."

"I did, and you were fine. As I said before, a good break is always helpful."

"Okay. Well, you ladies enjoy the rest of your day, and hopefully, I'll see you next time."

"I look forward to it," said MaKayla, tensing up as the words came from her mouth. "Why did I say that?" she asked, looking at Liyah.

"I would assume because you're looking forward to seeing him again," Liyah replied, smiling.

Jaron walked to his car and allowed the words to dance around in his mind. As he got into the car, the rain picked up again. He let out a sigh, closed his eyes, and sat back for a minute. There was a small rumble of thunder, which made him laugh a little, thinking about how the thunder had made her nervous. *I'd make you feel comfortable,* he thought. *But I wonder if she would want me to. Maybe she's just nice and has a guy.*

"But," came his mom's voice, "what if she's thinking the exact same thing? What if she's just as nervous about talking to you as you are? Or even more, what if she's waiting for you to make the first move?" Without a second thought, Jaron was out of the car and jogging through the rain back into the café. Liyah and MaKayla were still at the register, talking, when he walked back in, now dripping wet.

"I think you forgot your umbrella," said Liyah, smiling. MaKayla nudged her.

Jaron smiled. "I think you're right," he said, shaking off his sleeves.

"Did you forget something?" asked MaKayla, hesitant but hopeful as well.

"Actually, I didn't. Well, I guess I actually did. I came back because I didn't want to let the opportunity pass me by. I know I may be a little too forthcoming, and I apologize for that. It's not my nature. It's just that sometimes, you have to step outside of your comfort zone to get to where you're trying to go."

"Where are you trying to go?" asked Liyah, smiling, now more engaged than she had previously been. MaKayla turned to her and just gave her a face. "I'm sorry, I'm sorry. You were saying?"

"Well, to answer your question, I've wanted to be in this moment for a very long time. The first time I came to this café, I saw you. I'm sure you didn't pay me much mind, but you were the most captivating woman I'd ever seen. I couldn't bring myself to talk to you. It was like this was the opportunity of a lifetime, and I couldn't blow it.

"I mean, you're not just some ordinary woman. I know I may not know you well enough to say that as a fact, but sometimes, you just know, you know? The energy is there, and it all just makes sense, if you know what I mean." MaKayla didn't respond. She was too wrapped up in his words.

"So I ate and thought about what it would be like to talk to you. That's all. Nothing else, just to have a conversation. And then I left. Ever since then, I've hoped that just maybe, one day, you would be my waitress. I'd learn your name, and we'd just talk—nothing amazing or anything, just talk. I knew that would be enough for me."

"So I came back here every chance I could, but the opportunity never presented itself until the other week. Now we all know how that went. I mean, here was the moment I'd waited for, and this guy comes and treats you like you're the gum underneath his shoes. It took everything in me not to follow you out of the café that day. I mean, what would I have said? You didn't know me. I would've looked crazy, and I didn't want you to think I'm crazy or some stalker. You guys do have good food here too." He laughed a little.

"I thought I had lost the opportunity to talk to you forever. That's why I tried so hard to find you. Don't get me wrong, I did have to make sure you were okay, and I did need to apologize, but I also just wanted to see you again. I mean, you're beautiful to me—the way that loc falls over your face, just enough to cover your eye, like it's doing now." MaKayla felt like she was blushing. She put her head down and pushed her hair back. "I'm sorry," he said. "I just started talking, and things just came out. I didn't mean to overstep."

"No, no, keep stepping," said Liyah, leaning on the counter, hanging on every word. MaKayla elbowed her, and she stood up, rubbing her side.

"It's just, I was talking to my mom about you, and"—MaKayla perked up, interested even more at the sound of him telling her that he had talked to his mom about her—"and I realized that these situations are only what we make them. If you want something bad enough, you have to make it happen. You can't wait for it to happen."

Jaron took out his wallet and got a business card. "I know I've said a mouthful. I hope I haven't embarrassed myself too much. But if you don't already have someone special in your life, I was thinking that maybe you could call or text me sometime—if you're free, of course—and we could just talk. It's my office number at the top and my cell number at the bottom."

He handed his card to MaKayla, but she didn't move. She was frozen, unable to process what was happening. Liyah nudged her and gestured her head toward the card. MaKayla slowly reached for it but kept her eyes on him. She grazed his fingers as she took the card, and an enlivening sensation ran through her body. She felt warm.

"I look forward to hearing from you," Jaron said. "I mean, it would kind of suck if I don't, because that would mean I've made a complete fool of myself. Then I'd have to find somewhere else to eat lunch, because I couldn't bare the shame of showing my face here again." He let out a small laugh. "No pressure though," he said, smiling.

MaKayla still didn't respond. She just stood smiling at him in disbelief. Liyah pretended to clear her throat, and it brought MaKayla back to reality just as Jaron was turning to leave. "I look forward to hearing from you too," she said. He turned and flashed a smile, gave a brief wave as he put his hood on, and disappeared out the door.

"How, MaKayla, how?" asked Liyah.

"How what?" MaKayla asked, looking at the card.

"How are you going to hear from him? Did you give him your number or something? I mean, I was standing right here, and I didn't hear you say a word, so I'm not too sure how you'll hear from him."

Just then, it hit MaKayla, and she realized what she had said. "Why did you let me say that? Why didn't you stop me or something?"

"You see? I told you that's why he was looking for you. I was right. The one who says she always knows, and I was right this time.

Oh, look at you, just stuck. You couldn't even respond or acknowledge what he was saying. Man, you really got it bad, and I love it." Liyah just laughed. "And you want to talk about how I was when I met Darrell? Look at you, speechless."

"Oh hush, this is different, and you know it. He even had your mouth wide open."

"So, he wasn't talking to me," Liyah said, sticking out her tongue.

"Speaking of Darrell, we still have to finish talking about you using that L word."

"Saved by the customers," said Liyah as two women entered the café.

Chapter 20

Jaron sat in the car, smiling, the rain steadily working its way down the windshield. He was surprised that he actually gave MaKayla his phone number. He had thought about doing it for so long, but even as the opportunity was presented, he had no idea that he would do it. He hadn't thought about it. He was just going with how he felt. He replayed their conversations, from when they were sitting at the tables up to him walking out of the café.

He remembered the look of surprise on her face. After a few moments, he became very nervous. *Was that a look of surprise in a good way?* he thought. *Or what if she was surprised that I would even think that was okay? What if I had overstepped? What if I've made a fool of myself? What if she never calls or texts? I mean, what do I do then? I joked about it, but I really don't think I can come back here if I don't hear from her. It would be too uncomfortable for both of us, and I wouldn't want to put her in that position.* He was no longer excited and had suddenly thought himself into a nervous state. As he drove back to the office, he tried to calm his mind.

As he walked into the office, he saw Krystal sitting at the front desk, smiling while staring at her computer. Based off her smile, he assumed she was rereading her email from earlier. He made his way toward the elevator, and as the doors opened, Krystal looked up, startled.

"Oh, I'm sorry. I didn't hear you come in. I seem to have gotten myself wrapped up in imagining what my new apartment will look like."

"No worries," said Jaron. "I'm glad to see things are coming together for you."

"It's like you said Mr. Coleman. Sometimes, you have to wait a while to receive the best things."

"You know what? You are definitely right," said Jaron as the elevator door closed.

Jaron replayed his own words in his head as he made his way up to his floor. *I have waited a long time for this, so let's see how it goes. I've let my thoughts get ahead of me. I mean, we had a good conversation, and things ended nicely. She even said she looked forward to hearing from me too even though I don't have a way to communicate with her. Maybe she just meant seeing me again.* As the doors opened, Jaron could see everyone fast at work.

"Looks like someone forgot to take their own advice," came Tina's voice. Jaron realized she was referring to him being wet. "Why do you have an umbrella if you're not going to use it?"

"I had to run back into the café for a moment and forgot to bring it with me."

"Must have been pretty important for you to go running in the rain."

"Yeah, I guess you could say that," said Jaron, smiling, as he opened his office door. "Any messages?" he asked, taking off his wet coat and hanging it on the hook.

"Only one message—from Ms. Smith over at the college."

"Oh, I completely forgot about the internship program. I'd better give her a call now." Jaron picked up the phone and called Ms. Smith, the counseling chairwoman at the local university. After a few seconds of the phone ringing, Ms. Smith answered.

"This is Ms. Smith. How can I help you?"

"Good afternoon, Ms. Smith. This is Jaron Coleman. I seem to have missed your call earlier."

"Oh, hi Jaron. Yeah, I figured you might be at lunch."

"Yes, I was. But to be completely honest with you, the internship program had slipped my mind until Tina told me about your message. If you can give me the remainder of the day, I'll be sure to get back to you with a definite answer."

"Oh, I thought I should send a reminder email last week, but it also slipped my mind."

"Yes, I know how that goes. Things have been very busy around here, but I will get right on that for you."

"Thank you Jaron. I appreciate it."

"No problem. Are you looking at twelve interns again this year?"

"Well, there are actually ten for sure, but there are four other possibles. I will email you their names and majors to make sure you are able to find assignments that coincide with their majors."

"Okay. That sounds good," said Jaron. "We can set up a meet and greet this Friday. Just let me know what time works best for you."

"Alright. Let me talk with the students. Fridays are usually light for them, to my knowledge, so it should be easy enough to work out."

"I look forward to hearing from you later. Have a good day, Ms. Smith."

"You too, Jaron."

The internship program was something Jaron's father started a year after opening the company. He always told Jaron the importance of giving back to the community. Jaron did not want that to stop, so he picked up where his father left off. Plus, he had established a good relationship with Ms. Smith. The interns always seemed to work out with the company, and it was a great networking tool for them. It was actually where Krystal started before she began working there.

Jaron opened his laptop and began emailing the heads of the departments. He did not want to call them into a meeting until he was sure who would be available and who had too much of a workload to take on an intern.

*****

Soon after Jaron left, the café became very busy. MaKayla was going nonstop, but it did not prevent her from thinking about Jaron. Every time she had a table that was seated where he was seated earlier, she couldn't help but smile, not to mention the constant comments from Liyah. MaKayla didn't mind, though. She felt a sense of relief. She didn't have to wonder what he thought or how he felt about her, to some degree. But she kept telling herself not to get too caught up and allow her mind to go down the rabbit hole.

The first time she got a break, once things slowed down, she sat at a table near the window. She leaned her head against the glass, which felt very cool on her skin. It was a relieving sensation, which helped her body relax and calm down. She wondered what Jaron was doing and if he was thinking about her, if he was happy to have approached her, or if he was regretting it. She imagined him sitting at his desk, hard at work.

She pulled out the business card and read it for the first time. *Jaron Coleman, CEO Coleman Industries, leading the industry in innovative medicine technology, working to create a healthy future.* She smiled, putting the card back into her pocket. *What do I do now? I mean, he seems nice and genuine enough, but do I really have time to get to know someone right now?* she thought.

She saw a few teenage boys enter the café and went to help them. Before long, Liyah was standing next to her, helping make the boys ice teas. She couldn't help but smile at the way Liyah just stepped in to help without needing to be asked or anything. She was a great worker but an even better friend. She nudged her a little with her elbow, and they both smiled.

After the boys left, they stood at the front counter and stared outside, neither of them speaking. The rain had subsided, and the sun was working its way through the clouds. Cars glistened from the sun shining on their freshly rinsed surfaces as they rode past.

"I can't tell you ladies how much I appreciate you," came Mr. Stacy's voice from behind them.

"Well, I wouldn't mind hearing it." Liyah laughed.

"I've had a lot of people come through here for work—some students, some not—but I can honestly say I don't think I've met two women as dedicated, hardworking, and reliable as you two. I mean, sure, this one over here has a mouth on her, but I wouldn't trade you ladies for anyone in the world. You keep this place going. You know the ins and outs. No matter what I ask, you're always ready and willing. I guess what I'm saying is, thank you."

They were both silent. Neither of them knew what to say. They stared at each other before Liyah said, "Okay. What's the catch? What shifts do you need covered? Or, wait, is it time for inventory again? You know I love numbers, so you don't even have to butter me up for that."

He just smiled. "No, it's none of that. I was going through some old papers, and can you guys believe that today marks your three-year anniversary?"

"Wait. Did you say raise?" said Liyah. They all laughed.

"I'm sorry I didn't know before now. I would've gotten you ladies something for the occasion. I mean, no one has been here as long as you guys. Well, aside from Cliff, but he's my cousin, so he doesn't count. We've been cooking together since we were kids."

"Wow, three years already," said MaKayla. "I remember the first day we started. That was a pretty fun day."

"Yeah, and to be honest, I wasn't too sure you guys would make it. With you coming in with ultimatums, I had to hire both of you, give you both the same shifts, blah, blah, blah." They all laughed again.

"What would you do without this dynamic duo?" asked Liyah, putting her arm around MaKayla.

"Well, what you give me in headaches, you make up for in work ethic."

"Awwwwww," they said, giving Mr. Stacy a hug.

*****

After several hours of emailing back and forth with the department heads, Jaron found that he had more availability from his team than he thought. He wasn't sure if they were really free or if they just didn't want to tell him no. Their work ethic was already great, and he figured that his speech the other day had inspired them more than he had planned to. His objective was really just to calm the situation of not making the deal and reassuring his company that things would be alright. Either way, he was happy that they wanted to be available for whatever he needed.

He received a meeting invite from Keith scheduled for nine thirty tomorrow morning with the other people he planned to pull into the project they had discussed. There was no procrastination within the people he went to for assistance. Once he put a situation out to them, they hit it head-on.

Tina walked in. "Door was open, so I figured you weren't that busy," she said, smiling.

"Nope, just checking emails right now, trying to compile a list for the interns."

"Ooh, do I get one?" asked Tina excitedly.

Jaron looked up, smiling. "Do you really want one? You've never said anything about that before."

"Well, I just think it might be interesting to teach someone the importance of answering calls, schedule keeping, creating meetings, etc., etc., etc."

"Well, to be honest, we might have more people available for interns than interns themselves, so we'll have to see how it all works itself out."

"Okay. That's fine. Just know I'm available if you need me."

"As you always are. Speaking of schedules, how's the rest of my week looking?"

"Let me go and see," she said, walking out of the office and grabbing her laptop. "Well, Friday is all clear except for an 8:00 a.m. production team conference call. It's scheduled to go until 9:30. Tomorrow morning, you have that new vendor appointment over on Ninth at 9:00 a.m. There's no ending time for that. Thursday, you're free all day as well."

Just then, his laptop dinged. It was another meeting invite from Tim for Thursday morning at 9:00 a.m. "Okay. Thanks," he said as he accepted the invite and created a meeting request time change to noon for Keith's meeting. "Put me down for Thursday, meeting with Tim from 9:00 a.m.." His laptop dinged again. Keith had accepted his time change. "Tomorrow, meeting with Keith and department heads at noon. Then Friday, block off the entire day and book the large conference room for me, if you'd be so kind."

"Sure thing, bo—" Tina's voice trailed off, and her eyes dropped to her laptop.

"You were about to say something?" said Jaron.

"Oh, it was nothing," she said, smiling. "What event am I booking the conference room under?"

"You can say internship meeting, although it will be more than just that." Jaron too, was working on his laptop, sending an email to Ms. Smith with his team's availability and to find out what time on Friday worked the best. He also created another meeting event for Friday and invited everyone. He made the time from 10:00 a.m. but did not put an ending time, not knowing how long it would take to get through everything. Jaron sat back and let out a sigh.

"Is something wrong?" asked Tina.

"Not wrong, per se. It's just, things are about to get really tight, and I have to make sure I manage this the right way. There are a lot of moving parts, and I have to make sure they keep working well together, or it'll mess everything up."

"What do you mean?" asked Tina.

"Well, take this week, for instance. There's the impending deal with Mr. Thomas that the team's working on. Then there's the internship program that we're now adding to the mix. We just rolled out a new promotion, and I have special projects working on a few more items that we can put into works. I have Tim working on some new product ideas that I anticipate will probably be ready to roll out soon, and Keith is pulling people to work on new perspective locations for expansion."

"That's why this meeting Friday will be so long. We have to get updates and make sure we're all on the same page with these aspects. I have to ensure that no one's load is too heavy and that I'm not burning the team out."

"That is definitely a lot, but we've endured more. The internship program isn't new. The team is used to dealing with that. You and Tim are like a mad scientist duo at this point, always coming up with something interesting and innovative. They're really good too, by the way. The tea you gave me for my knee worked wonders. The new projects and promotions are all a part of business. We have to continually grow and evolve as a company. I'm sure they look forward to this challenge.

"The deal is just paperwork and technicalities now. You've already hammered out the hard part when it started with Wynstead." Tina frowned and then smiled. "So what's left, some prospective locations and running numbers?" She chuckled. "Isn't that what Keith loves to do? He probably does it in his sleep. We have a great company. This is a well-oiled machine. The parts fit and work well together. We bear the load for each other. So if you ask me, it just seems like another day at Coleman Industries."

Jaron sat back and smiled. "I already told you that your evaluation wasn't for a while and you're in good standings with me, right?"

"I'm being serious," she said, smiling. "But I was talking to Karla earlier, just checking on them like you asked. She said she's getting a personal masseuse and muscular fan guy who feeds her grapes. I'm more of a pineapple and watermelon girl myself."

Jaron sat up and shook his head. "You guys are crazy. I'll tell you what, if things go well with this deal, I'll look into a company spa retreat."

"Are you serious?" asked Tina in a startled voice.

"Yeah. I mean, I can't cover the entire bill for all the employees, but I'm sure I could cover a large enough portion to make it manageable for the rest of you. Then you and Karla can tell everyone it was your idea and you talked me into it."

"You see? That's why we're willing to go to the ends of the earth and back for you, because we know that you would do the same," replied Tina, getting out of the chair.

"Where are you going?" asked Jaron.

"Oh, I'm going to call Karla and tell her we're going to the Bahamas," replied Tina, laughing.

"You're crazy. I said spa retreat, not Bahamas."

"Oh, I thought that's what you meant," she said, coming back into the office, smiling. She typed a few things into her laptop and spun it around on his desk.

He pulled the laptop closer. "Is this the care package?" he asked.

"Yes. Isn't it nice?"

"It looks amazing. I'm sure they're going to love it."

"Yeah. It almost made me want to have a baby, but then I came to my senses," she said, laughing.

"Poor Trouble," replied Jaron as Tina walked out of the office.

Tina left for the day a little while later, and Jaron continued working until around seven o'clock. He hadn't realized the time until he looked at his buzzing phone. It was his little sister.

"Well, this is a pleasant surprise," he said as he answered the phone.

"Oh hush," she said. "How's it going?"

"It's going sis, it's going. There's a lot of work this week. Things are somewhat hectic."

"Is that because of that deal you were talking about?"

"Yeah, plus some other things we've been working on."

"Well, you have always seemed to thrive under pressure, to find a way to organize the confusion."

"I don't know. It's just something Dad used to always stress to me. 'Always keep your head when all about you are losing theirs. No matter how bad the storm or destruction is, it always passes, and the dust clears. You must be ready when that time comes.' He always told me that there would be times in my life when I would be looked upon to lead, to be a display of strength, that I had to prepare myself for those moments."

"Yeah, he was right. I remember how strong you were at the funeral, comforting us, comforting Mom. I never saw you drop a tear. I envied that. I didn't want to be weak. I wanted to be strong for him." He could hear his sister crying through the change in her voice and the sniffles. "I wanted to show him that he had taught me well and I'd be okay."

"Shannon," Jaron said through a sigh, "I wasn't strong because I didn't cry, and that didn't make you weak. To be honest, I thought something was wrong with me. I figured people would think that as well. I mean, who doesn't cry for their father? I think I was so numb to it all, and I hadn't come to terms with the fact that he was really gone. It was the most surreal thing I'd ever experienced. On top of that, I think a part of me was angry."

"You mean with the guy who killed Dad?"

"No, with Dad. I was angry with him."

"Why? Why would you be mad at Dad?"

Jaron was silent, and he could feel the tears falling, but he didn't wipe them. "I was angry that he left. I know it wasn't his choice, but I felt that he could've fixed it somehow. He always fixed everything Shannon. He was always there for us. He wasn't supposed to leave. I know he taught me so much, but I didn't think I was ready to live without him."

"Yeah," said Shannon through a small laugh. "But look at us, living and doing pretty well, if I may say so."

"You're right sis, and I know he's still here. He's living through us."

"I just wish he could be here to see it," she said. "Every time something big happens in my life, I want to share it with him and Mom to show him that I listened, that I'm succeeding."

"He sees you sis. I know he does. There are times when I'm unsure about things, and sure enough, here comes his voice with some cryptic message that he's planted in my mind at some point in time."

She laughed. "Yeah, he does me the same way."

"He knew how to prepare us, how to ensure he'd always be with us, and for that, I'm eternally grateful."

"Me too. I just miss him so much sometimes."

"Me too sis. Me too."

It had been a while since Jaron and Shannon had talked about their dad. There were things they had never discussed that came out in the conversation, and Jaron was happy to be having the talk with her.

"I know you give me a hard time because of how great I am." Jaron smiled. "But Shannon, I really love you, and I'm proud to say I'm your brother even if you may legally be a midget."

"I'm amazed that with a head that size, you can't be more creative. I know you must have the most vivid thoughts up there, huh, like 3D movies? It doesn't matter though, because I love you more."

They continued talking until Jaron made it home, catching up on how things were going with Shannon's new position and just random things in life. He had stopped and grabbed food on the way in. After getting off the phone, he took a shower and turned on SportsCenter and ate. He wasn't really watching the TV. It was more just white noise.

He reflected on the day and began to mentally prepare for the rest of the week. Then his mind went to MaKayla. *Is she still at work? It's kind of late, but maybe she closes. I wonder if she's thought about me today. Is it too soon to expect to hear from her?* He sat back and smiled. *What will Mom say when I tell her?*

*****

The rest of their shift went by fairly quick. Mr. Stacy left shortly after their conversation, and the traffic in and out of the café was at an average pace.

"See you later," said McKinley as she headed out the door.

"Later," they said, waving.

"Pretty good shift," said Liyah as she pulled out a stool next to the counter.

"Yeah, time went by, and I didn't even notice," replied MaKayla as she set up the registers for the morning.

"So now we can talk without being interrupted. I know I've been giving you a lot of crap since your boo left."

MaKayla flashed a stern look at Liyah, followed by a smile. "He's not my boo."

"Well, maybe not yet, but it sure sounds like he would like to be. Are you really considering not using his number? I mean, he's kind of put in a lot of work for it. He definitely seems to be serious about you."

"What do you mean he put in a lot of work?"

"Well, for one, he's been coming here for a while now because of you. Yeah, Cliff has it back there in the kitchen, but let's not be naive. Then he came looking for you all those days to make sure you were okay and to apologize for something he didn't do and, quite honestly, had no control over. Then he apologized and was extremely respectful about it. He wasn't just coming at you like you were a piece of meat, and that means a lot to you. I know it does."

"Then he came running in the rain for you just to give you his number, not even asking for yours in return, completely allowing things to move at your pace and on your terms. Plus, he notices little things about you, like that loc of hair that you can never get to act right ever since you let me cut it with those scissors when we were eight, trying to be a beautician. He thinks it's cute, so you can thank me for that," she said, laughing.

MaKayla smiled and closed the register drawer. "I don't know Liyah. I mean, I hear all of that. And when you say it that way, it feels good. But I really don't know."

Liyah got up as they made their final rounds, making sure everything was in its proper place before they left. "What exactly is it that you don't know? What are you so afraid of?"

"I mean, my plate is pretty full already."

Liyah stopped and turned, looking at MaKayla. "What?"

"It is. You know I have a lot going on."

"I'm not disputing that, but for someone who likes to eat as much as you do, the last analogy that you should be using is one about food."

MaKayla just smiled and shook her head. "I'm being serious Liyah. Getting to know someone isn't a simple thing. You have to invest time, and I don't know if I have the time to invest right now."

"I understand. You know I do. But you know we make time for what we want to make time for. We are on the journey of a lifetime. Just like it made us sad to have lost each other on that journey, and we've been putting in time to get back where we want to be. Obviously, we didn't lose each other on purpose, but our responsibilities made us think that we didn't have the time, but look at us now. We are making it a priority to be more involved with each other, talk to each other. Not one single thing has fallen by the wayside because of it."

"Yeah, but that's you. You're my sister, my other half. I love you. I've grown with you. You're not some guy that's going to take my focus off of my priorities for nothing."

Liyah didn't speak. She looked at the ground. "MaKayla, is this about Kaleb?"

MaKayla didn't say anything. She just looked away. "Let's just go. I know you have to get up early, and you still have to drop me off." Liyah didn't argue with her. She just shook her head and went into the back room to get her things.

Kaleb was MaKayla's first crush at the age of eleven. They became boyfriend and girlfriend their freshman year of high school. He was her first love, her first kiss, her first everything when it came to relationships, and her only real boyfriend. They broke up during MaKayla's sophomore year in college. He claimed that the distance wasn't working, but she soon found out that he had been seeing someone else back home. She was devastated, and although she had dated a few guys after him, no one really stuck. They all showed signs that, to her, resembled what she saw in Kaleb. Liyah was so upset that she threatened to beat up everyone back home if it would make MaKayla feel better, but nothing but time and school helped her move forward.

They rode to MaKayla's house without talking, just listening to music. MaKayla stared out the window, looking at the moon. The clouds were slowly floating through the sky. It occasionally covered up the moon, but for only a few seconds before moving on. MaKayla wished she could hide like the moon, but just like the moon, she knew she would have to come out to be seen again.

She hated that Kaleb still affected how she saw herself, that she still felt like she wasn't good enough, but she also knew that nothing she could have done would have changed the outcome. She didn't want to be in that position again. She didn't want her worth determined by someone else. She had done so much to repair how she felt about and saw herself. She was afraid that letting someone in would mess it up.

Jaron seemed different. He was right about the energy. She could feel it too. She wished she could easily open up and let him in. She wanted to be confident the way he was, but she was so unsure. She didn't want to make a mistake.

Liyah nudged her with her elbow. "Hey, what's on your mind?" she asked.

"I know we haven't talked about Kaleb in a while, but you were right earlier. I don't want this to be a repeat of that. You know how hard I fell for him and his words, how blind I was to what was going on. He broke me, and I don't want to be broken again. I'm not saying that I know this will be a repeat of that, but I'm afraid Liyah. I don't want to make a mistake. You know how long it took me to bounce back from that relationship. I don't want to risk that right now. I don't think I can. I wish I were strong like you, that I had your confidence, but I don't."

Liyah pulled in front of MaKayla's house and put her car in park. She sat quietly for a minute, then turned down the radio, exhaled, and turned toward MaKayla, who was looking down. "Hey," she said, smiling, picking up MaKayla's head. "There's no reason to put your head down. I completely understand how you feel."

She grabbed MaKayla's hands and looked her in the eyes. "You know you're my girl, and I may not always be the one giving out the advice, but hear me out. Kaleb was the past. Should you learn from it? Of course. But should it control your future? Not at all. He was a young, stupid boy—a boy, not a man. You got caught up in Kaleb's words, but Jaron is showing you action. He actually only recently started talking." They both laughed.

"Yes, I have confidence, because I know my worth. You know who helped me see that? You did. Now you see your worth, and you're afraid to give that worth to someone who you're not sure is worthy." Liyah smiled. "You see what I did there?"

"You're so silly," MaKayla said, shaking her head.

"But seriously, it makes sense to be cautious. How often do I tell you to talk to a guy?" There was a pause. "Never mind. Disregard that," said Liyah as MaKayla started to respond. They both laughed again. "This is different. He said he talked to his mom about you. How many guys do that if they're not serious, and how many would even admit to it?"

"I know. Trust me, I know Liyah. I want to throw caution to the wind and say, 'Forget it. I want to talk to him. I want to see where this will go.' I really do, but...but I don't know."

"If you want to, then do it. What's the worst that can happen, that he turns out to be a loser? Okay. You've dealt with losers before. But what if he's everything you've wanted? What if he's everything you've ever dreamed of? And I do mean dreamed." Liyah started smiling.

"I've never seen you so caught up over a guy before. There has to be something about him. There has to be a reason why you were dreaming about him and speechless when he talked or even had crazy responses when he was leaving. See what that reason is. Step out there. If time is the issue, you'll make time, or he'll understand and won't demand much of your time, or both. Who knows?"

"Before you respond with your fears, just think about it and if what I'm saying makes sense. Then promise me you'll text him. Don't think about it. Just do it and let the chips fall where they may. Don't miss out on the potential of what could be because of some immature little boy. I never liked him anyway with his perfect lining and pretty eyes. Mr. Kaleb with a *K*, not a *C*."

MaKayla let out a sigh, shaking her head, smiling. "You know, you really frustrate me, especially when you make sense."

"Do you promise MaKayla?"

MaKayla thought about it and sighed again. "I promise."

Liyah leaned over and hugged MaKayla. "Yay! I'm so happy for you. You're gonna have a boo. You're gonna have a boo," she sang.

"I only said I'd think about it and if you make sense, I'd text him. I haven't even thought about it yet, Liyah."

"No, no, no, you literally just said, 'You know, you really frustrate me, especially when, you, make, sense,' so you said I make sense already, so you're gonna get a boo," Liyah said, dancing.

"I'm going in the house. You let me know when you get home." Makayla said shaking her head and smiling.

"You let me know after you guys talk."

"Whatever. I'll talk to you later," MaKayla said, closing the door and walking toward the house. She felt better about the situation. Liyah had that effect on her, and the smile on her face said as much. Liyah blew her horn and waved as MaKayla walked into the house.

SPRING SHOWERS—THE BLOOM

MaKayla got in the shower and just stood under the water. She thought about the day, how nice it had all been, how even though it was only a talk, she missed Jaron. She replayed Liyah's words and tried not to think negatively, but it was hard. *I just really don't want to make a mistake,* she thought.

Just then, for whatever reason, her mom's words came into her mind: "It's okay to make mistakes, to take the wrong road. Most of the time, that's the only way to really get to where you want to go. You just have to realize that it's okay to stop and enjoy what's around you along the way. You don't have to rush to get to where you think you need to be. Just travel in the direction where you think you want to go. But keep your eyes open. Learn, experience, and enjoy along the way. Then, you'll see which way to go and if your destination is really where you want to be."

She remembered that day, the conversation, how she wanted someone to share her life with. *What if this is it?* she thought. "Don't think about it. Just do it," she heard Liyah say. She smiled as she dried off, wrapped her towel around herself, and walked into her bedroom. She grabbed her pants and took the business card out. She picked up her phone and exhaled. She put the number into the message box and typed, "Hey." She closed her eyes and pressed send.

About the Author

Steve Weatherspoon grew up in Chicago, Illinois. From the moment he was able to read, it was hard to find him without a book. His passion for reading grew into a passion for telling his own stories and expressing his thoughts through words. He's a lifelong writer who has been published in multiple high school publications under pseudonyms.

He is a first-time author, his debut novel being *Seasonal Storms: Spring Showers—the Bloom*, the first installment in the *Seasonal Storms* trilogy, which he began writing over six years ago. What began as a fun, small blurb, soon grew and was developed into a full-length story. Being a truck driver by profession, he used his downtime on the road to create a fictional story that we can all gravitate and relate to.

CPSIA information can be obtained
at www.ICGtesting.com
Printed in the USA
BVHW072316130922
646694BV00001B/3